AN IMPOSSIBLE IMPOSTOR

ALSO BY DEANNA RAYBOURN

Veronica Speedwell Mystery Series
A Curious Beginning
A Perilous Undertaking
A Treacherous Curse
A Dangerous Collaboration
A Murderous Relation
An Unexpected Peril

The Lady Julia Grey series

NOVELS

Silent in the Grave   *Dark Road to Darjeeling*
Silent in the Sanctuary   *The Dark Enquiry*
Silent on the Moor

NOVELLAS

Silent Night   *Twelfth Night*
Midsummer Night   *Bonfire Night*

Other Works

NOVELS

The Dead Travel Fast   *City of Jasmine*
A Spear of Summer Grass   *Night of a Thousand Stars*

NOVELLAS

Far in the Wilds
(prequel to *A Spear of Summer Grass*)
Whisper of Jasmine
(prequel to *City of Jasmine*)

AN

IMPOSSIBLE
IMPOSTOR

A VERONICA SPEEDWELL
MYSTERY

Deanna Raybourn

BERKLEY
NEW YORK

BERKLEY
An imprint of Penguin Random House LLC
penguinrandomhouse.com

Copyright © 2022 by Raybourn Creative LLC.
Penguin Random House supports copyright. Copyright fuels creativity, encourages diverse
voices, promotes free speech, and creates a vibrant culture. Thank you for buying an authorized
edition of this book and for complying with copyright laws by not reproducing, scanning, or
distributing any part of it in any form without permission. You are supporting writers and
allowing Penguin Random House to continue to publish books for every reader.

BERKLEY and the BERKLEY & B colophon are registered trademarks of
Penguin Random House LLC.

The Edgar® name is a registered service mark of the Mystery Writers of America, Inc.

Library of Congress Cataloging-in-Publication Data

Names: Raybourn, Deanna, author.
Title: An impossible impostor / Deanna Raybourn.
Description: First edition. | New York : Berkley, 2022. | Series: A Veronica Speedwell mystery
Identifiers: LCCN 2021038462 (print) | LCCN 2021038463 (ebook) |
ISBN 9780593197295 (hardcover) | ISBN 9780593197301 (ebook)
Subjects: LCGFT: Novels.
Classification: LCC PS3618.A983 I47 2022 (print) |
LCC PS3618.A983 (ebook) | DDC 813/.6--dc23
LC record available at https://lccn.loc.gov/2021038462
LC ebook record available at https://lccn.loc.gov/2021038463

First Edition: February 2022

Printed in the United States of America
1 3 5 7 9 10 8 6 4 2

Book design by Kristin del Rosario

This is a work of fiction. Names, characters, places, and incidents either are the product
of the author's imagination or are used fictitiously, and any resemblance to actual persons,
living or dead, business establishments, events, or locales is entirely coincidental.

For Danielle and Pam

AN IMPOSSIBLE IMPOSTOR

CHAPTER

1

Somewhere between Paris and London
April 1889

I do not care for infants, and even if I did, I should not care for this one. It is decidedly *moist*," I protested to Stoker, thrusting the child towards him. He took it with good grace and it emitted a sort of cooing sound. "It seems to like you," I observed.

I could not find fault with the child on that score. From his thirst for adventure to his avid intelligence, Stoker was an eminently likeable man when he was in good spirits. (The fact that he was superbly fit and partial to reciting Keats in moments of tenderness entered into my assessment of him not in the slightest. I am, after all, a woman of science.)

Stoker dandled the infant on his knee and it regarded him solemnly, eyes wide and round. I use the word "infant" in its loosest interpretation. It had, in fact, been born some nine or ten months before and possessed the appropriate number of teeth and skills for a child of that age. If we had permitted, it would have roamed the first-class compartment where we were comfortably ensconced en route from Paris to London. The fact that the journey included a Channel crossing via boat train was one of a dozen considerations in bringing along the child's nurse, a stout matron of something more than forty years. She was a calmly capable woman who managed her charge with a combination of ruthless efficiency and dollops of real affection. I had taken the precaution of purchasing leather leads to attach to the infant to prevent it from getting loose, but Madame Laborde assured me she was entirely capable of running it to ground should it escape.

Escape seemed the last thing on its mind as it wound its chubby fist around Stoker's index finger. As usual, the digit in question was stained with ink and smelt of honey and tobacco thanks to Stoker's inveterate habits. We had been in the child's company for only a few hours, but it had already ascertained that Stoker's pockets were a veritable hoard of sweets. It put out an imperious hand and Stoker shook his head. "You have had two already and you must eat your luncheon first."

The small person, I relate without exaggeration, narrowed its eyes and drew in a slow, deep breath. Then it opened its little maw and bellowed like a tiny bull. Hastily, Stoker thrust a hand into his pocket, rootling about until he extracted a paper twist of honey drops. He plopped one into the child's mouth just as it prepared to roar again. Instantly, the rosebud lips clamped shut and curved into a smile. It emitted another coo and the nurse sighed.

"Monsieur," she said evenly, "you must not spoil the child. He is headstrong enough without being indulged." She related this in French, as her English was poor, and Stoker shrugged, pantomiming that he did not understand the language. This was a patent falsehood. I had discovered him on numerous occasions reading saucy French novels in the original tongue. He claimed it made them more *romantique*.

I smiled at the nurse. "Madame," I told her in her native language, "you must excuse Monsieur. He lacks your fine Gallic common sense. He is half-Irish and they are a sentimental race."

Stoker opened his mouth and snapped it shut again without speaking. Officially, he was the third son of the late Viscount Templeton-Vane. Unofficially, he was the result of a passionate liaison between the viscountess and the portraitist who had come from Galway to paint her in oils. Stoker did not generally enjoy discussing his parentage, but he could not now object unless he admitted to understanding French, and it was a situation I decided to exploit to the fullest.

"He is the same with his dogs," I went on. "He lets them sleep in his bed and he feeds them from his own plate."

She shuddered. The French, I have observed, are devoted to their pets, but even they have limits. With a great deal of concentration, the infant took the sweet from its mouth and held it up to the light in one chubby fist, like a jeweler studying the facets of a rare gem. Then it popped the treasure back onto its tongue and began to pat Stoker's cheeks with its filthy hands. Suddenly, a noxious aroma filled the compartment. The cherub was sitting with a beatific expression on its face, as if it were not the author of the atrocity, but I knew better. I opened the window and gave the nurse a pointed look.

Madame Laborde hoisted herself to her feet and put out her hands for her charge.

"*Avec moi, mon trésor, s'il vous plait,*" she said briskly. She rattled off something about attending to the child's condition and took her leave with the creature. Stoker unearthed one of his enormous scarlet pocket handkerchiefs and began to scrub at the sticky marks on his chin.

"You are a natural with children," I said mildly. "I did not realize you had much experience with them."

"Oh yes. In the traveling show." Stoker had run away from his aristocratic home at the age of twelve and attached himself to a sort of circus, working his way up from amateur conjurer to knife thrower and prizefighter. "Violet, the Human Sow," he told me with a fond smile of reminiscence. "She was a lovely woman. Gave birth every year, usually to twins or triplets. The proprietor made her wear a pink singlet and a velvet snout to cuddle a few infant pigs while the rest of us carried her actual babies about."

"That is appalling," I said, preparing to launch into a righteous tirade about reducing women to their breeding capabilities, but Stoker forestalled me.

"Not as appalling as that smell," he replied, pinching his nose.

"Blame your small and unhygienic friend," I instructed.

He shook his head. "No, that odor was blown away with the fresh air," he said, nodding towards the open window. "The stench that remains is courtesy of *your* traveling companion." He fixed an eye upon the enormous item sitting next to me. It was a wheel of cheese, just short of an hundredweight, its rind washed in the sweet wine of the Alpenwald, a Mitteleuropean country that had proven the setting for the conclusion of our last adventure. We had performed a service for the princess of that country at great peril to our own lives and limbs, and in return, the lady had invited us to her wedding.* It had been a bittersweet time—the princess, poor soul, had married for the security of her throne rather than the dictates of her heart—but we had enjoyed the many courtesies extended to us. We had been away more than a fortnight and had fallen woefully behind in our work for the Earl of Rosemorran. We had been engaged at his lordship's Marylebone estate to catalog the collection amassed by his ancestors in

_____

* *An Unexpected Peril*

preparation for the creation of a museum designed to educate and entertain the masses. Housed in the Belvedere, a sort of freestanding ballroom of enormous proportions on his lordship's property, the collection was as varied as it was vast. Egyptian mummies jostled medieval suits of armor while caryatids looked down their aristocratic noses at the confusion. The bulk of the collection was devoted to natural history, animals stuffed and mounted from the furthest reaches of the globe and most in a state of moldering decay. The restoration of such mounts was Stoker's speciality, whilst mine was the preservation of the butterflies and moths. A lepidopterist by trade, accustomed to voyaging the world in search of specimens to sell, I had taken the position with the earl on the understanding that it would entail a certain amount of travel.

Instead, I found myself most days tucked into some cobwebby corner of the Belvedere, plucking out desiccated butterflies and inking labels. It was not entirely the earl's fault. He had vastly underestimated the time required to make the collection fit for exhibition, and my own activities had frequently interrupted the work. Stoker and I had developed the habit of murder—the solving of, I hasten to add. Not the commission of, although the earl's numerous and exuberant children might have tempted me to try. Their mother long dead, the children ran wild despite the best efforts of the earl and his sister, Lady Cordelia. The lady and I had become fast friends regardless of the differences in rank and experience, and I had been deeply honored that she had chosen me as her companion when she sojourned half a year in Madeira. I had anticipated long days spent with my butterfly net, pursuing the enchanting black and white spotted *Hypolimnas misippus*, but instead I found myself trotting out on endless errands, fetching remedies for morning sickness and swollen feet as the reason for Lady C's abrupt withdrawal from public life made itself apparent.

I held her hand through the worst of it, but there are scenes indelibly printed upon my memory, scenes of such barnyard specificity that no childless woman should be forced to witness them. But Lady C had delighted in her bovine contentment, so much that she altered her plans to have the babe adopted out. Instead, she arranged for a temporary situation until the child was fully weaned and could travel safely in the company of the French nurse she had engaged to care for it. The infant had been in Paris for some weeks, and Lady C wrote to me in the Alpenwald, requesting that I retrieve it for her, much as one would ask a friend to collect a piece of left luggage from a train station. She cleverly reasoned that, as the child had come from Paris, no one would connect it with her journey to Madeira. Presented as a French foundling, it could be "adopted" by her and raised as her own child, although without benefit of her name. The situation was not ideal, but it was far better than any alternative. I had little use for society and its various hypocrisies, but Lady C was deeply conscious of her brother's honor and the fact that her beloved nieces and nephews would be tarred with the same brush used to blacken her name should the truth come out.

And so, Stoker and I had stopped in Paris for a few days to enjoy the spring sunshine, pay a lengthy visit to Deyrolle—the taxidermical emporium where Stoker wandered in a state of considerable rapture—marvel at the hypnotic ugliness of the newly constructed tower by Monsieur Eiffel, and collect the child. It came with an abundance of *things*, rubber baths and traveling cots and tiny chairs and far more clothes than I owned. (I gathered from a conversation with Madame Laborde that Lady C had been lavish in sending presents.) But all the infant's impedimenta could not rival my own souvenir of the Alpenwald—the cheese. I had purchased it as a gift for the earl in recognition of his many kindnesses and inexhaustible patience with our detectival endeavors. I could never be persuaded from the course of justice, and as a result Stoker and I were forever haring off on some adventure or other. If we were not chasing a resurrected Egyptian god down a sewer or ballooning past Big Ben, we were being variously shot at, stabbed, abducted, or drowned. A nice wheel of cheese seemed a small price to pay for the earl overlooking our frequent absences.

Unfortunately, I had underestimated the most notable of the Alpenwalder cheese's qualities. It was renowned amongst gourmets for its aroma, earthy, with the slightest suggestion of goat. In short, it stank. And the longer one carried it about, through overheated train compartments and warm spring sunshine, the more pungent it became.

By the time we reached Calais, the odor of the cheese had taken on a sort of personality, a fifth traveler in our merry band, ensuring that wherever we went, porters ignored us and crowds parted. Stoker had been forced to carry it himself, his clothing now permanently imbued with the stink of it. He eyed me reproachfully, but I pretended not to notice.

We arrived back in London on a gloomy morning. A chill fog rolled off the river Thames, blanketing the city and muffling traffic. The odiferous cheese announced our presence, and before a hapless porter could make his escape, I cornered him and forced him to help us shift our baggage to the carriage Lady C had sent. We clip-clopped through streets shrouded in mist, and by the time we arrived at Bishop's Folly, the estate in Marylebone, we were damp and cold to the bone. Usually our comings and goings were of little note, but this time the entire Beauclerk family turned out to greet us. Lady C took charge of her child and the earl of his cheese, and the children of the quantity of Swiss chocolate Stoker had purchased for them.

Our bags were sent to our lodgings, two of the follies built by previous earls to cluster picturesquely around a pond. Stoker's was a pagoda while I had chosen to lodge in a Gothic structure reminiscent of Sainte-Chapelle, lavish with pointed arches and stained glass. But at his lordship's urging, we made straight for the Belvedere itself, our place of work and refreshment.

"I have a new acquisition and it has only just arrived," Lord Rose-morran announced, rubbing his hands together. Stoker flinched and I gave the earl a look of frank alarm. His enthusiasm was matched only by his fortune, and both were often in service of things only an eccentric nobleman could love. As soon as word of his intended museum spread, his aristocratic friends had taken the opportunity to clear out their own attics and country houses, sending along cartfuls of appalling things. Sorting through the detritus of some of England's finest families would have been enough to turn my hair white had I not been made of stern stuff, so I had, tactfully but firmly, insisted that his lordship promise to discuss future additions to the collection with us, his curators.

Catching sight of my expression, he hurried to explain. "Naturally, I would have conferred with the two of you, but you were in the Alpen-wald, and I had to act quickly, you see. Reggie Anstruther offered me a good deal, but only if I agreed to the whole lot and only if I took deliv-ery immediately."

Stoker's sigh was profound, but his lordship's excitement was un-diminished. He threw open the door of the Belvedere and stopped short. Packed almost to the entrance itself was a stack of crates, row after row, and enormous rolls of fabric, painted canvas that had been furled like sails.

"What, precisely, are we looking at?" Stoker asked politely.

The earl seized a pry bar and began to open the crates. "The entire collection from the French opera theatre Reggie owned. A fine fellow of business, Reggie," he said absently as he tossed aside the first lid. From Lord Anstruther's reputation, I would have said it was safe to conclude he was *not*, in fact, a fine fellow of business. Every month was a new scheme, usually something calculated to provide access to comely young women of some talent and flexible morals. He was forever in-vesting in dramatic companies and ballet troupes.

"Lord Anstruther has got out of the theatrical business then?" I inquired. The first crate appeared to be full of costumes, and the earl was busy inspecting his new treasures.

"What was that? Oh yes, at least, no more opera. He says singers are devilishly temperamental. The last one threw a shoe at his head and nearly took out his eye. So, he's sold off the opera theatre and used the money to invest in a troupe of girls who do tricks on horseback. It's very popular, he says. He means to take them on a tour of the provinces. Look here!" he called, diving into the crate. He emerged wearing a brown velvet donkey's head. It was sporting a wreath of flowers and a ridiculous grin. "Hallo, I am Bottom!" he proclaimed happily.

"From *The Fairy Queen*," Stoker agreed, holding up a program. A stack of them had been stuffed beneath the ass's head and he thumbed through them. "Odd to think of a French company performing Purcell, but then it seems they were quite catholic in their tastes. Some Mozart, Berlioz's *Les Troyens*, Massenet's *Le roi de Lahore*, ah, even Beethoven." He began to hum tunefully from *Fidelio*, and I turned to the earl, who was struggling to remove the donkey's head.

"Let me help you," I urged.

"Most kind," he said as I tugged at the velvet ears. It took a good deal of yanking—the donkey's head proving as stubborn as the animal itself—but at last the earl emerged, red-faced and a little sweaty.

"Jolly good fun. Must put that aside for the children," he said. "They might like to put on an amateur dramatical for midsummer."

I was not a little relieved to hear that his lordship intended at least some of the collection to find its way to the dressing-up box. Stoker had opened another crate and was half-drowned in a sea of silks and velvets—the peploi of Trojans, the embroidered robes of Asian kings, and an enormous panniered gown of spangled purple that could only have belonged to a Queen of the Night.

"But why," he asked the earl, "did you buy all of this if you only meant to give it to the children?"

Lord Rosemorran rummaged through the crates until he found the one he wanted. "Ah! This is why," he said, prying it open. Nestled in a heap of excelsior was a tangle of brown wooden limbs and heavy silk strings. "The marionettes," he explained, lifting one out. It was a harlequin, dressed in the distinctive multicolored diamond pattern, an enormous feathery pom-pom attached to its hat. "They are from Sicily, made by the Castrovinci family in the seventeenth century. Look here, a Tancred!" He plunged his hand into the excelsior and emerged with a puppet dressed in a suit of armor, the visor of his helmet thrown back to reveal a lavish set of black moustaches. "Ready to ride off on Crusade. You know, the Sicilian puppet theatre . . ."

What followed was nearly an hour of discussion on the history of the Sicilian puppetry tradition. I like to think it would have been diverting had I not been fatigued from the Channel crossing, but in fact, it would not. There was far too much explanation on the intricacies of choosing the *correct* type of olive tree for a marionette, and I reflected, as his lordship's gentle monologue continued to burble on, that no one should ever know quite so much about puppets.

At last, his lordship, reminded of the delicacy of the awaiting Alpenwalder cheese, wound down and left us amidst the litter of crates and excelsior. The canvas sails proved to be painted backdrops used to set the scene for the opera company, and the other boxes were packed full of furniture, props, costumes, and wigs. I made a few choice selections to hold back from the children's dressing-up box and Stoker scrutinized them.

"Why are you keeping those?" he inquired.

"Disguises," I explained. "We may not intentionally seek out adventures, but they seem to seek *us* and it is best to be prepared."

He lifted one garment between his fingertips. "This is a scarlet cassock. Veronica, exactly *when* do you plan on disguising yourself as a cardinal?"

"One never knows," I replied loftily. I tossed it into a crate with the other items I meant to keep and dusted my hands. "And now, food," I said with a decisive gesture.

Upstairs in the Belvedere was a sort of snuggery, fitted with a Swedish stove, Napoléon's campaign bed, and an assortment of cushions for the various dogs we had collected—Betony (the earl's Caucasian sheepdog), Nut (an Egyptian hound of Stoker's), Huxley (his bulldog), and my own noble Vespertine, a deerhound of great distinction. We took luncheon with them and later tea, spending the afternoon in a haze of cozy domestic bliss as we read through our correspondence, skimmed newspapers, and crumbled scones for the dogs. I glanced up to find Stoker deep in concentration as he read an editorial regarding the subject of votes for women—he supported the notion—and something thudded in my chest. At the time I put it down to indigestion. (The earl's cook was an accomplished woman, but occasionally her rock cakes were frankly indigestible.) Only later did I wonder if it might have been a premonition. For that afternoon was the last truly uncomplicated moment of happiness I was to know for a long time.

CHAPTER

2

The summons came the next day—a brief note from Sir Hugo Montgomerie, the head of Special Branch of Scotland Yard, delivered just after Stoker and I had settled to breakfast in the Belvedere. Stoker helped himself to a dish of eggs, arranged as usual on the sarcophagus we used as a sideboard, whilst I munched contentedly through a stack of buttered toast and read the newspapers, eager to see what I had missed during our travels abroad. A more serious soul might have reached first for the *Times*, but I have never claimed that particular virtue. I happily unfurled the latest edition of the *Daily Harbinger*, an illustrated periodical given to ludicrous flights of fancy complete with pictures of the most lurid variety. Stoker deplored my taste in newspapers, but I had found the *Daily Harbinger* to be highly instructive upon occasion. The fact that the pieces were only accidentally and intermittently based in truth did not alter my enjoyment. I had discovered the stories within were best taken with a hefty pinch of salt. But one thing I marked was the absence of any mention of the fiend whose reign of terror had dominated the headlines the previous autumn. After his orgy of killing early in November, it appeared the Ripper had slipped once more into the hell-bound shadows whence he had come, and London seemed to breathe a little easier as the spring commenced.

Not that the city was without its tensions. Parliament was sitting, and—unsurprisingly—the question of independence was on everyone's lips. *UNREST IN THE EMPIRE*, screamed the *Harbinger*.

"Whose independence?" Stoker asked in reply to my remark upon the subject.

I began ticking off the groups on my fingers. "Women. The suffragists staged a rally in Green Park, shouting loudly enough to be heard inside Buckingham Palace, although the queen was not in attendance. The Irish, predictably. There have been a spate of demonstrations in Dublin in favor of Home Rule. The Brazilians are thoroughly at odds with their emperor. And now the Indians. Apparently the notion of self-rule has gained popularity there as well. Members of the Commons intend to introduce bills to debate the idea of self-government for both countries, although not the vote for women," I added darkly.

"The queen won't much care for talk of India breaking free of the empire," he mused. "Rip says she quite likes calling herself empress."

Stoker's second brother, Sir Rupert—Rip to his family—had been knighted for services to the Crown. Officially the accolade had come for translating Chinese poetry, but Sir Rupert had confided one night after a third glass of whisky that it had actually been conferred for diplomatic work of the most discreet variety. Her Majesty was seldom seen in public, having withdrawn to Windsor Castle after the death of her beloved consort, but Sir Rupert still saw her occasionally, enough to note the creamy, catlike expression of satisfaction she wore whenever the subject of her Indian title arose in conversation. He was loyal to a fault, but upon this particular occasion, he had performed a marvelous impression of her, complete with a napkin draped over his head and an upended pudding dish in place of her tiny crown.

I pulled a face. "She mightn't have much choice. There was a bombing at a government office in Lucknow."

Stoker shied like a pony. "Anarchists?" We had had more than our share of trouble with such people, and I shared his reluctance to encounter more of them. In our experience, anarchists might claim to have the good of the people at heart, but they were often quite untidy in their methods.

"One of the extremist groups," I said, skimming the lines. "But a more moderate delegation has come to London for a series of meetings. They hope to achieve their means by peaceful negotiation." There was a photograph of the leader of the delegation—a maharani of mature years, which I applauded. It was far beyond the time when women should take their seat at the table of international politics, I believed. Unlike their masculine counterparts, women were far less likely to fling themselves headlong into war, to begin with.

I was about to hold forth on the subject when George, the hallboy, appeared, waving a letter that had just arrived in the second post. I slit it open with a fruit knife and skimmed the lines, noticing they had been penned in haste. Sir Hugo's handwriting, while always spidery, did not usually lurch quite so alarmingly.

"Sir Hugo asks us to meet him in Hyde Park," I said. "Near the Serpentine."

Stoker broke a sausage to pieces and fed the bits to the dogs. "Absolutely not."

I blinked at him. "Stoker, we cannot refuse. The Metropolitan Police force is the finest in the world," I said stoutly. "And Special Branch is its most illustrious division."

"Feathers," he said, piling more eggs onto his plate and adding a few deviled kidneys for good measure.

"*And*," I went on as if he had not interrupted, "Sir Hugo is the head of Special Branch. That makes him one of the foremost champions of law and order anywhere on the globe."

He sat heavily and plunged his fork into the heap of food on his plate, fixing me with a dark look. "I refuse."

"You have no reason to refuse," I said evenly. Stoker, being a male of the species, could not help occasionally erupting into irrationality. I had long observed that when a man does so, it is simplest to treat him with the same calm good humor one might employ when coaxing a stubborn horse or a slightly backwards child.

He put down his fork. "I can give you a score of reasons. I have been shot. I have been stabbed. I have been abducted. I have been very nearly drowned—"

I held up a hand. "For which you can hardly blame Sir Hugo. He did not drown you, nor did he abduct you. He has never shot you, and I am the only person who has stabbed you. It is illogical in the extreme to blame poor Sir Hugo for any of those inconveniences."

"Inconveniences?" His voice rose an octave. "You do recall that I very nearly died during one or two of those events?"

"Lower your voice, my love. You are alarming the dogs." I nodded to where the pack had pricked up their ears.

He picked up his fork again and stabbed a piece of bacon. "I know what this is about. You are feeling restless again. It has been two months since we last encountered a corpse and you nurture hopes that Sir Hugo will put us on the scent of fresh adventure." He waved his fork for emphasis.

"Do not point your breakfast meats at me, sir," I said in a tone of mild reproach. "I will admit only to a curiosity about what Sir Hugo wants and a willingness to put my talents, whatever they may be, at his disposal. For the good of England," I finished.

"For your own bloody amusement," he muttered, stuffing the bacon into his mouth. "Besides, I have a new mount to disassemble to-day. Lord Rosemorran spent hours playing with those benighted puppets and never even mentioned he has just taken delivery of a rather nice albino giraffe. From the Duke of Grasmere's collection. It's in filthy condition and apparently I am the only man in England His Grace trusts to repair it." He preened a little as he helped himself to more bacon.

I widened my eyes. "Heavens! How long has it been dead?"

He shrugged. "Sixty- or seventy-odd years."

"Then it will still be dead when you return," I said, smiling.

He growled and grimaced all the way through breakfast, but in the end, he put on his coat and came with me, although as a token of his annoyance, he made no move to pay for the hansom cab. Sir Hugo had instructed us to our rendezvous and I took care that we should arrive a few minutes before the appointed time. Sir Hugo could be as prickly as Stoker when vexed, and I hoped to find him in good humor. It had occurred to me to wonder if Sir Hugo had finally learnt of our Alpenwalder escapade. The events of that investigation had caused me to impersonate the princess of that country—a small crime, I supposed—and commit one or two other, much more significant acts. One might even be considered treason by an ungenerous person, I reflected. Sir Hugo, knowing the secret of my semi-royal birth, had been accommodating upon occasion, but I did not know if his indulgence would extend to criminal conspiracies, particularly those involving diplomatic relations. It seemed wisest not to test him if such a situation might be avoided.

And so it was a quarter of an hour before the designated time when Stoker and I passed through the gates of Hyde Park, where the plane trees were unfurling their soft green leaves to greet the spring with good cheer. Around the Serpentine, nannies pushed their charges in perambulators, both carefully polished. We passed a Sikh gentleman in a turban, quietly feeding bread crumbs to the ducks, and a woman of insalubrious appearance having a lengthy conversation with a red squirrel, whose ears twitched in response. I might have deplored the bustle and grime of the city, but London was also endlessly diverting, I reflected.

I had dressed in a town suit of heavy violet silk, the cut neat and just fashionable enough not to attract much attention. But venturing out with Stoker was rather like taking a pet lynx for a walk. He, too, wore a town suit—of excellent make, the aristocratic habit of good tailoring being one he could not bring himself to abandon. A closer look revealed the odd stain of wax or ink or custard cream due to his inveterate habit of wiping his fingers upon the nearest piece of cloth. But even if his suit had been in a state of pristine tidiness, he would have arrested attention. He was tall, reaching just six feet, and broadly muscled, his shoulders straining the seams of his coat. His hair, thick and black, waved to the bottom of his collar. His shirt concealed the myriad tattoos he had received whilst in Her Majesty's Navy, but the slim silver scar that ran from one brow to the cheekbone was silent witness to his encounter with a jaguar in the Amazonian jungles. That his eye had not been lost was a miracle. But the injury had left him subject to fatigue, and when that happened, he wore an eye patch, black as a pirate's heart. Coupled with the hooped gold earrings in his ears, the eye patch presented a creditable impression of a buccaneer, and I was not surprised when one or two nannies hurried their charges out of his path. I was even less surprised to see the expression of frank longing on the faces of a few of the maids. He is, without question, a striking-looking man.

To my surprise, Sir Hugo had already arrived and was sitting on a bench, well wrapped against the late morning chill. He rose as we approached and touched his hat.

"Miss Speedwell," he said, inclining his head in a courtly gesture. "Templeton-Vane."

As the third son of the late viscount of that name, Stoker was an Honorable and his given name was Revelstoke, neither of which he enjoyed. For as long as I had known him, he was Stoker to friend and foe alike. He gave Sir Hugo a cool nod in return.

"It is rather too brisk for sitting," Sir Hugo said. "Why don't we walk and I will tell you why I have summoned you." It was not a question. He put a hand under my elbow and propelled me forward. Stoker joined us on my other side and we moved onto a quiet path away from the nannies and their charges.

"We would have been happy to come to you at Scotland Yard," I began.

Sir Hugo held up a hand. "No. This is a private matter, not police business," he said. He paused a moment. "I should like to ask you for a favor. Of a personal nature."

Stoker's brows shot skywards, but he said nothing. "Go on," I urged.

We began to walk again, slowly, as Sir Hugo spoke. "It concerns my goddaughter, Euphemia. Or rather, it concerns her entire family. They are called Hathaway and they live at Hathaway Hall on Dartmoor. Miss Speedwell, are you quite all right? I think you stumbled there."

"A pebble in my shoe," I assured him. "No matter. Do go on."

"Well, I am a little vexed about the question of Euphemia," he said.

"And what is the trouble with Euphemia?" I asked in a deliberately casual tone. "Unsuitable suitor? Gambling debts?"

Sir Hugo pressed his lips together. "Euphemia is entirely above reproach," he said stiffly. "The whole family are guided by principles of service and duty. But they have known their share of tragedy. Let me begin with her grandparents, Lady Hathaway—Ada—and Sir Geoffrey, knighted for his service in India. Sir Geoffrey died last year, but Ada still lives at Hathaway Hall, although I understand her health is poor these days. She is very much in decline, I'm afraid."

"Who else lives at the Hall?" Stoker inquired. "Euphemia's parents?"

"No, they died in India some fifteen years ago. Euphemia was a small child. She scarcely remembers them. Her official guardian was her grandfather, Sir Geoffrey, but since his death last year, the Hall and its responsibilities have fallen to her elder brother, Charles. He, too, was in India, but he came to England upon inheriting the Hall. He has established himself there with his wife and young children, and they comprise the household along with the servants and Ada's companion."

He paused, giving me a quick sideways glance. "Euphemia wrote to me recently, a most extraordinary letter. You see, Charles was actually the second-born son by some years. The eldest, Jonathan, was the heir to Hathaway Hall."

I stumbled again, but Sir Hugo's tight grip on my elbow saved me. I turned to face him. "Jonathan? Jonathan Hathaway?" I said in a hollow voice. "But that's extraordinary. I know him. Or at least I did." My voice trailed off.

Sir Hugo's eyes were mournful. "Yes. I am afraid you did."

Stoker looked from one of us to the other. "What happened to Jonathan Hathaway?"

I was silent a long moment, thinking of the kindly young man I had known. "He died," I said finally. "In the eruption of Krakatoa."

Stoker took my hand in his. I did not often speak of the eruption. It had been a cataclysm that haunted me still. The very earth itself seemed to crack in two, heaving the world into chaos. Jonathan and I had been members of the same party traveling together when warnings had come that it was too dangerous to venture nearer the Sunda Strait, where the volcano was waking. I had heeded the caution of the local people, remaining at my lodgings in Sumatra, but Jonathan, with his cheerful certainty that all would be well, had gone ahead with another of our traveling companions. Neither had been heard from again.

"Of course, Jonathan's loss was devastating for the family," Sir Hugo went on. "His grandfather never quite recovered from the blow, and that is when Ada—Lady Hathaway's—health began to fail. Sir Geoffrey, dispirited, nonetheless understood that Charles was now his heir. The estate was not entailed, so the fact that Jonathan's body was not recovered at the time did not impede the settling of the inheritance. Sir Geoffrey drew up a new will leaving Hathaway Hall and the guardianship of Euphemia to her brother Charles. As I said, last year Sir Geoffrey died, and Charles came from India to take charge of matters. It was all handled as efficiently and as properly as possible," he said.

"Then what is the trouble?" Stoker asked.

Sir Hugo drew in a deep breath. "The trouble is that after six years, Jonathan Hathaway has come home."

CHAPTER 3

That is quite impossible," I said flatly. "He died in the eruption."

"How was it that his body was never recovered?" Stoker asked.

"It was pandemonium," I told him. "Utter chaos for months afterwards."

"Did you remain in Sumatra?" Sir Hugo asked.

"Yes," I said sharply. "My friends were missing. I stayed for some weeks, until it became apparent there was no point in entertaining hopes. They were lost."

"And yet Jonathan Hathaway survived," Sir Hugo said gently.

"But how?" Stoker asked.

Sir Hugo's brow furrowed. "I do not know the particulars. Only that a man has appeared at Hathaway Hall and Lady Hathaway has recognized him as her grandson."

I was quick to spot the discrepancy. "Only Lady Hathaway? Not the rest of the family?"

"The rest of the family did not know Jonathan well," he said thoughtfully. "As the heir, he was sent to England as a boy for his education. He stayed with Sir Geoffrey and Lady Hathaway at the Hall during school holidays whilst the younger children remained in India. Charles and Effie came to England later. Only Lady Hathaway is left of the family who knew Jonathan as a grown man."

"There must be servants," Stoker said. "A nanny? A gardener? Someone."

Sir Hugo shrugged. "Her ladyship closed up much of the house after Sir Geoffrey's death. It is an expensive place to run and she wished to economize. The family that had been in service the longest took the opportunity to emigrate—that was the gardener, the cook, and their housemaid daughters gone in one fell swoop. The housekeeper is still there, but she is a cautious woman. The house has since been opened up with Charles Hathaway coming to live there with his family, but the staff are almost entirely new, I understand."

"Charles Hathaway and his wife would not thank the housekeeper for recognizing Jonathan Hathaway," Stoker mused. "That would certainly upset the apple cart."

"It would indeed," Sir Hugo agreed. "The estate has come to Charles quite legally, and Jonathan—if it is indeed Jonathan—would have to challenge their grandfather's will in court. That would be an expensive proposition and I doubt he has the means to do it, but it would still sow enormous discord in the household. As yet, the inhabitants of the Hall seem divided. Lady Hathaway has recognized him and she has the support of one old family retainer, a nanny who lives in a cottage out on the moor. Her health is poor and her eyesight unreliable, so her opinion carries little weight, but it is something." He held up two fingers of one hand, then began to count off the fingers opposite. "Then Charles and his wife, Mary, are on the other side, doubting Jonathan's identity and fearing they are entertaining an impostor." He spread his hands apart. "That leaves Euphemia in the middle. She has not committed herself either way. She is not certain of what to believe."

"Was she fond of Jonathan?" Stoker inquired. "It seems curious a younger sister, who might well have idolized her elder brother, would not give full support to someone who could be he."

A faint smile touched Sir Hugo's lips. "Euphemia is a scientist—an astronomer, to be exact. It was Sir Geoffrey's avocation and she has followed in her grandfather's footsteps. She prefers to deal in facts, in that which may be quantified. She would believe nothing unless there is evidence."

"What sort of evidence?" I put in. "Do you mean to say this person has none of Jonathan Hathaway's papers?"

"He has documentation—letters and a passport—which appears to be in order, but these things can certainly be falsified."

"What does he say about his claim?" I pressed.

"That is the most intriguing part," Sir Hugo told us. "He says nothing at all. He appeared one day at Hathaway Hall, bruised and in a state of collapse. On the directions of Mrs. Hathaway, Charles' wife, the stranger was carried into the hall as an act of Christian charity. They bathed his wounds and put him to bed. In the hopes of identifying this stranger and perhaps notifying his family of his whereabouts, Mrs. Hathaway had his pockets searched and examined the papers that were found upon him. He had letters from Ada, much worn and tattered, addressed to Jonathan Hathaway in care of various postes restantes around the world. When Lady Hathaway discovered this, she insisted upon seeing the young man herself. She forced her way into the sickroom just as the fellow was regaining consciousness. He opened his eyes, said one word, and lapsed into insensibility again."

"What word?" Stoker asked.

"'Granna,'" Sir Hugo said. "It was an endearment all of the Hathaway children used for Lady Hathaway. That, coupled with a resemblance to Jonathan, was enough to persuade her that the man lying in the bed was her grandson, returned from the dead."

I shook my head. "It is too fantastical to be believed."

Sir Hugo's expression was sympathetic. "I know it must have come as a shock to you that someone purporting to be your friend should appear."

"How did you know he was my friend?" I demanded.

"My dear Miss Speedwell, I do hope you have not forgot what resources I have at my command," he said blandly.

"You investigated Jonathan Hathaway," I surmised. "And you discovered we traveled together."

"I was hoping to avoid involving you," he assured me. "I have dealt with one or two such cases in the past, and I understand how difficult they can be. But I must have the truth, for Effie's sake. For Ada's. Even for Jonathan's. If this man is an impostor, then he must be made to pay for his crimes. If it is Jonathan, then all shadow of suspicion must be lifted so that he can live his life in peace."

"And you expect Veronica to do that," Stoker said, folding his arms over his chest.

"Of course he does," I answered with a tinge of bitterness. "I am to be the test."

"You knew him," Sir Hugo said simply. "You traveled with him and were friends. Believe me, if I could have unearthed any other of his companions, I would have done so. I have investigated a dozen people known to have accompanied Jonathan Hathaway in his travels, and it came down to you and a fellow called Harry Spenlove."

I said nothing, but my breath was tight in my chest. Jonathan Hathaway. Harry Spenlove. Names I had not thought to hear again. They had been the best of friends, generous to me when our paths had crossed in New Guinea. Jonathan had had a passion for lepidoptery to rival my own, and Harry was simply game, always up for an adventure. What had begun as a lark, sailing to a new island on the hunt for *Papilio iswaroides*, had become a sort of good-natured rivalry. Jonathan and I would challenge one another, choosing a species and separating, meeting again at dinner to see whose hunt had been the more successful. Jonathan played a gentleman's game. He was heir to a fortune and had no need of the money our trophies would fetch from eager collectors. More often than not, his specimens found their way into my jars as he pleaded laziness. "I cannot be bothered to mount them properly," he protested. Or he claimed to have mislaid his chemicals, misplaced his materials, any excuse to pass his superfluous specimens my way.

He was not entirely altruistic, I remembered with a sharp pang. He often kept the most beautiful, the most unusual, for his own collection. But he had given me more than enough to earn my forgiveness. Coupled with his generosity, he had been a quiet, courtly companion. There was a serenity about him that belied the restless spirit that had sent him around the world, far from kith and kin. Unlike Harry, bright and reckless Harry, Jonathan had been restful. If Harry was a spark, Jonathan was a steady ember. I had adored them both in very different ways and for very different reasons.

"You have not discovered Harry Spenlove is alive, I presume?" I said, attempting a lightness I did not feel.

Sir Hugo shook his head. "Buried on the island of Java. I have telegraphed to the Dutch officials there and it has been confirmed. They have sent a rubbing of his gravestone, although one would prefer a photograph. Apparently, he died of a fever. Sanitation issues," he finished with a distasteful twitch of the nose.

"There was much illness after the eruption," I said dully. "I had not imagined that Jonathan survived."

"Krakatoa erupted six years ago," Stoker remarked. "Where has he been all this time?"

Sir Hugo pursed his lips. "Effie was not particularly forthcoming on that point. I gather the fellow was badly knocked about in the eruption. Suffered some injuries, worked his way across South America, that sort of thing. In due course, he made it to Bristol, where he was apparently involved in some sort of altercation with a few sailors. He took the worst of it and it seems to have aggravated his old injuries. He was in a state of confusion as he made his way to Dartmoor, using the last of his funds to pay his train fare. He alighted at the small moorland village of Shepton Parva. There is a goodish road, but the most direct route is across the moor. He was found in the summerhouse of the Hall. It marks the boundary of the garden from the moor itself. In fact, the summerhouse is the only way into the grounds of the estate from the moor. The rest is walled off for gardens and inaccessible by foot. He had collapsed by then, in a pitiable state, Effie says. No doubt that is what roused Mrs. Hathaway's pity, although I wonder if she regrets her impulse to take him in," he finished ruefully.

"If he is indeed Jonathan, he could well wrench her husband's inheritance away," Stoker mused. "To say nothing of her children's."

"And yet he makes no claim as yet," Sir Hugo said with a shrug. "He has apparently never told anyone to call him Jonathan Hathaway and answers to the name solely because it pleases Lady Hathaway."

"That is how things stand at present?" I asked.

"It is," Sir Hugo confirmed.

"And you want me to unmask him for you," I said.

"Or confirm his identity," Sir Hugo answered. "And if it is Jonathan, believe me, I shall join the Hathaways in killing the fatted calf. But such uncertainty cannot be endured. Miss Speedwell, you cannot refuse me."

Still, I hesitated. "Tell me more about your goddaughter," I said.

He paused, pursing his lips. "She is a curious girl, very curious. A first-rate mind, in the mold of her grandfather Sir Geoffrey. They are a curious family, most with a few abiding passions and the rare genius. Geoffrey was a genius. Unfortunately, his intellect seems to have passed by the next two generations entirely save for Euphemia," he added dryly. "She showed real promise as an astronomer, but without her grandfather's guidance, she has . . . drifted. She mourned him, far more than her parents or brother. I sent her a small dog, hoping to cheer her up," he added with a slightly abashed look. Why gentlemen so often feel the need to conceal their kinder impulses is a mystery only Nature herself could answer.

"That was thoughtful of you," I told him.

He pinked with pleasure. "It is only a little thing. An Italian greyhound. She dotes on the pup, dresses her in little jumpers, as the moorland climate is too cold for her. I thought having something to care for might bring her out of herself, but there is a quality about her letters, an elusiveness I cannot reconcile with the lively child I once knew."

"Have you visited?" Stoker asked.

Sir Hugo looked uncomfortable. "I could not attend Sir Geoffrey's funeral. There was a police matter which demanded my presence in London. By the time I was able to get away, some weeks had passed. I knew Effie was still quite melancholy, so I brought the pup with me. I thought to cheer her by taking her for walks and bringing books and paints. She showed no interest in anything other than the dog, and that only when she could spare time from dancing attendance on her sister-in-law."

"Mary Hathaway?" I inquired. "Charles' wife?"

"The same," he acknowledged in a dry tone that confirmed there was no love lost in that quarter. "I do not mind telling you I am no admirer of Mary Hathaway. She is too clever for Charles by half."

"How so?" Stoker asked.

"She is ambitious," he said, his mouth thinning in distaste. "Her father was in trade in Yorkshire, made his fortune in sweets—Fanthorp's Fancies."

Stoker brightened. "I love those—particularly the coconut drops."

"Yes, well, mind you don't mention that to Mary Hathaway. She is eager to put the origins of her father's money entirely behind her. She aspired to an old name, and in marrying Charles, she succeeded. There's little of the Hathaway money left, but that does not seem to trouble her. She has plenty from her father and she means to polish Charles up and make something of him."

"And how does Charles feel about that?" I inquired.

Sir Hugo pulled a face. "The boy likes sheep. All he wants is to restore the family flocks—they used to be legendary, the Hathaway Moorlands. But that is not grand enough for Mary. She expects him to stand for Parliament with an eye to a knighthood someday, and preferably a baronetcy."

"Lofty goals," Stoker remarked.

"Not if you have the brass, and Mary Hathaway does. Before she and Charles took charge of the Hall, it was a very quiet household. But since they settled, Mary has been making over the house and wants to try her hand at Effie as well. She uses the girl, morning to night, always asking her to fetch and do."

"Perhaps she likes lording her status over Effie," I suggested. "She wouldn't be the first sister-in-law to do so."

"Or she is simply trying to keep Effie too busy to bother with astronomy," Sir Hugo said. "Mary has convinced Charles that such studies are not 'genteel' enough and that Effie has been indulged far too much."

"And Charles goes along with it?" Stoker asked.

"Charles would agree if Mary told him the moon was made of milk," Sir Hugo replied sourly. "He is well and truly henpecked. When I was at the Hall, I am afraid I let my temper get the better of me. I accosted Charles and told him it was appalling that he permitted his wife to use his sister in such a fashion and that Effie ought to be allowed to continue her studies. Cross words, I am sorry to say, were exchanged. I have not returned since and I have been informed that any spontaneous visit on my part would not be encouraged. Effie has no money of her own," he finished. "Without funds, she cannot leave, so she remains there, a sort of drudge to her brother's wife."

"Poor girl," Stoker said with real sympathy.

I repressed a sigh. "She lacks gumption."

Sir Hugo's brows raised perceptibly. "How can you claim to know that?"

"She is in good health, is she not?"

"She is."

"And you have said she has had a good education. She comes from a good family. She might strike out on her own. She might teach or hire herself as a companion where at least she would earn a wage for her efforts. Instead, she does not bestir herself. She is content to exist in a sort of larval stage. She must be prodded out of her inactivity," I added firmly. I was a fervent believer in the restorative benefits of action.

"The girl has been grieving," Stoker reminded me.

"For more than a year, and that is quite enough time to mourn anyone," I told him. "I think we should undertake this mission to liberate Euphemia Hathaway from her torpid state."

"I have a walrus—an enormous walrus, to say nothing of my albino giraffe," Stoker said. His jaw was set in a line I recognized only too well. He was feeling decidedly mulish. He was longing to return to his workshop and immerse himself in his beloved trophies. We had only just returned from one of our little adventures, and I realized with a pang how often he had given way to my intrepid derailments of his plans.

"Sir Hugo, this is not the best time," I said, prepared for once to make the sacrifice Stoker so clearly wanted of me.

Sir Hugo turned to Stoker. "Since you cannot present yourself at Hathaway Hall as agents of mine, I thought you could go under false pretenses—at least not entirely false. You see, the original Tudor house was pulled down in the time of the Jacobeans. The building that took its place is dark and halfway to falling down of its own accord. The decades the family spent in India meant it was neglected, and Sir Geoffrey preferred to spend the funds on his observatory instead of mundane things like the roof. Charles has inherited a bit of a white elephant, and Mary has grand plans for the place. She wants it fully modernized—tiled bathrooms in the bedroom wings, flushing, er, appurtenances," he said, coloring a rosy shade at the idea of such indelicate matters as toilets. "Fresh wallpaper, furniture, all modern and comfortable. What she does not want is what she refers to as all the 'dusty rubbish' the Hathaways brought back from their travels. Charles and Effie's father was a natural historian. Not a particularly gifted one, but competent. He assembled a comprehensive set of mounts in his travels. As it happens, those mounts are still at Hathaway Hall, and I know that Mary Hathaway would be perfectly delighted to present his collection to Lord Rosemorran for his proposed museum."

He let the suggestion hang there, enticing as a juicy morsel of bait to a rising carp.

"I have specimens," Stoker told him. "More than I know what to do with, I promise you."

Sir Hugo smiled. "Oh, have you a thylacine then?"

Stoker stopped dead in his tracks. "You cannot be serious."

"As the grave," Sir Hugo assured him.

"*Thylacinus cynocephalus*," Stoker breathed, his eyes alight with the sort of unholy lust other men reserved for women.

"The Tasmanian tiger?" I asked. "I thought they were near to extinction."

"They are," Stoker said, his color high. "It is the largest carnivorous marsupial in the world. The power of its bite and the dimension of its jaw . . ." I need not repeat the rest. He went on in that vein for some time, to Sir Hugo's obvious amusement.

At length, I raised a hand to quell any further information about the creature, still grappling with Stoker's overly detailed explanation of the uniqueness of the scrotal sac in the male of the species.

"You are clearly in a state of desperation, else you'd not have cast such a tempting lure," I told Sir Hugo.

"I am," he said.

In spite of the words, his expression was—not quite pleading. Imploring. He wanted a favor, I reminded myself. And although justice would have been enough to spur me to action, the thought of Sir Hugo in my debt was a powerful inducement.

"Miss Speedwell," Sir Hugo said, "you cannot refuse me."

"You are right," I said, setting a mirthless smile upon my lips. "I cannot. When do we leave?"

CHAPTER

4

In spite of my insouciant response to Sir Hugo, by the time Stoker and I returned to the Belvedere, I was entertaining second thoughts. Not only had the mention of Jonathan and Harry revived the old, desolate feelings of panic and grief, but Sir Hugo's parting words had been none too comforting.

After explaining that seats had been reserved for us on the first train the following morning at his personal expense, he shook us each warmly by the hand, an expression of relief etched upon his features.

"I really cannot thank you enough," he said humbly. A sudden twinkle had come to his eye. "And if you find this possible impostor to be not enough mystery for you, you might turn your hands to an investigation of the supernatural variety. The moor is thick with ghosts, you know."

He left off with a laugh, clearly pleased to have successfully shifted the burden of this matter onto our shoulders. Anticipating our acceptance, Sir Hugo had already written to Charles, a conciliatory letter smoothing over their previous contretemps and explaining about Lord Rosemorran's plans for a museum. He had suggested that Charles write to us with an invitation to come and assess his collection with an eye to purchasing any specimens that would augment the pieces already in his lordship's possession. Charles had been so eager, Sir Hugo told us as he produced the invitation with a flourish, that he had responded by return post and we were expected the following day.

"We ought to refuse," I muttered to Stoker as we finished packing the oddments we would require. We were in the Belvedere some hours after dinner, collecting the necessary reference materials and tools of the trade.

"Why on earth would we do that?" he asked mildly as he surveyed a pair of calipers.

"This is a family matter of a most delicate nature," I protested. "It is hardly within our purview."

"Most of our investigations have been family matters and all extremely delicate," he said. "In fact, most of them have been connected with *your* family."

"I do not require being reminded of the fact," I replied in an acidulous tone. I chose a selection of fine brushes, a fresh notebook, and a magnifying glass and wrapped them carefully.

"Then why the reluctance?" There was something in his tone, a note that sounded just slightly off, like the string of a violin that has been imperfectly tuned and indifferently plucked.

I shrugged. "We have only just returned from the Alpenwald, and Lord Rosemorran has been very accommodating of our absences. I should not like to take advantage of him." I did not confess the truth, that an unease had settled over me, and I was reluctant to chase the ghosts of my past.

"It is hardly taking advantage if we secure specimens for his collection," Stoker pointed out. "I spoke with him after teatime and he is most anxious to acquire the thylacine if it is in acceptable condition."

I packed my things into a small carpetbag and paused, considering. Apart from the various varieties of fritillary, there were not many fine examples of lepidoptery to be found on Dartmoor, but the Rose-morran collection was a little thin on native British specimens. It was very early in the season, impossibly early, I reflected. It was likely that only *Boloria euphrosyne*, the Pearl-Bordered Fritillary, would be in flight before May, yet it was a sprightly little butterfly and a group of them might be worth the effort. I took up a box of minuten—the tiny headless pins used by butterfly hunters to secure mounts and by me to discourage men who tried to hold my hand without invitation. (A few tucked discreetly into the cuffs are wondrously effective.) I added the requisite killing jars, a tiny packet of cyanide salts, some cotton wool, and several specimen jars and boxes before selecting my favorite net. It was light and supple, crafted of ash, the bag sewn from the finest silk net I could afford. It was a thing of beauty, as much an artist's tool as an implement of science, and I felt something that had lain dormant within me come alive again as I passed my palm over the sleek grain of the wood.

"Besides," Stoker went on lightly, "I should have thought a ghost and a mystery would have been too much temptation for you to resist."

I managed a smile, but Stoker had already returned his attention to his own interests—namely, the thylacine. He had unearthed a recent issue of the *Semi-Annual Journal of the Natural Historian* in which one of his colleagues held forth at length on the subject of the elusive Tasmanian tiger and was sunk in happy anticipation of getting his hands upon a specimen of his own when I murmured something about a necessary errand and slipped out the door.

A short time later, I arrived on foot at the grand entrance of the Sudbury Hotel, one of London's most exclusive accommodations. A pair of doormen, smartly dressed in crushed bottle green velvet, sprang to attention, but I passed them by, nipping around the corner and down the alley until I came to the tradesmen's entrance. I scribbled a quick note and passed it to one of the boys who loitered in such places in hopes of small commissions. I presented him with a shilling—a more than generous sum, in my opinion, but the child had the skinny, pinched look of undernourishment—which he took with alacrity before disappearing into the working heart of the hotel. I had taken the precaution of wearing a veil, and in the ensuing moments I was grateful. More than one waiter gave me an assessing glance, no doubt attempting to ascertain if I had come to ply a very old and specific trade.

"If you are looking for a harlot, might I suggest the alley behind the Karnak Hall?" I said politely to the boldest. "Ask for Elsie. She is a friend." The fellow reared back and continued on his way, muttering about eccentric women, which I found rude in the extreme. Stoker and I had made Elsie's acquaintance during a previous investigation,* and she was a diligent practitioner of the amatory arts, but only for pay. And since a woman needs to earn a living, it seemed only considerate to send trade her way should the opportunity arise.

I was still ruminating on such thoughts when the door opened and a slender figure in a maid's uniform stepped out, casting sharp glances left and right.

"I have slipped away but I can give you no more than a minute before I am missed," she told me.

"It is lovely to see you too, J. J.," I replied. My friendship—if I may call it that—with J. J. Butterworth, lady reporter, was another souvenir of our adventures with the Tiverton Egyptological expedition and the events that occurred in Karnak Hall. Always in search of a story, she frequently disguised herself in order to gain access denied to her male counterparts. Her favorite masquerade was chambermaid at the Sudbury, a stratagem that permitted her to observe the great and good at close quarters—as well as the chance to examine the contents of their

---

* *A Murderous Relation*

wastepaper baskets, private papers, and bedsheets. Each of these, she had explained to me, could tell a story, and the *Daily Harbinger* paid well for them. She longed for the career of a serious journalist, but her way was too often barred by men determined to keep her out. So, in desperation, she often got her revenge by assuming one of her little disguises and delivering the type of story that a man could never secure.

J. J. grinned. "Back from the Alpenwald then?"

"And we are off again in the morning."

She lifted her brows. "So soon? On the trail of something?"

"Like you? I presume you are here in order to spy upon the maharani currently installed in the Empress Suite," I said.

She pulled a face. "Who told you?"

"No one. It was a guess which you have just confirmed," I said with a touch of—one hopes—forgivable smugness. "I saw your byline in the piece in the *Harbinger* about her and assumed she was staying here and that if I found her, you could not be far behind."

"Well done," she said, folding her arms over her chest. "You are a regular Augustine Dupin. Now, I have precisely two minutes before the housekeeper comes looking for me and has my guts for garters for standing about yammering when I am meant to be turning down beds. What do you want, Veronica?"

"I wanted to know if the name Hathaway means anything to you."

She paused, furrowing her brow. "Anne? Married to Shakespeare?"

"Not Warwickshire Hathaways. Devonshire Hathaways," I said in some exasperation. "They've a house called Hathaway Hall on Dartmoor."

She rolled her eyes. "Dartmoor? Nothing but sheep and rocks. Why the devil do they live there?"

"The same reason anyone lives anywhere," I said. "Inherited."

I gave her a minute while she thought. Watching J. J. Butterworth work through her immense hoard of knowledge was vastly interesting.

Stoker had once taken me to a demonstration of Mr. Babbage's computational machines. The whirring and clicking and sharp manipulation of information put me greatly in mind of J. J.'s efforts, her freckled nose wrinkling up as she screwed her eyes tightly closed, thinking.

"I did hear something, now you mention it," she said, opening her eyes at last. "A long-lost father or something."

"Eldest son," I corrected.

"That's it. Lost in a shipwreck or earthquake?"

"Volcano," I said.

She shrugged. "An act of God is an act of God. In any event, he died and is returned, resurrected as it were. My editor thought it might make an interesting story, but it is not mine. One of the new lads was assigned to it."

"When did it run?" I pressed.

"It didn't," she said. "It was meant to be only a small piece to run early this month, but Boulanger's flight pushed everything aside and heaps of articles were cut for space." I was not surprised. The French general Boulanger, nicknamed Général Revanche, had been at the head of his own political party—one that had nearly accomplished a coup and overthrown the French Republic. His reluctance to fully seize power when he had the chance in January had led to a warrant being issued for his arrest on charges of treason and conspiracy, and he had fled Paris at the start of April. Newspapers had been full of speculation as to his whereabouts—and what the French government would do to him if he fell into their clutches.

J. J. went on. "You were just in Paris, did you see anything of interest?" I recognized the sharp-eyed gaze of a hound upon the scent of a hare.

"No, apart from that appalling erection of Monsieur Eiffel," I assured her.

"It has not been formally opened. How did you see it?"

"It is impossible to miss," I said. "It dominates the city, quite dwarfing the Arc de Triomphe and Notre-Dame."

"It is a beacon of modernism and progress," she began, but before she could warm to her theme, the door opened and one of the errand boys peered out.

"You're wanted," he said to her before ducking back inside.

"I must fly." She bade me farewell but paused with her hand upon the knob. "There is one more thing about your Hathaways," she said. "I don't believe it was simply the Boulanger affair that killed the story."

"Then why was it never published?" I asked.

She rubbed her fingers together in an unmistakable gesture. Money. Then she vanished through the door without a backwards glance. J. J. had sound instincts, I reflected. If she believed her editor had been bribed not to run the story—and he was a bald man with as many scruples as he had hairs upon his head—then it was most likely the truth. And that meant that someone at Hathaway Hall was very keen for the story of the man returned from the dead not to become public knowledge.

CHAPTER

5

The next morning Stoker and I were on the train as directed, heading west as the sun rose behind us in a blaze of pink and gold. It was a breathtaking morning to be taking our leave of London, the sky dazzling enough to make us regret the necessity. The fogs had been blown away by a breeze fit to caress the cheek of a god, the earliest of the budding leaves spreading their bright green capes against a soft blue sky. We traveled in comfort, Sir Hugo's arrangements having extended to a first-class compartment and a hamper from Fortnum's filled with every conceivable delicacy.

Stoker spent the journey enthralled in the latest Arcadia Brown detective story—"to set the proper frame of mind," he explained—but the quarterly journal of *The Aurelian Sisterhood* remained unread upon my lap. I had thought to take the opportunity to catch up on my professional reading, but the vistas beyond my window were too distracting. The redbrick chimneys of the city, once unthinkably foul to me, now added a certain charm to the landscape for all their black-smoke belches, and I watched with a little pang as the narrow back gardens of the suburbs gave way to the wider stretches of open country. I was becoming a Londoner at last, I realized in some alarm. It had once been the greatest source of pleasure to put the vast metropolis behind me as I set out again upon adventures in uncharted climes. Now it seemed I hesitated to set foot outside its confines, trembling like a virgin sacrifice on the precipice of disaster. How could I, who had traveled with Corsican bandits and known the pleasures of camping with no other roof than the stars, shrink from a sojourn anywhere in these dominions? It was unthinkable. Had I, I wondered in horror, *lost my nerve*?

"I most certainly have not," I said aloud.

Stoker blinked at me over the top of his book. His cheeks were flushed pink, a sure sign that something saucy was happening on the page. "I beg your pardon?" he asked.

"Nothing," I assured him. "I am merely wrestling with a question of spirit. I fear I have become tame."

He snorted, marking his place in the book with a thumb. "You? Tame? My dearest Veronica, it would take a better man than I to accomplish such a feat."

I flapped a hand. "I did not mean *that*," I said. "I mean the yearning for open country and the freedom of a net in my hand and untilled ground beneath my feet. Apart from uneventful trips to Madeira and the Alpenwald, my escapades these past two years have all taken place within the confines of this island. And yes, I have encountered peril, but it is not the same as *adventure*."

He carefully laid the book aside. "Well, if it is adventure you seek..." He reached for me with a singularly determined look. He settled me across his lap, his lips brushing the pulsebeat just below my ear. "'Sweeter by far than Hybla's honey'd roses / When steep'd in dew rich to intoxication. / Ah! I will taste that dew...'"

Stoker frequently resorted to Keats in intimate moments, usually fitting his caresses to the appropriate lines, delivered in his rumbling baritone. I was powerless against the elegance of the poetry coupled with delicate debaucheries, and I did not refuse him. It was not at all the sort of adventure I meant, but it would do, I decided. Oh, it would do very nicely indeed.

The soft and lovely weather of London had subsided by the time we reached the other side of Salisbury Plain, growing progressively nastier until a proper gale was blowing as our train drew into the tiny station Shepton Parva. The Hathaways, expecting us, had kindly sent a conveyance, but it was obvious from the moment we settled ourselves inside that Charles Hathaway's lavish improvements at the Hall had not yet extended to the stables. It was an elderly vehicle, at least sixty years past its prime, with leaking roof and cracked windows, and a broken-down nag to pull it along at a snail's pace. Outside, the tempest roared, lightning occasionally illuminating a landscape of bleak moorland punctuated by lonely tors.

We journeyed into this no-man's-land for what seemed hours, and I thought of the man they called Jonathan Hathaway, making such an effort whilst in the grip of injury and illness. Did some primal knowledge in the blood draw him back to the land where his people had lived for centuries? Or had he merely stumbled into a fortuitous household where the lady of the house was prepared to do her Christian duty and entertain strangers unaware?

As we drew closer to the Hall, I became aware of a growing unease, a feeling not mitigated by the wildness of the landscape. The further we went, the more torturous the scenery, what little of it we could discern from the begrimed windows of the coach. The driver had been a dour sort, communicating only in monosyllables before taking his place on the box, and he seemed content to travel at the horse's painfully slow pace, although only an oilskin cape shielded him from the vagaries of weather. At last, he thumped once on the roof of the coach, calling in a harsh voice, "The Hall," as we paused—either for some dramatic effect or to rest the horse. The miserable creature stood a moment, and just then a sudden flash of lightning showed us our destination, a great monstrosity of a house, crouching against the landscape like a beast ready to spring itself upon unsuspecting prey . . .

(Stoker, who has been reading this account over my shoulder as I write, has just interjected. "For God's sake, Veronica, it was a *house*. Large and rather ugly with a few more gargoyles than strictly necessary, but it was a house." I have informed him that editorial criticism is not welcome within these pages, and I expect to hear no further commentary upon the veracity of my accounts. I should point out that I have long since ceased sharing my writing with him prior to submitting my accounts to the archive of the Hippolyta Club. He takes umbrage at my descriptions of his physique as well as any mention of physical intimacy between us. For all of his robust enjoyment of such activities, he occasionally demonstrates the fastidious prudery of a spinster aunt. It is a flaw I am attempting to remedy. In any event, I have banished him to work upon his newest acquisition and expect now to return to my account uninterrupted.)

. . . a great monstrosity of a house, crouching against the landscape like a beast ready to spring itself upon unsuspecting prey. A faint glimmer shone against three of the windows, but no blaze of light greeted us, no promise of warmth and welcome. In fact, we stood upon the step, barely sheltered from the worst of the driving rain, as Stoker applied himself manfully to a bellpull that resisted his efforts, clearly broken. He resorted to the knocker, an enormous affair of iron wrought in the shape of a ram's head—the Hathaway badge, as we later learned. Stoker grabbed it by the snout and dropped it heavily against the strike plate. The sound of it was barely discernible over the storm, and he was just about to raise it again when the door swung back on creaking hinges. The inside of the Hall was scarcely brighter than the tempestuous night, but it was enough to reveal a house-keeper, I presumed, with steel grey hair coiled above each ear in a style that had last been popular when Empress Eugénie was a bride. A chatelaine, heavy with keys, jangled at her waist as she moved.

"Oh, I am sorry! 'Tis such a filthy night, we expected you would have stayed the night at the village inn rather than make such a journey. Fair five miles it is in that rattletrap of Tom Carter's," she fussed, ushering us inside and towards a hearth where a single log smoldered.

"It is not the Hathaway carriage?" Stoker asked.

"Lord love you, sir," she said, "the family have a smart new carriage, but it cannot stand to our rough roads. The axle has been broken twice and one of the wheels came clear off yesterday. Now, stand you there, by the fireside," she instructed. She hurried back to the door, where the aptly named Mr. Carter was depositing our bags. Stoker proffered him a generous coin in gratuity and he took it, slouching out again and leaving the bags in a heap inside the door.

"Never you mind," the housekeeper said. "I will have your things brought to your rooms. I am Mrs. Desmond, the housekeeper." She guided us in, clucking a little like a hen over errant chicks. "The family have retired hours ago, and you must be worn to ribbons. Let me just turn down the beds and have hot bricks put in."

She hurried up a wide, oaken staircase. It was unusual in design, carved with decorations I could not quite make out in the gloom. Animals, I surmised, catching a glimpse of pointed fangs. Across the bottom of the staircase hung a pair of wooden gates, to keep the dogs from the upper floors, no doubt. But there were no dogs here now, warming themselves at the feeble fire. In days long past, there would have been a pack of hunting hounds, perhaps a lady's spaniel or two, lolling on a bright woolen hearthrug.

Now there were only the bare flags of the hall, upon which stood a pair of tall wooden chairs, enormous things with carved hoods over the tops, and a single suit of armor, rusting sadly in the corner. A large dining table had been set in the center, not half near enough to the fire for comfort, and a collection of worn sofas and armchairs that looked the worse for moth completed the arrangement.

A narrow gallery ran the length of one wall, and I saw Mrs. Desmond's head bobbing above the railing as she made her way to the private quarters of the house. A few odd bits of weaponry were hung upon the walls, and a tapestry frame—stripped of its treasure—showed where something grand had once hung. Picture frames had left their marks upon the stones, but only the nails were left. The room was a ghost of what it might once have been.

"So much for Charles and Mary Hathaway's modernizing," I murmured to Stoker.

He pointed to the swatches of bright new wallpaper that had been applied to one wall. They were various and hideous shades of mauve, all flowered, and I repressed a shudder.

"To do that to this grand old room is a crime," I observed.

"Then do not look at the new tiles heaped up in the corner," he advised.

Mrs. Desmond returned then and led us to our rooms. Theseus sprang to mind as she guided us down passages and up some stairs only to descend others. We turned, we twisted, we climbed. Some of the passages were laid with thick carpets, obviously new. These corridors were dotted with palms and aspidistras in heavy porcelain pots, and the walls, decorated with silks or gilded papers, were hung with paintings of fruit and landscapes, and Mrs. Desmond paused in front of each to recite the artist and subject, obviously having learnt them by rote and doubtless at Charles and Mary Hathaway's insistence. The sharp odor of new paint hung in the air in these corridors, but when we at last reached our destination, it was in a passageway with bare floorboards and doors painted in a faded, bilious green.

"This is the Maidens' Wing, and here is your room, Miss Speedwell," she pronounced, flinging open the door. I could sense rather than see Stoker's lips twitching. Maidens' Wing indeed! Mrs. Desmond went on. "All unmarried ladies stay here, but at present that is only yourself and Miss Euphemia. She is just down the corridor. And you have only to ring if you require anything," she said, motioning for me to enter. "Your bag has been brought up," she added, nodding to the carpetbag being unpacked by a young maid. The girl had already placed my clothing in the wardrobe and books upon the bedside table, and she adjusted the hot bricks under the sheets before bobbing a curtsy and scurrying away to the servants' stair.

"Thank you, Mrs. Desmond," I said.

The housekeeper pointed out the location of the bellpull and bustled away with Stoker, who winked at me behind her back. That little gesture warmed me, and I closed the door to take stock of my bedchamber. It had been furnished sometime early in Victoria's reign, I had no doubt, for there was an austerity to the heavy dark wooden furniture. It was thickly carved with motifs I could not quite make out, and the hangings were a dark ruby red. There was a needlepoint rug on the floor that might have been stitched by Methuselah's mother, and the cracked bowl of the washstand was lavishly decorated with garish red roses. There were few ornaments, the bulk of them having long been sold, I suspected, and what remained was of dubious quality.

But for all its faded grandeur, the house gleamed, every surface polished and waxed to perfection, every cobweb swept, every mantelpiece dusted. Mrs. Desmond clearly took excellent care to maintain the place, and my comfort had been anticipated. A merry fire burned hot upon the hearth, and cans of steaming water had been carried to the adjoining bathroom, where an enormous and ancient tub stood in pride of place. On a small table by the fire in my room, a covered tray waited. I lifted a dome to release the fragrance of hot chicken pie with vegetables and fresh bread. There were cups of custard, golden and eggy, and I knew if Stoker had a similar tray, he would be making low whimpers of pleasure.

In spite of the luxurious hamper on the train, I was hungry, the cold and wet trip across the moor rousing my appetite. I fell upon the food like a starveling, making short work of the late supper. My ablutions were swift, for the water had cooled as I ate. As I toweled myself dry, I cast an eye towards the bed. It was narrow as the devil and hard as a rock, stuffed with horsehair, I decided after an experimental bounce. The resulting shriek of bedsprings sounded like the proverbial banshee, and I realized that any private demonstrations of affection with Stoker would have to wait until we returned to London. Stoker had, upon more than one occasion, remarked upon my vocal expressions during lovemaking, which tended toward the exuberant and audible. With his natural delicacy, he would never attempt to engage in activities which might be overheard, and I was keenly aware of young Euphemia, no doubt slumbering peacefully somewhere along the same corridor.

I climbed into my high, narrow bed and burrowed into heavy sheets that smelt strongly of lavender. I might have appreciated Stoker's presence as a platonic bedwarmer, but the hot bricks had fulfilled their purpose, I realized as I sank into drowsiness. There are few comforts as satisfying as a warm fire, a cozy bed, and a delicious meal after one has been chilled to the bone with wind and rain.

Somewhere, in the depths of the house, a clock struck the hour and a floorboard creaked. Rain, which had lashed the windowpane, settled to a soothing hum, and at last, I slept.

CHAPTER

6

I woke to a tapping upon the door. It was early, the watery light just beginning to fill the room as I sat up in bed. Without waiting for a response, the author of the knock entered, a young woman dressed in a sober gown of dark flannel stuff. Her features were bony, her skin pale and starred with freckles. Dark, gingery hair had been plaited and wound to form an untidy coronet around her head. She was tall and slender and carried a tray in her hands. A teapot sloshed as she set it down with a bang.

"Good morning," she said, coming near to the bed. "I am Euphemia Hathaway. Effie to my friends."

"Veronica Speedwell," I said, smothering a yawn.

She poured a cup of tea and thrust it into my hands, a few errant leaves floating on the top. "You are the lady lepidopterist. I have read some of your articles," she told me, her expression avid.

"Are you interested in butterflies?" I asked, sipping at the tea. It was scalding hot, a rich Darjeeling with a dainty floral note. The Hathaways might live in a desolate and remote place, but they spared little expense in their food and drink, I decided.

"Not at all," she replied. "Flying worms, I call them. But I know where the best ones are on the moor. I can show you if you want to collect some specimens whilst you're here." She looked awkward standing beside the bed, so I patted the edge.

"Sit and tell me what does interest you if not butterflies," I invited.

She settled herself and I noticed her feet were shod in ungainly black brogues. A small lace collar had been pinned at her throat and she tugged it as she sat.

"My sister-in-law makes me wear it," she said with a grimace. "She thinks it makes me look respectable." I suspected the brogues were not Mary Hathaway's idea. They looked like a boy's castoffs, and Effie, seeing my gaze, waggled them, clicking the heels together.

"They are miles too big, but I stuff the toes with paper to make them fit," she confided. "They are excellent for walking out on the moor. Mary says they are definitely not respectable."

"And must you be respectable?" I took another sip of the warming tea.

"I should very much like not to be," she said, her hazel gaze holding mine. "I should like to have adventures. Like yours. You have seen the world. I read your expedition notes on your Costa Rican trip in *The Gentleman Lepidopterist*. Granfer used to subscribe to all of the major scientific journals. Your work is superb," she said.

"I am glad you enjoyed them."

"Of course, I have no interest in Costa Rica per se," she went on. "Jungles are no proper place to study stars. I am an astronomer, you see. I must have altitude and very clear skies. I should like a nice Greek island or perhaps a lovely desert . . ." Her voice trailed off wistfully.

"There are plenty of accomplished astronomers on these shores," I reminded her gently. "I believe the University of Edinburgh is considered to be a superior institution. You might study there. They have made great strides in educating women."

She rolled her eyes. "It would never be permitted. My brother

Charles is my guardian, you see, and while I might talk him around, Mary is a different matter entirely. She has *plans*." The last word dripped with scorn. "And if one is unfortunately relegated to the position of spinster, one must make oneself useful in every possible way at all possible times."

"Such as carrying early morning tea to the guests?" I smiled as I held out my cup. She filled it again and settled herself once more on the bed, companionably.

"Heavens no," she said, her eyes round. "I insisted upon coming myself because I simply could not wait any longer to meet you! You are the first woman of science I have had the pleasure to know—lady," she amended hastily. "Lady of science."

"I prefer 'woman,'" I told her in a mild tone. "'Lady' sounds better suited to a horse."

She grinned, a broad expression that revealed white teeth with a tiny gap in the front. "I feel as if we will be great friends," she said, leaping to her feet. "That is presumptuous and rude, and I shall be in terrible trouble if you tell, but I do not think you will."

She bounded to the door and stopped, her hand upon the knob. "I am meant to tell you that breakfast is in an hour's time, downstairs, in the Great Hall. It is drafty, so mind you dress warmly."

Before I could frame my thanks, she left, slamming the door behind her, a whirlwind in petticoats. I washed and dressed and made my way down to breakfast, making only two wrong turnings as I followed the aroma of fried ham and the sound of masculine voices. The table had been pushed near the fire, and it was laden with good country fare— eggs, kidneys, ham, breads, jams and jellies of every description, stewed fruit, porridge, and thick, fatty sausages that sizzled in the dish. A chafing dish of kedgeree stood in pride of place, and Stoker had taken a large helping of the savory rice and fish.

He was sitting at the table with a young man attired in the garb of a country squire, tweeds and gaiters. His broad face was open and friendly, the auburn hair brushed back from a high forehead that would grow higher with each passing year, I had no doubt. His plate was heaped high and I could see where the buttons of his waistcoat were straining slightly. He had put on weight recently, I deduced, and would no doubt gain significantly more if he continued to eat like a gannet.

He leapt to his feet as I approached. At the foot of the table, a diminutive young woman kept her seat. Her hair, almost white-blond, had been pinned firmly under an exquisite lace cap, and her wool dress, perfect for a chilly country morning, was a rich bottle green trimmed in fashionable Parisian passementerie. A pair of luscious pearls hung at her ears and she wore a tiny lace collar fixed with a brooch of pearls and small garnets. She might be domiciled in the wilds of Devon, but she had no intention of letting herself become a dowdy country mouse. All of this I surmised in an instant as her husband came forward, his hand outstretched.

"Miss Speedwell! How good of you to come," he said, taking my hand and pumping it furiously. "I am so very sorry we were not awake to greet you. We expected you would choose to stay in Shepton Parva on such a filthy night, and besides, we keep country hours here." He was broad of shoulder and tall, thickly set with muscle that would require exertion to keep toned. I could well imagine him, twenty years hence, fat and bald as an egg and entirely happy with his life. An air of contentment hung about him, but also a slightly bewildered look, as if he liked where he found himself but could not quite understand how he came to be there.

"Thank you for the kind welcome," I told him. "Mrs. Desmond was the soul of hospitality."

"I should hope so," Mrs. Hathaway said placidly. "It is one's duty to entertain angels unaware."

I gave her a smile intended to hide the fact that I loathed her on sight. There are few things I despise more than people who constantly quote platitudes. It demonstrates a painful lack of originality. Apart from that, she delivered her words with the overly refined diction of one who had been schooled in gentility but not born to it. There was no trace of the Yorkshire dales in her voice, and while I did not begrudge her the desire to improve herself, I suspected it had been undertaken out of snobbery.

I settled myself into the seat allotted to me and applied myself to breakfast. We spoke of pleasantries as we passed platters and bowls and worked our way through the heaps of food.

As the last cup of tea was poured, a nanny entered with a string of children. The oldest, a boy, looked to be about six. He was followed by a girl a year or so his junior. Behind them came a pair of nurserymaids, each carrying an infant of some six months or so.

"Geoffrey and Ada," Mrs. Hathaway said, beaming at her eldest offspring. "And the twins, Alice and Augusta." The maids presented the babies like entries in a county livestock show, and Stoker and I made appropriate noises. The children had, at least, all been scrubbed and polished, and no unappetizing aromas emanated from their persons, but the boy had a sly look about him, and the girl, Ada, stared with a gormless expression, her finger hooked firmly in her mouth until the nanny swatted it aside.

Mrs. Hathaway surveyed them and gave a nod. "Nanny, the moor is too muddy for a walk today. Air them in the garden."

"But I want to go to the moor," the boy child said, thrusting out his upper lip. He pulled out a crumpled ball of wire from his pocket and held it up to his mother.

"What have you there, darling?" she asked, smoothing down his cowlick with a practiced hand.

"A cage," he told her with ghoulish delight.

"And what do you need with a cage upon the moor?" she inquired.

"I am going to catch a faery," he said solemnly.

"Why do you mean to catch a faery?"

"So I can make it give me all its wishes," he said firmly.

"What a clever boy!" his mother said, turning to the rest of us with a fatuous smile.

"And what if the faery won't give you wishes?" his father asked, winking broadly at Stoker.

"I shall poke it with a stick until it does," his unlovely offspring said. "I shall poke it in the *eye*."

His father gave an uproarious laugh, but the child did not appear to be joking in the slightest, and I fixed him with a stern look.

"I think," I told him, "you might have confused faeries with djinns."

"I don't know a djinn," he said, thrusting his lip out further still.

"Djinns are nasty, foreign things," his mother assured him. She flicked me a glance. "If you want a faery, I am sure you will find one. But not today, darling," she added. His face puckered and she reached into her pocket for a small tin. "Now, have a few humbugs and go along with Nanny. If you are a very good boy, Nanny will take you out on the moor after luncheon when it will be dry, and then you can find your faery. All right, my darling?"

To my surprise, he capitulated, but only after extracting another pocketful of humbugs from his mother and a penknife from his father.

He surveyed the tiny blade with feverish pleasure. "I shall poke it in the *eye*," he murmured again as his nanny led him from the room. The girl child followed, sucking her forefinger once more, and the babies, stolid as lumps of lard, were borne away by the nursemaids.

"Children are an unparalleled joy," Mrs. Hathaway remarked to me. "Of course, being an unmarried woman who works for her living, you are denied such comforts, but you mustn't let that make you bitter," she urged.

Stoker smothered a laugh, choking into his eggs until Charles Hathaway clapped him firmly on the back.

"Quite all right there?"

"Yes, perfectly, thank you," Stoker assured him.

Mrs. Hathaway signaled a maid to remove her breakfast things and turned to us with an expectant air. "We are very glad you've come to assess the collection," she said, pitching her voice to a confiding tone. "There is so much work to be done on the house, and frankly, the greatest part of it is clearing away the old rubbish that is practically stacked to the rafters. We have had four bonfires already, and carted away a dozen loads of dreary old furniture and fittings."

Stoker's expression was pained. "Well, the specimens are not rubbish to Lord Rosemorran."

Charles Hathaway laughed. "Then he's a better man than I, he is. There are all manner of things in the collection, furry and fangy and completely unhygienic, as Mary says," he added with an admiring nod to his wife. "She doesn't want them about because of the children, you see. She thinks they will take fright from some of the more outlandish creatures."

"But they would be perfect for inclusion in Lord Rosemorran's collection," Mary Hathaway put in smoothly. "Perhaps with a nice little plaque to say where they were found."

"I am certain something could be arranged," Stoker told her.

I turned to Charles Hathaway. "I have had the pleasure of meeting your sister, Euphemia," I told him. "Are there any other members of the family?" It was not the subtlest of inquiries, but then Charles Hathaway was not a subtle man. He would not be offended by a little impolite curiosity, I decided. His sort would happily tell his life story to a stranger on the street. Jonathan had been much the same, I remembered with a pang. Ever ready with a smile and an invitation. His friend Harry Spenlove had been the quieter of the two at first, hanging back a little, while Jonathan had been an open book.

Charles Hathaway's brow furrowed. "Well, there is my grandmother, Lady Hathaway. My grandfather, Sir Geoffrey, was knighted for his discovery of a comet," he said proudly. "But Granna's health is poor and she may not make an appearance today. She has a companion, an Indian girl called Anjali. Do ask her if you need anything. She's a useful soul," he told us. "Mostly reads aloud to Granna and sews and listens to Granna's endless stories about life in India before the mutiny," he added with another braying laugh. I did not join in. I felt my lips thin at his casual way of speaking of his grandmother's companion. He went on, blithely unaware of my discomfiture.

"And then there is the man we call Jonathan," he said.

"You call him Jonathan?" Stoker asked easily. "Is that not his name?"

"That is precisely the question," Mary replied tartly.

Charles spoke up. "You see, Jonathan Hathaway was my elder brother. He took up exploring—a bit of lepidoptery, a little mountaineering here and there. Just gentlemen's hobbies, you understand. He was lost in the course of his travels in the Sunda Strait. The eruption of Krakatoa, a nasty business," he said with a visible shudder. "We assumed, naturally, that he was dead."

"Naturally," I murmured.

"But there never was a positive identification, no body to bury, no effects recovered. It was as if he had simply vanished," Charles said unhappily. "It was a dark time for us all. Granfer lost much of his enthusiasm for attending to his responsibilities, including taking a proper interest in this old pile," he said with a fond look about the room. He went on. "I inherited the house and its contents except for Granna's personal possessions."

"And the house was in an absolute state," Mary put in, flapping her hands. "Practically falling down, as you can see for yourselves. Just making it habitable has been a trial, and we've months of work left. Only our suite and the nurseries have been refitted with modern amenities. The entirety of the house requires attention, and the flocks have dwindled to almost nothing, outbuildings crumbling, cottages in need of repair. Charles has made a priority of the flocks, which is why you will no doubt find your rooms a trifle outdated," she added, color flaring in her cheeks.

"Now, Mary," he protested, but I had no desire to witness an example of marital discord.

"Mine is most comfortable and as clean as if the queen herself were coming to stay," I assured her.

She seemed mollified by this. "Mrs. Desmond is a treasure. I do not think she is entirely happy about all the changes, but then it isn't for her to object, is it? And it will make far less work for the staff once all of the rooms are completely modernized. Of course, Lady Hathaway does not wish hers to be modernized at all," she added with a confiding look. "And Euphemia would not notice if she bedded down in the piggery. She cares only for her astronomical instruments, and I am at my wits' end with her. It is such an unladylike undertaking to tax one's mind with science," she said.

I arched a brow and she went on. "Of course, it is different for you. You are some years her senior. But we might still make a bride of Euphemia if only we could curb her wilder habits. She is very young and terribly headstrong, you know. Like a moorland pony. But we have broken those to the saddle and I daresay we can break Euphemia as well," she added with a fond smile at her husband.

If anything of family loyalty or fondness for his sister gave Charles pause at the idea of bringing his sister to heel, it was obviously overruled by uxoriousness. He merely returned her smile and then beamed at us.

"Mary is quite the manageress," he said with apparent pride. "But then we need a bit of managing, don't we, my love?" He gave her a fond look and I pushed my plate away.

Something volcanic rumbled within me, and Stoker must have sensed it. He hurried to speak before I could vent my outrage at Mary Hathaway and her dismissive attitudes.

"You were telling us about Jonathan Hathaway's death," Stoker put in. "You have our condolences."

"Jonathan Hathaway is not dead," pronounced a sharp voice from the doorway. Situated as it was under the gallery, the door was in shadow, and we had not noticed the figure approach. She came forwards, her footsteps shuffling a little as she walked with the aid of a cane. It was a mahogany piece, highly polished and featuring the carved silver head of a ram. She was dressed entirely in black, the bombazine muting any gleam from the morning light streaming through the clerestory windows. The only touch of color was the white of her hair and the brooch at her throat. A chatelaine, like the housekeeper's but of rather more elegant design, hung from her belt. She was old, her face resembling a windfall apple, withered and wrinkled, the mouth set in an aggressive line, the chin lifted, and she regarded us with all the imperiousness of an empress.

Stoker leapt to his feet, as did Charles. I rose as well in deference to her age, but Mary Hathaway remained seated.

"Mr. Charles Hathaway was just explaining that," I told her.

She paused next to me and lifted the cane, prodding my hip. "Who are you?"

"Veronica Speedwell. And this is my associate, Mr. Templeton-Vane."

"They are natural historians," Charles said in a soothing tone. "They are here to look over Granfer's trophies to see if there is anything worth adding to the collection of Lord Rosemorran. I told you about it," he added with the merest touch of reproach.

She flicked him a glance. "I remember, Charles. I am not losing my faculties. But I am sorry to part with Sir Geoffrey's things. He had a connoisseur's eye."

"If you mean he bought anything that wasn't nailed down and shipped it home, then yes," Effie said, coming to stand beside her grandmother. Charles completed the introductions and suggested we begin our exploration of the collection at once. Mary Hathaway excused herself to write letters, leaving the rest of us to survey the trophies.

"I have instructed Mrs. Desmond to open up the Long Gallery and light a fire. We have kept it closed off to discourage the children from exploring," Charles said, his voice rueful. As he led the way to the older part of the house, I fell into step with Lady Hathaway on her slow progress to the Long Gallery.

"You were saying that your grandson Jonathan is not dead," I prompted.

She gave a sharp nod. "I never believed he was. A clever boy, our Jonathan. We never knew him until he was older, of course. He lived in India with his parents, but in due course, we insisted he be sent home to school."

"Are there no schools in India?" I asked innocently.

"None fitting the eldest son of such a distinguished family as ours," Lady Hathaway said. Just behind her, Effie rolled her eyes. Her grandmother went on. "In every generation, the eldest son has attended Harrow, and Jonathan was not going to be the first to break with that tradition. Naturally, his parents agreed and sent him to us. He spent every holiday here at the Hall, learning about his inheritance and the family traditions. He would have been a fine heir," she said, her lips trembling slightly. I glanced ahead to where Charles Hathaway walked, wondering if he had overheard. But he gave no sign of it, and I realized he had doubtless heard it all before. "After his schooling,"

Lady Hathaway went on, "Jonathan wanted to see the world. We were only too happy to oblige."

"Travel broadens the mind," I remarked.

"Yes, well, in Jonathan's case, it made it rather too broad," she retorted. "He developed a taste for life outside of England. No matter what we did, he found excuses to hare off again—always to the most outrageous of places." She lowered her voice. "Places not even colored pink on the map."

I suppressed a smile. Lady Hathaway might have spent decades in India, but she demonstrated the true provincial's wariness of any part of the globe that did not fly the British flag.

"He met with misfortune during his trip to Sumatra, and when that dreadful volcano erupted, we feared the worst. It has been six years, Miss Speedwell. Six long years, but never did I cease to pray and to hope that one day he would be restored to us. And at last! It has happened."

"Really?" I said in a faint voice.

"It has," she told me with a firm thump of the cane. "A few weeks past, a storm blew up, one of the late winter tempests that would try the hardiest constitution of man or beast. It was black outside and blowing a gale when Charles went out to see to his lambs. One had wandered away, and it was a large, handsome fellow. Charles couldn't bear to lose him, so he took a lantern and set off himself. Just at the edge of the garden, where the estate meets the moor, stands the summerhouse. And that is where Charles found him."

"The lamb?" I asked.

"Jonathan," she said in exasperation. "In a state of collapse, fainting with cold and fever just inside the door of the summerhouse. Charles did not recognize him, of course. It had been a dozen years or more since the brothers had met, but he did his Christian duty and had him carried inside. Mary immediately set to nursing him, having him put to bed and fed hot broth and calf's-foot jelly. They did not know who he was, you understand. It was not until Mary read the papers he carried that they learnt the truth. But I knew, the moment I saw him. He opened those great dark eyes and looked straight at me. And called me by name."

She paused and reached up her sleeve for a handkerchief to dab at her eyes.

"How extraordinary," I said.

"Indeed. Of course, he did not know where he was, poor pet. So spent with fever and injury from an accident that it was some days before we even dared to hope he would recover."

"Accident?" I asked, thinking of Sir Hugo's explanation of a dock-side brawl in Bristol.

"His conveyance overturned," Lady Hathaway said. I flicked a glance to Effie, whose mouth thinned in impatience. Either Lady Hathaway had been told a more genteel version of events, or she had lied to me in order to make Jonathan Hathaway's injuries sound more accidental than disreputable.

"And now he is home," Lady Hathaway crowed. "He is still not himself entirely, you understand. But he gains in strength every day."

"Will Mr. Jonathan Hathaway not have some objections to our assessing the collection without his approval?" I asked.

Charles Hathaway stopped instantly and whirled. "The collection, Miss Speedwell," he said, bristling, "is mine to dispose of as I see fit." He turned back and gestured towards a double door. "In here, if you please."

We followed him inside. Mrs. Desmond had taken down the shutters and kindled the fire as Charles Hathaway had indicated, but the room was a study in sadness. A chill born of long neglect seemed to have penetrated the very walls of the place. It was quite dark, being paneled in heavy Jacobean oak, and the only illumination came from the pale morning sun.

"I will tell Mrs. Desmond to bring lamps," Lady Hathaway said. What she meant was that she intended to delegate the chore, for she gave a signal to Effie, who huffed out a tiny sigh and left, clearly annoyed at being left out of whatever grand discoveries she imagined we would make.

The room was full of figures shrouded in dust sheets, and Stoker circled them in anticipation.

"Sir Hugo mentioned there was a thylacine in the collection," he ventured. His pupils were dilated and his breathing was uneven. Anyone who did not know him might imagine him in the throes of amatory anticipation, but I understood exactly what had roused his passions—the prospect of coming face-to-face with the elusive Tasmanian tiger.

Charles Hathaway plucked away one of the dust sheets to reveal a rather morbid-looking stuffed monkey. "A thylacine? That's the big bird, isn't it? The one with the devilish claw on its foot? Stands as tall as a man?"

"You are thinking of a cassowary," Stoker corrected tightly. "*Casuarius casuarius.* I am referring to *Thylacinus cynocephalus*, the Tasmanian tiger. A distinctive-looking animal, stripes on the pelage. Perhaps four feet in length with another two for the tail. Standing just over two feet tall and weighing perhaps sixty pounds?" Stoker had been sketching the dimensions with his hands, but Charles gave him a shrug.

"I am afraid I cannot say," he said. "It must be here somewhere, though," he added brightly.

Lady Hathaway planted her walking stick and wrapped both hands around the ram's head at the top. "My husband, Sir Geoffrey, was a distinguished collector," she informed Stoker loftily. "He acquired all manner of specimens on his travels throughout Asia and the Antipodes. When we returned from India, many things were simply stored here and never completely unpacked. His priority was building his observatory," she added, pointing upwards with the walking stick. "I daresay he would have got round to sorting the specimens eventually."

Besides the trophies huddling under dust sheets, there were innumerable crates and boxes, pasted with shipping labels and clearly untouched since the Hathaways had resumed living at the Hall.

Stoker looked about him with a faint air of desperation.

"We will search them all," I soothed.

"Certainly you will," Lady Hathaway put in. "There are treasures to be found in these crates, no matter what *Mary* might say." She spoke her granddaughter-in-law's name as if it were a swear word, and Charles made the sort of soothing noises one might make to settle an upset cow.

"Now, Granna, you know Mary just wants the Hall to look its best. The sooner these dusty old things are cleared away, the sooner we can hang the new wallpaper and the paintings she has been buying." He turned to us. "This is to be the picture gallery. We mean to commission a painting of Mary and the children to hang here with her collection of still lifes. Very fond of still lifes is my Mary."

He turned away to help Stoker find a pry bar, and Lady Hathaway muttered under her breath, just loudly enough for me to hear. "One must question the taste if not the actual intelligence of a woman whose greatest interest is painted bowls of *fruit.*"

I turned to her. "You do not approve of Mrs. Hathaway's planned changes to the Hall?"

She shrugged. "It is a matter of indifference to me. The Hall is nothing, *nothing* compared to our house in India. That was a palace," she said. She leaned near and I could smell aniseed pastilles on her breath. "An actual palace. In my day, people knew how to treat their betters," she said, her mouth turning down. "The Indians were grateful to us, you understand, Miss Speedwell. We brought roads and medicine and education. We showed them how to *live.*" I resisted the tart rebuttals that came to mind and began to count to one hundred as she carried on. "It is all quite different now, of course. The mutiny saw to that." I realized with a start that she was speaking of the Sepoy Mutiny.

"But that was more than thirty years ago," I pointed out. "Surely some things have changed for the better."

"Well, India is firmly part of the empire now, so one must be pleased about that."

No, one must not, I thought but did not say.

"But so much else has changed for the worse. I do not approve of these new practices, Miss Speedwell," she said sternly. "It is bad enough that Mary wants a folly on the moor and a conservatory, but she intends to install flushing water closets," she added in a furious whisper.

"I have one at home," I told her. "It is far more convenient."

"Convenient!" She sniffed. "What is convenience compared to decency? It is not at all nice to think of *pipes* and what may be in them. And do you know what else that means? Drains, Miss Speedwell. One cannot think of drains with equanimity."

I made a noncommittal noise that I hoped might pass for something akin to sympathy.

She shook her head, the jet beads at her ears trembling in outrage. "No, these modern ideas are decidedly not in good taste, but what can you expect from a person not born to the station she now occupies? Mary has married up, you see. Her father was in *trade*." The last word was a harsh whisper.

"But, Lady Hathaway, I, too, earn my living," I replied with a tinge of malice.

She curled her lip. "A trifling formality, Miss Speedwell. My grandfather was a marquess, you know. I can spot good breeding at fifty paces, and *you* have the bones of someone who was very gently bred."

Exactly how gently was something I had no intention of sharing, so I merely murmured a thank-you. She flapped a hand. "No call to thank me, child. I simply speak my mind. I have always been thus. I cannot abide deceit. One must speak the truth and shame the devil, as my dear mama always used to say."

It was astonishing, I mused, how often people claimed to be honest when they were simply making a virtue of excessive rudeness. I thought, too, of the possible impostor beneath her roof and wondered exactly what she would say if it were revealed that he were, in fact, not Jonathan Hathaway.

As if intuiting my thoughts, she leaned closer still, clearly in the mood for confidences. "I will be glad for you to meet my other grandson, Jonathan," she said. "He is a very different type to Charles. One loves Charles, of course. He is, after all, family," she said with a sigh. "But he is entirely in the thrall of his wife. Jonathan is his own man," she added proudly.

"It must be a great consolation to you to have him back," I remarked.

Instantly, the withered-apple face suffused with pleasure. "He is the delight of my days," she said. To my astonishment, her eyes filled with tears. "I had missed him so," she whispered.

Impulsively, I covered her hand with my own. She let it lie there a moment, not offended at the familiarity, and then gently withdrew it. She took a large handkerchief from her pocket and applied it to her nose, blowing it with gusto. The corner of the handkerchief flapped, and I could see the cipher that had been worked on it with tiny stitches. A series of pretty French knots and her initials in dark blue.

When all traces of moistness had been removed from her face, she tucked the handkerchief away and straightened her shoulders just as Charles Hathaway gave a little crow of triumph.

"Here now! I have found something," he cried, tearing one of the dust sheets free. The specimen beneath proved a dusty camelid, some South American creature with too many teeth and a pelt that had clearly proven irresistible to moth. One fluttered free, darting wildly as it searched for a way out.

"How damnable," Charles Hathaway muttered as he clapped his hands, crushing the moth between his palms. He opened his grip and peered at the silvering remains. "Got him!"

I peered into his hand. "*Tineola bisselliella*," I informed him. "Your homicidal effort was quite in vain."

"Eh?" he asked, his brow furrowing in puzzlement.

"The common clothes moth, Mr. Hathaway. You have killed a creature which does not feed in its adult stage. Only in the larval form does it take nourishment and wreak havoc with one's woolens. Or in this case, one's camelids." I turned to Stoker. "What is it meant to be?"

Stoker surveyed the long, crooked neck, the glass eyes that seemed to be staring in opposite directions, and the ear that drooped sadly as it dangled by one small shred of hide. "It seems to be an alpaca of some sort, but I shouldn't like to wager on it. Whoever mounted it has done a criminal's work here."

He poked it with a tentative finger and another moth erupted. This one flapped lazily about, circling Charles Hathaway's head before settling back onto the ersatz alpaca's nose.

"Not a very promising start, I'll grant you," Hathaway said as he dusted his hands. "I will leave you to get on with the specimens at your leisure. And when you have had your fill of the things in this room, there are a few other items that may prove interesting to Lord Rosemorran," he said, giving Stoker a cryptic glance.

"I hope that you are not speaking of my jewels, Charles," his grandmother put in tartly.

Charles gave a start as if he had forgot she was with us. He summoned a smile that was not entirely convincing. "Oh, certainly not, Granna. I was thinking of the equipment in Granfer's observatory."

There was a crash in the doorway as Effie dropped an unlit lamp, splashing oil onto the threadbare carpet.

"Have a care, child," said Lady Hathaway. "That carpet is an Aubusson."

If it was an Aubusson, it was a particularly nasty one, I thought, and slightly improved by the enormous dark stain from the oil.

"Never mind," Charles muttered.

"You mean to sell Granfer's astronomical instruments," Effie said, the second lamp trembling in her hands. Stoker moved forwards with his usual catlike grace, taking it from her before she could drop this one as well.

Charles Hathaway gave his sister an impatient look. "Effie, it is impolite to discuss such matters in front of our guests."

"They know why they are here," she returned, her freckles livid against her fair skin.

"Very well," said Charles, pushing a hand through his gingery hair. "Yes. There is no point in keeping items that are not in use."

"Not in use! *I* use them," she protested.

"As a hobby, my dear," he began.

"It would not be a hobby if I could go to school," Effie retorted.

Charles shot us an apologetic look. "Effie, this is not the time."

"For what? For our guests to find out that I am your penniless drudge? That I labor here, unwaged and unappreciated, because all I am is—"

"What you are is a helpmeet to your brother's wife," Lady Hathaway cut in. "As an unmarried girl, you ought to be grateful to Charles and Mary for continuing to provide a home for you. Instead, storms and tears, that is how you repay them."

Effie looked from her brother to her grandmother and back again before bursting into choked, angry sobs and running from the room.

Lady Hathaway sighed. "She is entirely ungovernable. I wonder if I ought to have dosed her more as a child. Castor oil has an improving effect upon the demeanor when applied in large amounts."

With that pronouncement, Lady Hathaway wandered out, leaving us to stare awkwardly at our host.

"Families, eh?" he asked with a sickly smile.

"Yours is much less trouble than either of ours," Stoker told him truthfully.

"That is good to know," Charles said. "I despair of Effie. Granna calls her unmanageable. Any time that she has spare, she spends in Granfer's observatory, working with his telescopes and other such things. As Mary says, it is unwomanly," he said with a little twist of the lips. "I should be perfectly happy to see the things cleared out. Mary wants the observatory for a sewing room, you see. And it would remove the temptation for Effie. I think she would cease to pine then and settle properly to her domestic obligations."

What obligations? I nearly demanded. As far as I could see, Effie Hathaway had done nothing but have the misfortune to be born into a family distinctly lacking in imagination and grit. She had originality and spirit, and she was in grave danger of having her mettle ground away to nothing.

"I am afraid we are thoroughly unqualified to assess any such instruments for the purposes of acquisition for Lord Rosemorran's collection," I said. I gave Stoker a hard look and he cleared his throat, turning to Charles Hathaway with an apologetic gesture.

"Miss Speedwell is entirely correct. Not our area of expertise, as it were," he said.

"Oh, well, that is a pity. Perhaps you will change your mind," Charles said. He glanced around the depressing room and seemed to shake off the little drama his family had just enacted. "I should leave you to it. If you need help at all, just send for Anjali. As I've explained, she is Granna's companion, but she will do anything you ask of her. A very biddable and docile creature, always quick to help."

With that, he left us. I turned to Stoker, who lifted one heavy brow in query. "Astronomy is the only life that poor girl has. We are not going to be the means of annihilating it," I told him.

"If Mary Hathaway has her heart set on using the observatory for her own purposes, I am quite certain Charles Hathaway will find a means of getting rid of the scientific instruments," he replied as he peered beneath a shrouded figure.

"Perhaps," I said firmly. "But there is no reason for us to aid him in his endeavors."

CHAPTER

8

We spent the next several minutes in silence, removing dust sheets and acquainting ourselves with the lay of the land, so to speak. The Long Gallery was, as its name indicates, a chamber some fifty feet in length and perhaps twenty in width. A narrow carpet, once scarlet—although it was impossible to be certain between the hearty appetites of the moths and the wear of many feet—stretched from one end to the other, indicating a path the ladies of the house might once have trod on inclement days. A few smaller patterned rugs were scattered about, none matching. Like those of the Great Hall, the walls here had been hung with paintings, the marks of the absent frames still visible upon the cracked and warped paneling. A few chairs and benches, heavy with Jacobean carving, were dotted about, but otherwise the room had been given over to displaying the treasures of the natural world. Wardian cases, the glass streaked and murky, stood by terraria whose plants had long withered to dust. I did not dare to peer too closely into the fishbowls.

I had just uncovered a particularly nasty trahira—that is a Brazilian wolf fish—when Stoker spoke. "You do not like him."

"Of course I do not like him. He has an ignoble face," I said, gesturing to the wide, grinning mouth that displayed rather too many sharp teeth.

"Not him, *him*," he said, jerking his chin towards the door through which our host had taken his leave.

"He is a type," I said, dropping the dust sheet to conceal that grinning mouth. "Very John Bull, everything for England, 'God Save the Queen' sort of fellow."

"Like every other man you meet in this country," Stoker said.

"Not you," I protested.

"Well, I am remarkable." His voice was distracted now, and I turned to see he had bent over an unexpectedly lovely little marmot.

"That you are," I agreed. "I do not like the way he speaks to his sister and I certainly do not like the way he speaks *of* his grandmother's companion—Anjali, I believe he said. He talks of her as though she were some useful thing to be loaned—a book or a horse."

"Don't be ridiculous," Stoker said absently. "That sort of man would never loan a horse." He flicked me a quick smile, and I saw that he was attempting to sweeten my mood. I had been cross ever since we had arrived at Hathaway Hall—no, it was decidedly earlier. When had I first noticed the lowness of spirits that had settled over me?

At the first mention of Jonathan Hathaway's name, I realized. I had mourned when I thought him dead along with Harry Spenlove. To hear from Sir Hugo that there was a possibility Jonathan had survived was almost more than I could bear. It touched a rawness within me that I had long buried. I had covered my grief and my anger at their fate. I had moved on with my life. But like most wounds left in darkness, this one had festered. There were too many emotions warring within me, and I liked none of them. Grief, guilt, sorrow. And rage. That one surprised me. As a woman of science, I prized intellect and reason. I had always attempted to keep my emotions in check whenever they threatened to interfere with logic. I gave vent to them when it was acceptable to do so, of course. I succumbed to laughter, to whimsy, to affection, to desire. I had been exalted in my happiness and occasionally maddened to frustration. But I had only rarely permitted myself to be truly angry. Anger robbed one of sense and perspective, I had always thought. And while I might hone the blade of my tongue, it was always in the service of impatience, annoyance, irritation.

And yet the knowledge that Jonathan Hathaway might have survived the eruption had caused a cataclysmic sort of rage to present itself, simmering just below the surface. My very skin felt hot, as though my blood were fevered. And yet I must master this irrationality lest I jeopardize the very reason I had come to Hathaway Hall. If Jonathan had survived, then a grave wrong had been done for his younger brother to have taken his inheritance. Charles Hathaway might be playing Jacob to his Esau, and I would see justice done.

But if some bounder had inserted himself into this family, unlikeable though I found most of them, I would turn that rage upon him, I decided.

"Veronica," Stoker said. I detected from his tone that it was not the first time he had attempted to get my attention.

"My apologies. I was woolgathering," I said.

"An apt occupation in this place," Stoker said. "They are sheep mad."

Just then, a soft tap at the door heralded a newcomer. A woman entered, dressed in sober grey. Her hair must have been glossy once, but it was a dusty grey now, although she had troubled to plait it neatly and coil it at her nape. She wore smoked spectacles, which rested just above a small, crescent-moon birthmark on her cheek. With her eyes obscured, it was impossible to judge her age. Based upon the colorless hair, I guessed her some years older than Mary Hathaway, although she moved with a quick, capable grace.

"Good morning, Miss Speedwell," she said in a low voice. "Sir," she added, inclining her head to Stoker. "Lady Hathaway has requested I come and make myself useful. I am Anjali."

"Do you have a second name, miss?" I gave her an expectant look.

If my request startled her, she was too polite to show it. "Anjali is fine, madam."

I held up a hand. "If we are to work as equals, then we shall certainly speak as equals. I am Veronica. That is Stoker."

She inclined her head once more, with all the poise of a duchess. "Very well. I have brought dustcloths and a basket of supplies," she added. "Brushes, neat's-foot oil, beeswax. A few things that might be helpful in cleaning off the worst of the dirt so you can see what is here."

"Bless you," Stoker said, coming to take the basket from her.

She moved to the board of mounted butterflies I had just unveiled. "I know these!" She bent near, her smile wide. "They used to flutter about my grandfather's garden when I was a child."

"*Junonia orithya*," I told her. "The Blue Argus. Handsome little things."

"Indeed," she said, surveying them raptly. "I remember once finding a number of purple caterpillars on my grandfather's violets. I thought to pluck them off and save the pretty flowers, but he scolded me terribly and explained that if we wanted the pretty butterflies, we had to leave the caterpillars alone. He brought me back every day to watch them as they formed their chrysalides and emerged as the loveliest little butterflies with the patches of blue on their hindwings. Such handsome spots they had, like orange eyes!"

"You have the makings of a lepidopterist," I told her.

She smiled, a rueful expression as she looked over the collection. "These poor fellows have had a time of it. Half of them with the wings broken."

"They were imperfectly stored," I explained. "They ought to have been mounted under glass to protect them. But they are a common enough species. I myself have netted hundreds of them. They would be easy for Mr. Charles Hathaway to replace."

Her smile turned enigmatic. "I do not think he is devoted enough to natural history to make the effort."

"Is nothing salvageable?" Stoker inquired.

"A few," I told him. "And there is a lovely specimen with unique characteristics that would be a good addition to Lord Rosemorran's collection." I pointed it out to Anjali. "See here, where it has the rather subdued brown coloration of the female on one half and the more flamboyant traits of the male on the other? It is called gender duality and it is rare in butterflies. Always worth preserving if possible."

She leant near. "How curious that the female should be so drab compared to the male."

"A clear demonstration of the value of the female," Stoker told her over his shoulder as he uncovered another shrouded case.

She blinked behind her smoked spectacles. "How so?"

"The female can be small and unremarkable and still attract a mate," I replied. "But the male requires something special to secure her attention."

"It is the same with most species," Stoker said, not looking up. "The male must always be vigilant that he has shown himself at his best lest a rival secure a place in her affections."

There was nothing pointed in his words, and yet I felt a glissade of some new coolness in his manner. Anjali looked from him to me, her expression frankly curious, and I dusted my hands briskly. "Apart from the dual-gender specimen, there is nothing in this case worth saving."

"I fear it is much the same with the small mammals," Stoker said, frowning at the case he had just uncovered. "Unless we have need of a family of red squirrels dressed as Crusader knights—complete with a tiny castle."

"You cannot be serious," I began, but Stoker pointed and I saw to my horror that he had not exaggerated. A tall mahogany case with large glass panels housed a tableau of twenty or so red squirrels garbed as Crusader knights. They had been arranged in front of a miniature castle, and perched upon the parapet was a little princess squirrel with a hennin, the veil held aloft by stiffened wires.

"It is appalling," I breathed. "I must have it."

"Veronica," he said, a note of warning in his voice. "I will not have that monstrosity in the Belvedere."

"Not for myself. For our dear friend Mr. Pennybaker," I corrected.

Instantly, his objections dissolved at the mention of the kindly little man who had saved Stoker's life through his swift thinking and skilled intervention at the conclusion of a particularly nasty investigation.*

"I shall purchase it myself as a present for him," Stoker said.

I pointed to another, smaller case. "There is a tiny convent of dormice nuns with a rat abbess. Mind you buy that for him as well."

Anjali worked with us, removing dust sheets and folding them with care, dusting where instructed as Stoker and I worked, assessing and making notes. We stopped for luncheon—taken in the Great Hall with Lady Hathaway. She explained that Charles was out seeing to his sheep, Mary was with the children, Effie had gone to visit her old nurse in a cottage on the moor, and Anjali naturally did not eat with the family.

"And Mr. Jonathan Hathaway?" I asked casually. "Does he not take luncheon with you?"

"He does, but today he was feeling a little stronger and thought to take a walk over the moor. The moorland air has recuperative powers,

---

* *A Murderous Relation*

you know. When it is warm enough, I encourage him to go, each time a little further than the outing before so as to build up his stamina. He was desperately ill for so long. His color is much better now," she said with satisfaction. "You may put that down to my excellent nursing."

"Oh?" I said, spooning up a bit of thick soup.

"Indeed," she told me, fixing me with her beady bird's stare. "I sat at his bedside and read to him for a quarter of an hour every day without fail. And I instructed Mary and Anjali and Effie how best to care for him, how often to change the bed linen, when to feed him beef tea and nourishing jellies, how much mustard to put into the plasters for his chest. I was extremely thorough. I quite overtaxed myself in my zeal to care for him," she added with a martyred air. "And now I must walk with a stick until I have recovered my health."

"You must have a greater care for your own strength," Stoker said, keeping his expression entirely serious. "It is very dangerous to let oneself become overtired. It makes you susceptible to all variety of ailments."

"Ailments! My dear Mr. Templeton-Vane, do not speak to me of ailments, I have so many," she said plaintively. "I suffer so. The damp, you see, is a trial to my bones. And we shall not speak of my gout. Some days it is utterly beyond my abilities even to rise from my bed. Only my devotion to my grandchildren and my own will sustain me. I cannot be enslaved to this feeble body," she said, striking one hand against a drooping breast. "I must rally myself in order to see to them. I have no wish but to make certain they are happy."

"How fortunate that your eldest grandson has been returned to the fold," Stoker said gently. I grimaced into my soup. Stoker's natural sympathy with women was a dangerous thing. From infants in the pram to women with half a foot in the grave, they fell at his feet, swooning. I put it down to the strange juxtaposition of his appearance—that of a mildly dangerous Elizabethan buccaneer—with his exquisite manners. He was courtly as a Spanish grandee, with an innate kindness that spelt instant attraction for the fairer sex. To encounter a man who looked like a ruthless brigand only to find him sublimely courteous was as intoxicating as it was unexpected.

And Lady Hathaway was already thoroughly enchanted with him, I realized as I finished my soup. It was to our advantage, of course. The more she liked Stoker, the greater the possibility that she would confide in him, share details of Jonathan Hathaway's story that might provide us with an opportunity either to confirm or deny his identity. I had little doubt that in her desire to acknowledge the putative Jonathan, she would dismiss any snippets of information that indicated he was a pretender. The situation called for rationality, logic, and a dispassionate assessment of the fellow's bona fides.

"It is the answer to prayer," she said, touching the exceptionally ugly jewel at her throat. I had noticed the brooch—it was impossible not to, for the thing was the size of a child's hand—but only then realized it was a piece of mourning jewelry. She beckoned me to come close and inspect it.

It was carved of jet, with loops of ebony beads set in gold. The large central medallion depicted a skeleton weeping over a gravestone, its hideous face grinning out from behind its bony hands. I deplored the current fashion—begun by my grandmother, Queen Victoria—for exuberant mourning, and this piece was one of its more gruesome examples.

"Very moving," I said, returning to my seat. Mrs. Desmond had just served a succulent-looking roasted duck and I was determined to eat it hot.

CHAPTER

9

After luncheon, Stoker and I returned to the Long Gallery, but I found I was in no fit state for the work. I poked and prodded and scribbled notes, yet my mind wandered continuously. I had just mistaken a tray of *Aphrissa statira* for *Eurema hecabe* when my attention failed completely. I flung my pencil aside, breaking the point.

"I must have air," I told Stoker. He was on the far end of the room, his head under a dust sheet as he examined some enormous trophy. He grunted a reply and I left, not bothering to stop for a hat as I strode out of doors. The gardens of the Hall were extensive, planted in the Italian style with shrubs instead of flowers, perhaps a wise choice in the difficult growing conditions of the area. Long lawns led to a summerhouse, which gave onto the rise of moorland beyond. This must be the summerhouse where they discovered Jonathan Hathaway, I realized as I passed inside. It smelt strongly of new wood, the lavish gingerbread trim so freshly installed it was still shedding sawdust and had not yet been painted. Nor had all the repairs been completed, I saw. A bench sagged along one wall, piled with cracked, empty flowerpots and a large tin watering pot that had once been gaily painted but had faded to an indeterminate grey. New boards were neatly stacked against another wall, along with a variety of woodworking tools.

The structure, for all that it was open to the elements, felt oppressive, overlooked as it was by all the rear windows of the Hall. There would be little privacy anywhere in the gardens, and privacy was what I craved. I hurried out onto the moor with a sense of escape. It was a different world here, wilder, with long swathes of heather and grasses forming a sort of patchwork against pockets of bracken that swayed in the wind. The expanse was punctuated by boulders that rose from the earth, shrugging off the damp soil like giants rousing themselves from sleep. Narrow paths crisscrossed the moor, and a signpost indicated the direction of the nearest village—Shepton Parva with its tiny railway station—and the closest tor.

Feeling a climb would be just the thing to blow the cobwebs from my head, I chose the latter, glad I had worn stout boots instead of slippers. I began to climb, pausing only once to look back at the Hall. It was rather less forbidding by day. In the light, it seemed almost embarrassed at its own decline, the very walls appearing to draw back against the hills rising on the other side. The uneven roofline was dotted here and there with gargoyles that I could now see were a sort of stylized sheep, nothing monstrous at all. Against one stone wall, a series of scaffolds had been erected, no doubt for the purposes of repointing and cleaning, for the ivies and mosses of the ages had been tidied away, and the stone glittered starkly grey in the afternoon light.

I turned and continued on my way, fairly scampering up the side of the tor. The air was crisp here, smelling of peat and new grass and sheep. The sound of the bellwether rose on the wind, guiding me upwards, and I stopped to admire a small flock in the distance.

"Those are our sheep," a voice called. I turned to see Effie Hathaway hurrying up behind. "I hope you do not mind," she said, raising her chin. It was almost a challenge, and I was glad of it. She seemed to have recovered a little of the spirit Sir Hugo had missed, if his description of her lowness had been accurate. "I saw you leave the Hall and thought I would join you."

"You are a most welcome companion," I assured her.

"Say rather I am a guide," she corrected. "The moor is dangerous for those unfamiliar with its perils."

She raised her hand to point out the dark patches dotted about the moor, some quite near to the paths. "Bogs," she pronounced. "You must be very careful not to stray into one. They have claimed any number of the sheep, poor stupid things."

"I shall be entirely careful," I promised her.

"You must not venture here without one of us," she insisted. "It looks safe, but it is deceptive."

"I have traveled the world in the course of lepidoptery, Miss Hathaway. I am familiar with every sort of terrain—jungle, forest, alpine meadow. I can acquit myself perfectly well here," I said, beginning to lose patience. In my current state of agitation, I was not prepared to endure a lecture from someone half a decade my junior. I had been in such difficulties before—the jungles of Costa Rica, while teeming with butterflies, are also lavishly dotted with patches of quicksand. I had been taught by my native guide how to extricate myself safely and indeed had done so upon numerous occasions, though not without incident. Quicksand, it must be noted, is almost always ruinous to one's hat.

She was not cowed. "The moor is different. It's haunted, you know."

I laughed. "Miss Hathaway, I am no schoolchild to be frightened with spectral tales."

"It is true," she insisted. "There is a grey lady that goes abroad in the night. No one knows what she portends, but such things are never good. Then there is the black dog which is seen roaming the moors when a Hathaway is going to die. There are faeries, as well, and piskies who steal babies and confuse travelers. And lately, folk have seen a spectral orb bobbing over the moor. A phantom ball of light that simply vanishes," she added, snapping her fingers.

"You are a person of science," I reminded her. "There must be a rational explanation for these sightings." In fact, I was far likelier than Stoker to entertain the notion that there might be more in existence than our mere mortal senses could discern. I am a firm believer in open-mindedness in these things. Stoker, on the other hand, holds such notions in rank contempt. Whether one should blame his gender or his education for this failure of imagination is a subject for debate at another time.

"Who has seen this spectral orb?" I inquired. "And where?"

Miss Hathaway pointed and began to climb. "Just here, along the path between the Hall and the little cluster of cottages on the other side of the tor. It has been seen several times by cottagers returning home from the village pub."

"Inebriates," I said firmly. "It is little wonder they have seen something which defies rational explanation. They are intoxicated. Besides which," I told her as the wind rose to a low moan, "the moor is an uncanny place. One's imagination could easily run rampant, particularly in the dark."

She laid a hand upon my sleeve. "I have done my part, Miss Speedwell. I have warned you that this is no place to be careless. Oh, look!" She pointed towards the tor. "A butterfly!"

It took only a quick look at the mazy flight of the winged thing to identify it. "A fritillary," I corrected. "A Pearl-Bordered Fritillary, if I am not mistaken, although it is impossible to be completely certain at this distance."

"And you without your net!" she lamented.

"Never fear. They are quite common, and it is just the beginning of the season. Where this one leads, legions shall follow."

We made our way up to the top of the tor, following the meandering path of the fritillary. She flapped away on the wind just as we achieved the pinnacle, but it was no matter. The view was extraordinary, affording a sweeping survey of the landscape in all directions. From above, it was easy to see that the Hall lay nestled in a little depression, a small green island in the more muted sea of purples and browns and greens that made up the moorland palette. The Hall had been built of heavy grey stone, austere and forbidding, with its few embellishments serving to accentuate its severity rather than softening it. The steeply pitched roof was laced with carved stone coping and pierced with tall, narrow chimneys. Above it all rose a tower, a singularly unique addition, topped as it was with a sort of glass dome.

"That is the observatory," Effie Hathaway told me, a note of pride ringing in her voice. "Granfer built it for his studies, and I use it now. At least for the present," she added bitterly. "Mary wants it for a sewing room because the light is so very good," she said, her voice rising to cruel mimicry of her sister-in-law's refined tones. Without waiting for a response, she turned her face to the north. "There is the village of Shepton Parva, where you left the train. To the east, that small cluster of cottages belongs to the estate. Some are let to villagers, but the largest belongs to our old nanny."

"I should like to meet her." There were few retainers as close to a family as the nanny. If she had cared for Jonathan Hathaway in his youth, no doubt she could provide insights that might prove valuable.

Effie looked startled. "She is very old and not always amenable to visitors," she began. "And I thought your interests were those of natural history."

She was entirely correct, of course. Our ostensible purpose for being at the Hall was to evaluate the specimens and perhaps acquire a few fresh exemplars for the lepidoptery collection.

But I had the advantage over Effie Hathaway in that she was, for all her awkwardness and grievances, a girl from a good family, which meant she had been trained to be polite in all circumstances. I had not.

I bared my teeth in what might have passed for a smile. "I must insist," I told her, setting off down the path.

As there was no cordial way to refuse me, Effie fell into a sullen silence as we trudged down the path to the east. Smoke spiraled out of the cottage's chimney, and warm light glowed behind the thin curtains.

"I will go ahead," she called back over her shoulder as she charged through the tiny wicket gate, stomping along in her heavy black brogues. "Nanny Burnham sometimes sleeps in the afternoons, and I should not like to wake her if she is resting."

It was a pointless excuse—surely the old woman would be woken by Effie bursting into her cottage—but she went on ahead and I stopped to admire the small garden. The building itself was low, of native stone, and as austere as the main Hall. But the planes of it had been softened by climbing roses and gentle creepers, their leaves just beginning to waken to the spring warmth. A little patch of rhubarb had been planted to take advantage of the sunny side of the cottage, and the front step had been swept and scrubbed to gleaming.

After a long moment, Effie appeared in the doorway. "Nanny Burnham would be very happy to make your acquaintance," she told me.

I stepped inside, taking a moment for my eyes to adjust. The day outside had been gloomy, with clouds scudding their shadows over the moor, but the heath outside had been brighter than this dim cottage. The lamp in the window and the fire on the hearth did little to dispel the shadows. And yet the cottage gave an appearance of coziness and warmth. A plump calico cat slept in a basket on the hearthstone, and two armchairs had been drawn near. An elderly lady sat in one, a rug spread over her lap to hold her knitting. On the mantel, a neat row of highly polished pewter pieces had been arranged with a few bits of flowery china. A door led off this main room, tightly closed against drafts, I was certain. From the rafters hung an assortment of bundled herbs which scented the air.

The woman made to get up, but I made a swift gesture. "Please, do not trouble yourself. You must be Nanny Burnham."

"Aye, and you are Miss Speedwell," she said, resuming her knitting. "Effie, fetch the lady some of my damson wine," she instructed as the needles clacked together. "It is just the thing for a body when the wind blows from the east," she informed me.

Effie did as she was told, taking a bottle and two tiny glasses from a small cabinet in the corner.

"What a comfortable home you have," I said to Nanny Burnham.

"Aye," she remarked placidly. "I was accustomed to living in the Hall, of course," she said with a disapproving twist of the lips. "But when Mrs. Charles Hathaway came to live, I was informed my services would no longer be required and I was given this cottage. It is small here, but I have all that I require, especially when the young ones come to see me," she added with a fond glance at Effie. The girl had poured out our wine and carried the glasses over on a small papier-mâché tray. *A SOUVENIR OF BRISTOL* was painted around the edge of the tray in scrolling letters.

"Bristol," I said, grasping at conversational straws. "I believe that is where Mr. Jonathan Hathaway entered this country after his recent travels."

Nanny Burnham kept her eyes on her stitches, her lips moving soundlessly as she seemed to count the row. "It is a fair port," she said finally. "Most every soul who comes to England from the west enters there."

"How unlucky for him to have encountered an accident," I said. "I believe he has had more than his fair share of troubles on his journeys."

Nanny Burnham's thin brows rose. "That he has, missus. A volcano in some godless place was the death of him," she said.

"Or so we thought," Effie put in quickly.

"Aye. He has returned to us," Nanny Burnham said, adding a few more stitches.

"It is not a godless place," I said quickly. "The people in Java have their own deities, to whom they are every bit as devoted as any Anglican to the Church of England."

Nanny Burnham raised astonished eyes. "Heathens! As devout as good Christian folk, why I never heard such a thing."

I hastened to change the subject. "I am surprised you are not still in service at the Hall," I said with more candor than tact. "With so many youngsters in the nursery, a nanny of your experience, and with such strong family feeling . . ." I let my voice trail off suggestively and she rose to the bait.

"Mrs. Charles Hathaway thought someone *younger* might be better," she said with a sniff. "And an Irishwoman at that!" She stitched on and I thought she was finished, but when she turned the row, she picked up the thread of the topic once more. "My rheumatics have been troublesome," she allowed. "And the Hall is terribly drafty—at least it was until the nurseries were redecorated. I hear there are carpets up there now, thick ones, up to your ankles," she added in a scandalized tone.

"I understand the nurseries are very comfortable," I agreed.

"Comfortable!" She snorted. "Children do not require comfortable nurseries. They need plenty of fresh air and wholesome food and exercise. And when they are sad, they need a bit of a cuddle," she added with a fond look at Effie.

The girl rose and dropped a kiss to her old nanny's cheek. "I never lacked for a cuddle with you around, Nanny B."

"Of course not, poppet," the old woman said, patting her. "Now, I am tired and I've dropped more stitches than I have set. Take your friend and leave me for a little doze, won't you?"

I rose at once, and as I bade Nanny Burnham farewell, I heard a thud behind the closed door. "Just the cat," she said, waving us on.

Effie and I emerged into the afternoon light. A soft breeze had blown up, smelling of heather and harebells. Effie was looking fierce and I gave her a questioning glance.

"I get so angry with her sometimes, I could scream with it," she told me, her hands curling into small fists.

"Nanny Burnham?"

"Mary," she said with an outthrust lip. "She is the reason Nanny B has to live in that tiny cottage instead of up at the Hall."

"Nanny Burnham seems comfortable there," I ventured.

"It is smaller and warmer," she allowed, "but Mary has decided to move her again. She means to pull down the cottages on this side of the moor and put up a folly. A *folly*," she said in obvious disgust.

"Where will Nanny Burnham go?" I asked.

"Mary is having Charles build a row of new cottages in Shepton Parva. It will be miles further to walk to see Nanny B," Effie said. "But Mary says they will be better for Nanny and the shepherds to live in because they are *hygienic*."

She carried on, cataloging her complaints about her sister-in-law, a litany to which I only half listened. I was too busy thinking of the thud behind the door and Nanny Burnham's insistence that it had been the cat. I was thinking too of the plump calico that had been curled up on a hearth cushion, never moving for the duration of our visit. And I wondered exactly why Nanny Burnham had lied.

CHAPTER
10

Dinner that evening was a quiet affair. We ate with the family once more in the Great Hall. It had become clear that this room served a variety of purposes. With the long table at one end, it was the dining room during mealtimes, but the cluster of armchairs and sofas at the other end, grouped about the hearth, meant that it also served as a sort of drawing room where the family gathered after dinner. Charles Hathaway explained that he worked from his estate office, a small room near the kitchens, and that the main public wing, comprising library, breakfast room, drawing room, and ladies' parlor, was in the process of renovation, as evidenced by the reams of wallpapers, carpets, paint pots, and scaffolding.

"And so the Great Hall must serve for now," he said as we rose and made our way to the table. "But we are hardly within the walls these days. I am always out and about, either supervising the flocks or meeting with prospective constituents, and Mary is here, there, and everywhere, seeing to the renovations and the children. And of course, Granna has her suite, where she is able to keep herself quite comfortably."

"Yes," Mary Hathaway said with a tight smile at her grandmother-in-law, "Lady Hathaway is very happily settled in the master suite. We would not dream of asking her to move."

It was painfully apparent that this was exactly what she wanted, but Lady Hathaway seemed blissfully oblivious. She merely reposed herself in the most comfortable chair—nearest the fire, I noticed—and waited for the rest of us to sit. "Jonathan returned with a headache this afternoon, but I have sent Anjali to ask him to come to us if it has eased," Lady Hathaway told us. "He ought to join our little party."

Charles and Mary exchanged glances but said nothing. Disposing of the natural history collection was entirely within Charles' rights as the heir to the Hall, but it might appear tactless to make a show of doing it in front of the brother whose birthright he had usurped.

Effie noticed the glance and gave her brother a sly smile. "Well, that might put the cat amongst the pigeons," she said. "You are selling off the Hall's treasures without Jonathan's approval."

"I do not require his approval—" Charles began heatedly.

"Indeed you do not." The voice came from the shadows under the stairs, and I began to wonder if the Hathaways kept that particular doorway dark solely to accommodate dramatic entrances. A tall figure stood there, his broad shoulders blocking what little of the light shone from the hallway behind. He moved forwards into the warmth of the fire, the golden light playing over his features. I had wondered if I would recognize him, expecting that after six years and experiences that must have left their tragic mark upon him, I might find it difficult to say with certainty.

But I knew him. His eyes settled curiously on me as Stoker rose and introductions were made. Hands were shaken. He came to me then and put out his hand.

"Miss Speedwell, how do you do?" he said warmly. There was nothing of recognition in his gaze. He looked at me with the same polite dispassion he had demonstrated in greeting Stoker. I was a guest of his family and nothing more. Whatever accidents and illness had be-fallen him, they had seemingly robbed him of his memory. I, who had known him so well, was a stranger to him.

"How do you do, Mr. Hathaway?" I replied faintly. He shook my hand, a good, firm shake, and then seated himself at the table, careful to take the furthest, coldest, hardest seat.

"So, I understand you are here to assess the natural history collec-tion?" he asked, turning from me to Stoker. If he had taken offense at his brother's precipitous action in ridding the Hall of some of its trea-sures, he did not betray it. His voice held no malice and his expression was one of interest but not antagonism.

Yet Charles Hathaway must have been pricked by guilt, for he hur-ried to speak, a dull pink tinge rising in his cheeks. "I didn't like to trouble you. You have been unwell and the arrangements were made quite suddenly."

Jonathan Hathaway smiled easily. "It is not my affair in any event, Charles," he said in a mild tone. "The estate and the contents of the Hall are entirely yours."

"Quite right," Mary Hathaway put in. "Now, you must tell me what you think of this preparation of oysters, Mr. Templeton-Vane. I have had a dreadful time finding good help, you know. French chefs are not inclined to come and bury themselves in the country, so I must make do with a cook, but I think these oysters rather good."

Stoker reassured her as to the delicacy of the dish, and—having successfully turned the conversational tide to gentler waters—she car-ried on, introducing a new topic for each course and ensuring the talk remained general rather than allowing any of us to speak quietly with our dinner companions. Each subject was designed to be a thoughtful prompt to engaging discussion, as formal and predictable as if she had followed an etiquette guide, which upon reflection, I realized she most likely had. With soup we discussed the forthcoming Exposition Universelle in Paris, while the fish overheard us chatting about the Lyric Theatre—opened in London the past December—and the merits of comic opera versus grand opera. The carving of the roast introduced the subject of the United States and its plan to permit a land rush in the Unassigned Lands of the Oklahoma Territory.

"And with four new states this year already!" Mary Hathaway said in a tone heavy with disapproval. "It is unseemly."

"My dear Mary," Jonathan said gently, "they are a young nation. They are still finding their way."

She gave an audible sniff, thereby dismissing all things American, and the conversation turned, with the serving of the salad, to travel at large. Stoker related a few amusing anecdotes of his time in Egypt, and Jonathan, who had participated in the conversation, fell silent, studying his plate with a furrowed brow as he laid his fork aside.

"Jonathan," his grandmother said, prodding him. "You have remembered something?"

He shook his head slowly. "I cannot say. It was a flash of something, like a magic lantern show. Just an image, and only for a moment. I saw a tall tower, a minaret, I believe it is called, although how I know the word, I could not say. I heard a strange call, unlike an English voice, and there were palm trees in a line next to a broad river of shifting colors. Dark green and brown. And upon the sandbank, a crocodile with a small white bird perched atop its head."

He had spoken in a low monotone, his eyes fixed upon his plate, but as he came to an end of his recitation, he must have realized we were all attending to him, for he darted a look at his sister-in-law. "Forgive me, Mary. I seem to have got quite carried away. This salad is delicious. What is it dressed with?" he asked with an urgent sincerity. It was a fortuitous question, for Mary had had the receipt from the cook of a viscountess, and she held forth until the sweet course on the proper method.

When we finished the sweet course, the ladies did not withdraw, there being no suitable room to withdraw *to*, as Mary Hathaway remarked with a tight smile. She was clearly chafing at the limitations of entertaining before her grand renovations were complete, but a few of the menservants appeared to move the table aside and group the chairs near the fire. Mrs. Desmond brought dishes of chocolates and nuts to arrange on small tables with coffee. Mrs. Hathaway dispensed the cups and fell into conversation with her husband and Stoker about the plans for the hygienic cottages to be built upon the moor. Lady Hathaway was dozing gently in her chair, but I felt restless and took a turn about the room. Jonathan Hathaway brought me a cup of coffee, which I detest, but accepted to be polite.

"Miss Speedwell, for you," he said with a gallant gesture. His gaze dropped quickly to the cup and saucer and then rose again, holding mine for only a few seconds but with such intensity that I could not possibly mistake his intentions.

I thanked him, and he turned away at once to take his own cup from his sister-in-law's fair hand. I meandered about the Great Hall, moving from one rusted sword to another until I reached the furthest point from those gathered about the fire. With my back to them, I lifted the cup and found a tiny piece of paper, which I transferred instantly to my pocket. I poured the coffee into a handy aspidistra which seemed to be suffering from anemia or melancholy, for it drooped in its pot, its etiolated leaves brushing the floor.

I completed my turn about the room just as Lady Hathaway rose to say good night. Mary excused herself on the grounds that she wanted to look in on the children, and I took the opportunity to escape as well, leaving only the gentlemen to carry on, no doubt with port and cigars now that the ladies were absent.

I had just reached the stairs when Stoker caught up to me. "Well?" he asked, gripping me by the elbow.

"Well?" I blinked at him.

"Veronica," he said patiently, "you are here to determine if Jonathan Hathaway is an impostor. Well? Is he?"

I shook my head. "I am afraid I cannot tell you."

"But you knew him—"

"Six years ago," I reminded him. "He was scarcely more than a boy when I knew him and would be more than thirty now. Men change a good deal. The passage of time and the gaining of experience leave their mark."

"True," he said, stroking his chin. He had been clean-shaven that morning, but a shadow of a beard darkened his jaw. "I am a little suspicious of him," he said, leaning towards me with a conspiratorial air.

My heart drummed a slow, heavy beat in my chest. "Are you indeed?"

He leaned closer still, his eyes bright with strong emotion. "Has it not occurred to you that he may be an altogether unscrupulous person?"

My face was hot, the blood warm in my cheeks. "Of course. Sir Hugo suggested as much. If he can raise the necessary funds, he might be planning to lodge a legal claim against the estate or perhaps he simply means to appeal to the Hathaways' sense of decency to give him a share—" I began.

Stoker shook his head. "No, nothing so straightforward as that. I mean something altogether more nefarious."

The drumming in my chest was loud enough I was certain he could hear it.

"Nefarious? In what manner nefarious?"

He shrugged, and his expression, usually open and forthright when we spoke, was decidedly oblique. "He is likeable, immensely so. And yet it is surprising how often such an open and amenable character may conceal something entirely different."

I swallowed hard, my throat unbearably dry. "I do not know what you mean."

"Have you never known men who smile and then play the villain? The sort of men who lay claim to what does not belong to them?"

Our eyes locked, and for a long moment, neither of us spoke. "Of course," I said at last. "We both have. Of what criminous activity do you think him capable?"

His expression became, if possible, even more inscrutable. He opened his mouth, then gave a quick shake of the head. And when he did speak, I had the strongest sensation it was not what he intended to say.

"What if he is after my thylacine?"

"Your thylacine?" I asked, rearing back in surprise. He was smiling thinly, and I realized it was meant as a jest. I forced an answering smile to my lips, summoning a bright and bantering tone. "As if anyone would want such a nasty-looking mammal."

"Not merely a mammal—it is a marsupial, a member of the order of Dasyuromorphia," he informed me loftily. "And far more interesting than any of your little butterflies. Not even Rajah Brooke's Birdwing can touch it."

"*Trogonoptera brookiana* is one of the greatest marvels of the natural world, worth every crime one might commit to own it."

He tipped his head, regarding me solemnly. "Not all crimes can be justified, Veronica."

Before I could respond, he brushed a kiss to my blush-warmed cheek, leaving me to wonder at the oddness of his conversation as I hurried on to my room. Mindful of the time, I carefully worked a goose feather from inside one of the pillows and extracted a small bottle of bath oil from my toilet case. Using the feather, I oiled the squeaky hinges of my door until it opened soundlessly. I did not undress. Instead, I lay, fully clothed, atop the coverlet for a long while, thinking. At last, long past midnight, I heard a door open and close next door— no doubt Effie retiring at last.

Then followed the sounds of her readying herself for bed—various drawers and cupboards opening and closing, and a continuous low monologue directed at the dog Sir Hugo had given her, I surmised, who answered with a few brisk barks, which she corrected. At last I heard the protesting creaks of aging bedsprings as she settled in. I counted to a thousand in Greek, then slipped off my own bed and picked up my cloak—long and full and dark blue—before moving to the door. A small pad of cotton wool fitted into the bolt hole ensured that it closed as quietly as it opened on its newly oiled hinges, and I passed into the corridor, careful to keep to the shadow of my doorway until my eyes became accustomed to the gloom. A series of clerestory windows admitted the flat white light of the waxing moon. After several minutes I could make out the shapes of the furniture that lined the hall—a few tables, the odd chair, an aggressively ugly statue. I used them as landmarks as I made my way to the staircase. The house made few sounds as I descended to the main floor. There was the dull chime of a clock striking the quarter hour, the groan of wooden beams felled centuries before settling into old age like elderly bones. I remembered what Effie had said about grey ladies and black dogs and cast more than one look over my shoulder as I moved through the house.

But the only ghosts that walked with me were my own. The door from the Hall into the side garden had been left unlocked, and I passed through, my feet making no sound upon the flagstone terrace. The heavy dew from the grass soaked through my slippers as I crossed to the summerhouse, my cloak pulled tight around me. There was no light inside, but I knew he was there.

I slipped inside and closed the door carefully behind me. It was dark as a tomb inside the summerhouse, yet I could smell hot metal and knew he had brought a lantern. He eased open one of the shutters and a small bar of light fell over my face, dazzling my eyes. He put the lantern on the floor and stepped forwards, smiling.

"Hello, wife."

CHAPTER

11

Harry Spenlove," I said stiffly. I brandished the scrap of paper he
had slipped between my cup and saucer. "I got your note." The
scrap of paper held a single word, dashed off in pencil. *Summerhouse.* No time had been indicated, but I had guessed he would want
to meet as soon as possible.

He tipped his head, his expression almost apologetic as he smiled
at me. "I do hope my presence here is not distressing to you. For my
part, I cannot tell you how good it is to see you."

He put out a hand as if to touch me, but paused at the last moment. "I could scarcely believe it when I walked into the Great Hall
and saw you standing there. It seemed a dream."

"It was rather unexpected on my part as well," I said tartly. "You
are supposed to be dead. Jonathan Hathaway is supposed to be dead."

"Jonathan *is* dead." His lips pursed. "Poor fellow. I quite liked him,
you know. He was a good friend."

"But you buried him under your name? I have had a few hours to
work it all out," I said. "Somewhere on your travels, after you abandoned me, Jonathan died and you took the opportunity to begin anew
under his name."

"Well, I had creditors," he began.

"You had a *wife*," I spat. "Or did it strike you as a trifling matter to leave me behind with everything else you had grown tired of?"

"Tired of you! Never," he said fervently. "But, Veronica, things were insupportable. You even said as much when I bade you farewell. If I hadn't died, you were going to leave me in any event."

"But you did not die," I pointed out acidly. "You survived and did not see fit to tell me. Did it never occur to you that I might want to know?"

"Yes," he said, so simply and with such conviction that I felt the wind ebb a little from my sails. He stepped closer. "I know you think poorly of me, but you must believe me—I never thought you would be in danger. Like everyone else, I thought that volcano was just kicking up a bit. I thought Jonathan and I would have a chance to go to Java and perhaps make a bit of money. I intended to send some to you," he added. "I know it was a villainous thing to leave you without warning, but I couldn't bear another argument, another moment of you looking at me—well, exactly the way you are looking at me now. So when Jonathan suggested we take a little trip to Java, it seemed like the best possible thing for both of us. But poor Jonathan contracted a fever on the ship. He was half-dead by the time we docked, and he went straight into hospital. That was a very dark time, the hours I spent at his bedside. I thought of all our grand adventures, suddenly at an end. He was the best friend I ever had, you know." He paused and wiped at his eyes. "I sat with him while he died. He was delirious with pain and fever, and he kept calling for this place, for his grandmother. And then he just . . . slipped away. I spent my last coin on a bottle of the best champagne I could find to share with him. A toast to the afterlife," he said ruefully. "I was rather the worse for wear when he finally died. The nursing sister who had been attending him had just left, you see. The new one brought a ledger, some ghastly bureaucratic necessity. But she was young and inexperienced and my Dutch was as bad as her English. She was confused, you see, as to which of us had died. I opened my mouth to correct her, but then I thought suddenly about the creditors still hounding me. I thought about the papers Jonathan had given me as he lay dying—his passport and signet ring and a packet of letters from home. All things that could establish my credentials. And the description in the passport applied equally well to both of us. Brown hair and eyes. Medium build. I was a little slighter, but with his clothes hanging a trifle loose, it was easy to convince people I had just recovered from a fever. I was a trifle shorter, but not enough to matter so long as I stood up straight. So, I wrote out the forms in the name of Henry Spenlove, and Jonathan was buried under my name."

"But if he were buried as Harry Spenlove, then how did the Hathaway family hear of his actual death?"

"I cabled them, in the name of a British doctor," he said, managing to look a little shamefaced. "It was only slightly dishonest," he went on hastily. "Jonathan was, after all, *gone*. As soon as I sent the cable, I had well and truly crossed the Rubicon. I was Jonathan Hathaway from that moment on. My life as Harry Spenlove was finished."

"As was our marriage," I remarked.

His smile was bittersweet. "I think that was well and truly done before I left. You made it quite clear you were having doubts. I took that badly. I knew I had behaved poorly, but I thought with Jonathan's name I could put it all behind me. I could be different. And my family are all gone," he said simply. "There was no one to hurt by the loss of Harry Spenlove. Jonathan and I had planned to go on to South America together, so I booked passage to Santiago. When I arrived, the Chilean authorities accepted my masquerade. I collected Jonathan's letters from the poste restante, and there was one waiting from his grandmother with a five-pound note in it, bless her. I was stony broke by that point, you understand, but with that note I was able to feed myself and buy a new set of clothes and take a comfortable room. And I was grateful to the old dear. I felt sorry for her. I realized the news of Jonathan's death would be difficult for her to bear. So, I read the letters he had given me. Long letters from her full of news of home. I got to know Lady H, you see. It was one-sided, of course. I longed to write to her, but I could not. I was living as Jonathan and he was supposed to be dead and buried. But I read those letters over and over again, and, well, I became quite fond of her, really."

"Fond of her!"

"I know it sounds ludicrous, but you must understand. For the past six years I have traveled, mostly in the Americas, never staying very long, never really getting to know anyone. It has been a lonely life, Veronica. Lady Hathaway has been my only constant."

I shook my head.

"You have done the cruelest thing imaginable, Harry. Jonathan is dead but you have given them hope."

He winced. "It was never my intention, believe me. Matters got entirely out of hand. I only meant to get out of Sumatra with my skin intact and lay quite low. South America, I decided. A good place to start over as Jonathan Hathaway. I bought a small farm and tried my hand at growing coffee."

"You? A farmer?" I tried to keep the scorn from my voice, but I was not successful. "You have not done an honest day's work in the whole of your life."

He looked affronted. "I will have you know that I applied myself, Veronica. I cleared land, I plowed. I had blisters upon blisters and calluses that would have made you weep for the state of my hands. As it happens, I was unlucky. The rains that year were positively monsoonal. Wiped out the whole crop and I was ruined. I had to flee, once more with creditors on my heels. I set up again in the Argentine. I planned to open a gambling den, but the authorities were a little too curious. So, I tried again—Mexico, then America. I thought I could lose myself in the west, prospecting for gold in California."

"And how did you manage to ruin that?"

"I believed a pack of lies," he said darkly. "To hear them tell it, nuggets of gold are simply waiting to be plucked from the riverbeds. The truth is rather more bleak. It must be dug out, slowly and painfully. Almost as bad as opal mining in Australia."

"Which is what you had just given up when I first met you," I reminded him.

His face lit. "So it was! Heavens, that was a lifetime ago. I shudder to think what might have happened if Jonathan and I hadn't met in Sydney and decided to travel together. Of all the benighted countries I have known, Australia must certainly be the worst."

"What is your intention here, Harry? You realize all I need do is walk into that house and tell them the truth and your little charade is over."

"Oh, you mustn't!" he said, his voice anguished. "Not yet. It isn't finished."

"If you think I intend to stand by and watch you fleece these poor people out of their estate—"

"Good God, that's not what I want! I have had quite enough of land, thank you very much. I do not comprehend why everyone is so enamored of land. Do you have any notion of how much *work* it is? No, indeed."

"Then what do you want?" I demanded.

He ducked his head, and when he spoke, his voice was low. "You won't believe me."

"Then be persuasive."

"Very well. I . . . I have grown fond of Lady Hathaway. She is the nearest thing I have to family. Sir Geoffrey's death hit her terribly hard, and her health has suffered," he added, looking away. He suddenly clamped his mouth shut, as if damming strong emotion, a small muscle working furiously in his jaw.

"And you think she ought to spend her last months with someone pretending to be her grandson?"

"But to her I am Jonathan. So why can't I be?" The question was presented, as Harry presented all his most outrageous schemes—in so reasonable a tone that it seemed perfectly plausible.

"Because *you are not Jonathan Hathaway*," I reminded him.

"What does that matter? Jonathan is dead. If I am exposed, then she has lost him, forever. So long as she calls me Jonathan, then she has a grandson, and what is in a name?"

"And that is justification for lying to her, for leaving her brokenhearted—"

"Who said a word about leaving?" he asked, his mouth quirking into a crooked, winsome little smile I remembered only too well.

"You cannot be serious."

"As the grave, my dear. It is a comfortable enough place, although gloomy, I grant you. And Mary is dreadfully bossy, and her children are frightful, and Charles is so dreary, constantly wittering on about sheep. But I am content to remain here as long as Lady Hathaway lives."

"And when she dies?" I demanded.

He shrugged. "I will spin a pretty tale for the family. I will simply tell them that it is difficult to remain here with Lady Hathaway gone, and I suspect, with the greatest irony, that it will actually be true. I will leave them as I came, quickly and without fanfare. Perhaps the odd postcard on my travels, but nothing more. I will be a footnote in the family folklore, the brief candle who flickered once again to life before slowly fading. I will ask nothing else of them," he finished firmly. "And

I will make Lady Hathaway entirely happy for the remainder of her time."

"That might be years," I pointed out.

He shook his head mournfully. "No, I am afraid. The poor old darling has an extremely bad heart. She has died more than once, you know. The last time in my very arms."

"You are joking."

"I most certainly am not. I had to pour brandy down her throat to get her to come round again. The physician says it is a matter of months if not weeks. Half a year at most. I will be on my way again by Michaelmas, I will wager."

I said nothing for a long moment. That was the trouble with Harry Spenlove, I reflected. He made everything seem thoroughly reasonable until you escaped the circle of his charm, and then it was like waking from a spell.

He moved half a step closer. "Veronica, please. She is the nearest thing I have to family. Do not make me leave her. Not now—forgive me. I do not like to beg, but if that is what you wish, I will."

His voice broke a little, and unshed tears shone brightly in his eyes. He averted his head, clearly overcome by strong emotion.

"She is a deeply unlikeable old woman," I pointed out. "How is it that you have become so attached to her?"

He grinned. "I was reared by a woman very much like her—my own Granny Spenlove. As mean as the devil and twice as cunning. But her prickliness made it all the more meaningful when she decided she liked you. And she liked me very much. I was her favorite. I had almost forgot what it is like to be cared for," he finished, looking sharply away.

I tipped my head to meet his gaze and put a finger under his chin, lifting gently. "Harry, I am deeply impressed by what you have told me."

He looked sincerely hopeful. "Are you, love?"

"Yes," I said in a sober voice. "I am impressed that you can still lie with such conviction."

He gaped and then pushed my hand aside. "What the devil do you mean?"

"You do not have a sentimental bone in your body. There is a greater chance of faeries dancing upon the moon than you telling the truth, but I must insist you attempt it. Tell me, sincerely this time, why do you wish to stay here? Does it have anything to do with the altercation in Bristol?"

He opened his mouth, then snapped his teeth shut, grinding them. "Very well. Yes. I managed to run afoul of a particularly nasty pair. I thought I had eluded them, but they caught up with me in Bristol. They decided to provide a little demonstration of their feelings about me in the way of bruises," he said sullenly. "It was not an especially enjoyable interlude. I got free of them as soon as I could, but they knew where I lodged and I dared not stay. I knew they would immediately suspect I had gone to London to lose myself, so I headed west instead. It was only after I had boarded the train that I realized I was near to Hathaway Hall. Suddenly, the most elegant solution presented itself. I would simply take refuge here and enjoy her ladyship's company."

"And her trust," I added.

"I have taken nothing from this family apart from borrowing a room that would otherwise go unused and eaten their food, the price of which I have more than earned as a confidant and companion of Lady Hathaway." He suddenly seized my hand. "Veronica, I will swear upon whatever you like—whatever I hold sacred. I have told you the truth. I am in grave danger if I am forced to leave this place. But so long as I am here, I am safe. And Lady Hathaway is happy. Can you not simply let this particular sleeping dog lie in peace?" He had given up pleading. He simply held my hand close to his heart and waited.

"I suppose you could force me," I said quietly.

His expression was sincerely affronted. "If you are referring to your companion, I assure you, I have no interest in raising the fellow's ire. He is obviously besotted with you, but I should like to point out, he is *considerably* larger than I and you know how protective I am of my person."

He took a step closer still. "Veronica," he said in a low, coaxing voice, "please. Jonathan was a good fellow. His grandmother loved him dearly and she has been so very happy to have him back. Let me do this for her. And yes"—he paused, holding up a hand—"I know it will benefit me as well. I do not pretend to be nobler than I am. But to wrench that old dear's dream from her would be cruel, and say what you like about me, I am never that."

This much was true. Feckless, reckless, and utterly unreliable, but he had never been vicious. His failings were all the more painful for being delivered by someone who missed being a truly good man by so little. He wanted only a trifling bit of backbone, of moral courage, to be the man he ought to have been.

He went on. "No one ever need know that we have been acquainted. We can continue on with our polite fiction of having just met, and you and the enormous Mr. Templeton-Vane can finish your work and be on your way. What happens after will be just as I described it. I will allow Lady H to fawn and fondle as much as she pleases, and when her life draws to its natural close, I will be there, holding her hand, her devoted grandson to the very end."

"And then what? Perhaps brother Charles will set you up with a tidy annuity before you leave. Is that what you hope? Payment for services rendered."

"How cold you've become!" he said, his tone gently mocking. "But I suppose that crime may be laid at my feet. You must have grown up very quickly in the aftermath of the eruption."

"Not that it seems to have concerned you." I could have bitten my tongue as soon as the words escaped me. They were petulant and I had hoped it was beneath my dignity to care what he thought.

To my astonishment, something like remorse flickered in his eyes and he took my hand. "Veronica, you were always my greatest regret. Do not let me be yours."

I snatched my hand back. "You assign yourself greater importance than you should. I do not regret you, Harry. I do not think of you."

Likely sensing he had gone too far, he stepped back. "I understand. I hurt you deeply. And for that I am truly sorry."

"You *left* me during a cataclysmic disaster. I might have died."

"Of course you weren't going to die!" He seemed genuinely shocked at the suggestion. "Veronica, you were, even then, the most resourceful person I have ever known. At twenty you could manage your affairs with as much aplomb as an army general planning a siege. It never once occurred to me that you mightn't survive—and I was right. Look at you! More ravishing than you were then and entirely mistress of your own destiny. You have employment that suits you, a companion who clearly worships your very hem. You have health and beauty and a wit so sharp a man might cut himself and think the bleeding a privilege."

I rolled my eyes at the transparency of the flattery, but he gave a good impression of a man speaking his mind. He put out his hand as if to seize mine again, then drew it back.

"I am at your mercy, sweet Veronica."

"How very like you! To plead your case when you know I am as vulnerable as you," I said bitterly. "You always did like to turn the tables. I suppose if I refuse, you will tell everyone the truth."

"If you reveal my identity, then how we are acquainted with one another will, of necessity, be revealed," he said evenly. "I will not deny it, and I will not lie."

"Harry Spenlove, drawing the line at a lie—that is a new development!"

"You were always clever, Veronica, but you were never small. It is one of the things I admired most about you. There was never pettiness in you, and I do not believe you have acquired the habit of it. If you keep silent, then both of us will benefit, but most of all, a harmless old woman who cherishes her grandson will die happy. If you speak, you will bring pain to us both and perhaps hasten her death. I leave it to you to judge if that is a weight your conscience can bear."

He moved to the door of the summerhouse and closed the lantern, plunging us into darkness. When he opened the door, moonlight flowed in, just bright enough to illuminate the path back to the Hall.

"Go first," he urged. "I will wait and make certain you are not seen."

I had to pass him to exit the summerhouse, and when I did, I felt rather than saw him move towards me. It was a brief gesture, just a quick touch of one finger along my arm, but it raised shivers.

"Whatever you decide," he said softly, "I will not blame you."

CHAPTER

12

After my conversation with Harry, I did not sleep easily. Too many memories had been resurrected. I sifted through them all, remembering the first time I had met him—with Jonathan, aboard a steamer leaving Sydney. We were all bound for Sumatra and they presented themselves as rivals for my affections, albeit good-naturedly. Before we passed through the Coral Sea, it became clear that something had quickened when Harry and I looked at one another. The air seemed to shimmer with possibility, and Jonathan took it with his usual grace. He and I formed a friendship of our own, founded upon our mutual love of lepidoptery. We exchanged stories of our best finds and our wish lists of specimens yet to be netted. We talked long into the night of birdwings and swallowtails, debating the merits and beauties of Papilioinidae versus Pieridae.

But at the end of our conversations, after we had said good night and gone our separate ways, Harry slipped into my cabin and we passed the rest of those nights in a very different manner. I had been enchanted with Harry's easy manner; there was a lightness to him that indicated this would be a charming dalliance to offer refreshment to my spirit and body and nothing more. To my astonishment, he proposed marriage. I did not know then what troubles had befallen my mother upon this score. A hasty and intemperate marriage had led to her destruction, but it would be some time before I came to learn of this. I knew only that marriage, as an institution, was a thing to rouse wariness in my breast. The bearing of brats and ironing of shirts held little charms, I explained to Harry. But he kissed away every objection I made, promising that our lives would never be little or dull, that we would travel the world, making our own adventures, forever ardent lovers instead of allowing ourselves to fall into complacency. In the end, he wore me down, enticed me with a pretty picture painted from his words. I said the vows and signed the papers and let him slip a slender cold band of gold upon my finger.

Within a month the ring was gone, pawned to pay a debt, and I realized what I had done. I had shackled myself to a man who could not be trusted, upon whom I could never truly depend. Too late, I understood the magnitude of a woman's vulnerability in marriage, how every particle of her happiness depends upon her choosing well. And I had chosen unwisely.

Jonathan had understood. Harry would frequently vanish, taking with him some small trinket or other to buy his way into a game of cards. Jonathan, who might have gone with him, often stayed carefully behind. I never quite knew what he intended. Was he guardian? Friend? Did he nurture hopes to be more should circumstances arise? Or did he simply act out of guilt or pity for a neglected bride whose rosy, romantic dreams had been shredded?

He never behaved badly, never put a finger upon me nor murmured a word to cause unease. Only once, after we had spent a particularly lovely afternoon filling our jars with the most extraordinary specimens of *Troides vandepolli*, did he, flushed with success and spurred by high spirits, permit his hand to linger too long upon my arm. I looked up at him and saw a jolt of surprise, awareness springing to life before a deliberate closing of the shutters.

Jonathan and I were never alone again after that day. He took great care always to invite others to join our expeditions, and even tried to leave once or twice himself. Harry always talked him round, but as our fledgling marriage crumbled even further, Harry seemed eager to escape. When Krakatoa began her fateful rumblings, it was Harry who arranged their jaunt to Java. It was meant to be a trip of less than a week, but a fortnight later I was still in Sumatra, twiddling my thumbs and waiting, growing more impatient with every passing hour. I was unaccustomed to ordering my life to suit another, and I had found I did not like it. I was preparing to make my own arrangements to leave when the volcano erupted in spectacular fashion. It is a time I seldom think on and never with fondness. Water and food were scarce and unpalatable, and hygienic arrangements were unspeakable. The most rudimentary civilities were obliterated in the volcano's wake, everything drowned in soot and mud and boiling seawater that heaved upon the beaches, leaving dead and rotting things behind. I stood at the stern of the boat as we sailed away, gripping the railing to stare behind until the palm-fringed islands fell beyond the horizon.

I had never presented myself as a married woman; I had never called myself Spenlove, and Harry had taken my wedding ring. There were no photographs, no love letters, no tokens we had exchanged. There was nothing and no one to remind me of my foolish foray into matrimony. And so, I forgot it. At least, I tried. I worked hard, day and night, driving myself into exhausted and dreamless sleep, until at last, Harry began to fade, like a snippet of a song, long since heard and half-forgot.

Never again did I refer to Harry. From that point on, I looked only to please myself, keeping my heart firmly locked away. I dallied, I flirted, I enjoyed myself immensely, but at all times, I made certain my activities were undertaken to suit my own inclinations and not those of another. If I took one excellent lesson away from my marriage, it was that wifehood was not my calling and was one I vowed I would never undertake again.

And for a number of years, my resolve was never threatened. I had met a number of charming men, some more distracting than others. Some I enjoyed for an afternoon, some for a fortnight. But never longer and never at home. I reserved my escapades for my travels, always knowing I could retreat to England should I feel myself in danger of falling prey once more to my softer feelings. And yet it was in England that I met the man who was more myself than I was. I had observed before that if the rest of the world's folk were made of mud, Stoker and I were quicksilver, able to catch one another's thoughts as easily as a swallowtail may be netted on the wing. We did not require one another, for neither of us was deficient. But we enhanced one another, we bettered one another.

I had always refused to entertain the possibility of marriage, and he had respected this, having had his own unwholesome encounter with that state. But I knew that in his heart of hearts, there was a most traditional and conventional part of him that would have married me if I were willing to have him. In spite of his pain and his scars, he would have taken me as his wife, and the knowledge that I could not, would not, do the same troubled me. Was my love the lesser because I would not risk myself to keep it? Was I selfish or pragmatic? Was I true to my own nature or was I everything nature abhorred, a woman who would not tie herself to a mate for the duration of her life?

And now Harry had returned, blithely stepping into my life as a reminder that every day I had spent with Stoker had been a lie, a stain upon my conscience because I had withheld from him the facts of my own past. Stoker had, in due course, laid himself bare, giving me every part of himself, no matter how imperfect. And I had returned the favor by drawing a veil over that which I wished to conceal. I had not trusted him, and so I was repaid in betrayal, I reflected bitterly.

It was with considerable self-loathing that I at last tumbled into an uneasy sleep full of fitful rest and broken dreams. I woke to find another grim morning had begun, the sun nowhere in evidence, hid as it was behind a bank of gloomy grey cloud. I completed my ablutions and went down to breakfast, my footsteps slowed by dread. I did not anticipate telling Stoker the truth with anything like pleasure. In fact, I was not at all certain of what words I should employ. How does one even *begin* such a conversation?

And of course, there was the obvious temptation not to speak of it at all. For all his failures of character, Harry did have a certain soft charm, and whilst I did not doubt for a moment he had come to Hathaway Hall for his own mercenary purposes, I also knew he was entirely capable of following his capricious heart. That Lady Hathaway had roused his affections, I was certain. I had observed his little courtesies to her at dinner when he thought no one was looking. The dropped spoon he retrieved, silently exchanging it for his own so she did not have to wait to enjoy her pudding. The steadying hand when she rose to leave the table. The quick, assessing glances when her color rose or faded. He was adept at playing the attentive grandson, but even Harry Spenlove was not so gifted an actor as that. He did sincerely care for the old harridan, I was convinced. And unmasking his deceit would unquestionably devastate her, a distinctly unhappy possibility given her state of health.

And beside the matter of Lady Hathaway, I had excellent reasons of my own for not exposing Harry's masquerade. When we had been married, the secret of my true parentage was one I had not yet penetrated. Now that he had returned, the revelation that I was the semilegitimate daughter of the Prince of Wales was not information I cared to share, least of all with an opportunistic estranged husband. My father and I had never formally met and I had never been acknowledged, but I had upon more than one occasion been called into service for the family, lending such talents as I possessed. Ours was an uneasy partnership, and I did not even know if I wanted my father's acknowledgment. But if there were ever to be a chance of a relationship with him, Harry could never know. Guarding my own secret seemed a good deal likelier if I gave Harry a wide berth, I reflected. Although I had made up my mind that I must somehow find the words to explain my situation to Stoker.

Breakfast provided no opportunity, for Stoker had already finished and begun his work in the Long Gallery, according to Charles Hathaway. "I was hoping you might go to the observatory, Miss Speedwell," he continued. "My sister is still rather sullen about the notion of giving up our grandfather's celestial instruments, and I thought she might be a little more amenable to giving them into your care. She admires you so," he added with a little sop to my vanity.

I repressed a sigh. All my sympathies lay with Effie, and I had little inclination to be drawn into family quarrels. But before I could frame my refusal tactfully, Mary Hathaway appeared with a few of her offspring. "Children, say good morning to Miss Speedwell. You remember her, my darlings. The lady scientist."

She managed to make the phrase "lady scientist" sound faintly obscene, but my greater objection was to the children themselves. Geoffrey was still carrying his cage, although I was relieved to see it contained nothing living, and the unlovely Ada was once more sucking at her finger. Her long, straight hair was tied back with a bow so enormous it looked like ears.

"Come, children, let us show Miss Speedwell where the observatory is," she urged. "She is going to speak with your aunt Euphemia," she told them firmly.

I had promised no such thing, but there seemed little chance of escaping Mary Hathaway's domination as she herded us all up the stairs. Geoffrey walked next to me, one hand clutching my skirts as he waved the little cage at me. I realized then how much it looked like a gibbet and shuddered.

"So, no luck catching faeries then?" I asked meanly.

He gave me a dark look. "You couldn't see it if I had. Faeries can be *invisible* when they want."

"Then how will you know when you catch one?"

"Because it will scream when I poke it with my stick," he assured me.

We had come to the top of the stairs and Mary Hathaway looked fondly at her children. "Such a consolation, children," she said. "And such a responsibility. The rearing of them is extraordinarily taxing," she confided as she handed them off to their nanny and a small cadre of nursemaids.

"I have no doubt," I said, twitching my skirts out of Geoffrey's sticky grasp before he trotted off with his nanny.

"That is why I appreciate you speaking with Effie," she said. "The sooner those instruments are out of the house, the better."

"But why? Surely there is no harm in Miss Euphemia having a hobby," I protested.

Her mouth was set in a firm and unflattering line. If she kept up the habit of disapproving of things, she was going to age very poorly, I reflected.

"It is not, I am afraid, merely a hobby. If it were, no matter how unladylike, I might be able to condone it. But Effie wants to pursue science as an occupation, and that is simply not acceptable."

"I am doing it," I told her roundly.

Her expression turned frankly pitying. "And that is certainly admirable in your case. Spinsters must, after all, earn their crust of bread somehow. But Effie has family and ought to have a husband. She has no call to earn a living. Besides, her unwomanly pursuits have led to other bad habits," she said, pursing again. "She consorts with servants, particularly that Anjali who attends Lady Hathaway. I have attempted upon numerous occasions to put a stop to it, but unfortunately Effie is entirely ungovernable, and Anjali is engaged by Lady Hathaway and I have not the authority to remove her."

"You would dismiss her over her friendship with Miss Euphemia?"

"Friendship?" The word was uttered on a genteel shriek. "Miss Speedwell, I beg you, do not use such a word. It is unthinkable. And I will have my way in the end," she added with the complacency of a cat surveying a plump mouse. "But for now, please do what you can to reconcile Effie to the fact that the observatory will be cleared out—whatever her thoughts on the matter."

She leaned near enough that I could smell her toilet water. Something heavy with the fragrance of lily, which I have never liked.

"Effie, I do not mind telling you, has been only one of my trials here, Miss Speedwell. Lady Hathaway is occasionally imperious, forgetting that she is no longer mistress here. One wants to be *tactful*..." She trailed off and I made sympathetic noises. I hated giving any sign of encouraging confidences to someone I found frankly odious, but Mary was, after all, a source of information.

"And, of course, with the sudden appearance of Jonathan Hathaway," I began.

She rolled her eyes heavenwards. "You have no notion the trouble it has caused us! I will not say he has been anything other than helpful with Lady Hathaway. His attentions in that quarter have been entirely welcome. He entertains and soothes her in a way none of the rest of us can. He has saved me a tremendous amount of work, I can tell you. But the scandal if it were to become public!" She put a fingertip to my sleeve. "I know I can trust your discretion, Miss Speedwell. After all, you are part of an earl's household," she added in a tone of respect. I understood her better then. She had the merchant class's view of aristocracy—awed to the point of idiocy. Aristocrats, as I had excellent reason to know, put their trousers on exactly the same as everyone else, and sometimes with far less skill or assistance. That Lord Rosemorran and Stoker's eldest brother, Viscount Templeton-Vane, were decent fellows was the exception, not the rule, for noble gentlemen.

But I assumed a smile I hoped she would interpret as one of agreement. "You must live in terror of the story being published in the newspapers," I suggested.

Her own smile was one of accomplished smugness. "Would you believe, Miss Speedwell, one of those dreadful daily tabloids intended to write about it? But my father handled the situation, and we need have no further worry in that quarter," she added, pressing her lips together. So, her papa's fortune was a source of embarrassment until she had need of it to purchase the *Daily Harbinger*'s silence. I had not thought it possible to dislike her more, but this new hypocrisy had managed to do the trick.

Perhaps regretting the mention of her father—or else remembering that it was common to consort with anyone below one's own social station—she drew herself up and bustled away, entirely forgetting to give me instructions on how to reach the observatory, but I did not call her back. I was perfectly delighted to be rid of her, and I fled in the general direction of the observatory. I followed the long corridors of the Hall until I came to the small black door set under the portrait of Sir Geoffrey. The knob gave way in my hand and I bent double to pass through the doorway. Immediately beyond lay a narrow staircase of lacy black metal that twisted upwards, spiraling around itself into the furthest reaches of the tower. My skirts somewhat hampered my progress, but I climbed steadily onwards until at last I reached a small door with a notice pinned to it. The words were printed in heavy block capitals.

DO NOT ENTER ON PAIN OF DEATH

I smiled and rapped once on the door. Through it, I heard a hasty scrabbling. There was a long delay before a voice called for me to enter.

CHAPTER

13

A table sat in the middle of the room, stacked high with charts and books and an orrery, a small model of the heliocentric universe with the various heavenly bodies fixed to brass arms. It was an impressive piece, the clockwork mechanism ticking as the small golden planets revolved around the larger sun. I had seen such an instrument only once before, in a private collection in Florence, where I had been shown the various intricacies, the way each hollow planet could be unscrewed and detached from the golden arms so that it might be packed away for traveling purposes. The continents and oceans of the Earth were identified with etched Latin names, so minute as to be visible only with the aid of the magnifying glass attached by its own arm at the equator. The whole thing was fitted with a clockwork mechanism so that the planets might revolve, each in its own time, with a tiny alabaster moon hovering gently about the Earth. It was meant to educate, but so lovely and intricate a device must be admired simply as a thing of beauty as well.

Effie perched upon the table, an open book resting upon the back of the Italian greyhound curled up in her lap. It lifted its head when I entered, gave a great sniff with its pointed noise, and settled again, clearly unimpressed. The walls had been fitted with enormous windows, and Anjali stood beside one, flapping her hand at the open casement, and the room's atmosphere was thick with a pungent and distinctive odor.

"If you mean to disperse the smell of cigarette smoke, keep a dish of strong vinegar about," I advised. "It does wonders to clear the air."

Anjali pressed her lips together, but Effie burst out laughing. "Do you really not mind then? You won't tell?"

I advanced into the room and closed the door carefully behind me. I extracted my own cigarette case and struck a vesta. "I think not."

After that, we were entirely convivial. Anjali still demonstrated the caution I have often noticed in upper servants. Not entirely staff and definitely not family, companions—like governesses—were neither fish nor fowl. They enjoyed too many privileges to permit intimacy with the rest of those employed in the household, but too few to allow them equality with their masters and mistresses. Yet she seemed genuinely fond of Effie, and I was glad the poor girl had at least one person in the house who seemed to support her interests in science.

Not only support them, but share them—for Anjali was well-read, and we had a spirited conversation on the relative merits of Galvani versus Volta and Lamarckian versus Darwinian theory. She was passionately enthusiastic about Darwin and most appreciative of my recommendation of the work of Antoinette Brown Blackwell.

"I shall make a point of reading her efforts," she promised. "Although so long as she is a critic of Lamarck, I have no doubt I will find her writings instructive."

"I am delighted to hear such reasonable views," I told her. "Mr. Templeton-Vane is decidedly too fond of Lamarck for his own good."

Just then, the mantel clock struck the hour and Anjali smoothed out her skirts, resuming once more the sober mien of an upper servant. She inclined her head to Effie in what might have been interpreted as a bit of light mockery, for her lips twitched as she bobbed a curtsy. "Miss Euphemia," she murmured. She turned in my direction. "Miss Speedwell."

She left us then, and a peaceful silence settled over the observatory. From this vantage point, one might watch sheep and clouds, both formless masses of white, gathering and shifting over the moor. The clock ticked on, and there was a muted wet snuffle from the dog.

"It is nice that you have a companion," I told her, gesturing towards the dog. As if sensing she was under discussion, the pup lifted her head and gave me a lofty look.

"A gift from my godfather—Sir Hugo Montgomerie," she said with a tinge of pride. "But you must know him. He corresponded with Charles to arrange the sale of the collection to Lord Rosemorran."

"I have made his acquaintance," I temporized.

"I do not see him very often," she said. "He sends me five pounds on my birthday every year and he brought Al-'Ijliyyah as a present the last time he visited, but he and Charles quarreled so I do not think he will come again soon."

"Al-'Ijliyyah! You have given her an Arabic name?" The dog put her nose forward tentatively and I ventured to hold out my hand for her to smell.

"I called her after Al-'Ijliyyah bint Al-'Ijliyy, an astronomer who lived in Aleppo before the Crusades. Can you imagine?" she asked, her eyes shining. "She was making scientific instruments a thousand years ago."

"A worthy namesake," I agreed.

She rolled her eyes. "Mary doesn't like it. She refers to her as Jilly and now everyone else does. Only Anjali calls her by her correct name."

"She seems a good friend," I began.

Effie let out a sharp bark of laughter that startled the dog. "Did Mary ask you to speak to me?"

"How did you know?"

"Because she does it with anyone she thinks might be able to persuade me to listen." She pitched her voice into an exact impression of her sister-in-law's affected tones. "'Effie, you mustn't consort with the help. It simply is not done and it sets such a bad example for the children.'" She rolled her eyes again. "As if I care about setting an example for the children."

"You are not fond of your nephew and nieces?"

"I loathe the little horrors," she said frankly. "The twins are babies and therefore unspeakably dull. Little Ada just *stares* with a sort of terrifying intensity as if she is trying to see underneath my skin. And the less said of Geoffrey and his obsession with putting things in cages the better."

"I have never been inclined to like children myself," I admitted. "I am far more content with butterflies and dogs."

Al-'Ijliyyah nosed closer to me, shoving her snout under my hand until Effie laughed. "She wants you to scratch behind her ears. She is a peremptory little beast, but I am fond of her."

I obediently scratched behind the dog's ears, earning myself a delicate little lick when I was finished. I looked about, surveying the stacks of notebooks and instruments arranged on a series of low shelves so as not to impede the view from the vast windows. A telescope, ancient-looking with a wide, cracked lens, stood in front of one of the windows. The expansive vistas made the small room seem quite spacious, and I was conscious for the first time since arriving at the Hall of a sort of quiet peace.

"I like it here," I told Effie. "I see why you have made this your bolthole."

"When it is clear, you can see almost to Torquay. And at night, the stars are as numerous as grains of sand upon the shore."

My gaze fell upon the orrery, the planets still making their revolutions around the sun, some of them almost imperceptibly slow.

"It was Granfer's. And it was meant to be mine." Her complexion flushed, an unbecoming color on one with gingerish hair.

"I am sorry," I told her truthfully. "Perhaps it need not go," I began.

"Charles insists. The telescope is worthless now," she said with a nod towards the cracked instrument. "But the orrery is in excellent condition and rather rare. Italian in origin. Worth a considerable amount of money, so naturally Mary and Charles are interested in it. I have made my peace with it," she added quickly, and I wondered whether to believe her. She went on. "Besides, I have Granfer's research notebooks, and they are more valuable, at least to me. I am continuing his work."

She paused and made a vague gesture towards the notebook in her lap.

"What is the work?" I inquired.

Her eyes narrowed suspiciously. "Do you really want to know? People ask, but they never listen when I tell them."

"I can believe that. One only has to watch someone's eyes glaze over as you try to explain the distinctions between lepidopterans to know that such queries are seldom sincere. Mine is, I assure you. Tell me."

She resettled her spectacles on her nose. "Very well. Granfer was fascinated by the work of Lockyer and Janssen in discovering an element they detected in the emission line of the sun's atmosphere. They called it helium."

"After Helios, the sun god?" I asked.

"Exactly," Effie said. Her face was suffused with enthusiasm, eyes agleam as she spoke. She explained that while her grandfather was content to search for traces of helium on earth, she was more intrigued by the fact that it had been discovered during an eclipse.

"With the developments in scientific instruments, the observations that could be made during eclipses would be orders of magnitude greater than anything that has been possible before. We might further our understanding of how fast the stars are moving, what comprises them, and if it would ever be possible to reach them."

Her dream of humankind sailing amongst the stars seemed far-fetched at best, but I was in a mood to humor the girl. Too many people had been content to shatter her illusions; I would not be one of them.

"And what would it take for you to continue your research?"

"Well, it would help a very good deal if Charles were not selling my equipment out from under me," she replied tartly. "But if I am honest, there are more advanced instruments with which I could do more. I have clung to Granfer's orrery because it is of sound quality, and it is so beautiful. Its very antiquity is what makes it valuable to Charles. But a proper observatory with the latest, most sensitive telescope would enable me to do so much more." A rueful smile touched her lips. "There is no point in wishing. Such a laboratory is quite beyond my means."

"Yes, I understand a proper telescope alone is costly," I mused. "I belong to a club for extraordinary women—philosophers, botanists, mathematicians, that sort of thing. We have a pair of astronomers amongst our members and only last year we were able to finally provide funds to establish them in an observatory of their own. It took a good deal of effort, but we secured enough contributions to purchase a tiny ruined castle on the shores of Loch Doon. Apparently the night sky there is quite unsmirched by the fogs and smogs of the cities."

"Are you speaking of the Marvell sisters?" she asked, her eyes rounding.

"Oh, do you know them?"

"Know them! They are legend," she breathed. "And you have met them?"

"Once or twice in the course of raising the funds necessary to establish them in Scotland." The Marvells, Henrietta and Lucy, were somewhere beyond forty, vague, wispy-looking women with flyaway hair and the habit of trailing off in the middle of sentences as though they had lost the thread of their thoughts. Privately we joked that it was the result of spending too much time lost amongst the stars, but we jested only with the deepest affection. I went on. "I am afraid we shall see nothing of them now they have their Scottish aerie. They send monthly reports to the club and seem thoroughly content."

"I am not surprised," she said, her small hands curling into fists. "They have managed to make a life for themselves doing what they love. As you have."

I smiled at her. "It was rather easier for me. Lepidopterists require only a butterfly net and a good deal of perseverance—along with considerable luck."

"Sometimes," she said, her eyes quite blank behind the smudged spectacles, "you have to make your own luck."

I made my way to the Long Gallery to speak with Stoker. The time had come, I told myself firmly, and I must seize the moment, grasp the nettle, take the bull by the horns. I had exhausted my catalog of metaphors, so I paused on the threshold, steeling myself. There were few moments in my life that had ever required such courage, I reflected. I had been shipwrecked, menaced by villains, abducted—more than once, in fact. In short, I had been in peril so many times I could scarce count them.

And yet. Nothing frightened me so badly as the notion of revealing to Stoker what I had taken such pains to conceal.

"This will not do," I said aloud, summoning all my resolve. I put my hand to the knob and turned it, striding into the room as I began to speak. "Stoker, I must—"

"Veronica!" he called in a tone I had seldom heard him employ outside of intimate congress. He was, in a word, enraptured. His eyes shone, his color was high, even his hair seemed to wave more exuberantly. He was standing on the far side of the room, his attention fixed upon something I could not see. "Come and see!" he urged. "It is magnificent."

I went to him and saw that he had found it at last. "The thylacine!" I exclaimed.

He must have only just uncovered it, for the dust sheet had been thrown back, motes still dancing in the light of the lamps.

"*Thylacinus cynocephalus*," he breathed. "At last."

It was rather smaller than one might have expected for the ferocity of its reputation, scarcely larger than a medium-sized dog, but its expression belied any domestication. The snout was pointed, and the lips curled back to reveal a set of teeth clearly meant for ripping. The ears were small and neat and slightly rounded, the jaw heavy. Stripes, subtle near the head, became more pronounced as they proceeded to the back, ending in a long, whippet-thin tail.

"I quite understand what you mean about the jaw," said a familiar voice. I realized then that we were not alone. I had been sufficiently distracted by Stoker's discovery to have overlooked his companion. Harry, in his guise as Jonathan Hathaway, was standing in the shadows behind Stoker, peering around him to look at the creature.

"Is it not a glorious sight, Hathaway?" Stoker asked, his voice as contented as a cat's.

Hathaway. He did not correct Stoker, but then I had not anticipated that he would. He was smiling at me, but I caught the pleading expression in his eyes and turned away.

"A most impressive creature," I told Stoker. "Is it male or female?"

"Male," Stoker pronounced. "But unlike other Antipodean marsupials, the male has a pouch into which it can withdraw the scrotal sac for defensive purposes during an attack. It is an extraordinary specimen. It ought to have been mounted to display the full range of its bite."

"Eighty degrees," Jonathan put in. "Is that not what you said?"

"More or less," Stoker agreed. "You can see here—" He was off again, pointing out the intricacies of the animal's anatomy, from its remarkable jaw to the jaunty angle of its tail.

"I will leave you to it," I said quietly. They both made the appropriate noises, but they scarcely seemed to notice when I withdrew to the far side of the room in order to examine the cases of lepidoptery specimens. Those I had already found were old, from Sir Geoffrey's time, and, due to the deleterious effects of shipping and improper handling, had noticeably deteriorated in quality. But as I moved on, I received a shock, for the next case was much newer, and I recognized the hand that had inscribed the labels.

Ornithoptera euphorion, I read, tracing the neat penmanship. I remembered Jonathan Hathaway laboring over this particular case, mounting the pretty set of Cairns Birdwings he had netted in Australia. It had been raining in Sumatra and butterfly hunters do not give chase in the rain. We had settled in for a long afternoon of writing up our journals and labeling our collections, exchanging stories and admiring each other's handiwork. I had been assembling a particularly lucrative collection of Saturniidae for a gentleman in Scotland with a passion for moths and had just secured the largest exemplar of *Attacus atlas* I had ever seen. Nine and a half inches across, it was enormous and almost wildly beautiful with its rusty colorations and geometric patterns. Jonathan had insisted upon toasting my success while Harry had speculated on the amount of the bonus I could expect for capturing such a beauty. Jonathan had finished his case of birdwings that day and shipped it home to Hathaway Hall, but I had carefully stowed my Atlas with the rest of the moths. Within six weeks, they would be destroyed in the eruption, and I never did see the payment for the days I had spent roaming the jungles of Sumatra. But what I remembered most of that day was the genuine pleasure Jonathan Hathaway evinced at my success.

I glanced up to find Harry standing behind me. "I recall that day," he said softly. "It was the day I decided to ask you to marry me."

"Don't," I ordered. "Or I will tell him this instant."

"You were never more beautiful than when you were on the hunt," he went on.

I rose, but his hand came around my wrist. "Can you bear to destroy his happiness?" he asked, flicking a glance to where Stoker stood, working on the thylacine. He was taking notes, calipers and magnifying glass at hand, singing "The Maid of Amsterdam" with a few particularly explicit additions he had doubtless learnt in the navy. He looked utterly content, and I wrenched my wrist free from Harry's grip.

"Do not test me," I hissed. But even as I left the room, I realized how easily Harry had discovered my Achilles' heel and how true had been his aim.

A fter dinner that evening—more delicious food and bland conversation—we gathered again for coffee around the hearth. This time Effie joined us for dinner and Anjali had even been permitted to appear when coffee was served. After the first cups had been drunk, Lady Hathaway snapped her fingers at Anjali. "Go with Effie. She knows what I want."

Anjali bowed her head and followed Effie from the room.

"What are you on about, Granna?" Charles asked affectionately.

Lady Hathaway gave him a slow smile as she folded her hands over the top of her walking stick. "Just you wait, boy. I do love a surprise."

"At your age!" Mary said with more candor than tact.

Lady Hathaway's mouth thinned. "When you have reached my advanced years, Mary dear, I do hope you will have acquired a little wisdom to compensate for the loss of your good looks."

Jonathan's lips twitched with a suppressed smile, but Mary seemed not to notice how thoroughly she had been put in her place. There was a complacency to her, the self-satisfaction of the young, I thought. She knew well enough that in a short while, she would be undisputed mistress of Hathaway Hall. Her things would be moved into the master suite, no doubt after she had redecorated, stripping away every last reminder of Lady Hathaway. By virtue of her age alone, she would triumph. Viewed in that light, it was rather sordid and a little sad, I decided. Lady Hathaway had clearly been a person of some influence, accustomed to wielding power over those around her. With the passage of time, she had become smaller until all that remained were the tiny tyrannies of the elderly inflicted upon the young.

It all made me exceedingly grateful that I had no proper family to speak of. I enjoyed the smug solitude of an orphan, with no obligations to trouble me and no expectations to stifle my whims. It might be lonely at times, if I were entirely honest, but how much better to be alone with my dignity intact than at the mercy of my relations!

It was only a few short minutes until Effie and Anjali returned bearing a small casket. I was not familiar enough to distinguish among the various styles of Indian workmanship, but the artistry was clearly from that part of the world. It was wrought silver, badly tarnished but still lovely. Effie presented it to her grandmother with a flourish while Anjali handed over a key, an enormous thing with a thick silken tassel attached to one end.

"Granna," Charles Hathaway began, half rising from his seat, "is that—"

She waved him back to his chair. "It is indeed, Charles. Do not fuss." She settled the casket on her lap and fitted the key to the lock. It turned with an audible protest, and Effie had to help, but at last there came a decisive click and the lid sprang free.

Lady Hathaway beamed down at the contents, an expression of

fondness warming her features. "There you are, my darlings," she crooned. "It has been a long time." She reached a hand into the casket and brought it up again, dripping in rubies.

We gasped as they caught the light, flinging it back again, the glittering scarlet sparks warming the pale, withered flesh of her hand. She gave a delighted laugh and dipped her hand again, this time emerging with a string of emeralds. Pearls followed, long strands of them looping about her arm. She presented earrings and brooches and bracelets, all set with the same gems, and a turban ornament in the shape of a peacock's tail, paved with rubies.

"Do you see that little hollow?" she asked us, demonstrating the empty chamber at the top of the turban ornament. "That is where a plume would go, always an ostrich feather of purest white. And here," she added, touching a spot just above the elaborate scarlet tail, "this is where the heart of the peacock belongs."

She reached a last time into the casket and drew out a velvet box. She handed it to Jonathan. "Open it, lad," she ordered.

He gave her a questioning look, but she flapped her jewel-laden hands at him. "Do as I say."

He looked at the group. My own expression must have been one of wide-eyed wonder, for I had never seen such an assemblage of jewels and I had once worn the crown jewels of the Alpenwald. The others looked frankly astonished at the magnificent display heaped in her ladyship's lap.

Jonathan took a deep breath and opened the box. He caught his breath, and I knew he was not pretending. His awe was entirely sincere. With reverent fingers he drew out a stone, an enormous thing, as red as blood and shimmering with the crimson glow of a still-beating heart.

"The Eye of the Dawn," Lady Hathaway said as he held the gem up to the light. "Perfect pigeon's-blood color and without flaw. It was mined in the mountains of Persia and has a fascinating history. It was given by the Shah of Persia to a maharajah as a peace offering after years of violence between them. It is said that the stone was originally a diamond but turned to a ruby from the blood shed between these two warlords. The maharajah had it set into the turban ornament to display it proudly, but he wore it for only a month before he died. His son and successor wore it less than a year. After that, it was believed cursed for men to wear it, and it was removed from the turban ornament and placed into a necklace instead for the maharani. Eventually it passed into the hands of a particular maharani whose husband was instrumental in the Sepoy Mutiny. During the confusion of the rebellion, the jewels came into my husband's possession. He presented them to me, of course, and they have been mine ever since."

Stoker and I exchanged glances. Her ladyship had not been forthcoming on *how* the jewels came into her husband's possession, but it was presumably not through legitimate means. Colonials had used the mutiny as an excuse to seize property owned by the native royals, and more than one upstanding English family had found itself the richer for it, albeit no one ever admitted publicly to behaving like privateers. If priceless gems and expensive bric-a-brac suddenly found their way from palace strongrooms to the necks and drawing rooms of the British in India, who would complain? Certainly not the various nobles whose possessions had been plundered. The collapse of the mutiny had left many of them in the precarious position of having openly supported the overthrow of the authorities who were firmly entrenched in India. A few ropes of pearls or blooded horses were a small price to pay to avoid serious repercussions for having been on the losing side of the rebellion. Whether Sir Geoffrey Hathaway had stolen the gems outright or exerted pressure upon the prince to hand them over, they had certainly not been given freely, I surmised.

"Magnificent," Effie breathed.

"It is," Jonathan Hathaway said in a low, reverent voice.

"It will be yours, lad," Lady Hathaway told him. "I have sent instructions to my solicitor and the necessary codicil has been signed." Jonathan opened his mouth but Lady Hathaway held up a hand. "Do not fuss. I mean to keep them until I am dead, for I do like to look at them now and again, but when I die, they are yours."

Mary gave her husband a sharp look and he interjected. "But, Granna, surely you recall that the jewels were being fetched from the bank so that Mary might wear them for her portrait," he began.

Lady Hathaway curled a lip. "The jewels are my own private property, Charles. And it is not your concern what I do with my property," Lady Hathaway said firmly.

"Of course," he replied, holding up a hand. "Certainly. Right you are."

Mary said nothing, but her lips were clamped tightly together. She rose and smoothed her skirts. "If you will excuse me, I must look in on the children."

Charles looked after her as she left, clearly unhappy at being caught between his wife and his grandmother. He fell to fiddling with his pipe, turning out the ashes onto the hearth and tamping in a fresh plug of tobacco.

"Well?" Lady Hathaway prodded Jonathan. "What do you think?"

Jonathan replaced the stone gently, almost reverently. He closed the box slowly, as if loath to take a final look at the ruby. He handed the box back to Lady Hathaway. "A most extraordinary stone," he said in a soft voice.

She nodded towards the casket. "All of this will be yours. Consider it amends for the loss of your birthright."

Jonathan covered her hand with his. "You are too generous. Perhaps we should discuss this later."

Charles looked up from where he had finally got his pipe to light. "Do not wait on my account. One of the ram lambs has wandered off and I meant to see if he'd returned." He rose and shambled out, looking more than ever like a forlorn sheepdog.

Jonathan's gaze followed him. "I think your gift will bring trouble in its wake," he told Lady Hathaway.

She gave him a sharp glance. "What do I care? I shan't be here to see it. I shall be dead and moldering," she added with a smile.

"Well, I certainly won't fuss," Effie put in. "The jewels are most likely still cursed and I've no intention of bringing that sort of thing down on my head."

"And you call yourself a woman of science," her grandmother jeered.

Effie colored slightly. "I *am* a woman of science, although precious little good it does me in this family."

Her grandmother wagged a finger, sharp color rushing into her mottled cheeks. "Do not take that tone with me, Euphemia. I will not stand for it, do you hear me?"

She seemed a fair way to working herself up, but Anjali stepped forwards. "It grows late, your ladyship," she said quietly. "Would you care for hot milk tonight or a tisane?"

"Hot milk," the old woman said irritably. "Mind you sweeten it properly and none of your foreign spices."

I felt a rush of sympathy for Anjali, trapped as she was in employment with such a disagreeable old person, but she merely inclined her head serenely. "Of course."

Lady Hathaway thrust the casket at Effie. "Carry this up to my room so I can lock it away properly. Anjali, give me your arm." She struggled to her feet, making use of her walking stick as she rose. Anjali dipped her knees a little to better support her ladyship. They bade the rest of us good night and left. As the door closed behind them, Jonathan let out a long sigh.

He seemed lost in thought, his attention fixed upon the fire. The light of the flames played over his face, shadows chasing one another as they flickered. I steeled myself. The time had come. I rose and looked at Stoker, opened my mouth to ask him to accompany me to my room, where I would tell him everything.

"I say, this has all been a bit much. Would you mind playing a game or two of billiards? A little distraction would not go amiss," Jonathan said to Stoker.

"Certainly," Stoker said. His innate courtesy would require him to oblige. Besides which, he adored billiards and was always complaining he could never get a satisfactory game since I am, in his words, "entirely lethal with a stick" and "not to be trusted anywhere near a billiards table." (It is the rankest lie. I have only broken two windows in the course of playing with him and they were not particularly valuable ones at that.)

"I was hoping to speak with you," I said, turning to Stoker. He paused by my chair and pressed a kiss to my hair.

"I will look in on my way to bed," he promised. Behind his back, Jonathan gave me a long, level look and shrugged by way of apology. As I suspected, he had known exactly what I intended and had cleverly managed to put off my confession for at least a few more hours.

"Feathers," I muttered as they left me. I sat for a long while, watching the flames die to embers, the room growing cold around me. At last the falling temperature drove me to my room where the fire had been kindled and a hot brick placed in my sheets. The warmth tempted me, but I was determined to stay awake until I had a chance to speak with Stoker. The weight of my secrets pressed upon me and I was eager to be free of them, no matter the consequences.

CHAPTER

15

In spite of my resolve, I must have drifted into the arms of Morpheus, for when I opened my eyes, a bleak grey daylight shone at the window. I was cramped, excruciatingly so, for having spent the night curled in the window seat, and it took several minutes to untangle myself and bring movement to my stiffened limbs.

As I stretched my neck, I caught sight of a piece of paper that had been thrust under my door. It was half a sheet of foolscap, and I knew the hand well, even in a hasty scrawl. It was from Stoker, a few words to explain that he and Jonathan had stayed at billiards until an unconscionably late hour and though he had tapped, I had made no answer. He explained that he was in need of specialist packing materials for the purposes of protecting the thylacine, and as none was to be had nearer than Exeter, he had taken the earliest train and would return after luncheon.

I tossed the letter aside with a few choice words that would have scandalized the rest of the household had they heard me. Now that I had made up my mind to confess all to Stoker, every hour the action was delayed had become torture. I felt suffocated by the burden of the truth, and even the air in the Hall seemed thick with my deceit. I could bear it no longer. Without Stoker at hand, I realized there was slim purpose to my working in the Long Gallery alone. There was little work to be done with the butterfly collections and I could easily manage it whilst Stoker was occupied with his beloved thylacine. The rest of the Hathaways would doubtless be engaged in their regular activities and I had no wish to join them. I was, in a word, free.

With alacrity, I donned my working costume of tweed trousers and shirtwaist, buttoning over this a fitted waistcoat and a jacket. A narrow skirt, which could be buttoned up and out of the way if necessity demanded, concealed the immodesty of the trousers, while flat boots buttoned to the knee protected my legs. I took up my equipment—net, killing jars, cotton-wool pads soaked in a cyanide solution, and a small wicker hamper like a fisherman's creel. A packet of minuten, the tiny headless pins of the lepidopterist's trade, were neatly fitted into my cuffs, and for good measure I slipped my favorite knife into my boot. I wore no hat, content to feel upon my face whatever sunlight might oblige. I stopped in the kitchens long enough to ask Mrs. Desmond's cook for supplies for my little hamper. She complied with generous wedges of cheese and fruitcake, apples, a bottle of cold tea, and sausage rolls. I waved her a cheerful farewell and burst from the door with the same sense of escape as a prisoner released from his confinement.

In a bound, I was through the summerhouse and onto the moor. It was early in the season yet, but I knew the watery meadows which lined the bogs were home to the pretty jeweled specimens of Dartmoor—fritillaries of every variety, hawkmoths, hover flies, hairstreaks, skippers, and even a few of my beloved swallowtails. They were domestic butterflies, much smaller and less brilliant than those of the tropics, but they were among the varieties I had chased first, with my child's net. It kindled a keen sense of nostalgia to be in pursuit of them once more, scrambling over rocks and through puddles after the flash of a soft blue or gentle purple wing. I had thought once that I had lost my taste for netting specimens, content to rear them by hand in my vivarium. But as I ran and climbed, intent upon the chase, my blood rose, and I felt a rush of familiar exaltation.

At noonday, I took my rest amidst a few standing stones atop an escarpment. The climb had been demanding, leaving me breathless with both exertion and delight as the countryside fell away before me. I could spot the various moorland folk about their business—shepherds moving amidst their flocks, peat cutters working the bogs for the slabs of peat used for the cottage fires. I perched above them all, sitting atop a standing stone that had conveniently toppled over, providing me with both seat and table for my picnic luncheon. The sausage rolls were squashed but delicious, the cheese flavorsome, the cake richly studded with fruits and spices. There was nothing like physical activity to heighten the pleasures of food, I reflected, dusting the crumbs from my fingers and draining the last of my tea.

I had just tucked the bottle back into my hamper when I spotted a familiar figure upon the moor, walking with careless grace, his hands thrust deeply into his pockets as if he hadn't a concern in the world. A rush of emotion flooded me and I snatched up my things to intercept him, flying down the little escarpment on winged feet.

So rapid was my pace and so stealthy my steps that he was taken by surprise.

"Veronica!" he exclaimed, obviously startled. He smiled, but I could tell from the quick dart of his eyes to the side that he was evaluating his odds of escaping.

"If you think we are not going to have this conversation, you are entirely mistaken," I informed him. "You lied to me, Harry."

"Veronica, that is a dreadful thing to say."

"Your expression of wounded astonishment is most convincing. Tell me, do you practice it in the mirror for just such an occasion?" I asked.

He clucked his tongue. "It is a sad thing when a woman turns to cynicism. It's very aging, you know." I started forwards, but he raised a hand. "Peace, I beg you! Let us not quarrel, wife."

"Do not call me that," I spat. "And do not change the subject."

"What we were speaking of?" he asked, furrowing his brow.

"Your mendacity. You lied when you said that you merely wanted to remain at the Hall to enjoy the company of Lady Hathaway and give succor to her in her old age."

"Not at all, and I am frankly offended you should think so."

"The jewels," I hissed. "You knew about the jewels."

He winced. "I did not *know*."

"But you suspected."

"Well, I did surmise," he admitted. "Jonathan told me there were some extremely valuable things lying around, and I thought if the old dear wanted to make me a present of them, I would certainly not offend her by refusing."

"Aha!"

He sighed. "You needn't look so triumphant. We both know my character, Veronica. I acknowledge my flaws. I am an opportunist. I am feckless and a bit of a coward at times."

I began to tick items off on my fingers. "You lie. You gamble. You cheat. You steal."

"I most certainly do not!" he returned indignantly. "Is it my fault that I am so personable that ladies often want to make me presents? Sometimes quite lavish ones?"

My mouth went slack. "Is that what you do? Persuade ladies to part with their fortunes?"

"Well, I am not proud of it, but a fellow has to make a living and I was blessed with two assets—a passably handsome face and an exquisitely persuasive tongue. Now that I think on it, there is a third asset that has proven most useful—"

I held up a hand. "I have experience of that particular asset, and the less said, the better. The point is, you explicitly said that your purpose in staying here was to rest and to find a way to get onto your feet in a legitimate way."

"And that is still my intention," he said firmly. "But I did not know specifically about the jewels until the sweet old dear opened the box last night and dropped them into my lap."

"I do not believe you," I told him.

He shrugged. "There is nothing I can do about that. I am, in spite of your convictions to the contrary, telling the truth. I knew there were a few choice items in the Hathaway collections, but I thought perhaps a nice dagger set with gemstones or a few antique rugs, maybe a statue I could flog. I had no idea whatsoever that her ladyship was nesting comfortably upon such a clutch of golden eggs. And they are *her* golden eggs," he added firmly. "She owns them free and clear. What she does with them is entirely her business."

"Meaning that if she wishes to give them to you, she may do so."

"Meaning exactly that. I did not expect such a stroke of luck, but believe me, I will not take kindly to any attempts to block it," he said, the pleasant smile still touching his lips.

"Do you mean to threaten me?" I was incredulous. "Harry, you forget that all I need do is drop a word into Lady Hathaway's ear—or Charles'—and your time here is finished."

"Which you will not do," he said, moving a step closer. "I had a lovely chat with your inamorato last night," he told me as the smile fell away. "We were rather far into our cups and got to know one another. It is astonishing what a few stray remarks can reveal."

My breath sat heavily in my chest. Stoker and I had so many skeletons lurking in our cupboards, they rattled like Spanish castanets. I could only hope that one secret in particular was still my own.

"What do you mean?" I asked. I raised my chin in a gesture of bravado, but I did not think he found it convincing.

"Charles Hathaway's library is an interesting place. He never uses it, you know. He prefers the estate office for conducting his business. That means no one is ever in the library, and it sits there, a dusty repository of all kinds of interesting information—the sort one finds in old newspapers and books like *Debrett's*."

I forced myself to breathe calmly as he went on. "It took only a few hours of poking about this morning to discover that your Mr. Templeton-Vane has been married. A very nasty divorce, that," he said in a tone of speculation. "I imagine it has left him rather shy of the notoriety that comes with the attention of the press."

"Guttersnipes," I said stoutly.

"Yes, but useful nonetheless," he replied. "I imagine there are a few who might be interested in knowing that the infamous younger brother of the Viscount Templeton-Vane is living in mortal sin with a woman who is not his wife—who is, in fact, married to another man."

"But we are not—" I bit off the words before I could finish the thought.

His brows shot up. "You are not living in mortal sin? Only by the thinnest of technical margins, my dear. You have not committed bigamy, and for that I congratulate you. But I would like to point out that what you are doing is presumably worse, at least for Templeton-Vane. He is consorting with a woman to whom he is not married—a woman with a husband. It paints the fellow in a very bad light indeed, I should think. I can only imagine what the newspapers would make of *that*."

I thought of J. J., my opportunistic friend who had, at least thus far, resisted spilling my secrets to the world. But how much greater a story it would be if it were revealed that the semi-legitimate daughter of the Prince of Wales not only existed but had a husband and was comfortably sharing her favors with another man. Perhaps even personal loyalty would not be enough to still J. J.'s pen. And I would not be the only one destroyed by the lurid headlines. Stoker had experienced the viciousness of the popular press, and it had nearly killed him. I would not permit the hounds to tear at him again.

My hands curled into fists. "You would not dare, you—" The exact word I used has no bearing on this narrative, but it was enough to cause Harry to adopt once more a wounded expression.

"That was entirely uncalled for," he protested.

"You are blackmailing me," I countered. "I think it entirely justified."

"I am not blackmailing you—I would never do such a thing." He seemed genuinely affronted. "Blackmail would require that I demand money or services in exchange for keeping your secret. In point of fact, I am asking you to keep *mine*."

I opened my mouth and snapped it closed again. In that completely unnerving way he had, Harry had neatly turned the tables upon me.

"I had forgot," I said slowly.

"Forgot what?"

"That talking to you is like staring into a carnival looking glass. Up is down, down is up. Nothing makes sense."

"Of course it does." His voice was gentle and his smile back in evidence. "Veronica, do you think I *enjoy* playing the villain? I loathe it. I want only to be left alone, but like any creature, I will fight if I am cornered. I know you do not trust me, but I wish, how I wish that you would! I have endured so much these past years. I long for peace. And you know, as well as anyone, peace can only be purchased at a price. I am destitute. Would you see me beg in the streets?"

"Of course not," I murmured.

"Then let me have this chance," he pressed. "I vow to you, on anything you hold sacred, that I will not take so much as a crust of bread that has not been given freely to me."

"And Lady Hathaway's jewels?" I asked, curling a lip.

"That is a question for another day," he said smoothly. "She may change her mind. Charles and Mary may persuade her to keep them with the estate for the benefit of their children. Effie might coax her into giving them up as a dowry. Or the old dear might pawn them to take a holiday on the Riviera with Mrs. Desmond," he added, his smile deepening to reveal the dimple at the side of his mouth. "For now, all I ask is that you do not interfere with me."

"And in exchange you will not interfere with me?" I asked. "You will not speak to the newspapers?"

He reached out to take my wrist. His fingers wrapped around my cuff and he drew back with a sharp exclamation of pain as the minuten pierced his skin. Tiny drops of blood beaded his fingers. "Some things never change," he said with a rueful look at the prick marks on his hand.

"I am never entirely without defenses, Harry. You should remember that."

I stalked away from him, anger lending speed to my steps and distracting me from my footing. I walked for some time, over rises and down hillocks, until at last I had run out my rage. I set my foot down, expecting to find solid ground beneath me, but the earth itself seemed to shift. I had stepped into a puddle of mud, I realized, and made to withdraw my foot. Instead, it stuck fast, with all the tenacity of a hand gripped about my ankle.

"Blast and damnation!" I muttered, dropping my net to the firm path and bending over to plant my hands in such a manner as to gain purchase to pull my foot free.

But I had underestimated the strength of the suction of this little patch of bog. It crept up my nether limb, seizing foot, ankle, then shin in its embrace. The weight of the mud dragged at me, slowly, inexorably. I reached out for my net and drove it hard into the nearest bit of firm ground. Taking it in a firm grip, I pulled with all of my might, pushing down with my free foot in order to break the seal of the bog.

With a violent crack, the pole of the net snapped in my hands, sending me flying backwards as my free foot slid out from under me. I caught myself at the last second, wrapping my hands in a tuft of moor grass to prevent my body from being sucked entirely into the mire. My leg was now imprisoned up to the top of the thigh, and my free leg was inching perilously close to it. Something in the grasses I held gave way then, and I slid backwards, my second leg now firmly in the grip of the bog. I moved it experimentally and felt myself slide further still, the mud cold and heavy against my hips.

"This will not do," I said severely. I still held half the pole in my hand, and with an Herculean effort, I plunged it once more into the ground, taking care to bury it deep enough this time. I wrapped both hands around the small portion that remained aboveground, pulling myself forwards, one painful inch at a time. Time moved with the slow thickness of treacle, but it was most likely only a few minutes before I was able to feel solid ground beneath my hips. Danger still lurked, I reminded myself. One false move and I should slip back into the welcoming embrace of the bog mud.

With infinite care, I pulled the makeshift stake free and drove it home again, stretching out my arms to secure it as far into safety as I could. I inched forwards again, this time hearing my feet come free with a decidedly loud sucking sound. A person with little experience of such places might have attempted to stand at this point, but I knew better. I pulled my legs to my chest and rolled, over and again, until I was on trustworthy ground. Then I sat, breathing hard and cursing myself for a fool. As I had explained to Effie Hathaway on our first day, I knew well enough how to care for myself in such situations. And yet. The first rule my guide had impressed upon me was the importance of avoiding such peril in the first place. "The easiest quicksand to get out of, Miss Veronica," he had said with an emphatic gesture, "is the one into which one never gets." I had always enjoyed his unique turns of phrase, and that was one that had remained with me always.

At least until now, I reminded myself with some bitterness. It has been my experience that when one is accosted by a lowness of spirits due to some failing in one's character, it becomes a habit to seek out and prod any other failing. Self-loathing is a habit, and one I could not afford to indulge. I doubt I should have castigated myself so thoroughly on my mistakes in the bog had I not already felt akin to a worm in light of my association with Harry Spenlove. I was not entirely certain which I deplored more—the fact that I had married him in the first place? The knowledge that I had not been completely truthful with Stoker? The opportunity I had not seized to tell Stoker the full story the previous night? Or the sordid little scene in which I had just engaged with my erstwhile husband? I was tempted to keep his secret, not solely to protect Stoker, I reflected as I lay in the moor grass. My exertions had stripped me of my emotions and pretenses, leaving me to face the unwelcome truth: I was inclined to protect Harry because I believed there was a grain of truth to his story. It might well have been no more significant than a speck of sand in an hourglass, but it was enough to cause me considerable consternation.

With a muted roar, I rolled onto my stomach and thrust myself onto my knees and then to a standing position. I was covered in mud and would no doubt be sore when the agitation of the experience had worn off. I required a hot bath and clean clothes. My attempt at adventure had come to an ignominious end.

CHAPTER

16

I had no sooner entered the Hall than I encountered Stoker, still dressed in his frock coat, wrenching his collar free from his shirt, neckcloth in hand. He stared in consternation at my dishevelment.

"Veronica! What has befallen you?" He would have embraced me, but I put up a hand to prevent him.

"Do not touch me, I am dripping in moor mud," I said. "I am unhurt. Merely a mishap."

"A mishap! You are covered from brow to boot in the stuff," he added, wiping a thumb over my cheek.

"I was careless," I said truthfully. "I stepped into a bog. No matter. I extricated myself. Nothing lost but my pride. And my equipment," I added, brandishing the pieces of my broken net.

"You have others," he said by way of consolation.

"But this was my favorite. I could only afford the most inferior equipment on my first expedition, but with the sale of a rather spectacular set of luna moths, I was able to afford this," I explained, looking at the sad ruins. A net is not merely a lepidopterist's tool in trade. Over rills and rocks, through meadow and marsh, the net is never out of one's hand. It is the constant companion, the partner in chase, the accomplice in victory. I had carried this particular net for six years. Next to the tiny grey velvet mouse in my pocket, a legacy from the father who would not acknowledge me, it was my most treasured possession. Nay, not possession. Friend. My net knew my failures; it had witnessed the places where my courage had deserted me. But it knew also my triumphs, the moments when I had faced down insurmountable adversaries and set my teeth against the storm, determined to carry the day.

He glanced about, to make certain we were alone, I think, for he pitched his voice low. "Mrs. Desmond said Jonathan Hathaway has gone for a walk upon the moor. Did you see him?"

"I did," I admitted. I had no wish to expand upon the conversation, but with the windows of the house overlooking the moor, it was entirely possible that we had been spotted.

"And?" Stoker pressed, his expression searching. "Were you able to form any conclusions as to his veracity?"

"I cannot say," I replied.

He thrust an impatient hand into his hair. "I suppose that is understandable. You last saw him under extraordinary circumstances more than half a decade ago. People change."

"But still you wish I had a more definitive answer to give you," I suggested.

He smiled obliquely. "I am content to remain with my thylacine for as long as it takes to secure him for travel, but the minute he is safely packed, I shall want him back in London so I can examine him properly."

I silently cursed the thylacine even as I fretted over Harry Spenlove's true motivations in playing at being Jonathan Hathaway. When I was with him, it was entirely possible to believe his intentions were semi-honorable. To come to tranquil rest after years of racketing around the world, to enjoy the benevolent affections of a grandmotherly figure—these were understandable, even laudable intentions. Upon occasion, in the darkest of the small hours of morning, I would lie awake and wonder how I had come to be enthralled by such a devious and unprincipled character. He had charm, to be sure, and a certain vivacity one could not help but admire.

And yet. Alone, personal attractions had not been enough to win my hand. I was too wary, too like a butterfly, content to sample the many delectable offerings in a field of particularly enticing specimens. But Harry had been different, and with a rush of unpleasant self-knowledge, I understood why. Like Stoker, he had a slender ribbon of pain woven into the fabric of his soul. He troubled to conceal his—whilst Stoker, when I met him, was content to display his foul temper to anyone—but the root of the suffering was the same: abandonment. Two such different men, yet their wounds were very nearly identical. I had been drawn to them as wounded things, not to heal them, but because I sensed in them kindred spirits, for my own soul bore lacerations of its own, and with that realization came a sudden and ungovernable anger. I had existed, in almost perfect contentment, for quite a long time without that knowledge, and the implacable storm of it breaking so swiftly over my head left me adrift. For a tuppence, I would have boarded the first train out of Shepton Parva and left them all.

"Will it matter?" I burst out.

"Will what matter? The thylacine? Of course it does; the thing is damned near extinct in the wild. Getting hold of a trophy like this one is the find of a decade for a natural historian," he said.

I rolled my eyes in exasperation. "Not the thylacine. Jonathan Hathaway. What if I cannot ever say with certainty it is or is not he?"

Stoker thought a moment, then shrugged. "I suppose if you cannot, then it may not be helped. Perhaps Sir Hugo can find someone else who knew him. A school friend? Another traveling companion?"

"But it might be too late at that point," I said. "If he is a villain, bent upon some scheme, he may already have accomplished his aims and preyed upon this family."

"How?" he asked bluntly. "His grandfather's will was quite specific. With Jonathan Hathaway dead, Charles inherits all. Now that Jonathan is come back—if it is indeed he—he cannot take the house. He cannot get his hands on any of Mary Hathaway's money, for that comes from her father. The land goes with the house, and I suppose, with expensive legal counsel, he might make a claim for a few head of sheep, but I cannot fancy him with a shepherd's crook and a dog at his heels," he added with a smile.

"No, nor can I. But there are valuable things in Sir Geoffrey's collection," I began. I was thinking aloud, torn between my desire to protect Harry from his own worst impulses and my duty to expose him for what he was. Neither prospect filled me with pleasure, and I was unaccountably irritated with Stoker that he had not intuited my unsettled feelings. What, I began to wonder, was the point of allowing a gentleman access to one's bed and heart if he could not interpret a lady's most irrational moods?

He went on just as if I were not standing in front of him, glowering like a thundercloud.

"Of course, any zoologist would know, the thylacine is the most precious thing in the house, but it will take a proper crate and a few men to move it. And even if he managed to lay hands upon it, what would he do with it? There is no one to whom he could possibly sell it if he wanted to retrieve even half its value without us getting word of it. The world of natural history is a small one," he reminded me. "And he is not known within its confines. Too many have been swindled by fakery. Collectors with money to burn are cautious now. It is no longer the heady days of Mr. Barnum and the Feejee Mermaid."

I shuddered thinking of Mr. Barnum's repellent specimen. He had presented it during the height of the fashion for cryptids, creatures half out of myth, displayed to a gullible public audience for the price of a small coin. This particular item had been fashioned from sewing a fish's tail to the torso of a monkey. One look at the thing and any person of science would have rejected it out of hand, but the average individual yearning for entertainment would be more persuaded by novelty than accuracy. There had been a fad for such things after the publication of Mr. Darwin's text. When *On the Origin of Species* had first burst upon the scene, many misread its premise of a common ancestor shared by man and ape to mean that men were descended from monkeys—a perfectly ludicrous notion. But the idea was just sensational enough to persuade people to part with their hard-earned money to see proofs in the shape of horrible hominids, patchwork mannequins fashioned of simian limbs and human features. The fact that such grotesqueries were displayed at fairgrounds and pleasure palaces instead of respectable scientific institutions should have been sufficient to ensure their ridicule, but too often I had seen perfectly intelligent and rational people convinced by one of these repellent fakeries. Our intrepid journalist acquaintance, J. J. Butterworth, had even written a series of articles after spending a fortnight with a traveling show. She had pasted false hair onto her face and arms and displayed herself under the bill of the Ape Woman of Nova Scotia, for which she was paid the princely sum of ten pounds.

Before I could return to the subject of Jonathan Hathaway, Stoker dropped a heavy hand to my shoulder. "In any event, all you promised Sir Hugo was that you would try. You made him no guarantees of success," he reminded me. He dropped his hand and gathered up his stack of paper parcels. Several were marked with the label of a scientific supplier, but the smallest bore a bright red and white string and an illustration of a dancing sweet.

"Honey drops," he said, grinning. "And now I am for my thylacine," he told me with an unholy light in his eyes.

I might have stopped him then, told him I had something of importance to discuss. But his attention had already wandered; he was with *his* thylacine—I had noted the use of the possessive pronoun. Whatever price Lord Rosemorran paid for it, I was certain Stoker would always take a proprietary interest in the beast.

"Go on, then," I said, forcing a smile to my lips. "I must clean myself before I befoul Mrs. Desmond's carpets any further."

He left me then in a swirl of frock coat and honey drops. I made my way to my room on leaden feet. But in half an hour I had rung for hot water and washed myself thoroughly, dressing in my blue gown once more and sending my tweeds down to be cleaned along with my boots. The pieces of my butterfly net were wrapped in a spare petticoat with the same reverence the Egyptians of old gave to their mummies. I laid the bundle in my carpetbag with a sigh of regret. That net had collected as many memories as butterflies—trekking the lush foothills of the Andean alps, venturing to islands beyond the edge of the world, sunrises and sunsets and every moment in between. How I missed my adventures!

I dashed away a sudden bit of moisture from my eyes and stiffened my spine. This would never do. Being with Harry had resurrected so many ghosts, and my emotions were in tumult as they had never been before. I had prided myself on knowing precisely who I was and what I believed. Yet in the two years since I had come to London, that had been tested, over and again, the bond between my image of myself and my own identity stretched until it had at last snapped. I would have said firmly and without hesitation that I was a forthright person who valued honesty and plain speaking, that I would stride boldly into difficult situations and face them head-on, prepared to take my stand whatever the cost. Instead, I found myself beset by emotion at the sight of a broken butterfly net, hiding in my room as I kept a terrible secret from the one person I ought to have told. Why this devilish concealment? Was it pure cowardice? I searched my heart and found that it was not reluctance to endure Stoker's wrath which decided my course. I had withstood his temper often enough—in fact, I have admitted in the pages of my recorded adventures more than once that I found his displays of spleen to be invigorating as his eyes shone and his muscles flexed with indignation or fury. Had I any expectation of his committing any violence, it would not have been so. But Stoker, more than any person of my acquaintance, would never harm me. I knew that as well as I knew my own name. He was incapable of inflicting suffering upon me.

But, oh, how I despised myself for inflicting it upon him! I knew that concealing my past from him would divide us, but the truth would be wounding, I had no doubt of it. It would come as a blow, both the fact of my marriage and the fact of its concealment. I would have to deliver the strike in a time and place that would permit him the agonies he would no doubt experience. Anger, wounded pride, betrayal—these were uneasy sentiments and he deserved to grapple with them privately, not in the company of strangers such as the Hathaways.

At least, that is what I told myself as I left my room, justifying my choice to delay telling him the truth. I was also mindful of Jonathan's—how quickly I had come to think of him by that name!—unsubtle hints as to his intentions should I reveal his secrets. I split no hairs; I appreciated no sophistry. He could twist it however he liked, but the plain fact was that he had chosen blackmail. He trusted not in my long-dead affection for him but in the fervor of my feelings for Stoker to shield him from the consequences of whatever crimes he chose to perpetrate. And for all his pretty speeches about Lady Hathaway and new beginnings, I did suspect he nurtured some less wholesome scheme to divide that lady from her wealth.

There was only one proper course to be taken, I decided. In order to protect Stoker for as long as possible and to keep Lady Hathaway from becoming the victim of Jonathan's villainous plot, I would have to remain at Hathaway Hall, keeping a watchful eye upon everyone, ready to unleash my own particular hell in defense of those who did not understand what sort of viper they nursed within their bosom.

Refreshed if not wholly persuaded by my logic—I am keenly aware of my own hypocrisies even as I indulge them—I bathed my tear-swollen eyes and dressed for dinner in the one silk gown I had brought. It had been freshly sponged and returned to my room, and I fancied the violet silk flattered my eyes and skin. I took extra care with my hair, plaiting and coiling it atop my head. I felt once more in posses-sion of myself, and it was with fresh resolve that I descended to dinner, determined to keep a firm grip upon my emotions and apply rational principles to my situation. I would watch Jonathan (*Harry!* I corrected myself sternly) with the keenness of a raptor. I would harden my heart against his protestations of innocence and remind myself that he had engaged in a polite exercise of extortion in order to get me to do his bidding. Well, two could play at that sort of game, I decided. All I re-quired was to find the weakness in his armor. I am, it has been noted by criminals of the loftiest distinction, a worthy adversary, and al-though it would pain me to view Harry in that light, I would balk at nothing to keep Stoker free from his clutches. Thus determined, I went to dinner in a mood of dangerous optimism.

CHAPTER
17

I was, unfortunately, destined for disappointment. Harry was, in a word, delightful. He flattered Mary, complimenting the dinner as well as the elegance of the table although both were entirely due to the efforts of the sterling Mrs. Desmond. He asked thoughtful questions of Charles about sheep and insightful questions of Stoker about advances in the taxidermical arts. He attended Lady Hathaway with a closeness that would have been called fawning under other circumstances. He even, I was nauseated to see, indulged his erstwhile nephew and nieces when they appeared, washed and brushed and dressed in starched nightgowns to present their scrubbed cheeks for kisses before they retired for the night. He permitted little Ada to search his pockets for sweets while urging young Geoffrey to display the gruesome little cage and its new inhabitant (an unlucky mouse). Even Effie came under his spell as he expressed interest in viewing the rising moon through her decrepit telescope before it began to wane.

He flattered, he cajoled, he entertained—in short, he had them nibbling from his palm. And the occasional glance he darted my way, a blandly innocent look delivered from under his demurely lowered lashes, showed that he knew exactly what he was doing. He even forestalled my plan to speak with Stoker by challenging him to another game of billiards.

Stoker hesitated, looking at me, but Harry went on, smiling. "You must allow me the chance to win back the money you took from me last night," he said, laughing. "It is only sporting."

If there is one thing against which an Englishman is powerless, it is being thought unsporting. Stoker gave me a shrug and followed Harry into the billiards room whilst I took myself upstairs for a sulk. I was determined to wait up as long as it might take to speak privately with Stoker, although I knew Harry would do everything in his power to prevent it.

So I took up a book, the latest Arcadia Brown adventure, filched from Stoker's carpetbag, and resumed my post in the window seat, fully dressed. The moon was high, peeking out from behind the scudding clouds and shedding a silvery glow upon the gardens below. My book proved rather less interesting than I had anticipated—no fault of the intrepid Arcadia, who was on the hunt for a villainous wretch who had abducted her sidekick and loyal companion, Garvin—and I found myself watching instead the shifting shadows. As I peered into the darkness, one of the shadows seemed to detach from the stone wall, moving into the moonlight, gliding over the dew-spangled grass. I watched as it drifted in the direction of the summerhouse at the end of the gardens. From my perch, I could see the edge of the moor beyond, a vast, inky emptiness. It was uncanny enough in the daylight, but at that hour, it seemed not entirely impossible that it might play host to all manner of spectral things.

As if conjured by my very thoughts, at that moment, a tiny ball of light appeared on the moor. It proceeded towards the summerhouse, growing larger as it came closer, bouncing erratically, as if propelled by some supernatural movement. Light upon the moor could well be a shepherd searching for a lost lamb, but a lantern would have shed warm, yellow light. This illumination was fed by cold fire, a chill and lifeless blue light that glowed with an unnatural fury.

I threw down my book and took to my heels, blessing the instinct that had caused me to remain dressed. I had no weapon, for what weapons may one employ against the spectral? I had no light, and as I pounded down the stairs to the garden door, I realized I needed none. The clerestory windows permitted enough illumination to guide my way, and I found the garden door unlocked and standing slightly ajar.

I burst through, putting on as much speed as my evening frock and thin slippers would permit. I had gathered the skirts into one hand, lifting them free of my feet, but I tripped nonetheless just as I emerged into the garden and fell heavily. I swore loudly and looked ahead to where the dark, cloaked figure was just opening the summerhouse door. It turned and seemed to stare directly at me from across the green sward, its face shrouded in the shadows from its hood.

"Hold there!" I ordered. The figure in black seemed to hesitate upon the threshold of the summerhouse, indecision writ in every line of its posture.

"There is a spectral ball of light upon the moor!" I cried, forcing myself to my feet.

Even as I spoke, the blue light approached the summerhouse door that led out to the moor. The figure in black turned and seemed to shrink away from the light as it came near.

"Go away!" called a feminine voice. "You are not wanted here!"

I rushed ahead to where Anjali—for I recognized from the voice it was she in the black cloak—trembled upon the threshold of the summer-house. As I ran, I heard a dull rattle and wondered if the phantom was attempting to enter the summerhouse.

Gathering my skirts well above my knees, I hurtled past Anjali and into the summerhouse, giving an imitation of a Viking berserker cry. (I have upon occasion had recourse to employ the battle cries of the Maori, the Celt, and several of the indigenous peoples of the Americas. I have found them all equally effective.)

In this instance, the orb of blue light seemed to float then vanish before my very eyes. I would have given chase, but behind me, Anjali emitted a shriek and fell heavily into a swoon.

"Anjali!" I cried, gathering her into my arms. She was entirely unconscious but seemed otherwise unharmed. Just then, Stoker and Jonathan burst into the garden through the door from the billiards room.

"Veronica!" Stoker exclaimed, dropping to his knees beside me. "Are you all right?"

"I am fine, but we must pursue the apparition! It was a ball of blue light," I insisted, pointing in the direction it had vanished. Stoker leapt into action while I thrust Anjali into Jonathan's arms and commanded him to look after her. "Mind you do not let her take cold," I added as I pushed myself to my feet and followed hard upon Stoker's heels.

He had stopped just beyond the summerhouse, peering into the bleak emptiness of the moor. I shoved past him, feeling the stone-strewn grasses beneath my slippers. This was where the landscaped order of the gardens gave way to the empty wildness of the moors beyond. They stretched like some sort of alien world, the menhirs silvery white against the ceaselessly moving darkness of the terrain. Of the phantom orb there was no sign. I peered into the night, straining my eyes for any sign of the spectral presence. "Perhaps behind one of the stones," I said, starting towards the nearest.

Stoker grasped my arm. "Don't be a fool. You cannot possibly venture onto the moors at night. It would be suicide." I made to wriggle free, but he held my arm fast.

"Drat and damnation," I muttered. But, of course, he was correct. I recalled my own unfortunate experience with a bit of mire earlier that day. Only experience and a steady nerve had seen me out of it safely. Rushing in the dark would be unspeakably foolish and unnecessarily dangerous.

With bad grace, I returned with Stoker to the gardens, where Jonathan had carried the still-senseless Anjali. He looked up with anxious eyes. "What is wrong with her?"

"Shock, I imagine," Stoker told him. He put a finger to her pulse and listened to her breathing. "Her pulse is quick but strong. I can find no injury. Carry her inside so she does not take a chill. She cannot remain upon this damp grass."

Jonathan struggled to his feet, upon which Stoker reached out and swung the motionless form into his arms with as little fuss as if she were a feather.

"What the devil is all the furor about?" Charles Hathaway, imperfectly attired in nightshirt and hastily donned trousers, a nightcap settled askew on his head, lifted a lantern as he emerged from the house.

"It was a phantom, Mr. Hathaway," I told him.

"Phantom!" It was too dark to see properly, but I was certain he had paled at the word.

"An orb of blue," I added helpfully. "I saw it as plainly as I see you now. Anjali did as well, and the sight frightened her so badly she collapsed."

"Ruin," Charles Hathaway said faintly. "It means ruin to see one of the phantoms of the moor."

I went to him and pinched him hard upon the arm, at which he jumped. "Madam!"

"You looked decidedly unwell and we simply cannot have two people unconscious at once," I told him.

"I am composed now," he said, although his voice still quavered.

"Good." I turned once more to Anjali, who was beginning to stir in

Stoker's arms. "Upstairs with her. I presume she has a room near Lady Hathaway's in case she is needed in the night."

Charles Hathaway confirmed this and we made our way inside, a strange little procession. He paused at the doorway and gestured for Stoker to carry her inside. Stoker settled her gently on the bed.

"Leave me to it," I instructed. "This is woman's work."

He hesitated. "She may be distressed when she regains her senses."

"I will not leave her," I promised. I looked at Charles Hathaway. "You might send Effie. In case she requires anything."

He nodded, seeming glad to have something to do. Jonathan had melted away, but I was not surprised. Harry Spenlove had never been good in a crisis, I reflected bitterly. Stoker offered once more to help, but I waved him off, conscious that this was hardly the time to embark upon the discussion that was now long overdue.

I glanced about the room. It was small and stingily furnished, with a narrow bed and a table and chair, neither of which matched the washstand. A thin screen across one corner of the chamber was the only concession to privacy. The Hathaways were the sort of folk who did not even permit a lock upon the door for the servants, I noticed with a rush of resentment on Anjali's behalf. I went to the small hearth and poked up the fire that had fallen to ash, building it until it could take a few tiny logs. It made only a little difference to the chill of the room. Anjali was lying motionless upon the bedcover where Stoker had placed her. She, like me, was fully dressed. I removed her damp shoes and set them near the fire, but not near enough to scorch. Her hem was wet as well, and the back of her dress. I should have to wrestle her out of her sodden things, but it would go a good deal easier if she were awake.

Although I was in evening dress, I am never entirely unprepared for misadventure, and I reached for the narrow blade that rested in a tiny scabbard tucked into my décolletage. I unpinned a lock of my hair and in one quick motion sliced off the last few inches. It was quick work to twist the hair into a knot and set it on fire. I waved the burning knot under her nose and she came to at once, choking a little against the smell.

She asked no questions, but simply stared up at the ceiling for a long moment. "I must have fallen senseless," she said at last. "What happened?"

It was the question of every swooning heroine in every Gothic novel. I had little patience with the predictability of it and conducted a swift evaluation of her physical state whilst I replied.

"Mr. Templeton-Vane carried you," I informed her. I peered into her pupils but they were the same size, large in the dim light of the room. "We found you in a state of collapse in the garden. Did you strike your head when you fell?" I asked.

"I do not believe so," she told me. I reached a hand to the back of her head, probing.

"I feel no lumps or abrasions," I said at last. "That is good. How is your vision?"

"Perfectly fine," she assured me.

"Headache?" I pressed. "Rebellious stomach? Trembling?"

She put out her hand and I saw that it did not move. "I am well, thank you."

"Good. You need out of those wet things," I said. She sat up and I would have helped her disrobe, but she hurried behind the screen and removed her dress and stockings. I brought her a thin flannel wrapper and she clutched it about herself as I draped the dress and stockings over the screen to dry.

"You are very kind, Miss Speedwell," she said, smiling faintly.

I settled her onto the bed and took advantage of her gratitude to sit beside her. "What did you see before you collapsed?"

"I—" She opened her mouth, then closed it sharply and shook her head.

"It might help you to speak of it," I urged.

"I saw nothing," she said, her mouth set mulishly.

Just then, Effie Hathaway appeared, her freckles standing out in sharp relief in her pale face. "Anjali! Are you ill? Charles said you had taken a tumble in the garden. What on earth were you doing outside this time of night?"

She went to the bed and Anjali gripped her hand, the knuckles going quite pale. "I am quite well. I did not mean to disturb anyone. Her ladyship—"

"Granna is snoring," Effie assured her. "It would take the opening of the seventh seal to awaken her."

Anjali gave her a small smile. "I am glad." She closed her eyes then, and Effie put a hand to her brow.

"No fever, thank heaven. But I still do not understand," she began.

"It is nothing," Anjali told her sharply. She gave Effie a meaningful look and they fell into an uneasy silence.

Since neither of them seemed inclined to speak again, I rose.

"If you mean to stay with Anjali, then I will leave," I said. From the bed, Anjali murmured her thanks and I beckoned Effie to step outside the room with me. She pulled the door almost closed behind us, leaving only a small crack.

"I will stay with her," she said.

I nodded. "I will be brief. Anjali saw a phantom orb, a sort of ball of blue light on the moor," I told her.

Effie's color sharpened suddenly, bright ruddy spots rising in each cheek. "Did you see it as well?" she demanded.

"I did. I pursued it, but it vanished upon the moor."

"You *pursued* it! But it was a phantom," Effie protested. "You ought to have been too frightened to attempt it."

"And you are a woman of science, which means you ought to know it is likely some phenomenon of a natural variety," I replied. Whilst I was perfectly willing to entertain all possibilities, I found myself taking a decidedly contrarian position with Effie. Her insistence that the moor was full of supernatural creatures had no doubt been intended to provoke reactions in the Hathaway children, but it seemed Anjali had fallen victim to the notion of such horrors as well. Such a dramatic reaction was surely the result of a mild hysteria, certainly stoked by Effie's haunted tales of the macabre.

She must have been thinking along similar lines, for she colored slightly. "I know it is irrational and contradicts all that we know of logic and reason. And yet . . ." She paused and glanced outside the window to where the moon hung, full and ripe. "I am a modern woman, like you, Miss Speedwell. But I was reared here, and the moor is full of ghostly tales. Runaway coaches with phantom horses, highwaymen who ride in search of their heads. And our own grey lady and black dog. I have told the children the stories, but I confess, I cannot help but sometimes wonder if perhaps there is not a grain of truth to these legends."

She looked very young just then, her freckles standing out starkly against her white skin as the flush ebbed from her cheeks. I felt a rush of pity for her, particularly when I considered that the woman lying on the bed was perhaps her only friend in the house.

"Atmosphere and setting can make believers of us all," I said in what I hoped was a gracious tone. The truth was, I had often expressed just such a notion to Stoker, much to his amusement. I was unwilling to dismiss all things supernatural simply because we had no explanation for them.

Effie gave me a level look. "No doubt you think me very foolish."

"I understand how easily one's belief in the rational world may be overcome by the sight of something spectral. This was an uncanny apparition."

"But you do not believe it *was* an apparition," she pressed. "What do you think it was? You must have some thoughts on the matter."

I shrugged. "I do not say that such things are utterly impossible, but this particular manifestation was making use of the door to the summerhouse. Why should it have need of such a thing if it were indeed incorporeal?"

Effie continued to stare at me, her hands working into small fists at her sides. "I do not know. But I can tell you that it is supposed to be an omen of evil tidings to this family when such things are seen. Everyone in these parts knows that. The sensible thing when something frightful is abroad on the moor is to lock your doors and draw your curtains."

"Surely such precautions are pointless against an entity which is completely supernatural," I argued. "Ghosts and phantoms do not exactly stop at locks and doors."

"No, but you are supposed to stay inside and leave such things strictly alone," she said stubbornly.

I reflected that Effie, like all the Hathaways, had a considerable exasperating streak. She seemed annoyed that I questioned the spectre, and yet she was the one who had warned me of such things to begin with. Perhaps, I decided, she was a little embarrassed at being a woman of science who indulged in such superstitious fancies.

Suddenly, it all seemed terribly pointless, and I realized I was very tired after my earlier exertions on the moor. I longed for nothing as much as the comforts of my bed just then.

"Is there anything more I can do for Anjali? If not, I shall leave her in your hands."

Effie shook her head, her expression relieved—no doubt that I was not pressing her further on the matter of scientific inquiry where the phantom was concerned. "You have already been most kind, Miss Speedwell."

"It was understandable. I myself found the spectre unnerving," I assured her. I bade her good night then and made my way to Stoker's room. I was fatigued, but I could not in all decency avoid the conversation we needed to have on that pretext. I should, I knew, rest easier for having it over and done with.

The clock was striking the hour as I raised my hand to rap upon Stoker's door. But just as I did so, I heard a gentle snore. He was already asleep, and if there was one thing he hated, it was being roused from his slumbers. I told myself it was out of consideration for his rest that I did not waken him, but it was the purest cowardice. I spent the next few minutes loathing myself vigorously as I returned to my room and prepared for bed. I ought not to have slept well, given all that weighed upon my conscience and the events of the evening, but I did.

I passed peacefully into the arms of Morpheus, where I lay quite happily until the next morning—when hell itself seemed to break loose within Hathaway Hall.

CHAPTER

18

I was first aware of some uproar when I left my room, having made my ablutions and dressed for the day. I had dressed in a becoming blue wool day dress trimmed in black passementerie and pinned my hair in a style Stoker particularly liked. I did not probe deeply into my motives in doing so for fear I would discover I had made myself attractive in order to please a man—a disturbing notion to be sure.

"That is the beginning of domestication," I told myself darkly as I descended the stairs. But before I could complete the thought, I heard raised voices from the direction of the Great Hall. Anjali was coming up the stairs and passed me, carrying a watering pot.

"You are up and about your duties early," I said with a smile.

She inclined her head in the direction of the Great Hall. "It seemed best to give the Hathaways a little time to themselves this morning," she said as Charles Hathaway's unmistakable voice rose.

"Troubles?" I asked.

She pressed her lips together. "I should not speak of it," she said with great tact. "Besides, you will hear of it soon enough."

I searched her face. She seemed paler than usual but otherwise none the worse for her nocturnal adventure. "I hope you are quite re-covered from last night."

She ducked her head. "I feel very foolish."

"Anyone might have fainted at seeing such a thing," I assured her. I tipped my head thoughtfully. "I suppose you went outside for a ciga-rette?"

She flushed. "Lady Hathaway does not mind, but Mrs. Hathaway would be very upset if she knew that I indulged."

I laid a hand upon her arm. "Your secret is safe with me."

A tiny smile played about her lips. "You are very kind, Miss Speedwell."

She stepped aside and I passed her then, bracing myself for what-ever uproar might be in evidence. When I entered, I saw Stoker, sitting quietly at his place, consuming a vast amount of kedgeree whilst Charles thundered.

"I cannot believe this, the blackguard! The very devil!" He caught sight of me and flushed. "My apologies for my language, Miss Speed-well. It appears my brother"—he larded the word with sarcasm—"has disappeared."

My heart thudded, striking my ribs so loudly I was certain they must have heard the thump.

"Disappeared?" I asked, arranging my face in a quizzical ex-pression.

"No note, no explanation. He has simply vanished from the house." Charles lapsed into silence as he threw himself into his chair. His plate was full but he pushed it away uneaten. From her seat, Mary Hatha-way sipped quietly at her tea while Effie sat buttering slices of toast she did not eat, piling them at the edge of her plate.

"Surely he has simply gone to town," I began.

"He did not order the carriage," Mary said, setting her cup down with a gentle clink. "Which means he must have crossed the moor in the dark. His bed was undisturbed," she added primly.

"And Granna is convinced he must have fallen to his death in the bogs," Effie put in.

"Euphemia!" Charles said in a warning tone.

"Well, it is what she thinks," Effie protested. She looked at me. "But there is more." Something in her face warned me before she said the words.

"The jewels," I breathed.

"Yes," Charles said grimly. "He has gone—and the Eye of the Dawn has vanished with him."

Breakfast was an uncomfortable meal. Stoker said little and Mary Hathaway even less, but there was an unpleasant serenity to her, as if something of a mess had been tidied away to her satisfaction. Justifiably distressed, Lady Hathaway had rung for breakfast in her room, carried by the faithful Anjali, and so we were free to speculate on what might have happened. The Hathaways seemed inclined to follow the dictates of Occam's razor: the simplest explanation is the likeliest. And the simplest explanation was that Jonathan Hathaway had helped himself to his grandmother's diamond and left.

"I suppose he might have taken it to be valued," Effie suggested.

"It is not his to take," Charles reminded her coldly. "And for God's sake, stop buttering toast if you don't mean to eat it."

Effie surveyed the pile of buttered toast. "Don't scold, Charles. I will put it out for the pigs," she said in a contrite tone. "It will not go to waste."

Charles made a harrumphing sound.

Stoker cleared his throat and addressed Charles. "In view of the current distractions, I think it best if Miss Speedwell and I return to London at once. You will not want strangers in your midst just now."

Charles gave him a narrow look. "But you will take the thylacine? On Lord Rosemorran's behalf?"

Before Stoker could reply, Mary Hathaway spoke up. "I say, take it with you. I doubt his lordship could resist the beast once he's seen it if it is as remarkable as you say. And then perhaps his lordship might see his way to giving it proper pride of place when his museum is complete. Perhaps even a Hathaway wing?" she suggested.

For all her pretenses to gentility, Mary Hathaway had the keen instincts of a merchant, I realized. She had realized how much likelier Lord Rosemorran was to keep the trophy once it was already in his possession, a fait accompli, and it was apparent that she harbored a wish to associate the Hathaway name with the far more august Rosemorran title.

Stoker nodded. "Certainly, if you wish. I will build a suitable crate and pack it up this morning."

Mary excused herself to supervise Mrs. Desmond in the stillroom with the making of jam whilst Charles went to find a railway timetable. Much discussion of trains followed before Stoker turned to me. "I trust that meets with your approval, Veronica?"

I blinked. I had been woolgathering, and for all I knew, he was asking if I wanted to take a slow train to John o' Groats. I forced a smile. "Of course. I haven't much to pack. I need only finish the list of the butterflies I believe Lord Rosemorran should acquire and I shall be entirely ready."

"Very well," Charles Hathaway said as he rose. "If you will excuse me, I have things to do. The farmwork will not wait simply because my brother decided to play the villain."

He rose and threw down his napkin. Effie, who had been watching silently, collected his full plate and her own and excused herself to the piggery.

"Do you suppose the pigs got at him?" Stoker asked conversationally.

"I beg your pardon?" I surveyed him across the breakfast table.

"Pigs. They're notoriously voracious eaters."

"But an entire man—"

He shrugged. "Simplest thing in the world for a pen full of hungry porkers."

I pushed aside my plate, staring suspiciously at the sausages as I did so. "That is revolting."

"That is nature," he said, finishing his kedgeree. He regarded me over the rim of his teacup. "You realize this means the fellow we have known as Jonathan Hathaway can be no such person?"

To busy my nerveless fingers, I took up a piece of toast and began to butter it. "Why do you say that?"

"If he has taken the trouble to steal a jewel he was meant to inherit anyway, he is clearly an impostor. And that would explain why you were uncertain of his identity, as were his relations."

"Lady Hathaway believes in him," I said.

"Lady Hathaway is elderly and no doubt sees what she wants to see," he returned. He sat back in his chair and gave me a long, level look. "The more important question is, Who is this man pretending to be Jonathan Hathaway?"

The butter knife slipped through my fingers and crashed onto my plate.

He went on. "Well, I suppose it hardly matters now."

"Doesn't it?" I asked, retrieving the knife and plunging it once more into the butter. It was easy to pretend it was Harry Spenlove's heart, I thought darkly.

"The theft of the jewel is a family matter, not a criminal one, since Lady Hathaway certainly does not mean to bring charges," he said evenly. "Whether he ever returns again or simply vanishes into the night with his diamond, he cannot be arrested unless Lady Hathaway insists. And that will clearly not happen. So," he finished with a broad smile, "that means we have survived this little favor to Sir Hugo without being stabbed, abducted, shot, or otherwise assaulted. I shall consider that a victory."

As soon as Stoker had prepared the thylacine, we made our goodbyes and the household saw us off. Lady Hathaway and Anjali stood at her ladyship's window, waving, while Mary brought her children to lisp an interminable farewell poem. Every time one of them forgot a line, she made them begin again until at last I could bear it no longer.

"What clever children!" I exclaimed, interrupting them with a bright smile. "Stoker, I think they deserve some of your excellent honey drops."

His expression darkened. "This tin is the last of them," he protested in a whisper.

"Sometimes sacrifices must be made for the general good," I returned. I put out my hand for the tin. He rummaged in his pocket before handing over the candy with ill grace. I plucked a large piece out for each child, cramming it into their greedy mouths before Mary Hathaway could protest. Instantly, the gooey mess stuck their little teeth together, rendering them blessedly silent.

I handed the tin back to Stoker, who would have sulked except for the fact that a pair of strapping farmhands was just emerging from the Hall with his trophy. He supervised their handling of it as they secured the crate on the back of the carriage. He leapt up, clearly intending to ride thusly to the station at Shepton Parva, perched next to his beloved thylacine with the air of Achilles gloating over the still-warm body of Hector.

Before I could remonstrate with him, Effie emerged from the house carrying a large wooden box. She thrust it into my startled hands.

"The orrery," she said, flushing.

Charles gave her a surprised look. "Why, Effie—" he began.

The expression on her face would have suited one of the lesser martyred saints. "I know it has to go, Charles. You are quite right. But I cannot bear to keep it if I am only going to lose it in the end."

"Well, I think you might have it for another month or two," he said kindly. "Lord Rosemorran may not even offer for it."

"Then let him have the thing!" she burst out. "If I am not permitted to study, then Granfer's instruments are a mockery. They should all be cleared away." She flicked me a glance. "Good-bye, Miss Speedwell. I think you meant to be kind."

I had not time to reply before she returned to the house, clearly on the verge of tears. Charles Hathaway looked a little embarrassed, but his embarrassment was tinged with relief.

"It seems she is benefiting from your helpful example, my dove," he said to his wife.

Mary was too busy applying a damp handkerchief to her children's faces to respond. We said our farewells and I clambered into the carriage, clutching the unwieldy box. The driver clicked his tongue at the horse and the conveyance lurched into motion. I turned to wave farewell at the assembled Hathaways, feeling as though we had just made a timely escape, but from what I could not say. Mary fussed over her children under her spouse's genial eye—it would never occur to him to help, I reflected as she darted after little Geoffrey, who slipped, eel-like, out of her grasp. Anjali and Lady Hathaway had already disappeared, but as we bowled along the drive, I saw a gingery head at the window of the observatory. Effie must have fairly run up the stairs to watch us leave, I realized. And she remained there as long as the carriage was in sight, until the little rise of the hills beyond carried us away from Hathaway Hall and its curious inhabitants.

CHAPTER

19

As the miles fell away behind us, I was conscious of a lightening of my spirits. I had spent the better part of the morning packing up my things and heaping metaphorical ashes upon my head. My silence had allowed Harry to abscond with the diamond, an eventuality I ought to have foreseen, given my familiarity with the man and his character—or lack of it. Furthermore, upon reflecting on the appearance of the spectral sphere of light, I had at first wondered if it might have been Harry, roaming the moor in pursuit of some dastardly purpose of his own.

Of course, this was impossible, as I had seen him, with my own eyes, emerge from the house with Stoker, where they had been engaged in a spirited game of billiards. But I had not inquired deeply of Stoker as to whether Harry might have absented himself from the game for any period of time. Any gentleman might, I reasoned, withdraw pleading the urges of nature. It would be a simple matter to slip out of the house and venture out onto the moor—but for what purpose?

To meet with a confederate! I sat forwards on my seat in excitement. Surely this was the likeliest explanation. The moorland might provide inspiration for tales of supernatural conjurations, but as a scientist, I must always employ logic first when unraveling such a puzzle. And since any criminous activity was within Harry Spenlove's purview, I reasoned, conspiracy might dwell there as well. Perhaps he had stolen the jewel and spirited it out to the moor, delivering it quickly to a partner in crime—a clever precaution in case the house was searched for the missing diamond. With a bit of luck and excellent timing, he might well have managed it, and would have got away entirely undetected were it not for Anjali's untimely desire for a cigarette.

But why then disappear? I wondered. If he had successfully purloined the gem and passed it to a fellow thief, why leave? And why bother with the intricacies of handing it off to another if he meant to disappear at the same time?

I puzzled over the question for a long while, until it finally struck me that I did not have to know and was, in fact, likely never to do so. My gaze fell then upon Stoker, settled in the seat opposite. His brow was furrowed as he studied his newspaper, but he glanced up, catching my gaze with a look that seemed to pierce my very soul. Guilt at the lies of omission I had committed rose within me, choking me. This was the chance to tell him the truth. I opened my mouth, but before I could speak and without preamble, he moved forwards suddenly, covering the distance between our seats, touching his mouth to mine.

It was, as ever, spark to a powder keg. I put my arms about his neck as I fell into the kiss, which encompassed some duration and considerable enthusiasm. When he pulled back, we were both flushed and a little untidy.

"Whatever brought that on?" I asked with a lightness I did not feel.

He smiled, his gaze intent. "Perhaps I am simply grateful."

"Grateful?" I searched the floor for a missing hairpin and thrust it into place.

He took my hand and began to speak. "After Caroline, after all that happened in the Amazon," he said, invoking the name of the former wife who had left him for dead, "I was so mired in misery that I could not see my way. Days, weeks, months, bled into one another. I cannot recall them. Not a single moment stands out in my memory as different from the rest. It was an endless twilight. Nothing seemed to matter. Until the day you burst into my workrooms and turned my life entirely upside down."

"Stoker," I said, but he laid a finger upon my lips.

"Let me finish. You madden me. You distract me. You enrage me. I cannot think of any person of my acquaintance who has so often and so thoroughly driven me to the brink of endurance. And yet you saved me. Whatever that melancholy state, it has been banished, and I know it is because I wake every day knowing that you are there."

I looked into his eyes; I knew then I could never tell him the truth. To explain Harry's true identity would be to take a sledgehammer to his happiness, and I simply could not bring myself to inflict such pain upon this man whom I loved as fiercely as I had ever loved anything in my life.

When we arrived back in London, it was to a predictably chaotic environment. Courtesy of the Easter holidays, the children were home. Lady Cordelia, distracted by the maternal joys of having her own child to tend—albeit in the guise of a foundling left in her care—let them run positively wild, and for all his fondness, Lord Rosemorran was never an attentive parent. Being opportunistic by nature as all children are, the younger Rosemorrans had been left to their own devices. The eldest, Viscount Launceston, heir to the title, was contentedly teaching himself Greek with an eye to excavating antiquities in the Peloponnese. Apart from the odd bit of digging in the herbaceous borders to perfect his field techniques, he troubled no one. His sister, Lady Juno, was also of a scientific bent, although her experiments in chemistry resulted in assorted repellent odors and the odd explosion, which the rest of the family accepted as all in a day's work. The rest of them were variously involved in shipbuilding, arboreal management, photography, stage illusions, and Egyptology. This meant that no matter where one ventured on the estate, there was bound to be a child constructing a yacht, up a tree, developing photographic plates, sawing a sibling in half, or attempting to mummify a rat thoughtfully provided by one of Cook's cats. These were all acceptable and even laudable endeavors, being undertaken in the pursuit of knowledge. (One might quibble about the value of mastering the tricks of stagecraft, but putting this point to the child in question resulted in a lengthy lecture regarding the intricacies of light theory and something to do with prisms. I endured the conversation for a quarter of an hour before reeling away for the revivifying consolation of strong drink.)

But the most impetuous and precocious of his lordship's children was the youngest—Lady Rose. Even now I cannot write those two words without a shudder. To pronounce the name "Lady Rose" is to conjure an image of feminine delicacy and refinement, but there was no more savage and ruthless creature upon the earth. I would, with delight, welcome a thousand eruptions of Krakatoa before enduring a minute longer than necessary in her company. She has, from the first moment of our acquaintance, made it her mission to thwart me. I have found my bedsheets soaked with ink, my hair tonic replaced with treacle, the toes of my shoes stuffed with pins.

It is not in my temperament to permit such treatment to pass unremarked upon, but Lady Rose has a decided advantage over me: youth. It is unseemly for a grown woman to embark upon a war of wills with a child of eleven, but I frequently daydreamed with real pleasure of hoisting her to the top of the tallest monkey puzzle tree by her petticoats or feeding her a tart laced with syrup of ipecacuanha.

The casual reader may wonder why Lady Rose took a position of instantaneous and implacable hatred towards me, but the reason is quite simple: Stoker. Lady Rose had, from the cradle, entertained a fiendish adoration of the man, fueled by his generosity with sweets and his willingness to let her play with the more outlandish supplies in his workshop. More than once I had come upon them, heads bent near as Stoker explained the proper way to fit a glass eyeball. She had developed a genuine and impressive enthusiasm for natural history, with a particular gift for bones. The child could take one look at a long bone and pronounce its genus and species. Her father was content to indulge her until she ordered a copy of all fourteen volumes of Bertrand's *Mammalia* at astonishing expense and charged it to his account at Hatchards.

By way of punishment, he suspended her pocket money, which led her to a few fairly outlandish schemes. First, she stripped the larder of food, filling a small wagon and pulling it down the street as she sold off half a ham, a cold roast of beef, grouse from his lordship's Scottish estate, various imported cheeses, and the rock cakes Cook was saving for teatime. She turned a particularly impressive profit on the Alpenwalder cheese I had carried home for his lordship, and the earl felt the loss of this anticipated treat so keenly, he confiscated every coin she earned. So, Lady Rose, mindful of her sister's fashionable new gown with beetle-wing embroidery, had embarked upon a new plan—one she did not share until we reached Bishop's Folly to find the entire garden throbbing with small greenish orbs winging their way from leaf to leaf as they solemnly consumed everything in sight.

"Rose," her father said faintly. "What have you done?"

"I was breeding beetles," she said, standing with her feet astride like a tiny Colossus, hands in fists upon her hips. "I was meant to sell them to dressmakers for pocket money."

The gardener, staring at the carnage, resigned on the spot, and his lordship went after him, good gardeners being difficult to find and even more difficult to keep within the confines of the city.

"A very clever idea," Stoker told her kindly.

"But pointless," I put in. "The beetles most commonly used for embroidery are wood-boring varieties such as *Sternocera aequisignata*. Unfortunately, these are common rose chafer beetles. You have managed to unleash approximately a thousand *Macrodactylus subspinosus* into the garden instead."

"I did not unleash them," she replied darkly. "They unleashed themselves. I had them in a very nice Wardian case until they found a way out."

I gave a start. "A Wardian case? Do you mean you were breeding them in the Belvedere?" After knocking the arm off a particularly rare and elegant caryatid—Lady Rose could be accident-prone—she had been forbidden from the Belvedere unless specifically invited by either Stoker or myself.

"I couldn't exactly breed them in my bedroom," she protested. "I share with Juno and you know how she is about bugs. It isn't fair, either, for she's always blowing things up or mixing solutions that smell like rotten eggs, and no one ever seems to mind."

"She," I returned acidly, "has never destroyed an entire garden. I went to great trouble to secure those particular succulents for Patricia. What is she meant to eat now?" I asked, gesturing towards the Galápagos tortoise that lumbered sadly by. Lady Rose and I had once reached an entente based upon my sharing with her a method to induce a harmless bout of vomiting in one of her brothers who had been particularly annoying, but the fragile bond of understanding had well and truly snapped. I was especially fond of Patricia. Tortoises do not have much personality to speak of, but Patricia was gregarious, as tortoises go. She had recently suffered a disappointment in love, and I had consoled her by planting a row of her favorite succulents, the last pulpy leaf of which fluttered to the ground at my feet, shorn free by the rapacious beetles.

"I didn't mean to," Lady Rose insisted.

Stoker put a hand to her shoulder. "I know. Come, there are a few violet creams left in my cupboard in the Belvedere, and I've brought home a real find and I will need help with the uncrating."

"What is it?" she asked with narrowed eyes.

He bent near, pitching his voice to a conspiratorial tone. "A thylacine."

Her mouth dropped open into a perfect O. "A thylacine! You're joking."

"I never joke about Tasmanian tigers. Now, go and wash your hands because I'll not have my specimen befouled, and we will eat violet creams and admire the fellow."

Lady Rose hurried off and I stared at him in amazement. "How do you do it? She is an unrepentant monster, and yet with you she is a model of obedience and good humor."

He cocked his head to one side. "She puts me greatly in mind of what you must have been like as a child."

"Heaven forbid!" I cried.

Stoker merely grinned as he turned away to supervise the unloading of his thylacine. As promised, he gave Lady Rose a lengthy examination of the beast, drawing her attention to its enormous jaw capacity and distinctive ears. Having heard entirely enough of the delights of this particular mammal, I retired to my folly to wash off the grime of travel. I ought to have unpacked, but I could not face the remnants of my ruined net just yet. I left my carpetbag and the box containing the orrery and returned to the Belvedere to enjoy my tea whilst I opened the mountain of correspondence that had arrived in our absence.

Once word had got out about his lordship's intention to open a museum, Stoker and I had become the target for every collector in the kingdom—and further afield. We regularly received letters from as far away as the Americas, describing decrepit collections and offering items for sale. Many of these the earl dealt with himself, being as acquisitive as his ancestors when it came to unearthing treasures. But dozens of missives were dropped on my desk each week—often with an accompanying enticement in the form of a sample of the collection—and it was my thankless task to sift through them, penning gentle letters of refusal to the least promising whilst scrutinizing the others for any possible delights Lord Rosemorran might have overlooked. He could be entirely single-minded in his pursuit of statuary and most neglectful of the other arts. He had been known to refuse a first-rate Gainsborough if it meant securing a third-rate Bernini model instead.

I was pleased to find this lot contained, amidst the flotsam and jetsam, a fine group of Roman coins from a parson in Northumbria, an enormous fossil from a lady fossil collector in Dorset, and a luscious set of cameos commissioned by a Pamphilj pope. The latter were of particular interest to me, arriving as they did in a scarlet leather box stamped with the papal tiara in faded gilt along with the Pamphilj arms. The accompanying note—from the owner, a papal marquise from Gubbio—explained that the cameos had been a gift from Innocent X to his sister-in-law, Olimpia Maidalchini. The formidable Signora Maidalchini had been the power behind the papal throne during the pontificate, and the pope had showered her with honors including making her Princess of San Martino. The cameos were a set of twelve, carved from the lava of Vesuvius and polished to a high sheen, each representing one of the Muses complete with the corresponding nymph's emblem. From Euterpe's flutes to Melpomene's mask of tragedy, each was beautifully rendered in perfect detail. The cameos had been fitted into settings of fine, granular gold dotted with pearls, a lovely gift for the woman suspected of being the pope's mistress.

I set them at the corner of my desk and listened with half an ear to Lady Rose's questions—most of them surprisingly intelligent, I was forced to admit—as I sorted letters and plucked the occasional beetle out of my tea. At length, George the hallboy came to fetch Lady Rose, as she was very late for teatime, the one hour each day his lordship insisted upon spending with all of his offspring. She left, smudged with chocolate and bits of fur and beaming. Stoker was likewise in excellent spirits and helped himself to a large handful of sandwiches whilst I gestured to the teapot.

"It will want hotting up," I advised him. "It has gone quite tepid during the course of your lecture."

"I was not lecturing," he said, pouring himself a cup of the lukewarm beverage. "I was merely pointing out to Lady Rose—"

At that point I stopped listening, knowing Stoker was thoroughly capable of repeating his remarks of the last two hours verbatim.

"Oh God, not the bloody Tasmanian tiger again," came a muffled voice.

Stoker and I exchanged startled glances. The voice seemed to be coming from the sarcophagus we used as a buffet. It was of mediocre Greco-Roman design, the mummy long since lost. It could hold an admirable selection of hot dishes as well as stacks of periodicals. But I noticed that it had been swept clean, the usual piles of papers moved to the floor. Furthermore, the assortment of prosthetic limbs—historical examples of wax, wood, and even clockwork metal—that usually resided within had been stacked beneath the trestles upon which it rested.

"Stoker," I said slowly, "I believe we have an intruder."

"What sort of intruder would conceal himself inside a mummy case for the better part of two hours only to announce his presence?" Stoker asked.

"The sort who did not realize how blasted heavy the lid is and is now trapped," the voice replied.

Stoker bolted to his feet to render aid. The sarcophagus, meant to hold the dead with a minimal amount of decay, would have been sealed when first used in order to protect the mummy from the effects of light and air. Ours, fortunately, had been lightly damaged. The toes had been sawed off at some point, no doubt for ease of packing the unwieldy thing, but this had the benefit of permitting a bit of air to circulate within, although I imagined it would have grown unbearably stuffy after a while.

Of course, had I realized who was inside, I might have been inclined to leave him there, but Stoker was already engaged in an heroic rescue. He snatched up a pry bar and wedged the narrow end beneath the lid. One great shove and it slid open enough to reveal the last face I wanted to see ever again.

"Jonathan Hathaway, what in the name of the oozing wounds of Christ are you doing in there?"

CHAPTER

20

The fellow in question blinked at the sudden light. "I say, would you mind terribly helping me out before we begin the inquisition? And might I trouble you for a bit of food? I've had nothing all day and I am famished." He said this with the winsome air of a stray pup begging for scraps, and Stoker was instantly moved to oblige.

Within a very few minutes, our visitor was ensconced upstairs in the little bolt-hole we fondly referred to as the snuggery. He looked thoroughly disreputable, unshaven and dressed in evening clothes that were creased beyond redemption, a deep violet bruise darkening one eye. But he appeared entirely at ease, seemingly viewing the entire experience as some sort of grand adventure. He draped himself on Napoléon's campaign bed, and the dogs had come to investigate him, smelling as he did of the ancient and interesting confines of the sarcophagus. He tolerated their snufflings and licks with good humor until Huxley, the undisputed chieftain of this particular clan, turned away and settled at Stoker's feet, clearly content to let the intruder remain. Having witnessed this imprimatur, the other dogs relaxed. Betony, the Caucasian sheepdog, took up a post near the stairs, whilst Vespertine sat at my feet, her heavy head resting upon my knee. Nut, the Egyptian hound, settled herself daintily next to our visitor, now and again looking up at him in adoration as he fed her scraps of ham. I had always maintained that Nut was a dreadful judge of character, and her instant affection for our guest confirmed it. He eased into a comfortable position, one hand wrapped around a fresh cup of gently steaming tea, the other holding a half-eaten sandwich. It was his fourth. He no sooner finished one than he began the next, giving a gentle moan of satisfaction as he helped himself to Cook's best efforts.

"This ham is particularly delectable. Do you know if she smokes it herself?" he asked brightly.

"Stop making polite conversation," I ordered.

Stoker gave me a startled look, as well he might. I had been by turns either silent or shrewish with our visitor. The fellow gave me a hurt look and finished his sandwich, putting out his hand for another. I jerked the plate just out of reach. "You have had enough. It is time to sing for your supper. What are you doing here?" I demanded. "How did you even know to come to this place? And where is the diamond?"

Stoker might have thought my approach unconventional, but the questions were valid and he turned to the subject of my interrogation with a curious gaze.

"Well?" Stoker pressed.

"To answer your first question, I saw the address in Charles' correspondence," he admitted. "As to how I came here, when I left the Hall, I crossed the moor and caught the milk train at Batleigh, just before the stop at Shepton Parva. I had heard enough of your situation from Charles to know it was as good a place as any and better than most to hide myself."

"But why?" Stoker asked.

"Because I knew I should be suspected of stealing the diamond," he said. He sipped at his tea and the warmth seemed to stiffen his resolve. "I did not take it, although I cannot expect you to believe that, sir. I give you my word that I did not."

"And yet as soon as the diamond was taken, you fled the Hall and now are currently hiding out? In a sarcophagus?"

"I picked the lock of the Belvedere, thinking this would be a safer place to hide away until you returned, but the girl was always here," he replied in some frustration. "I did not wish to frighten her, so I hid, but she is a most curious child."

Lady Rose, I mouthed to Stoker.

He nodded. "But if, as you say, you did not steal the diamond, you must see that fleeing presents evidence of your guilt."

"I am aware of that. Yet I will swear upon anything you like that I am innocent. I merely hoped that my prior acquaintance with your— with Miss Speedwell," he amended hastily, "would persuade you both to act on my behalf."

Stoker's brows shot skywards. "Then you do know him?" he said, turning to me.

I opened my mouth to reply, but he forestalled me. "We met briefly on our travels. I think she remembers me now, although it was a distant association and long ago," he said smoothly. With Stoker's head turned away from him, he gave me a long, deliberate wink.

I smoothed my skirts. "No. It will not do. This has been too weighty a burden upon my conscience. I will carry it no longer."

Harry's eyes went wide as he looked at Stoker's impressive physique, rather more in evidence than usual given that he had stripped off waistcoat and jacket along with his neckcloth to work. His sleeves had been rolled up to reveal his sinewy forearms, his collar discarded to bare the strong column of his throat. Harry, I knew from long experience, was assessing Stoker's ability to harm him.

He squirmed backwards a little on the campaign bed as Stoker's gaze swung from me to Harry and back again. "What burden?"

I cleared my throat. "I recognized this man as soon as I saw him at Hathaway Hall, but he is not Jonathan Hathaway. He is the second man Sir Hugo spoke of. This is Harry Spenlove." I paused and drew in a great breath.

Stoker canted his head inquiringly.

"I did not admit to knowing him because there was at one time an attachment between us. In fact—"

"For God's sake, don't do it," Harry begged, pulling his legs up in front of him in a defensive posture. He upended his empty teacup and held it like a shield.

Stoker looked amused. "Sir, I beg you, calm yourself. I am aware that the lady has had previous attachments on her travels. This is the first I have made the acquaintance of, but I hope I may remain a gentleman with regards to liaisons that may have been undertaken well before I even met her."

"I am glad to hear you say that," I began.

"Veronica!" Harry's voice rose to a shriek.

I turned to him. "You are the one who said he should know. I am merely agreeing with you." I turned back to Stoker. "You are correct. Harry and I formed an attachment whilst we traveled—"

Stoker held up a quelling hand. "Stop," he ordered. "I do not need to know anything more."

"But I feel obliged to tell you," I protested.

"I do not wish to hear it," he countered. "Veronica, I knew that you had lived a life before our paths crossed, and I am glad of it. No conventional woman would have been prepared to accept me for all that I am," he said, gesturing vaguely towards his stained clothes, his eye patch, his tattoos. "But I do not crave the specifics. It is enough that at some point you were fond of this fellow, and that attachment clearly faded or you would not have left him in the past."

"Well, she did think I was dead," Harry put in.

"Exactly so," Stoker replied. "And I've no doubt she grieved for you. But you, sir, are her past. I am her present and future. Your arrival here does not threaten that."

Harry broke into a broad grin. "I quite like this man, Veronica," he said.

"Your opinion is entirely immaterial," I said coldly.

"Well, I call that unfriendly," he protested. "And I came here to throw myself on your mercy."

"Mercy is not a quality for which I am renowned," I reminded him.

"I would like to clear my name," Harry replied. "I did not steal the diamond."

"It is entirely too coincidental that it should have disappeared at the same time you did," I argued.

"Not necessarily," Stoker put in quietly. I turned to him in astonishment.

"You cannot say you believe him," I began.

Stoker shrugged. "I do not know what to believe, but I have a good guess as to why he left Hathaway Hall with such speed." He turned to Harry. "You were in mortal fear, were you not?"

Harry gaped at him. "How did you know that?"

"Simple deduction," Stoker said. "I took the liberty of examining your room at the Hall before we left."

I blinked at him. "You did?"

"I did," he went on smoothly. "There was money in the washstand drawer—forty pounds to be exact. A thief would certainly have taken the money along with a change of clothes," he added, gesturing towards Harry's evening suit.

Harry nodded slowly. "I must say, that is a first-rate piece of deduction. I left as if all the hounds of hell were after me, with nothing but my notecase and its four shillings in my pocket. You see, I had discovered that the diamond was missing. And I knew I would be suspected."

"How?" I demanded.

He reached into his pocket and retrieved a handkerchief—marked with the initials "JH" and a pattern of French knots, all worked in dark blue silk.

"Jonathan's handkerchief? But why should that make a suspect of you—" I broke off, understanding at once. "Oh, of course. The thief left it with the empty jewel case."

"Exactly," Harry said with a shudder. "You've no idea the fright it gave me, knowing that someone had taken the Eye of the Dawn and meant me to swing for it."

I looked to Stoker. "Is jewel thievery still a hanging offense? One forgets."

Harry went on. "Does it matter? The intention was that I should be branded a criminal in the eyes of the Hathaway family, most particularly Lady Hathaway. Her good opinion of me would have been entirely destroyed."

"I daresay it was not improved by your leaving so precipitously just as her diamond was stolen," I told him tartly. "After all, one must presume you have not an innocent reason for opening her jewel case in the first place."

He opened his mouth, then snapped it shut quickly, like a rising carp. "Oh, very well. I did mean to take it, I admit it. I went to Lady Hathaway's dressing room. It was quite late and she was already abed, snoring like a hound, bless her," he added with a fond smile. "But I can move like a cat when necessary. So I crept in and opened the casket."

"How?" Stoker inquired.

"I have certain skills of long practice," Harry replied smoothly.

"This is not his first criminal enterprise," I added.

"Such a nasty word, 'criminal,'" Harry mused, rolling his eyes heavenwards so that he looked like one of the younger martyred saints.

"Such an apt one," I countered.

He went on as if I had not spoken. "In any event, I was able to open the casket and I discovered the Eye of the Dawn was missing. The rest of the parure was intact, but the only thing inside the diamond's box was the handkerchief."

He brandished the item in question and Stoker took it, gazing at it thoughtfully.

"What are you thinking?" I asked.

He shook his head. "Nothing precisely, just that it is a remarkably childish attempt to throw suspicion upon one party in particular—the sort of imagination that might read sensational thrillers." He looked at Harry. "This was taken from your room?"

"Or the laundry," Harry said. "Or I dropped it. I am forever leaving them lying around. Anyone might have collected it."

"And anyone might have disliked you enough to see you implicated in the theft," I said sweetly.

"Very true," he said in a genial tone. "I am accustomed to people deciding to take a sudden dislike to me. It is regrettable, but one cannot help it."

"Not if one is engaged in criminal enterprises," I replied.

"Might I inquire," Stoker said politely, "if this is your usual business or merely a hobby?"

Harry looked pained. "I have tried to make an honest living, but it is difficult."

"It can be," Stoker agreed.

"So," Harry went on, "I have very often been obliged to return to my less-than-laudable ways. Fortune has not always been kind to me."

"And so you intended to defraud Lady Hathaway of her diamond as your latest criminal enterprise?" Stoker asked.

"Things," Harry said coldly, "did not go according to plan."

"Obviously," Stoker replied, his gaze resting upon Harry's bruised eye.

"After I left the Hall in some distress, I met with certain associates of mine who had a vested interest in the diamond. It disappointed them that I was unsuccessful," Harry said. He prodded the bruise gently with his fingertips. "One of my associates tends to be demonstrative with his fists when he is disappointed."

"You were stealing the diamond to order," I said, my understanding suddenly illuminated. "It was a conspiracy!"

"The word 'conspiracy' implies a certain egalitarianism," Harry corrected. "I was very much operating at the behest of another party—a party whose attentions I hoped to avoid by leaving the Hall as soon as it became apparent I could not fulfill my commission."

"You were running away to avoid the thrashing your partners were sure to administer for your failure." I poked his empurpled cheekbone, provoking a shriek. "A thrashing they managed to inflict anyway."

"My flight from the Hall did not go unnoticed," he said dryly. "I was apprehended as soon as I alighted at the station. They took me to a villa somewhere beyond Hampstead, where they made their feelings about the situation perfectly clear."

"And then they let you go?" Stoker asked.

"I let myself go. There are only two of them, and the fellow who did this"—he gestured towards his bruises—"left me on my own for a little while. No doubt taking a leisurely dinner to fortify his strength before he came back to finish the job. I did not think it would be a wise strategy to test my hypothesis, so I effected an escape."

"And you came *here*?" I said.

"You needn't sound so incredulous. I haven't been to London in many years. It would take time to locate friends who might take me in. And, as I said, I had seen your address on the letter Charles had. He showed it around, you know, pleased as punch that a lord had written him. He made each of us ooh and aah over the bloody thing as if it were a holy relic. I remembered the name of the house and thought I might lie low here for a bit, just until I got my nerve back. I never imagined you would be returning so soon, although I must say I am rather glad you did. I was in real danger of suffocating in that monstrosity," he added with a shudder.

"The sarcophagus has holes in it," I told him coldly. "Your only danger was cramp."

"Still, I have had a thoroughly unpleasant time of it and I want nothing more than to sleep just now and then eat again, something hot this time. A nice bit of roast beef," he said, his eyes shimmering with longing. "Do you know how long it has been since I had a nice bit of roast beef? The Hathaways eat far too much lamb. I am heartily sick of it."

"Tell us more about these colleagues of yours," Stoker urged. "A fellow who is free with his fists, you mentioned."

Harry nodded. "Göran, an enormous Swedish fellow whom I have only ever heard communicate in grunts. Swedish is a distinctly un-mellifluous tongue. He answers to *her*."

"Her?" I inquired.

Harry shuddered. "Isabel de Armas MacGregor," he said, whispering the name.

"She is not here, you utter coward," I said.

"You do not know. She is capable of anything. *Anything*. And right now she is put out with me. Very angry indeed. I promised her the Eye of the Dawn, and I cannot deliver."

"Why did you promise her the diamond?" Stoker asked.

Harry's expression was pained. "There was a little scheme in South America, some months back." He paused thoughtfully. "How much do you know about the Brazilian Empire?"

Stoker shrugged and I interjected, mindful of the article I had recently read in the *Daily Harbinger*. "The emperor, Pedro II, is ailing and elderly. He has only a daughter to succeed him, and power is shifting increasingly towards the coffee growers and the generals in his army."

Harry's look was one of admiration. "That is a far sight more than most English bother to know. Yes, the emperor is failing, and not likely to hold on to his throne for much longer. He worked for many years to abolish slavery in Brazil, a very unpopular position, it must be said. The landowners complained it would destroy the economy, but slavery was ended last year and, in point of fact, the economy has flourished. That ought to have improved the emperor's popularity, but it has not. He is living out his own obsolescence. All of Brazil turns to the future instead. And that is where Isabel de Armas MacGregor came in." He paused as if to steel himself. "Isabel never believed the end of slavery would damage the economy. In fact, she rather thought Brazil would enjoy a boom of sorts, expansion in technology and transportation, new investments, that sort of thing. As it happens, she was correct, and if she had had money to invest, she would have made quite a nice packet. But Isabel is not inclined to invest in the normal, aboveboard way. She had a different plan—a railway. From the Atlantic to the Pacific."

Stoker stared in stupefaction. "A trans-Andean railway? Man, it cannot be done."

"You know that. I know that. I daresay even these dogs know it," Harry said, ruffling Nut's elegant head. "But the Brazilian coffee growers can be a bit greedy, particularly when one dangles the possibility of opening new markets to the west via a pretty new railway designed to move their crops to the coast of Chile and beyond."

"And they believed her?" I asked.

"Isabel is a very persuasive woman," Harry said with a faraway look in his eye. "She had them convinced, in part because she presented herself, most convincingly, as a lady of royal parentage. She appeared one day in Rio de Janeiro and distributed calling cards identifying herself as Her Royal Highness, the Princess Isabella de Armas de Gonzaga-Palmela. Now, an attentive person might have noticed that she cobbled together that title out of Spanish and Italian and Portuguese names, but that was actually quite intentional and rather a stroke of genius. No one could say for certain where she was meant to be from, so it was difficult for anyone to denounce her as an impostor. She presented a letter of credit to the bank in Rio de Janeiro drawn upon the Bank of Scotland and settled into the most expensive hotel in town, entertaining lavishly. It was all most convincing. Naturally, the businessmen who would not give a farthing to Isabel de Armas MacGregor were falling over themselves to write cheques to the Princess Isabella. At least, they said they would. When it came to it, they were reluctant to give the money directly to her on the grounds that it was distasteful to do business with a lady, even one of such august rank. So, she decided to find someone to play the part of a respectable man of business to collect the payments, present them to the bank in exchange for notes, and give them to her in exchange for a percentage of the proceeds."

"Enter Harry Spenlove," I guessed.

"Indeed." He smoothed a hand over the stubble at his chin. "I assumed my most toffee-nosed accents and my soberest suit of clothes and took a suite of offices in the most expensive building in the city. Within days they were lining up, bringing me piles of money. I gave the first few lots to Isabel, but there came a day when the wealthiest gentlemen, a group of five who were very good friends and making the bulk of the investment, were scheduled to come together to present their monies and receive in exchange their certificates of ownership in the nonexistent railway. I took their funds and poured champagne and we all toasted to how rich they were going to be, and they staggered off to have a grand luncheon—to which I was not invited, by the way—and I sat there looking at the pile of cheques. Well, I am not *proud* of what I did next—"

Stoker held up a hand. "We can guess."

"Yes, I suppose you can. Isabel, I will admit, did not take things in a sporting fashion."

"I expect not," I said. "How much did you swindle out of her?"

Harry murmured a figure and I felt my eyes go wide. "Good heavens. And where is it now?"

"Gone," he said cheerfully.

"Gone where?" I asked.

"I spent it."

"How in the name of seven hells could you have spent that amount of money?" Stoker demanded.

Harry ticked off the items on his fingers. "First-class passage to New York. The best suite at the Fifth Avenue Hotel. Dinner every night at Delmonico's. Then I took a cottage in Providence for the summer," he added. "A lovely Italianate-style palazzo I had from a Vanderbilt. Deathly expensive, but worth it. And then there was the yacht."

I held up my hand. "Never mind."

"And to travel in such circles, I needed the right clothes, everything from suits to cravat pins and watches. I tried my hand at polo but I must say I didn't much care for it. I sold the ponies at a loss. I came back to the city for the autumn and stayed through the New Year, but America had lost its charm for me by then. New York is a rich man's town, you know. One simply cannot enjoy it in an impoverished state. Besides, by that time I had got word that Isabel was on my trail, and I thought it wise to elude her as it seemed she was holding a grudge."

"How do you know that?" Stoker put in.

"She sent a rather vivid caricature. She is not a bad little artist, although I cannot say I much cared for the subject matter," Harry said with a shudder. "So I had a little wander about Canada for a few months to see if I could lose her, but she tracked me to Halifax. I had quite a narrow escape that time. I booked a steerage ticket for the very next steamer to England, which she must have anticipated. As soon as I disembarked at Bristol, they were waiting for me, Isabel and her pet Swede. She made it perfectly apparent that she was still angry, which I told her was not very understanding and that she ought to take it like a man."

"But she isn't a man," I said.

"You needn't remind me," he replied. "The female of the species is indeed more venomous and far more capable of bearing a grudge. She gave her associate, the taciturn and disagreeable Göran, carte blanche to do as he pleased with me. He has a fondness for working with blades." He broke off with a shudder. "In any event, Göran was preparing to murder me on her orders when I suddenly remembered Jonathan Hathaway and the pretty little collection of jewels his grand-mother owns. And I recollected the story he told me of one stone in particular—the Eye of the Dawn. The plot was not a sophisticated one, but I thought of it on the spur of the moment, and for something born of purest desperation, it really wasn't all bad," he mused. "It was work-ing quite well too. The jewels were inaccessible—Lady Hathaway kept them in a bank vault in Exeter, and whilst I am proud of my talents, I confess breaking into bank vaults requires skills I do not possess. I had only to wait comfortably at Hathaway Hall until Lady Hathaway decided to send for them. I was racking my brain, trying to hit upon a scheme that would entice her to do precisely that, but there was no need. Charles had already decided to commission a portrait of Mary and suggested she ought to be painted in the jewels. Rather ironic that it was on my behalf that Lady Hathaway actually brought them out, is it not? In any event, once they were in the house, it should have been the merest child's play to lift the diamond, make my escape, and present it to Isabel with my fervent apologies. That diamond was the price of my head," he added darkly. "And now it is forfeit."

He gave a great yawn and slipped sideways, the cup tipping gently from his hand. His eyelids drooped, and I raised my hand to slap him smartly, but Stoker caught my wrist. "We have not finished our discussion," I protested. "I merely meant to rouse him."

"Let him sleep," Stoker said, not dropping my hand. "We have much to discuss."

CHAPTER 21

S toker and I repaired to the main floor of the Belvedere, picking
our way amidst the costumes and set pieces and leering marionettes. "I shall have nightmares," I grumbled as I set aside a particularly venomous-looking donkey puppet.

Stoker perched atop a camel saddle, swinging one booted foot as
we talked.

"I hardly know where to begin," I said.

"I think we may agree that your taste in paramours has vastly
improved," he said soberly.

"Quite, although in the interest of perfect clarity, I ought to
say—"

I looked up to find Stoker regarding me with an expression of cool
detachment. I had seen his face arranged in precisely the same fashion when he stared at the thylacine's scrotal pouch, I realized. It was
an indication that he was assessing, dispassionately. Whatever confession I had intended to make died upon my lips. I could confide
many things, but none of them to that face, I decided.

"Yes?" The voice was as cool as the expression.

"I was merely going to say that I was not aware of Harry's character when first we were acquainted. He is entirely mendacious and not to be trusted."

Stoker pondered this. "Oh, I do not know about that," he said casually. "I am rather a good judge of character. I think he may be relied upon."

"You cannot mean to say that you believe that Banbury tale he just spun? What sort of a villainess is called Isabel? And a Nordic giant with a penchant for blades? It is like something torn from the pages of a sensational novel—and not one of the well-written ones. One of the cheap, pulpy variety available for purchase in provincial train stations."

Stoker shrugged one heavy shoulder. "I find him credible. After all, his bruises are real enough. I am a surgeon," he reminded me. "He cannot have faked those."

"No, but he may have inflicted them," I replied darkly.

"How hard you are upon him!" Stoker mocked. "Anyone would think he had broken your heart."

"I— I—" I gaped at him, then took a few calming and restorative breaths to gather my nerves. "I should hope that I am a woman of sufficient character not to bear grudges of anything as insignificant as a failed love affair."

He bared his teeth in a smile. "I am glad to hear it. Now, I think it is perfectly obvious that we must help him."

"Help him!" The words were incredulous and slightly shrieked. One of the dogs howled in protest.

"Help him," Stoker repeated firmly. "One might even consider it our duty. After all, we blundered in and may have overset the plans in motion that could have won him his freedom from this nefarious pair."

"We had nothing to do with the theft of the diamond," I replied.

"But his compatriots do not know that. This is all a muddle at present, and he is in the middle of it, poor lad."

"Poor lad?" I shook my head, wondering if I had possibly struck it without realizing I had done myself an injury. "You do not say that you are in sympathy with him?"

Stoker canted his head thoughtfully. "Well, I have never run afoul of a lady jewel thief, but I have experience with mendacity in the form of a woman."

For one terrible moment I thought he had discovered the true nature of my attachment to Harry, but then I realized he was speaking of Caroline, his wretched former wife who had cuckolded him and left him for dead in the jungles of Amazonia. I marveled that Stoker and I could have both chosen so poorly in our first attempts at matrimony. (It also occurred to me that a fitting revenge upon both of our spouses would be to introduce them to one another and let nature take its course, but that does not reflect well upon my attempts to rise above trivial resentments, so I will draw a veil over this particular notion.)

Stoker went on. "I understand how badly one can underestimate the gentler sex. Indeed, even referring to them as 'the gentler sex' is a misnomer of the most grotesque variety. When one considers the praying mantis, for example, *Mantis religiosa*, and how the female of the species will happily bite the head off of her mate after copulation—"

I held up a hand. "I am perfectly familiar with the practice," I began.

"I am certain that you are." The tone was bland, but I darted him a suspicious look. Before I could inquire, he went on. "Which is to say, I do sympathize with the fellow. He is clearly in fear of his life from a mortal adversary who is both tenacious and clever. She has tracked him, remember, from Brazil to New York, Canada to Bristol. And now to London. We would do well not to underestimate her determination. No, it is quite apparent that Harry Spenlove is in need of our help if he is to elude this murderous fiend."

I folded my arms over my chest. "What do you propose?"

He shrugged. "It has been a long day and we are all of us tired. A good night's sleep and we shall convene a council of war. Amongst the three of us, we should be able to devise a plan that will see Harry cleared of this obligation and set upon his way again."

My mind raced, but I could see from the pugnacious set of his jaw that there was no point in arguing. "Very well," I said with an obliging nod. "If you are so persuaded that this is the proper course of action, we will offer him our assistance."

"I am glad you see it my way," he said cordially.

"However," I added as if he had not spoken, "you must believe me when I say that he is capable of any mischief. The Belvedere is a treasure house of sorts, and none of it belongs to us. We are custodians of Lord Rosemorran's possessions and, as such, responsible for them. If Harry decided to help himself to something small and valuable to fund his escape, we should be obligated to his lordship."

"Agreed," he said, running a hand over the whisker shadow at his jaw. Suddenly, he broke into a mirthless smile. "I have it. We will sleep here. With him."

"We will do what?"

"We will make ourselves comfortable here in the Belvedere. If Harry decides to get up to some mischief, we will certainly hear him and be in a position to stop him. I would offer to mind him on my own, but you know how deeply I sleep, and two pairs of ears are better than one," he added.

"An admirable solution," I said, and my voice sounded hollow to my ears. "Although I suspect neither of us will enjoy comfortable slumbers. We have only campaign beds to avail ourselves of."

"No matter," he said, dropping to his feet noiselessly. "After all, we can always think of it as an adventure."

. . .

Any hope I had of sleeping well was thwarted by the oddness of the situation in which I found myself. Stoker put the matter to Harry with as much tact as possible under the circumstances. It is, after all, no easy thing to insinuate that you intend to sleep near a man because you do not trust him with so much as a hatpin.

But Harry, being so often the object of vituperation, was remarkably inured to insult.

"My good fellow, think no more of it," he assured Stoker. "I should do exactly the same in your position. In fact, I will move myself here, to the furthest reaches of this delightful snug, so that in order to reach the stairs, I should have to pass both of you." To demonstrate his resolve, he tucked a narrow mattress under the eaves, as far from any egress as possible.

"If you do not murder us in our sleep," I muttered as I arranged a coverlet and pillow on the campaign bed. If either of the men heard me, they gave no sign. I settled into my couch with Vespertine whilst the other dogs collected themselves around Stoker. Apart from Nut, that is. Once more the little pharaoh hound attached herself to Harry. She had begun life as the pet of a criminal, and I was not entirely surprised at her preference for Harry. She must have had an affection for duplicity.

Stoker doused the lamps and in a short while I found myself the audience for a veritable symphony of snores, snuffles, snorts, and susurrations. Two men and a pack of dogs do not a restful night's sleep make, I reflected as I lay wakeful long into the night. At length I was forced to my usual remedy of counting in Persian. I must have drifted off at last, for I found myself dreaming that I was once more in Sumatra, hunting butterflies on the slope of a volcano. They were enormous things, those butterflies, purest white and with a wingspan wider than my reach. I chased them, but my net was broken and the volcano was rumbling ominously. I had just followed one to the rim of the crater when a plume of lava jetted skywards with a roar that ended on a thud.

Curiously, the thud was realistic enough to jolt me to wakefulness. Beside me, Vespertine lay, head up, ears pricked. I glanced about the snug—deeply shadowed but not entirely black thanks to the efforts of the moon peering through the skylight above. The other dogs were alert as well, although both men slumbered on.

Like any freestanding structure in the midst of a lavish garden, the Belvedere was afflicted with mice, and Stoker and I waged a constant war against their depredations. They cavorted and capered with abandon, and I was well accustomed to their various scribblings and scrabblings. But were they capable of making a proper thud, loud enough to rouse one from sleep? Entirely unlikely.

I peered hard into the gloom, straining eyes and ears for some further disturbance when at last it came—the faint yellow glimmer of a light on the main floor below. An intruder!

I eased myself out from beneath the coverlet. I had retired fully dressed thanks to Harry's presence, but I had left off my boots for the sake of comfort and dared not resume them now. Stocking feet would serve my purpose better, I decided as I slipped off the narrow bed. Vespertine stirred, but I motioned her back and she subsided with a reproachful look. She had, in the months since we had come to live together, taken a protective interest in me. But she was a well-trained creature, and although she did not care for being left behind, she obeyed, emitting only the softest of whines in protest.

The other dogs, tucked comfortably around Stoker and Harry, merely watched as I picked my way to the staircase, a winding affair of elaborately decorated iron. With no wooden stairs to creak beneath my weight, I stood a good chance of descending without attracting the attention of our visitor so long as I was cautious. I edged onto the top step, casting an eye over the expanse of the Belvedere's main floor. It was, as ever, a jumble of statuary, Wardian cases, taxidermy mounts, scientific instruments, books, paintings, coin collections, and other assorted items, all made orders of magnitude less orderly by Lord Rosemorran's latest acquisitions—the theatrical props and costumes. Their packing cases had been piled higgledy-piggledy, obstructing my view. But near my desk, I could just espy the nimbus of a single flame, moving erratically. Our intruder was there then, doubtless rifling my drawers, I reflected in some irritation.

I crept down the stairs, edging around the packing cases until I came to a gap. Keeping to the shadow, I studied the figure bent over my desk. It was a man, slender of build and moving with the suppleness of youth. He was dressed, as all good burglars ought to be, in black, a muffling scarf wound about his neck. A cap had been discarded on the desk and he held a candle high as he shifted a stack of correspondence—the late post that I had merely dropped atop the wooden box I had carried from Hathaway Hall. Putting this aside, he picked up the box, not an easy feat whilst juggling the candle, and I heard a gentle swearword escape his lips.

He turned, and the candle illuminated his face for a moment. I had been correct about his youth; he could not have been more than twenty. His features were pleasant, or might have been were they not twisted in a mask of concentration. A drop of candle grease fell to his hand, and he gave a quick gasp of pain, dropping the candle and plunging us into darkness. With the realization that I suddenly had the advantage, I raised my head and gave a short, sharp whistle.

Pandemonium erupted. In response to my whistle, the dogs hurtled down the stairs in a thunder of snarls and barks. The intruder gave a small scream and attempted to flee, but I had placed myself between him and the door, stepping out from behind the packing crate, putting my body directly in his path. We collided with extraordinary force, knocking me to the floor and sending the box flying. The intruder must have fallen as well, heavily from the sound of it. But he was quicker than I, for almost immediately I heard him recover his feet and rush to the door. I thrust myself to my feet to follow, but instantly I was surrounded by dogs and knocked to my knees again. Vespertine was the worst offender, bowling me over and sitting upon my stomach to reassure herself that I was quite all right. She remained there, an immovable force, giant paws resting on either side of my head as she licked my face.

"Get off, you daft monster," I ordered as I attempted to shift her. She moved only slightly, just enough to crush me a little more. The other dogs circled around, setting up a howl until Stoker and Harry appeared, rubbing their eyes.

"What the devil—" Stoker began.

"Intruder," I gasped. I made a flailing gesture towards the door, but Stoker was already in pursuit. Huxley, the bulldog, alone of all our pets, had given chase, and I was glad at least one of the beasts could be relied upon. Harry stayed behind to pry a reluctant Vespertine off me. I rolled over and whooped air into my lungs until I could breathe freely again, whilst Harry lit a few lamps and tried to settle the rest of the dogs.

I was just patting Vespertine—one cannot hold a grudge against dogs, after all—when Stoker returned. He had followed the intruder as he had risen from his bed, shirtless and bare of foot, and he bore the traces of the pursuit when he came back.

"He went through the pond and out through the back hedge," I surmised.

Stoker nodded.

Harry gazed at Stoker in perplexity, then turned to me. "How do you know that?"

I gestured. "The only part of the property with thorns, mud, and moss is the hedge on the other side of the pond. You will observe the scratches on his torso—just the right height for a hedge. His feet are stained with mud and moss, and there is a lily pad lodged in his trousers."

Stoker plucked bits of filth off himself as he spoke. "He is a fast runner, our visitor. I think the sound of the dogs spooked him, for he made straight for the water, no doubt hoping it would wash away his scent. In any event, he blundered out the other side and crashed through the hedge before climbing the wall."

"And you couldn't catch him up?" Harry asked.

Stoker's nostrils flared in irritation. "I had an encounter with a tortoise that impeded my progress."

I pointed to the torn knees of his trousers. "Patricia," I informed Harry. "His lordship's Galápagos tortoise. A venerable old thing, but a hazard sometimes. She is very keen on shrubbery and must have been taking a rest under the hedge."

Harry shook his head. "This is the most astonishing and maddening place I think I have ever been."

"And you have only been here a day," I reminded him. I paused, remembering the crash I had heard when the intruder and I collided. The wooden box must have gone flying, for I found it on the other side of the packing crate where I had concealed myself. It had been smashed to bits. I was surveying it mournfully when Stoker and Harry joined me.

"What happened?" Harry inquired, leaning over the wreckage.

"He was attempting to steal this," I said, moving one of the shattered boards aside.

"The Hathaway orrery?" Stoker asked.

I nodded as I examined the pile of splinters. "A pity. It is quite wrecked," I began. But as I sifted through the broken bits of metal and wood, I saw something glint with unmistakable fire.

"Why on earth would a housebreaker come after an orrery?" Harry demanded. "What was so special about it?"

"This," I said, simply. I stood up and opened my hand. On my palm, sparking and shimmering, lay the Eye of the Dawn.

"Bloody hell," Harry breathed.

"Indeed."

CHAPTER

22

Harry put out a hand to take it and Stoker intervened, neatly plucking it out of reach. "I think I will take custody of that," Stoker said in a tone that dared him to oppose.

Harry's smile was ingratiating. "Of course."

"I presume these were your associates bent upon the diamond's recovery," Stoker said to him.

Harry shrugged. "If it was a giant Nordic fellow, then I suppose so, but how they found me or knew the diamond was in the orrery is unfathomable."

"You might have told them," Stoker pointed out.

Harry sighed. "But I didn't *know*. I will be perfectly honest with you: had I known, I wouldn't be here now. I would have taken the bloody thing, given it to Isabel, and got on with my life. That diamond is the price on my head, if you will remember."

I looked at Stoker. "As much as I hate to agree with Harry, it does make precious little sense for him to have arranged a confederate to break in and steal the diamond if he knew where it was. It would be a simple enough matter for him to take it himself."

"Thank you," Harry said, attempting to look appreciative.

"Do not place your gratitude in me; it is misguided," I informed him. "I grant you common sense but nothing more. Besides, the intruder was not your Nordic fellow. Does this Isabel creature have no other associates?"

"None that I know," Harry said.

"She might have hired one," Stoker pointed out.

"And thereby risk being double-crossed again when Harry has already cost her a fortune? I do not think so," I said slowly. "I understand the female mind better than either of you. I suspect her methods will be completely personal, just herself and her most trusted companion—this pet Swede of hers."

"Göran," Harry reminded me darkly. "His name is Göran."

"As it ought to be," Stoker replied. "A good Scandinavian name."

"I have always preferred Odin," Harry said idly.

"For a dog perhaps, but it lacks a certain dignity for a human," Stoker replied.

I cleared my throat. "If we might return to the matter at hand. I saw the fellow. He was most definitely not a Scandinavian. In fact, his was a most decidedly Indian face—and a good-looking one at that."

"Indian?" Stoker's gaze sharpened and I knew what he was thinking.

"Anjali," I said in agreement.

Harry looked from me to Stoker and back again. "What has just happened?"

"Stoker and I had a conversation," I told him.

"But you did not say anything."

"We did not have to. A gentleman of Indian origin has this night attempted to steal the diamond—also of Indian origin—from its place of concealment. And one person with access to it at Hathaway Hall was the third factor of Indian origin."

"Anjali," Stoker finished. "She has access both to Lady Hathaway's room whence the jewel was taken and to Effie's observatory. She might easily have taken the diamond from her ladyship's room and secured it into the orrery, thereby ensuring it would reach London and not be discovered should Charles insist upon a search of the Hall," Stoker added.

"Then who is the fellow who broke in here?" Harry demanded.

"A confederate," I deduced. "It would be a very easy thing to send a quick cable to a fellow conspirator waiting here in London to receive the diamond, giving him its location."

"Terribly risky," Harry said.

"Audacious," Stoker agreed. "They could not be certain we would not inspect the orrery immediately."

"But it was unlikely we would," I said. "We had traveled up from Devon and arrived rather late. What more natural than that we should put it aside in favor of your thylacine and the post that had arrived in our absence? Which, I shall remind you, is precisely what we did. And an attempt has been made to recover the orrery the very first night we have returned to London. To wait longer would be a far greater risk. This was audacious but not reckless. A calculated gamble. A throw of the dice by a desperate young woman."

"Anjali?" Harry asked.

"Effie," I corrected.

"Effie!" Harry looked affronted.

"A most unhappy soul," I said. "Continually belittled, made to feel small. Her accomplishments and talents given little value in that house. She is, to them, a pair of hands and a strong back, no better than a pack animal. If the Hathaways have their way, she will be nothing more than livestock to them, domesticated out of every impulse towards genius."

"She does seem to resent being pulled away from her studies after her grandfather's death," Harry put in. "Poor girl."

"Quite," I said briskly.

Harry cocked his head. "What exactly do you mean to do with that?" he inquired, his avid gaze resting on the jewel still clutched in Stoker's hand.

"I shall keep it safe until we have determined what must be done with it," Stoker said. "It is late and there is too much at stake to make rash decisions. We should all go back to bed and salvage what we may of the night's rest. Tomorrow we will discuss it."

"A council of war?" Harry said in a light voice. But his smile was tight and I suspected he resented Stoker's taking charge of the situation.

"Exactly that. Stoker's suggestion has merit, and to ensure that we all cooperate, I will go with you, Harry," I said, pushing him towards the staircase.

Over his feeble protests, I stayed hard upon his heels along with the dogs, all of us herding him back to bed. For some minutes we heard various clangings and bangings from the floor below, where Stoker was clearly attempting to mislead us as to where he concealed the jewel. I heard the ring of metal—a suit of armor—the bright shudder of a glass pane closed too quickly—a tall clock rescued from a château during the Revolution—the soft splash of the aquarium where a pair of fat, lazy goldfish spent their days swimming over assorted pebbles. He shoved the drawers of an apothecary chest from the Italian Renaissance, slammed the door of a Spanish cardinal's prie-dieu, and even clattered a few of the Sicilian marionettes that Lord Rosemorran had recently acquired. For the better part of a quarter of an hour he rampaged about the place, laying false trails until at last his dark head appeared at the winding stair leading to the snuggery.

"Have you quite finished?" I asked pleasantly. "Only it seems one or two of the walls are still standing."

"I was merely ensuring a good hiding place," he replied. "No offense was intended by my thoroughness."

"None taken," Harry assured him. He had stretched out on his mattress, Nut tucked at his side, both of his hands laced behind his head. "Although one might wonder if your precautions were not a *trifle* overenthusiastic."

"You ought to be thanking him," I retorted. "If our intruder were to return and secure the diamond, he would be signing your death warrant. I presume Mrs. MacGregor would not be best pleased if the thing were nipped out from under her nose."

Harry shuddered. "She would not."

"Then let us rest," I suggested, snapping my fingers at Vespertine to come and lie beside me. "There are only a few hours left until daybreak. And who knows what fresh intrigue tomorrow will bring?"

Within minutes, the pair of them were snoring again, the dogs joining in the chorus. Beside me, Vespertine's breathing was deep and slow, and I rested one hand upon her deep chest. But sleep did not come so easily for me. As I lay, staring into the darkness, I continued to revisit the events of the night. My glimpse of the intruder had been brief, but I could not shake the feeling that I had seen him somewhere before . . .

I must have slept at some point, and heavily, for when I awoke, I was entirely alone in the snuggery. I washed in the tiny water closet that had been plumbed for our convenience and brushed the creases from the clothes in which I had slept. In spite of the fitful night, I felt a surge of energy. Adventure beckoned, and although I deplored spending any more time than necessary with Harry, I could only appreciate the situation in which we now found ourselves. A priceless diamond! A thief in the night! A man returned from the dead! A mortal enemy determined to ensure his destruction! It was all thoroughly satisfactory, I reflected. I descended to find Harry tucking into his breakfast with gusto while Stoker was already at work upon his thylacine.

"Your single-mindedness is astonishing," I told him as he grinned over the back of the beast at me. His shirt was already begrimed with sawdust and glue and any number of other substances I could not hope to identify. "How is it?"

He shrugged. "Salvageable. The hide is in excellent condition, although the original taxidermist's grasp of the anatomy is rudimentary in the extreme. See here—"

He launched into an explanation of the intricacies of *Thylacinus cynocephalus* with vigor until I held up a quelling hand. "I beg you, not before breakfast."

"Oh, there is a way to stop him?" Harry asked, looking distinctly bedeviled. "I had a twenty-minute lecture on the mandibular structure."

"Only twenty? Count yourself fortunate," I advised. "Stoker can speak at length and extempore on any number of subjects so long as he has access to proper hydration and copious amounts of sugar. The longest I have personally witnessed was six and a half hours on a walrus, but that was a special occasion."

"That particular occasion is the reason that Lady Torrington pledged a thousand pounds to build her own wing of the Rosemorran museum," Stoker said mildly.

"Indeed. And your thylacine is very nice," I soothed. "Harry does not appreciate it because he is a philistine. Perhaps you ought to mount *him* and add him to the collection."

Harry eyed me narrowly over the breakfast dishes. "You are in a distinctly jolly mood this morning."

"Nonsense," I said, pouring out a cup of tea. I sniffed the steam appreciatively. "I am never jolly."

"You are in higher spirits than when you retired," he amended.

"That I am," I agreed. I forked up a healthy bite of egg and savored it. I had, upon waking, and in that curious state betwixt dreaming and consciousness, finally placed where I had seen the intruder's face before. I was on the point of sharing the information when the dogs began to prick up their ears.

"Someone is coming," I said.

Harry groaned. "I already had to hide behind a packing case when the boy brought breakfast down."

"George is a good lad with too much work to poke about. The Beauclerk children have far worse manners," I said, whisking aside the breakfast dishes. "There is no time to climb up to the snuggery. Into the sarcophagus," I ordered.

Muttering all the while, Harry climbed in and Stoker had just settled the lid into place when there was a scratch at the door and it opened. "Hallo," called a familiar voice.

"Sir Hugo," I said faintly. "Whatever brings you to the Belvedere?" He entered, hat in hand, and smelling of fresh aftershave.

"I am on my way to Scotland Yard and thought I would stop in," he said.

"Marylebone is not on the way from your house to Scotland Yard," Stoker pointed out.

"I was not at my house," Sir Hugo returned. "I was in St. John's Wood clearing up a matter for the Home Secretary, but you did not hear that from me," he added. I flicked a glance at Stoker. St. John's Wood was where the great and good stashed their ladies of light virtue. Whatever the Home Secretary had been getting up to in that particular suburb, it was a rather good wager that Mrs. Home Secretary did not know about it.

Sir Hugo settled himself into Stoker's desk chair—the only other option being the camel saddle—and crossed one long leg over the other. His expression was expansive. He was clearly pleased with the results of his own night's work.

"I am sorry to say there has been a development," I began.

He waved a hand. "The diamond—the elusive and legendary Eye of the Dawn. Yes, I know. Effie wrote. That is how I knew you'd come back. She mentioned that a pair of natural historians had been to stay—she quite enjoyed meeting you, you know. But then this business of the jewel going missing set the cat amongst the pigeons and that was the end of your visit."

"Did she tell you anything else?" I asked. I was conscious of Stoker, continuing to work quietly on his thylacine as Sir Hugo and I talked.

Sir Hugo shrugged. "That my instincts were correct. This 'Jonathan' was an impostor and helped himself to Lady Hathaway's diamond before fleeing. Naturally, we are making inquiries. We know he crossed the moor and boarded the train to London at Batleigh, but the trail has gone cold at that point."

I could almost hear the sigh of relief from inside the sarcophagus.

"But you will continue to pursue the thief?" I pressed.

"Of course," Sir Hugo said, his brows raising in obvious astonishment. "The fellow has stolen a diamond worth almost as much as the Koh-i-Noor!"

"I imagine that sort of crime would carry a heavy penalty," I mused.

"Oh, to be certain, but of course, we do not hang people for it these days, more's the pity." A stifled noise came from the direction of the sarcophagus.

"What's that?" Sir Hugo asked, looking around.

"My apologies," Stoker called. "I sneezed."

"Ah, gesundheit," Sir Hugo said. He sighed. "To complicate matters, Lady Hathaway is being most obstructive. She refuses to cooperate, claiming she gave the stone to the fellow, although the rest of them maintain it was stolen."

"But without her cooperation, you cannot prosecute him," Stoker said from behind his thylacine. "She is, after all, the owner."

"Or is she?" I pondered aloud.

Sir Hugo blinked. "Whatever do you mean?"

"Only that Lady Hathaway was oblique as to how her husband came to be in possession of the parure. She said he acquired it during the confusion of the Sepoy Mutiny."

"Yes?" he prompted.

"'Acquired' is not the same thing as purchased," I reminded him. "Things were chaotic during the mutiny, and many Englishmen proved they were not above a little light looting. If Sir Geoffrey stole the jewels—"

"Stole!" Sir Hugo looked thunderous. "Now see here, Geoffrey Hathaway was a fine man, stalwart and loyal to queen and country."

"Yes," I said patiently. "*His* queen. *His* country. Not India. He wouldn't have been the first Englishman to help himself to something that didn't belong to him."

"Yes, well," Sir Hugo said, grumbling as he sat back in his chair. "I hope you are not implying that it is within one's rights to steal something from a person who has in turn stolen it. If so, you are sailing in muddy waters, Miss Speedwell. A veritable ethical swamp, if you will."

I bared my teeth in an attempt at a smile. "I was just thinking aloud."

"Well, perhaps you ought not to think if it leads you to such places," he said with a touch of his old pomposity. "In any event, I wanted to thank you for bestirring yourself to help in this private matter. Naturally, your efforts will not be reflected in the formal records of Special Branch as this was not an official assignment, but you have my personal gratitude, and you may rely upon me to remember it."

He rose to leave and I stopped him. "What of Euphemia?" I asked.

His expression was blank. "What of her?"

I stifled my exasperation. "When you first spoke of her, you remarked upon her dissatisfaction. I cannot see that it will be in any way improved in the future, governed as she is by her brother and his wife. She ought to be educated for her vocation of astronomy."

Sir Hugo shrugged. "I am afraid it is out of my hands. Charles wishes her to remain at home, and it would be inappropriate of me to interfere."

I faced him, my hands curling into fists at my sides. "She is your goddaughter. You have an obligation to her!"

His brows rose nearly to his hairline. "To her spiritual development, and she is a confirmed member of the Church of England. Beyond that, it would be the grossest intrusion upon Charles' authority within his own family for me to speak upon this matter."

"She is unhappy with her place," I began.

"She is a woman," Sir Hugo said simply. "And she has no money. It is up to her brother to look after her, and it is her lot to make herself happy within that."

"You cannot seriously believe that she deserves less happiness than anyone else simply because she is a *woman*," I said, my temper rising.

"My dear Miss Speedwell, I am merely pointing out that all of us must be useful if we cannot be independent. Now, I have every intention of settling a small annuity on Effie upon the occasion of my death. One hopes that by the time of that event, which I trust will be some years in the future," he said with a touch of acerbity, "she will have acquired the necessary discipline and self-control to conduct herself appropriately and manage her independence. Until then, it will be instructive for her to learn to master her wilder impulses."

"You speak of her as though she wanted to run away and join the circus," I retorted. "Sir Hugo, I can assure you, Effie does not want to tame tigers. She wants only to work, to establish herself as a scientist in her own right after a suitable course of study."

"And as I have said, it is not my place to interfere in her family's arrangements for her," he said dryly. "We must, after all, accept that they know best."

"Must we? I should like to point out that a few days ago you seemed concerned about her tendency towards melancholy. You dance to a different tune today and I am left to wonder why."

He flapped an impatient hand. "I have had a letter from Charles. He discovered that Effie has been writing to me and wanted to give me his personal assurances that she is improving."

"His assurances! Charles Hathaway is more concerned with his sheep than his sister, I can promise you. He is the very last person to understand a personality like Effie's."

Sir Hugo stroked his moustaches, his expression indulgent. "And you think that after the acquaintance of what was it? A day? Two at most? That you are better placed than her own brother to comprehend Effie?"

"Her own dog is better placed," I retorted. "And yes, it wanted only a very short acquaintance to make it perfectly apparent that she is a highly strung and thoroughly frustrated young woman who needs her talents to be appreciated and directed."

"And they will be," he countered smoothly. "Mary Hathaway will supervise her and ensure she is not idle. Charles thinks they have been too indulgent with her, allowing her to spend her days in fanciful pursuits and that this has led to her melancholia."

"It is not melancholia, it is grief! She has lost the only person in the world who seemed to understand her—her grandfather. And no one else bestirs themselves to know her. It is a wonder she has not drowned herself in a bog."

"She would not dare," Sir Hugo countered roundly. "The Hathaways are an eccentric family, but they have never been given to hysteria."

"She is not hysterical," I said through gritted teeth. "She is unhappy because she is treated like a child or a drudge when she wants only a little kindness and respect. She needs intelligent conversation like a plant needs the sun, and she will not find it in that house."

Sir Hugo threw up his hands. "I find we are at an impasse, Miss Speedwell. I can only thank you for your time and say that I hope you did not find the task too arduous." He rose and shot his cuffs. "Good day to you. Stoker," he called with a nod. He let himself out and Stoker went to liberate Harry from his sarcophagus. Harry emerged with a wheeze.

"Is it dusty inside?" Stoker inquired.

"No, no," Harry said, his expression bland. "I quite like the dirt. It adds a certain piquant charm. In fact, I am growing rather fond of the place. I am thinking of moving in permanently. Perhaps putting up a few shelves and installing a stove."

"Ass," I said distinctly. I turned to my correspondence and began to open envelopes with a silver fruit knife, slicing with a certain satisfying savagery.

"Whatever did those letters do to deserve such brutality?" Harry asked, plucking an apple from Stoker's desk. He polished it upon his lapel and took a healthy bite.

"Better the letters than your hide," I warned. "Or yours," I added with a glare at Stoker. "You were suspiciously quiet during Sir Hugo's visit. You might have spoke in favor of Euphemia Hathaway's liberation."

"To what end?" he inquired with a shrug. "Sir Hugo will do as he pleases. He is not to be shifted from his position."

"I do not remember his being so pompous," I said.

"He received a fair bollocking from the newspapers and Parliament over the Ripper affair," Stoker reminded me. "I think it has disarranged his confidence. He was comfortable taking risks, entertaining new ideas. But his failure to catch the Ripper has left him vulnerable.

J. J. Butterworth alone has written five pieces calling for his resignation over the past few months," he added, invoking the name of our sometime adversary, sometime friend. J. J. was an intrepid and engaging reporter, but she could also be the very devil if she were hot upon the heels of a story. She was the most ambitious creature I had ever met, and I was not surprised she had taken steady aim at the head of Special Branch.

Harry had been listening raptly as he ate his apple, his head swiveling from Stoker to me and back again. He swallowed, then looked at us brightly. "I say, does anyone want to explain why you are such close chums with the head of Special Branch? That was Sir Hugo Montgomerie, was it not?"

"It was, and no, we do not," I replied.

"Then perhaps we could discuss my diamond—its current whereabouts and when I can have it back," he suggested.

"It is not yours, and no, you may not," Stoker said calmly.

"You were the one who said we would have a council of war," Harry protested.

"I have changed my mind."

"That is hardly sporting," Harry began.

I leapt to my feet. "Newspapers!" I exclaimed. I scrabbled around my desk for the newspaper I had been reading the day we returned to London.

"Veronica, what are you on about?" Harry inquired.

"I have just remembered where I saw the face of our intruder," I said, thumbing hastily through the pages with ink-stained fingers until I found it. "Here! 'The Maharani of Viratanagar has arrived in London to participate in informal discussions with members of Parliament. It is rumored the discussions will touch upon the growing support for Indian independence,'" I read aloud. "'Photographed with her grandson and heir, Bhairav.'"

I pointed to the photograph. In the center was the maharani, a statuesque woman of some years. She had a long, elegant nose, giving her a distinctive profile, and a head of thick, dark hair. She was dressed in traditional Indian fashion, an elaborate arrangement of draperies and veils heavily embroidered with jewels. More gems were in evidence on her arms and bosom, hanging from her ears and encircling her fingers. She was a woman accustomed to commanding attention and authority, and her expression was one of cool detachment. Next to her stood a slender young man dressed in narrow trousers with a long, fitted coat that buttoned quite up to the throat. He had her nose as well as her sharp, assessing eyes, and was even more youthful in his photograph than he had been in person.

"They are staying at the Sudbury Hotel," I said. "We must lose no time." I reached for my hat as Stoker quirked up a brow.

"The word 'maharani' means high queen. Do I understand that you mean to accuse the grandson of a high queen of being a common burglar?"

"I do not mean to accuse anyone," I replied. "That would be grossly irresponsible."

"Then what is your plan exactly?" Harry asked.

"The first rule of any scientific endeavor is observation," I said, rummaging in the box of operatic costumes for a piece of veiling. I pinned it over my hat, obscuring my features. I did not think our young miscreant had got a very good look at my face, but it would not do to let him know we were onto him. "We will go to the Sudbury and simply observe to confirm it is in fact the maharani's grandson."

"We ought to speak with Julien," Stoker put in. "He is always a fount of information."

I smiled at the mention of the hotel's head pâtissier. "You mean gossip, but yes. He might well know something useful. But you cannot go like that. You are filthy with at least seven identifiable stains upon your shirt."

Stoker grumbled but went off to change as I turned to Harry. "You are no tidier than Stoker. You have traces of mummy clinging to your clothes and you are still in evening dress."

He pulled a face. "I have no other clothes, remember?"

I sighed, recalling his woeful tale of fleeing the Hall with the clothes upon his back and a few measly shilling notes in his notecase. I went to my desk and unlocked the drawer which held my own purse, fishing out a handful of notes.

"Take this. You cannot walk around London like that unless you mean to attract exactly the wrong sort of attention. Outfit yourself and meet us at the Sudbury."

His fingers closed around the notes slowly, almost reluctantly, I fancied. He shoved them into his pocket, then scribbled a few lines on a piece of paper and signed it with a flourish.

"What is this?" I asked.

"An IOU," he informed me. I felt a mocking response rise to my lips, but something in his gaze stilled my tongue. He seemed, to my astonishment, embarrassed at being made a loan, and I realized his intention to repay me was serious.

"How long do you require to make yourself presentable?" I asked politely.

He shrugged. "Two hours? I will stop in and get a proper shave as well," he added, rubbing a hand over his bewhiskered chin. "I feel an absolute ape."

"The hotel has an exceptional barber," I advised. "They even manage to get Stoker's chin smooth and that is an Herculean task. Go there after you have found suitable attire and let them finish you off."

"An excellent notion," he said. We were like characters in a farce, I realized, saying very polite things to one another and studiously avoiding anything of substance.

As if guessing my thoughts, he reached out a sudden hand, stopping just short of touching my sleeve. "Veronica, I wanted to thank you—" Before he could finish, Stoker appeared, adjusting a fresh collar as he tugged on his jacket.

"Have I interrupted?" he asked with a bland, mirthless smile.

"Not in the slightest," I assured him. I reminded Harry to slip out of the grounds of the Belvedere undetected when he left, and we decided upon a time for our rendezvous. Stoker made no comment upon the arrangements until we were in Marylebone High Street, hailing a hansom.

"You realize we have left him alone with the diamond," he remarked in a bland voice.

"He has two hours in which he must find a new suit of clothes, get to the Sudbury, and have himself barbered. Hardly time for him to make a proper search. Besides, I am entirely certain you have hid the thing well enough he would not find it in a fortnight," I answered.

"Oh, I rather hope he does," Stoker said. A tiny smile played over his lips, but he said no more and I dared not ask.

"My friends!" Julien exclaimed, coming to shake hands with Stoker. He eyed my veil and lifted it to kiss me on either cheek. "One cannot hide such beauty, my dear Veronica," he murmured into my ear.

I grinned. Julien's flirtations were as innocent as they were obvious. He would happily kiss hands and cheeks and drop compliments like bonbons, but he was surprisingly monogamous when his heart was engaged. He had recently become enthralled with a widow of comfortable means, and his erotic attentions were reserved solely for her.

He brandished his pastry bag. "I am very nearly finished here, but the gâteau St. Honoré waits for no one," he said gravely as he applied a series of piped embellishments of stiffly whipped cream around the edge of a circle of puff pastry. *Pâte à choux* had been piped atop this and the entire thing was topped with profiteroles, held in place with sticky golden strands of sugar transformed by the alchemy of heat and time into amber caramel.

"Beautiful," Stoker breathed.

"My friend, you cannot see the most luscious part. The inside is filled with *crème chiboust*," he teased as Stoker made a whimpering sound in his throat.

Julien handed him a bowl of leftover *crème chiboust* and a spoon. "Come," he beckoned. "We will go where we may be private."

"How do you know that is necessary?" I asked.

He gave me a knowing look. "With the two of you, it is always necessary."

Julien issued a series of rapid instructions to his crew and then shepherded us into his private room, a sort of study where he kept his cookery notebooks, bottles of exquisitely expensive syrups he concocted himself, and assorted mementos from his travels. A pretty religious statue had been added to the collection, a churchman clutching a baker's peel.

"You have a new friend," I observed.

Julien gave the saint a fond look. "Saint Honoré, the patron of pastry chefs. You will note his mitre? He was bishop of Amiens in his day, and not to be confused with the patron of the *boulanger*, Saint Lazare. His feast day is in a few weeks, and I am making them always to practice his special cake," he added, nodding towards the pastry kitchen, where his assistants were still struggling to replicate the intricate gâteau St. Honoré.

He sat back in his chair, folding his hands expansively over his taut middle. For a pastry chef, Julien had a remarkably slender physique, fit and wiry in spite of the masses of sugar he consumed. He was dressed in a chef's coat of pristine white, but he never wore a toque, preferring instead a soft cap, usually of crimson velvet. Today's effort was new, still velvet, but a striking shade of cyclamen.

"A gift from your lady friend?" I guessed.

He smiled, broadly enough to show his dimples. "She makes me many gifts, *ma petite chou*."

"So you have entirely given up on the idea of wooing J. J. Butterworth?" I inquired. "It was only January when your head was quite turned by her charms."

He shrugged. "Dough cannot rise in the cold," he said cryptically. "But you did not come to discuss my love life. How are you, my friends?"

"In need of information," Stoker said. But, having scraped the bowl of *crème chiboust* clean, he allowed his gaze to drift to a small plate of enticing tiny glazed fruit tarts that shimmered like jewels.

Julien, attentive as always, offered the plate to me first, then thrust it into Stoker's hands. "You must try them. I am not unhappy," he said, high praise from such an exacting practitioner of the pastry arts.

My little tart had been filled with a bit of crème anglaise and then heaped with candied apricots and glazed, the whole affair topped with brandied sugar spun into a miniature bird's nest.

I swallowed the last delectable crumb and sucked the sugar from my fingers. "You are truly a master," I said with a happy sigh.

Julien waved aside the praise, but his pleasure was obvious. "Now, if I were to guess, you have come either to inquire about the opera singer who is currently in residence with her husband and her lover— or the maharani."

"Got it in one," Stoker told him through a mouthful of tart.

"Which?" Julien asked.

"The maharani," I said promptly. Under other circumstances, I would have been thoroughly entertained by a little salacious operatic gossip, but a lady and two men with claims upon her attentions struck a bit too near the bone for my comfort.

Julien tipped his head back and steepled his fingers. "A very elegant lady, the maharani. She favors silks in very strong colors which suit her. Not everyone can wear orange," he advised me. "With your complexion you should not attempt it."

"I never would," I assured him.

He went on. "But on her it is dramatic as a rising sun, a most enchanting effect. And her figure is very good. She is not so young, you understand, but with such excellent breasts—"

"Yes, thank you," Stoker said, flushing a delicate shade of rose.

"Do you not wish to hear about her breasts?" Julien asked. "My friend, they are delectable. Not too large, just beautifully formed." Once Julien began enumerating a woman's charms, he could go on for hours.

"Something besides her breasts," I suggested.

He shrugged. "They are lovely, but not as matchless as her eyes. Englishmen," he said with a moue of displeasure, "do not always appreciate the subtleties of difference in the shades of brown. They see skin and hair and eyes which are dark and think, 'Eh, this is all the same.' But no! God has wrought each with a poet's hand, giving tones and shades. One must look closely in order to see, do you understand? And no one sees as well as Julien d'Orlande," he added, puffing out his chest. "The maharani has eyes like polished gems, full of light and intelligence. She is accustomed to command. She does not drop her eyes modestly like an Englishwoman, but she lifts her chin and dares one to look away. I find her enchanting, although she does not eat enough," he added with a frown. "It is often the way with those raised in that part of Asia. They have not the habit of sugar, so their taste for sweets is fruit, always fruit! I tempt her with my delicacies and always she sends the maid to say, 'My mistress will have a mango.' A mango!" He rolled his eyes in despair. "Where is a mango to be found in England in April, I ask you?"

"So how do you satisfy the lady's appetites?" I asked demurely.

He grinned at the double entendre. "You converse like a Frenchwoman. I cannot give her the mango. Such a thing does not exist here in this season. So one day, in despair, I created one from marzipan. I took the almond paste and sculpted and painted and tinted until it was exquisite, impossible to tell from the real thing. I sent it up to her and she sent it back and asked it be given to the poor for their pleasure. But she dispatched her grandson to bring me her compliments."

"Her grandson?" I asked, widening my eyes.

"A nice enough boy—a man, I should say. Perhaps twenty or a little more. He is shy, but the sort of shyness which means he sees much. His grandmother is a strong personality, you understand. He has not many opportunities to put himself forwards. But it is easy to see that he adores her and she him. He is learning her ways."

"What sort of ways?" Stoker inquired.

"The way of the leader," Julien replied succinctly. "The maharani is a most alluring woman, but she is not languid. She does not lie about and order her servants to attend her and think of nothing but her clothes. She entertains often, many men of politics and business. For her, India should be free. She speaks openly of such things. It was the mission of her husband, you understand. But he was killed, many, many years ago."

"Was it, perchance, thirty years ago?" Stoker asked.

"Something like that," Julien said. "I do not know the details, only that she has been a widow for a very long time, and she carries on his work, speaking out for the independence of India."

"Like Lakshmibai," Stoker said.

Julien tipped his head. "Who is this?"

"Lakshmibai was the Rani of Jansi, a place in northern India. During the rebellion in 'fifty-seven, she led her own troops into battle. She fought and died for the independence of her people. Britons think of her as a dangerous rebel, but to Indians who want to be free of our empire, she is quite the heroine. They say she is buried under a tamarind tree and that her spirit inspires those who would cast off their oppressors."

"A most interesting woman," Julien observed.

"Indeed, and any woman who follows in her footsteps is bound to make a stir," Stoker said.

"All the travel to whip up support, the quiet efforts to arm those who embrace resistance—I imagine it must all be terribly expensive," I mused.

Stoker nodded. "Certainly. Anyone truly committed to the cause cannot spend their days farming or breeding livestock or doing any other work to make money. They must be supported. And, as you say, weapons are costly."

"The maharani is staying at an expensive hotel," I went on. "I am curious about the state of her finances. Many of the Indian princes are fabulously wealthy." I was thinking particularly of the Nizam of Hyderabad and his extravagant lifestyle. It was said an entire wing of his palace was devoted to his clothes, for he never wore the same ensemble twice. Other princes, however, lived in much quieter style, scarcely more affluent than the average English squire. I wondered where the Maharani of Viratanagar fit into this picture.

Julien brightened. "But I can tell you that," he said with some pride. "Her clothes and jewels are extraordinary, but she does not have many. She dresses like the queen she is, yet I have seen her already in the same ensemble though she has been here only one week. She eats simply, rice and vegetables, and her jewels are those handed down through the family. When one of the rajas from Uttar Pradesh comes, he takes the whole of the upper two floors, every suite for his family and his court officials. They order everything on the menu, and his wife and daughters spend every day shopping. The parcels that are delivered—they come every minute of every hour, dresses, boots, ribbons, furniture. Not the maharani. She does not shop. When she entertains, it is over tea, made with spices over a brazier in her own rooms. She has serious conversations with serious men."

"She might be short of money," I ventured.

Stoker shrugged. "Or she is simply frugal and bent upon her purpose in coming here."

"Whatever that may be," I finished. I rose and pulled on my gloves. "Thank you for your time, Julien. It has been pleasurably instructive, as ever."

He kissed me again on both cheeks and pressed a wrapped packet of marzipan mice into Stoker's hands for the journey home. Our business finished earlier than we expected, we left a note for Harry with a porter, informing him that we were returning to the Belvedere and telling him to meet us there. I believed what I had told Stoker regarding the unlikelihood of Harry discovering the Eye of the Dawn in our absence, but I saw no point in tempting fate. The sooner we were back in the Belvedere, the sooner we removed any temptation from Harry.

We gave the note to the porter and emerged onto the street. Stoker fished the packet of marzipan mice out of his pocket and tore into it with gusto.

"Really, you cannot wait until we are in the cab?" I began, lifting my arm. Before he could respond, the driver of a vehicle waiting at the curb lifted his whip to acknowledge me. I opened the door just as I noticed the unusual height of the driver, possibly six and a half feet, I would have guessed, with bright blond hair under a greasy cap that had been jammed low on his head. I paused, one foot on the step, my hand on the open door as I stared into the dimness of a compartment whose windows had been entirely covered with heavy black oilcloth.

"Miss Speedwell," said a low voice. "Get in." I had not seen the figure, shrouded in black and tucked into the shadows of the far corner of the conveyance, but I could just make out the glint of a small revolver aimed at my head.

The hand tightened around the gun as I hesitated. "If you do not, I will shoot your companion, and I daresay I will not miss at this distance," the voice went on.

I heaved myself into the carriage, taking the seat opposite.

"What the devil—" Stoker began. He broke off mid-sentence as soon as he caught sight of the revolver.

"Yes," I said with a sigh of annoyance. "We are being abducted. Again."

CHAPTER

24

As soon as Stoker climbed inside, the driver reached down and slammed the door shut, sliding home a bolt from the outside. He sprang the horse and we jolted into traffic. Stoker was next to me, his thigh pressed to mine, for the conveyance was not large. Across from us sat our abductor, a woman dressed in sober black, a heavy veil concealing her features.

"Mrs. MacGregor, I presume," I said politely.

She threw back the veil with her free hand and she was smiling. "So Harry has talked about me, has he? He always was indiscreet."

"Quite," I agreed.

"If you know my name, you presumably know what I want," she went on.

Her voice was low and rich, the sort of voice which would have suited the stage or a courtesan's boudoir. It was a voice which could coax people into doing things. Her face was almost unremarkable except for an arresting pair of eyes, dark and watchful, and I realized then what Julien meant. Where Effie Hathaway's brown eyes had been pellucid as a country stream, Isabel de Armas MacGregor's eyes were bright and fathomless, and she used them to wonderful effect. A man could drown in such eyes, I reflected, and possibly quite a few women.

She was aware of my scrutiny and she smiled at it, revealing small, white teeth with sharp little canines. I was glad of those teeth. They stopped her from looking too sweet. Her cheekbones were high and broad, her mouth wide and richly colored. In all, she was a chameleon. With a sober gown and the properly demure expression, she would be as meek as a parson's mouse. But arrayed in a scarlet satin gown of fashionable cut with painted lips, she would have been any man's most depraved fantasy.

"Do I look the part?" she asked, batting lashes at me that I fancied had been enhanced with a bit of soot applied with a burnt match. It was a trick I had myself employed from time to time.

"I should think you could look whatever part you chose," I told her honestly.

She preened a little. "How very kind of you. I do so appreciate when these situations are conducted politely."

I glanced pointedly at the gun in her hand and she gave a little laugh.

"I believe you think my weapon impertinent, Miss Speedwell, but I assure you, it could have been much, much worse." There was an unholy gleam in her eye that told me she was speaking the truth. She turned to Stoker, canting her head.

"You are an unexpected delight," she said slowly, letting her gaze linger on a few of the choicest parts of his anatomy. He blushed again and she smiled widely. "How utterly adorable. It would be the gravest pity to shoot you, my dear," she said, dropping her voice even lower as she looked at him from under her lashes. "Mind you don't force me to."

He said nothing and she laughed again.

"It is good to find another woman who enjoys her work," I remarked, drawing her attention away from Stoker.

"Indeed," she said, looking as frisky as an April lamb. "I think we are going to be very great friends indeed."

"Perhaps then, as a friend, you might see your way clear to telling us where we are going?" I suggested.

The smile turned lightly mocking. "You presume too quickly upon our friendship, Miss Speedwell. All in good time. Now, if you would be so good as to toss your reticule onto the seat next to me. I know exactly what a lady can get up to with a hairpin."

Hairpin, stiletto, clasp knife. Unfortunately, I had precisely none of these upon my person. I had dressed in a fashion suitable for the Sudbury, that is to say, dully respectable in a high-necked ensemble of violet velvet with tidy little boots of turquoise leather, chosen for the luscious poppy embroidery rather than function. I had no doubt the slender Louis heels would snap if I tried to kick her in the stomach, and there was no way to predict what might happen to a loaded revolver in the confines of the carriage.

So, I did as instructed, pitching my reticule onto the seat next to her. She smiled. "How very cooperative of you, my dear. Now, let us settle in and be comfortable. We have a bit of a journey ahead of us."

The drive was of considerable duration—longer, I suspected, because we were being taken by a circuitous route to confuse us should we try to determine our whereabouts. We performed four left turns in a row, I noted, and then two complete turnabouts. Following this was a long pull uphill which I detected by noticing the slight inclination of my torso to pitch forwards as I was sitting facing our captor. I had hoped she might let her attention wander, providing an opportunity to overpower her, but she was alert as a fox at all times. In fact, something in the set of her chin caused me to suspect she would welcome such an attempt, and I was determined not to oblige her.

Stoker and I had been in far worse situations, I reminded myself, and we had always emerged—if not unscathed—then at least alive. There was no reason we should not do so again, and as I considered the vast amount of unanswered correspondence heaped on my desk, I could not bring myself to entirely regret the diversion.

At last, the brisk clip-clop of the horses' hooves slowed and stopped. The carriage rocked heavily as the driver alighted, booted feet landing hard upon what sounded like loose chippings. Immediately, the door was wrenched open, the wan sunlight dazzling after the gloom of the darkened carriage. A gloved hand beckoned and our hostess gestured with her gun that we were to obey. Stoker climbed out first, and I noticed the driver was careful to keep a body's length between them should Stoker be inclined to engage in any sort of physical assault. I followed, and Mrs. MacGregor brought up the rear. We were in the drive of a large and unlovely private house. It had been built in the worst excesses of the Neo-Gothic movement, like a miniature Strawberry Hill, with gardens to match. Everything was overgrown and tangled and untended. Weeds sprouted through the gravel at our feet, and long iron red streaks marred the whitewash of the villa's walls. A few gargoyles leered from above the portico, where a pair of potted palms sat, mournfully shedding leaves.

"Why is it always gargoyles?" I murmured.

Mrs. MacGregor ignored me. She gestured towards her cohort. "This is Göran. He will attend you, and he has a dreadful temper, so mind you don't provoke him. He will show you the way to your quarters and I will follow with this," she said, brandishing the gun, "just to make certain everyone is cooperative."

We looked at Göran, who gave us a broad grin as he fondled his clasp knife, polishing it with an exaggerated gesture on his lapel. When he had made his point, he pocketed the blade and unlocked the front door whilst we stood a little way behind. I listened for any sign of neighbors, but there was nothing to be heard except country sounds—birds twittering in the bushes and the new green leaves of the trees rustling in the wind. Clouds were building, scudding across the sun and throwing the house deeply into shadow as Göran threw open the door.

The house was exactly as I feared—a veritable architectural wedding cake with every possible extravagance and embellishment worked in plaster. With care and good furnishing, it might have been acceptable, for the proportions of the rooms were suitable for a large family home. But the roof must have been damaged, for every ceiling was bubbled and cracked, the plaster crumbling away. The floors were stained with watermarks that ruined the elaborate parquet, and I distinctly heard mice scrabbling about in the walls.

"What a lovely home you have," I said to Mrs. MacGregor, baring my teeth in a smile.

She returned the gesture. "Rented for a song from an owner who has almost forgot the place exists. The nearest neighbor is six miles, so there is no one to hear you," she added with an unmistakable note of menace, all the more disconcerting for being delivered with a smile.

I decided against goading her further, and we followed the taciturn Swede down a corridor and through a door, down a flight of stone stairs and through another door. Through it was a small chamber, cut into the earth and built of stone. The seams in the stone floor were packed with black dust, and I realized we were standing in the former coal store. A trapdoor high in the wall above us showed where the stuff had once been delivered, but I could see the shiny new hinges even at a distance. No doubt the hasp and lock on the other side were new as well, and the inside of the coal store had been fitted out as a sort of jail. A pair of narrow mattresses festooned with dubious-looking stains had been thrown down, and a chamber pot stood expectantly in the corner. In the center of the room, a cast-iron column was bolted to the floor, running the height of the room and through the ceiling some fifteen feet above. Around it were lengths of bright new chain, heavy stuff, with shackles to match. While Mrs. MacGregor watched from the doorway, Göran secured the shackles around our arms and legs. Wound as the chains were about the column, we were free to shuffle about the room but could not make it as far as the door. A single lantern had been lit and hung on a peg next to the door, well out of reach.

"We will bring food in a while," Mrs. MacGregor said brightly. "I do hope you will be comfortable." With that she slammed the door, and I heard the familiar, desolate sound of a key turning in the lock.

"Well, here we are again," I said calmly. "This is usually the point at which you become hysterical."

Stoker stared at me. "I have never become hysterical. I have, upon every occasion, reacted with perfect candor and appropriateness to the situation at hand."

"You shout a great deal," I reminded him.

"Because I am usually in pain," he retorted. "I have been chained, stabbed, shot, beaten, nearly drowned, and subjected to every possible insult regarding my upbringing, breeding, conduct, appearance, and intelligence. I think that is quite enough to send any man into a froth of emotion."

"See, you admit. You are prey to your emotions. And you, a man of science," I added, tutting audibly.

My remarks, as the clever reader will no doubt have already deduced, were designed to distract Stoker from the predicament at hand. The fact that we had been abducted was not in itself surprising or particularly alarming. That sort of thing had been occurring with such regularity, I had almost come to expect it. But during the course of our investigations the previous October, Stoker had been the recipient of some particularly nasty attentions on the part of our abductors. Ribs had been broken, a cheekbone fractured, a lung punctured, along with various and sundry abrasions and contusions, any one of which might have felled a lesser man. He had not even begun to recover from the depredations when he had been shot, a wholly unnerving experience on my end and one I did not wish to repeat. (Stoker will protest that his was the more harrowing ordeal, but as he was unconscious for most of it whilst I was left to worry, I think I may claim the greater share of distress.)

Malefactors, I had observed, were seldom as unchivalrous as one would expect. Despite often being deprived of my liberty, I had yet to be boiled in oil, stretched upon a rack, poked with hot pins, or subjected to whatever tortures were in fashion at the time. I was usually left to worry through the long, lonely hours of darkness when Stoker was off being tormented, and the experiences had left me with nerves flayed to ribbons. I did not anticipate this new ordeal with any great fortitude, I must admit. The Swede was a tall and muscular fellow with a neck like that of a slightly malnourished ox, and I did not like the gleam in his eye when he looked at Stoker. He would take his time with it, I feared, and perhaps even subject Stoker to a few new experiences. He looked entirely too fond of his knife, I decided, and whilst I cherished each and every scar upon Stoker's excellent physique, there was no great need to add more.

There was no way to anticipate precisely when the tortures would commence, but the time would pass more quickly in spirited conversation, thus the prick to Stoker's temper. I thought to distract him, and I did a masterful job. He spent a good while giving vent to his various resentments, cataloging his numerous umbrages until his voice was almost hoarse, and he suddenly broke off in mid-rant.

"You are doing this on purpose," he accused.

"Of course I am," I returned calmly. "There is no possibility of escape at present, and we needed to pass the time."

"How do you know there is no possibility of escape?" he demanded.

"We have been in similar peril upon enough occasions that I know how to evaluate a makeshift prison when I see one," I said. "To begin, the floor and walls are stone, solid and immovable. There is no window to permit egress, and the door is six inches of good English oak, locked from the outside. That leaves the coal doors," I said, pointing upwards, "which are no doubt padlocked from the outside even if we could reach them, but there are no handy bits of furniture or ladders, and the stone walls are too smooth to permit even the tiniest fingerhold in order to climb them."

He grunted his agreement. "I don't suppose you have a weapon stuck somewhere on your person?"

I glowered a little. "No."

His brows steepled upwards. "Not even a corset stay you've sharpened into a stiletto?"

"I am, for your information, wearing a new corset and I have not had the opportunity to alter it to my satisfaction," I replied in considerable annoyance. It was a new fashion, the ribbon corset, and had been the product of a Parisian corset maker's atelier. I had swooned at the delicate latticework of the satin ribbons, and I had taken immense pleasure in the greater liberty of movement it permitted.

His eyes took on a significant brightness. "Is it the rose-colored one from Paris?"

"It is," I replied. He stared off in the middle distance for some time, the rose corset having proved a particular favorite of his—in fact, on the occasion of its first appearance, he had not removed it at all, preferring to tender his attentions while it and the matching rose garters remained in place—until I snapped my fingers to get his attention.

He came to with a start, but a smile of fond reminiscence still played about his lips. "And you are quite certain you have nothing upon your person which you can use against our captors?"

"I do hate to dash your hopes, but I am afraid I am dressed for calling at the Sudbury, not my working costume," I said, plucking at the heavy violet velvet of my day dress. "I have no knives, no pins, not even a handy bit of garrote wire."

"Garrote wire?" he asked in a choked voice.

"I purchased it during our trip to the Alpenwald," I explained. "I was studying a cheese wire one day, and it occurred to me what a nice garrote it would make with those lovely little wooden handles. And so easy to tuck into a pastille tin! Unfortunately, it is in my reticule," I added darkly. "Which that woman has taken."

Stoker looked distinctly unnerved. "Do you really mean to strangle someone with a cheese wire?"

"No one ever thinks it will be necessary until it is," I replied calmly.

"Touché. But as to your assessment of our predicament, you are entirely correct. And they have left us here a few hours, enough time to come to terms with our situation and become a little uncomfortable. Soon, they will come, either to bring food or to take me out and begin their interrogation."

"To which I say, give them what they want," I told him.

"I beg your pardon?"

"Give them the Eye of the Dawn. You know where it is hid. I do not. Therefore, it is up to you to tell them the truth. The diamond is what they want. And possibly Harry. Give them both and let us go and have a nice dinner."

His laugh was incredulous. "Veronica, do you really expect them just to let us go after that? We have seen their faces. We can identify them. Hardened criminals do not let witnesses live."

"How do we know they are hardened?" I countered. "They engage in financial schemes and plots. They may be most reluctant to actually shed blood. Besides, I am quite certain they are anticipating trouble from us. If we are amenable and cooperative, it might prove profitable for all of us."

"And the diamond? Are we simply to hand over a jewel of immense wealth that does not belong to us?"

"I would give them half the earth if it stopped them harming a hair of your head," I said fiercely.

He wrapped his arms about me, clumsily because of the chains, which clinked and clanked. It was a noisy but ever so effective embrace. "I have no intention of giving them the diamond. It belongs to the maharani," he said in a tone that brooked no argument. "And I will see justice is done."

Just then the door opened and Mrs. MacGregor appeared. "What a charming picture of domesticity!" she said in an arch voice. She came near to us, an action she dared since her compatriot was standing directly behind her, arms folded, a revolver now stuck into his belt. It was a much larger weapon than hers, and something in the gleam in his eye told me I might have misjudged how willing the pair might be to engage in an act of violence. Mrs. MacGregor was holding a key, tapping it idly against one cheekbone as she circled us.

"Where to begin?" she mused, almost more to herself than us. She stepped up to Stoker and surveyed his face, running her gaze from the dark tumble of his overgrown locks to the silvered scar that ran from his eye to the sharp plane of his cheekbone. She put out a finger to trace it, making a sympathetic sound deep in her throat.

"Whoever did this to you ought to be horsewhipped," she said softly. "To mar such handsomeness is a crime."

"I killed the creature responsible," he replied.

The lovely mouth curved into a smile of pure delight. "I am glad to hear it." She cupped a hand under his chin and lifted it, turning his head this way and the other. She was looking at him the way Stoker looked at his thylacine, and I did not much care for it.

She ran her hand down his shoulder and the length of his muscled arm, pausing only when she reached the iron cuff at his wrist. Slowly, she slid the key into the hole of the cuff, pushing herself forward so that her torso was almost touching his as she turned it. With a decisive click, the cuff sprang open and she gave a breathy sigh. She repeated the process for the cuffs on his legs and rose with a slow smile.

"There. Is that not better, my lamb?" she asked. "Now, you will come with me for a little conversation. Göran will walk behind us, so you must not think to misbehave," she warned. Stoker gave an anguished glance back at me, but she poked him in the back with the key. "Walk on, my dear. She will be perfectly fine without you." Once he had passed through the door, she came back to where I stood. "When we are settled, Göran will bring you food. Try not to be too lonely," she said with a wolfish grin.

"Oh, do not worry about me," I said carelessly. "My only fear is for Stoker. You are precisely the type of woman to bore him to sobs."

I had judged, correctly, that she prided herself on her allure. The very suggestion that her charms might not appeal would prick her temper like nothing else. What I had not judged was exactly how she might give vent to that temper.

Still smiling, she reached out and slapped me, hard enough that tears sprang to my eyes. Later, when questioned about what happened next, I maintained that returning her blow was the only possible course of action. I laced my shackled hands together and landed them with a crack and set her back upon her heels. Her head snapped, shaking loose a few of her lush dark curls, and when she touched a finger to her lips, a bead of blood bedewed the tip.

If I had been free of my restraints, I daresay I would have bested her. I had been, after all, educated in the rudiments of physical combat by a genial Corsican bandit with whom I spent a most illuminating few weeks. He favored a sort of unhinged recklessness that I admired, although the Chinese monk with whom I shared a lifeboat after a modest shipwreck in the South China Sea counseled discipline and technique. When entering the fray, I have frequently forgot the monk's training—I suspect regular practice is necessary in order to quash the natural impulses to mayhem. I have, as I have related, instead generally launched myself into the fracas with some fair imitation of a Maori battle cry or an Irish war whoop. (Stoker deplores this vocal embellishment, but I maintain it is a highly effective means of unsettling one's opponent.) In any case, there was no opportunity for the sort of refinements I had developed in the course of my tuition. There was only rage, white-hot and rooted in the audacity of this woman to lay hands upon me after eyeing the man that I loved as if he were the prize bull at the market fair.

Of course, that was my mistake. Mrs. MacGregor had no horse in the race, as it were. She was simply toying with us, whilst my own emotions were very much engaged. That enabled her to step back and judge where her next blows might best be placed for the maximum impact with the least effort.

She doubled up her fist, the key gripped in her palm, and bent, pushing from the knees like any boxer of merit might have done. She hit me once, in the stomach, driving the wind from my lungs. I doubled over, twisting to avoid the next punch, but she had anticipated this and swung her fist in an expert arc, catching me neatly in the kidney. I dropped to my knees, whooping for air even as my hand grasped a bit of the slack chain.

"Oh, no, you don't," she said, stepping back smartly out of reach. "Sit down and mind your manners," she advised. "I do not think I will have Göran bring you any supper after all. You can eat when your gentle-man friend does. If I choose to leave you any teeth," she added, snapping hers at me for good measure.

She left then, the imprint of my hand standing out bright red against the pale olive of her complexion. It was a small satisfaction.

CHAPTER

25

The next few hours passed as slowly as any I have endured. I marked the passage of time by the candle as it burned away. The air in the room was close and warm, and I began to wonder idly about suffocation. But by peering at the coal doors, I could just make out slender gaps between the boards through which the setting sun drove the last rays of light, and if light could enter, so could air. It was long after these gilded bars had faded to blackness that the door opened once more. I had tortured myself with thoughts of what Mrs. MacGregor and the taciturn Göran might be doing to Stoker, particularly in view of my intemperate provocations. I had failed to consider the woman might revenge herself upon Stoker, but the fact that she knew him to be dear to me would make him a perfect target for her ire.

I do not know how long I remained alone, but it required considerable discipline to keep my thoughts productive. I slipped once or twice into elaborate fantasies involving the many and comprehensive ways I could employ to inflict pain upon Harry Spenlove should our paths ever cross again, and this greatly cheered me when the hours dragged on.

I was just imagining him tied to a roasting spit, being turned in front of a merry blaze, basted in oils, a plump and juicy apple in his mouth, when the door opened. I expected Stoker, battered and bloody, but instead, Mrs. MacGregor stood in the doorway, dressed in an entirely different ensemble to the traveling costume she had worn before. As it happened, I had been quite correct about crimson suiting her complexion. She fairly glowed from the richness of the scarlet velvet against her skin—a good deal of which was on display. The garment she wore was a sort of wrapper or dressing gown, edged with lavish plumes of feathers dyed to match the velvet. It was cut far lower than decency would permit any garment to be cut, and the skirt was likewise split to her hip. Her hair was unbound, waving in a dark cloud to her waist, and I could smell even at a distance her fragrance—something musky and almost feral.

"I thought I would come to see how you are," she said in a conversational tone. A small, knowing smile played about her lips. She looked entirely pleased with herself, sleek as a cream-fed cat, and when she moved into the room, she fairly undulated.

"I find the accommodations perfectly acceptable," I assured her. "Although if you mean to make a habit of this sort of thing, you really must find some rats. All of the best dungeons, however makeshift, have rats."

She laughed, a rich, mellow sound. "Do you know, Miss Speedwell, I think if we had met under different circumstances, I might have liked you. Or perhaps I would still want to break your fingers one by one, who can say?"

"The feeling, Mrs. MacGregor, is entirely mutual," I replied.

She came near, circling the column to which I was bound, running her hands up the chains. "I am glad to see you haven't been misbehaving," she said, looking over the iron cuffs at my wrists and ankles.

"Not even a scratch from a hairpin. No obvious attempts to escape. What a biddable and obedient little prisoner you are!"

Still grasping the chains, she leant near, putting her face close to mine. Her lips were rosy and plump, her eyes bright. "I must congratulate you, Miss Speedwell, on your choice of companions."

"Harry Spenlove is no companion of mine," I retorted. She smiled.

"I meant Mr. Templeton-Vane," she said. She leant closer still. "So few men have mouths that taste of honey." Her mouth hovered near mine. "Can you smell him upon my breath?"

I sighed. "No, but your perfume is giving me a dreadful headache. If you could step back just a little," I urged.

She blinked, then laughed. "Oh, you think I am jesting." She edged aside the ruffled neckline of her gown, baring her throat to reveal a broad, plummy bruise.

"Do you recognize his handiwork?"

"Yes," I told her truthfully. "He is an enthusiastic practitioner of the osculatory arts."

"Not at first, if I am honest," she told me in a confiding tone. "He put up such a lovely struggle against kissing me back. But one is always at an advantage with well-bred gentlemen. That early training to be polite to a lady is difficult for them to resist, especially when the natural impulses are roused. In my experience, a direct approach is the most effective. They simply cannot find it in themselves to protest when an attractive woman puts her tongue into their mouths."

"I do not imagine such situations are often found on the syllabus at Eton," I agreed.

She smiled again, shaking her head. "He is such a delectable study in contrasts. The tattoos and the earring, the work-roughened hands— they suggest a certain coarseness. But the speaking voice! Such elegant diction in those deep tones of his. It sends a shiver down the spine. And the deftness of those hands . . ." She trailed off dreamily, but she watched me closely.

I yawned a little and she darted a hand in to rattle one of my chains. "Am I boring you? It is hardly sporting of me to keep you chained up like a little pet bird, is it?" She delved a hand into her cleavage and extracted a key. With a quick twist of the wrist, she unlocked one of the cuffs. It fell to the stone floor with a clatter.

"You know," she said in a conversational tone, "you are exactly the sort of woman Harry Spenlove might find diverting. There is something unusual about you, Miss Speedwell. I heard you were a lady scientist and expected something quite . . . different," she told me, her full lips curving into a smile. "So, I wonder, did Harry ever misbehave himself with you? You can tell me. It is, after all, just us ladies."

I rubbed at my chafed wrist with my other hand. It was still bound by its iron cuff; Mrs. MacGregor might claim she wanted to be sporting, but she was not stupid enough to set me free entirely.

"I understand exactly why Harry fell in league with you," I told her, ignoring her question.

"Oh?"

"He likes to be the most intelligent person in the room. You must have made him feel a veritable Cicero," I said.

I expected the slap, but it still stung when the blow landed. She anticipated I would retaliate, so she stepped back sharply and yanked hard upon the chain at my foot. I tumbled to my knees, cracking them hard upon the stone floor. The jolt rattled my teeth and she took the opportunity to seize my hair, pulling my head back until my spine cracked.

I did not see the blade, but I could feel the cool edge of it bite into the flesh of my throat.

"I thought, as women, making our way in a man's world, we might be in sympathy with one another," she said. "But I see I was wrong.

Very well. No more games, Miss Speedwell. Let us be quite clear. Your gentleman friend has been most uncooperative with regard to giving me Harry's whereabouts or the location of the diamond. I believe you know both of these things."

"I do not," I told her hoarsely. It was the truth, if only in a technical sense. I knew the Eye of the Dawn had been concealed in the Belvedere, but as to its exact location, I could search a dozen years and never find it amongst the heaps of boxes and barrels and crates. For a moment, the temptation to tell her at least that much rose within me. I could endure any torment she chose to inflict upon me, but not knowing where Stoker was or whether the villainous Göran was currently abusing him with knives was almost more than I could bear. But Stoker had insisted upon serving justice, and I would not let him down, I vowed. Restoring the jewel to its rightful owner was worth a bruise or two.

During these ruminations, Mrs. MacGregor seemed to grow impatient. She tightened her hold on my hair. "And if you did know where they were, would you tell me?"

"I should think not," I managed.

The edge of the blade bit in further and I felt a slow dampness seeping into my collar.

"You really are the most tiresome woman," she said.

"You are not the first to observe it," I admitted. She released me so abruptly that I fell forwards, landing hard upon my hands. I put my fingertips to my throat and drew them back, wet and ruddy.

"Do not worry, Miss Speedwell. It should not scar. But I can do much worse and for much longer." With that, she delivered a robust kick to my side, knocking me into the wall.

She did not bother to shackle me fully again when she left. I lay on the floor, forcing myself to breathe slowly and shallowly so as not to aggravate the pain in my ribs.

I had crawled to one of the mattresses and was lying very still when the door opened and Stoker was pushed inside. To my surprise, he did not look much the worse for wear. A few expected bruises were empurpling his cheek, and his hand was bandaged with what must have been the remains of his shirt, for he was naked to the waist. Mrs. MacGregor kept her revolver trained upon him whilst Göran locked him into his set of shackles, murmuring what I could only assume were threats in Swedish. He held up his clasp knife and opened it, putting the blade near to Stoker's face as he continued to speak.

"Yes, my God, man, I know. I may not be fluent in any of the Scandinavian tongues, but a threat of that sort requires no common language," Stoker told him in some irritation.

Mrs. MacGregor said something in Spanish—my grasp of the language is limited to formal Castilian and not the colloquialisms of South America—and Göran backed away, still smiling at Stoker. She turned on her heel, saying nothing in farewell, and Göran slammed the door, bolting it firmly from the outside.

"Stoker," I said calmly, "you seem to have misplaced some of your clothing. And I believe those are the marks of Mrs. MacGregor's fingernails upon your iliac furrows."

Stoker blushed to the roots of his hair. "Veronica," he began.

I held up a hand. "Let us pass swiftly through the accusation, excuse, and recrimination phase of this conversation. Mrs. MacGregor kissed you—against your will, which is decidedly an affront. No one should be handled against his will," I said primly. "But I perceived the lady's condition when she visited me earlier. It seems that you may have returned one or two of her caresses. And I am not angry if you did."

He blinked. "You are not?"

"No. I know why you did. You thought to elicit information from her by cleverly turning the tables. She intended to seduce you, so you decided that your best plan would be to play along with her, perhaps even introduce a few caresses of your own in order to lower her defenses."

He shook his head. "I may live ninety years and never will I understand how the workings of your mind can so closely intuit mine."

I shrugged. "I would have done the same in your position. In fact, I might have done the same with the wretched Göran, but he provided me no opportunity for seduction. It was the best strategy under the circumstances. And she is a most attractive woman. It is not as if the effort would have been unpleasant," I added, cutting my eyes around to where he sat, looking entirely miserable.

"Not entirely," he admitted in a low mutter.

I cleared my throat. "Then let us discuss its effectiveness. What did you learn?"

It was his turn to shrug. "Very little for the amount of time we spent together. Much of it was taken up with dinner."

"Dinner?" My stomach gave a hopeful rumble. Julien's fruit tart had been slender sustenance.

"Six courses," Stoker said. At my expression, he made an attempt at consolation. "But the champagne was an indifferent vintage and the duck was overcooked."

"Duck? I do love a nice duck," I said mournfully. "The house appears thoroughly decrepit. Where did you engage in such debaucheries as roast duck?"

"She has fitted out one of the rooms as a sort of boudoir," he said, blushing furiously again. "I daresay the walls are still crawling with damp, but there's a good deal of satin and scarves draped about to conceal it, and the food was brought in, I suspect."

"Salome could not have done better," I said brightly. "Now, what does she want?"

"The Eye of the Dawn, which we knew. And Harry. She does not know where he is at present, and she seems to be getting anxious that the diamond may be slipping through her grasp."

"She questioned me along the same lines, although she was rather less winsome in her attentions," I said sourly. "How did she even know to abduct *us*? We have never been in public with Harry, never been seen together. No one knows of our connection to him, although she suspects he and I may have known one another at some point."

"Apparently they have been keeping a weather eye upon Hathaway Hall. She said Harry was supposed to bring her the diamond and that she had been cheated. When he did not arrive to hand off the jewel, she sent Göran into the local pub, where he bought Tom Carter a few pints in exchange for any information about guests at the Hall. Carter obliged and said we had come just before the diamond was taken and left just after it went missing."

"So Göran does speak English? I suppose he thinks glowering at us in Swedish is more intimidating," I mused. "The Hathaways meant to keep the business quiet. How did Tom Carter come to hear of it?" I asked.

"His sister is one of the few maids left at the Hall. She has rather a soft spot for 'Master Jonathan' and decided it was far likelier that we had stolen the diamond than the long-lost heir."

"Stupid girl," I said with feeling. "So her indiscretion has caused village gossip to label us the malefactors?"

"It is a plausible enough story if one discounts Harry's Jonathan Hathaway as a possible villain," Stoker said evenly.

"It is ludicrous. One cannot be more suspicious than a long-lost heir returning to claim the family name and then disappearing precisely when the most valuable jewel in their collection goes missing. I should like to have a robust discussion with these villagers on the subject of Occam's razor."

"To them, the simplest explanation *is* the likeliest," he replied. "Strangers come, strangers go, the jewel leaves with them."

"Harry Spenlove is a stranger," I pointed out.

"Not to a village accustomed to the Hathaway name. It shields him where we are outsiders—outsiders who actually are in possession of the diamond, so they are not wrong," he added.

"That is hardly our fault! It was thrust upon us. Did you tell Mrs. MacGregor its whereabouts?"

"I did not," he said.

"Neither did I, although I admit I was tempted," I told him. "We need not be enduring a moment of this."

"Well, from my perspective, it's quite the nicest abduction we have ever had," he remarked.

A hot rush of rage fired my veins. "I have no doubt. You have been wined, dined, and caressed whilst I have been here, worried beyond belief that that woman was going to let her pet Swede twist your limbs into something resembling an Alpenwalder pretzel. Next time, I shan't bother."

"Next time?" He choked a little, and if we had not been confined in possibly mortal peril, I might have suspected him of laughing.

"Well, if you refuse to tell them, perhaps I should," I suggested.

He sobered instantly. "Do not even think of it. I am warning you, Veronica."

"Warning me. Warning me?" My voice rose to a register I do not usually employ, but before I could continue, a curious scratching sound captured my attention.

"What is that?"

"It was you, shrieking like an overexcited tamarin monkey," Stoker said.

"I do not shriek," I told him with considerable *froideur*. "And this was a scraping noise. There it is again."

I pointed upwards and he cocked an ear, nodding as the sound came again, a rasp like a chain being pulled through a handle. Then came a creak and the coal doors were eased open. After a moment, Harry Spenlove's grinning face appeared.

"Hallo? Ready for a rescue?"

CHAPTER

26

With a snap, a rope dropped into the room, uncoiling as it fell. One end had been secured outside the coal door and the other fell just short of the stone floor. Down Harry climbed, not as gracefully as Stoker would have done it, but silently and with a certain athletic vigor he often took pains to hide.

"Harry," I muttered as he leapt lightly off the end of the rope and came to me. "What fortuitous timing. You might have come before your inamorata broke two of my ribs."

"I thought she would never leave," he whispered. "I could not exactly make my presence known."

He came near and bent to the shackle at my foot.

"What are you doing?" I demanded.

He rolled his eyes heavenwards. "This is a rescue, you daft woman. I should have thought that was perfectly obvious."

"You are not the first person I would have chosen to play the role of hero," I pointed out. "You have always fled at the first inkling of danger."

"I am here now," he said, looking a little put out. He brightened. "I say, I have always wanted to play the hero! Isn't this fun?"

"Rather less for us," I pointed out.

"No doubt," he replied, looking instantly abashed. "But I did remarkably well under the circumstances. You see, I was just leaving the Sudbury barber shop when I saw the pair of you get into the carriage. I was about to hail you when I recognized Göran." He paused to shudder. "I knew at once what was happening and I realized I was your only hope of liberation. So I hailed the next hansom and was hot as any hound upon your trail."

Stoker held up his cuffed wrists. "And an excellent job it was, but do you think you might unlock us now? Your friends may return any minute, and it would be advisable for us to put some distance between us before that happens."

"I do not suppose you thought to bring a hacksaw?" I asked.

Harry dipped two fingers into his pocket and lifted out a key with the air of a professional conjurer. "How you do like to underestimate me, Veronica." He fitted the key to the lock and the cuff sprang free. He grinned. "I am an exceptionally resourceful man."

I was too fatigued and famished even to care how he had come into possession of the key. He repeated the process on the rest of the cuffs and I moved my limbs cautiously, stretching life back into them as he turned to Stoker's shackles.

There was a sudden snap and Harry swore, something loud and profane and thoroughly Anglo-Saxon.

"What is it?" I demanded, coming near to look.

"It seems Mr. Spenlove has broken the key off in the lock," Stoker said dryly.

"Rotten luck," Harry told him, peering into the keyhole.

"Harry," I began in a warning tone.

He backed away, hands held up as if to ward me off. "Veronica, it is not my fault."

"So we are just as abducted as we were before your arrival," I said.

"That is wounding, Veronica. It really is. I have done my best, and I needn't have bothered, you know. I could have gone to the Belvedere and spent these hours searching for the diamond and left you to your fate. But I didn't. I came here to free you."

I opened my mouth to blast him, but it occurred to me he was entirely correct. Mrs. MacGregor and her erstwhile companion were far angrier with Harry than they were with either of us, and we had endured considerable discomfort at their hands. Heaven only knew what they might do if they realized Harry was within their grasp.

"You are right," I told him in the spirit of contrition. "It was good of you to try."

He brightened. "Thank you. Although I am afraid of what will happen next," he added in a confiding tone. "Isabel is an impatient woman. She does not like to be thwarted."

He eyed the stains on Stoker's collar. "I see she has attempted to work her wiles upon you. No doubt you rejected her?"

"She did not get everything she wanted," Stoker temporized.

Harry shook his head. "She will only try that once. And now you've pricked her pride, she will not like that at all. I fear she will loose Göran on you next, and I am quite certain you will enjoy that much less." He paused, then rushed on. "She will let him hurt you. In ways you cannot imagine."

He fell silent whilst we imagined a few of those ways. Then Harry went on, haltingly. "I am sorry for this. She would never have come into your lives if it were not for me. I have blundered again, when all I wanted was to make things right," he said mournfully. "She will not rest until she gets that bloody diamond, and I know she will not hesitate to harm you both if you stand in her way. Perhaps if I offer myself up . . ." He let the sentence trail off suggestively.

Stoker batted it away. "She cannot get the diamond from you because you do not know where it is. And if she instructed Göran to torture you, it would do no good except to leave you bloody and injured in those ways we cannot imagine."

Harry shuddered and Stoker went on. "And, of course, it is entirely possible she will kill us anyway. We have seen her face. Really, it is just a matter of time before she gets frustrated enough to let Göran do away with us. There is a pond in the front garden. Do you think that is where she will have him dump our lifeless bodies?"

Harry's pale face had taken on a greenish cast. He summoned a brave smile. "For all her sins, she seldom turns to murder."

"*Seldom?*" I said, my voice rising.

"I cannot make promises, she is a little unpredictable. But she is a pragmatist. I do not think she would risk the penalties for murder if she has what she wants," he said, although a note of doubt had crept into his voice.

"And if she has the diamond, Stoker is not the only one she might be willing to let go," I ventured.

"Of course!" Harry exploded in a harsh whisper. "Yes, I am thinking of my own prospects, Veronica. Have you ever known me to do otherwise? But this serves all of us. Isabel gets her bloody diamond and you and Stoker are out of it. Everyone walks away with what they wanted. Otherwise—"

"Otherwise, she may very well make carp food of us all," Stoker put in cheerfully. "Do you think that pond *has* carp?"

Harry shuddered. "How can you speak of such things so calmly?"

"Because I know that is not going to happen," Stoker replied. Harry and I stared at him.

"How can you be so certain?" I asked. "We are all in agreement that Mrs. MacGregor is bent upon getting her hands upon the jewel and her henchman will do whatever she bids him. She is bound to be frustrated at this point, and seduction having failed, torture is indeed the next logical step."

"Yes, and one I do not mean to let her take," Stoker said. "I am going to tell her where the diamond is."

Harry sagged in relief. "Thank you. I think we can make her see reason if she has it. She might be persuaded to let you go free and to let me live if she is able to retrieve it."

"She would never find it," Stoker replied. "She has not seen the inside of the Belvedere. It would have to be someone who is familiar with the place. It must be retrieved for her."

"Well, that's only the three of us," Harry said. "And you are shackled."

"Then it will be left to you and Veronica," Stoker told him.

Harry and I both began to speak at once, but Stoker held up a quelling hand. "I do not like it, but it is our best chance of securing our freedom. Mrs. MacGregor will no doubt be willing to liberate us for the Eye of the Dawn itself. The pair of you will have a means of bargaining with the diamond in hand."

"Absolutely not," I said flatly. I jerked my chin at Harry. "He cannot be trusted."

"I say, that is ungrateful," Harry protested. He held up a hand with raw knuckles. "Do you see the blood there? I scraped myself to come to your aid. I've walked my feet raw, risked Göran cooking my kidneys, and do not even ask me what sort of horrors Isabel might inflict if she put her mind to it, because just the idea gives me the shudders."

Stoker fixed him with a piercing stare. "Stiffen your resolve, Harry. I know you've a history of fecklessness, but I believe you can do this."

Harry dipped his head, clearly pleased, and I spoke up. "As delightful as this scene of manly admiration is, I must know the reason for your change of heart, Stoker."

He flicked a glance in my direction. "My objection to telling her the location of the diamond was twofold. First, I had hoped to restore it to its legitimate owner, but that possibility grows more remote as each hour passes and Mrs. MacGregor becomes increasingly intemperate."

"And the second?" I asked.

"Without someone to retrieve the diamond for us, we had nothing with which to bargain. I did not trust Mrs. MacGregor or her Swedish blackguard to secure it without bringing some danger to Lord Rosemorran's family should they stumble upon these villains. You know how often the children are in and about the Belvedere even if it is forbidden. What chance would they have if they encountered Göran?"

"None," Harry put in. "He is a fiend, as I have good cause to know. That does make perfect sense, my dear fellow. With the diamond in hand, Veronica and I can rescue you and purchase my own life from Isabel as well. It is the best solution to an imperfect situation. If you do think I am up to the challenge," he added with a bashful look at Stoker. I had never known Harry to be so lacking in confidence, but I could also understand where the dogged pursuit of Mrs. MacGregor had worn him down. She had, after all, tracked him across three continents. Of course, comparing himself to Stoker would be a blow to his self-regard as well, I reflected. As it would be for most men.

I was silent a long moment, and Harry was clever enough to do the same, giving me a few precious moments to think. "We have never failed to see justice done," I told Stoker. "This feels like a failure. The first. And it is exceedingly bitter."

Harry put a hand over mine, and out of the tail of my eye, I saw Stoker flinch. "Veronica, I understand your convictions. I remember well how firm you are in matters of right and wrong. But surely you can do a small wrong like abetting the theft of a jewel in order to save him?"

I looked at our hands, clasped together, my knuckles bloody from where I had punched Isabel de Armas MacGregor. I did not look at Stoker, but I could feel his gaze upon us. And then I looked into the face I had once loved, the bright brown eyes, soft and almost pleading.

"My dear Harry, I would not abet a small crime to save him," I said with a smile. "I would commit a large one."

I turned to Stoker and straightened my shoulders. "Very well. I accept this is your plan."

Stoker inclined his head and the look he gave me was enigmatic. He turned to Harry and cleared his throat. "I would entrust her to your care except that I have rather more faith in Veronica to handle herself than I do you."

Harry smiled, a lopsided smile. "You are not incorrect." He hesitated, then stepped away. "I will give you a moment to say farewell," he added with unexpected delicacy.

I moved to where Stoker stood, chained like a Gaulish warrior. "I will come back for you," I vowed.

"I know." He bent his head so that his lips brushed my ear. To an observer it might have looked like he was murmuring endearments, but the words he said were not romantic burblings. He issued a swift series of instructions on where to find the diamond and then straightened. He put out a hand as if to touch me, then seemed to think better of it.

I forced a smile. "Soon," I promised him.

I would have stepped away then, but his control seemed to crack. He reached for me. "Look away, Spenlove," Stoker ordered hoarsely. When he released me, I staggered a moment as I tried to find my legs. Stoker turned away and settled himself on his mattress as if steeling himself for whatever ordeal was to come.

I moved to the rope where Harry was waiting. "My God," he murmured. "Little wonder you are so loyal to him."

I turned, my hand upon the rope. "I have not shot you yet, Harry. Do not make me regret that."

Climbing the rope with my injured ribs was an interlude upon which I do not care to dwell. It was accomplished only by a tremendous amount of willpower and determination on my part with Harry right below, shoving and cajoling until at last I heaved myself through the coal door and dropped to the grass beside it. I rolled over and began to heave. I was thus occupied for some minutes as Harry emerged and waited politely.

"Finished?" he asked brightly as I sat back, hand pressed to my side.

"I cannot think anything remains," I assured him in a grim voice. He put out his hand and helped me gingerly to my feet. Ordinarily, I do not care to be guided, but in this instance, I was content to let Harry lead.

"The road is easier going, but the fields are faster," he told me, eyeing my slippers in the moonlight.

"Just walk," I ordered, pointing to the nearest field. He did as I instructed, pausing twice to help me over stiles and once through a decidedly aggressive thornbush. My hat was gone, my face covered in bruises and scratches, and one sleeve was hanging by a thread by the time we reached the station of Pettibone, a tiny country halt that was mercifully deserted when we arrived. I hung back in the shadows whilst Harry purchased our tickets, but I needn't have bothered. The lone clerk was sleepy, barely rousing himself to make change. I kept my face averted, studying the map of the surrounding countryside. Marking the direction we had followed, I was able to plot the location of the villa and was pleased to discover our little station was not far from St. Alban's. We were not so far out in the country as I had feared, and we were, mercifully, on the correct side of the city in order to reach Bishop's Folly with ease. Our luck held, and the train arrived shortly after we did.

Harry guided me to an empty first-class compartment and I collapsed onto the seat with an audible groan. "It was clever of you to think of first-class tickets," I murmured. "No one to bother about us."

"You paid for them," he said with a grin. "It is the last of what you made me a loan of this morning."

Harry stripped off his coat and covered me with it, hiding the worst of my tatters as he gathered me into his chest and wrapped his arms about me. Beneath my cheek, his heartbeat was slow and steady. "Try to rest. I will take care of you."

I gave a derisive laugh, but it broke, ending in a cracked little sigh. He put a hand to my hair and rested his chin on the top of my head. "At least let me try," he said.

It would have taken strength to resist him in that moment—strength I did not possess. I felt myself relax into him, floating, drifting, and then I was away, and the last thing I felt was his thumb, gently stroking my hair.

CHAPTER

27

The next thing I knew, he was prodding me awake. "We are here," he murmured. I sat up and a lightning bolt of pain surged through my side. "Easy," Harry said. I forced myself to my feet and spoke through gritted teeth.

"I will take my ease when Stoker is free."

Harry, wisely, made no reply. He left his coat draped about my shoulders, and for all the unorthodoxy of our appearance, we attracted little notice as we moved through the throngs in King's Cross. A quick journey by cab saw us to the back street that bordered the far side of Bishop's Folly. Stoker and I had agreed that a discreet entrance would be the wisest course of action. Harry and I slipped in through a small door concealed in a wall of ivy, locking it carefully behind.

I had expected the dogs would assail us, but we were greeted by nothing more active than Patricia, the Galápagos tortoise, lumbering through the shrubbery like a boulder with legs. She lifted her head as we passed, but we did not stop. We hurried on, past the pond and the little arrangement of follies that Lord Rosemorran's father had assembled at the edge of it. The tiny Gothic chapel was my private domain; the Chinese temple was Stoker's. It seemed an age since I had slept in my own bed, and I was conscious of a new and unaccountable lowness of spirits as I passed my chapel.

Just beyond the pond was the vivarium, a vast glasshouse where I nurtured butterflies, rearing them from larvae to imago, and then collecting the specimens after Nature had taken her course and their brief life spans finished. I had been training George, the hallboy, to tend them in my absence, and I could just see his slender form through the misted panes of glass, moving about the drifts of foliage, setting out plates of cut fruit and rotting meat. (The latter was for the benefit of my little colony of *Apatura iris*, a luscious little violet butterfly that feasts on carrion. I was preparing an article for *The Aurelian Sisterhood* on the subject, and had set up an experiment testing their preferences by providing them with the carcasses of a frog, a mouse, and a rabbit. The frog, the interested reader might care to note, was by far the favorite.)

Atop the rise at the front of the property, the house itself glowed with light from the windows of Lord Rosemorran's study to the nursery floor, where his children were no doubt busily authoring mayhem. I wondered if Lady Cordelia were amongst them, putting her baby down for his evening sleep, and I felt another sharp pang. I did not envy her having a child—far from it. I had no maternal instincts whatsoever. But I envied her stability, her sense of place in the world. Wherever she went, whatever she did, she would always be Lady Cordelia Beauclerk, sister of the Earl of Rosemorran. She would always have a home at Bishop's Folly, and she would always move with the assurance of the class into which she had been born. My own sense of authority had been hard-won by experience, and I realized, perhaps for the first time, that it had begun to falter. Being confronted with the specter of Harry Spenlove had knocked my confidence badly. He had been the greatest mistake of my life, and seeing him, I was once more a girl of twenty, following her impulses straight into disaster. I had not been

myself since the moment I had come face-to-face with him at Hathaway Hall, and I was suddenly, blindingly furious at him for robbing me
of my carefully cultivated sense of sureness.

I put aside my ruminations as we reached the Belvedere undetected. The dogs leapt on us with lolling tongues as soon as we entered. Harry fended them off as I closed the door and lit a pair of lamps.

"Here, madam, be a little kind, I beg you," he said to an exuberant
Vespertine, who stood on her hind legs, front paws braced on either of
his shoulders. She was sniffing his face with a wary intensity.

"Harry, stop playing with the dog," I ordered.

"I am hardly playing," he protested. "I think she has designs upon
me." He pushed her gently away, and she dropped to all fours with a
low grumble.

He came to stand at my side as I surveyed the Belvedere. It had
been built as a freestanding ballroom more than a century before, a
Georgian pleasure pavilion with a staircase leading to the encircling
gallery above. The gallery, with its alcoves and vantage points, had
served as a suitable place for seducers and chaperones alike, I suspected. A gentleman might whisk a partner behind a bit of drapery for
an illicit embrace even as a cluster of spinster aunts perched on gilt
chairs to survey the dancers below. After the ballroom had fallen into
disuse, a previous earl had enclosed one of the alcoves and installed a
proper water closet in order to use the Belvedere as a sort of retreat
away from his domineering countess. He was the first to store the
London contributions to the Rosemorran Collection in the Belvedere,
while the present earl was the one who had ordered the various other
Rosemorran acquisitions brought from their country properties. It
was stacked with trunks, crates, and portmanteaux of every description, to say nothing of the statues, paintings, cases, and pieces of furniture that crammed every corner.

Harry gave a soundless whistle. "Thank heaven we do not have to search every inch of this place. We would have been here until the crack of doom," he said.

I gave him a narrow look. "Is that why you did not avail yourself of the chance to find the diamond whilst we were in chains?"

"I am hurt that you should suspect me *still*," he said in an ag- grieved voice. "But I will admit, if I had been tempted, the very thought of locating the diamond here brings to mind adages about needles and haystacks."

Without further discussion, I made directly for the thylacine, paus- ing only to take up one of Stoker's scalpels as I went. I tested the blade on my thumb, drawing a bright bead of crimson blood from the pad.

"Hold this." I thrust a lamp into Harry's hands. "I must have good light if I am to do this without damaging his tiger."

"He put the Eye of the Dawn into an *animal*?"

I was not surprised at his tone. When Stoker had whispered its location to me, my own reaction had been one of astonishment. But it made its own kind of logic, I had reflected. Few people had Stoker's enthusiasm for dead things, and it would be easily overlooked in such a place. Of course, its location also accounted for his reluctance for anyone except me to retrieve it. He would never have trusted Isabel or Göran with his beloved thylacine; his confidence in me was shaky at best.

But I merely shrugged at Harry and applied myself to the task at hand.

"Can you think of a place that might be better?"

Together we wedged ourselves under the trophy—somewhat awkwardly—as the dogs gathered around. Nut, apparently sulking that Harry had been absent for the better part of the day, was point- edly ignoring him whilst Vespertine resumed her examinations, snuf- fling at Harry as he tried to twist away.

"For heaven's sake, hold still," I scolded. "I nearly took off a finger."

"I am trying," he said in a strangled voice. "This creature is making me exceedingly nervous. I much prefer cats, you know. They are entirely indifferent to one's presence."

He broke off with a sort of strangled sound as Vespertine gave a breathy sigh and butted her enormous head into his stomach. The lamp swung wildly, but I had just broken the last stitch and the precision work was finished. I slid my hand into the pouch of the thylacine and my fingers closed instantly over a small parcel. The parcel was a piece of oilskin tied around a nest of cotton wool. I opened it and what lay inside sparkled in the lamplight. Harry struggled to look past Vespertine's head, but she was proving difficult to dislodge. I waved it at him and wrapped it up at once, knotting the string several times to hold it fast.

"Come on," I said, pushing myself to my feet with an audible groan. "We must get back."

"Not so fast," he said, putting a hand to my wrist.

"What are you doing?" I demanded, my gaze flying to his even as I clutched the parcel to my chest.

"Trying to take care of you," he said in a tone of mild injury. "Whilst you were sleeping, I studied the timetable. The next train does not leave for another hour. You have a few minutes to change your clothes and bathe the blood from your face. You will be more comfortable," he pointed out. "You should also take a little food. Something to sustain you. It will be a long night." He nodded towards the parcel. "Take the jewel with you while you get fresh clothes. I will find food."

"I have clothes upstairs in the snuggery," I said.

"Good. Go. I will keep watch of the time."

I looked at my bloodied hands and ruined gown and nodded. "You are right, of course. Thank you, Harry."

His mouth curved into a ghost of a smile. "You might take that dog with you before her attentions turn unpleasant."

I snapped my fingers at Vespertine, and she trotted obediently at my heels as I made my way up to the snuggery. I stripped out of my ruined clothes and washed, gingerly, removing the worst of the blood but revealing the blossoming bruises. I replaced my elegant ribbon corset with one meant for athletic activity. It fastened in the front, permitting a lady to dress without the assistance of a maid, and the support provided immediate relief from the pain in my ribs. I pulled on a fresh white shirtwaist and my spare hunting costume, this one of dark green tweed tabbed in dark leather. With my long boots under my skirt, I felt much more myself. I buttoned the parcel into my pocket and descended after only ten minutes.

Harry was sitting, feet propped on my desk and crossed at the ankle, dangerously close to the box of Pamphilj cameos. He was devouring fruitcake straight out of the tin. "Ambrosial," he pronounced through a mouthful of cake.

I swatted at his foot. "Take your feet down before you damage those cameos," I ordered. "And give me some of that cake."

He settled his feet to the floor and handed me a slice, thick with currants and dried peel and sticky sharp with brandy flavored cherries. I ate it quickly, without tasting. It was coal for my engine, I reflected, and nothing more. I gave him a dark look and he leapt to his feet.

"We can go now," he said obligingly. We doused the lamps and left the way we had come, slipping out the back gate of Bishop's Folly and into the darkened streets. This time we had no luck in securing a hansom and made our way on foot, arriving at the station with just enough time to board before the train left in a cloud of steam and smoke.

I was more exhausted than I had been on the previous trip, but I was wakeful, too conscious of the fact that every passing mile, every passing minute, brought me nearer to Stoker. I had not dared to think about what might befall him in my absence, but I was entirely certain

Isabel MacGregor would not be pleased to find one of her birds had flown the coop.

I sat forwards on my seat, urging the train faster, while Harry sat opposite this time, watching me with an inscrutable expression on his face.

"What?" I demanded.

He shook his head. "I was merely wondering if I should be jealous. I don't know that you would ever have cared so much if you thought I was in peril." He attempted lightness, but there was a lash of bitterness in his tone.

"I did think you were in peril," I reminded him.

"How did you . . . Never mind," he said. "I do not think I want to know. No answer could possibly make me feel better. If you were destroyed by losing me, then I am the greatest monster imaginable. And if you were not, then I am the unworthiest."

"You are determined to think poorly of yourself."

His smile was mocking. "I have had years of practice, my dear. Believe me when I tell you, no matter what you think of me, my own opinion is always worse."

"That is a cold comfort, Harry. Besides, I mourned you."

"The more fool you, Veronica," he said lightly.

"I did," I insisted. "I might have regretted our marriage. I might have misjudged the man you were, but I never hated you. I never believed you beyond redemption."

"Then why were you so content to let me leave?" he challenged.

"Because it was not my place to redeem you. The only person who can do that is you."

He shook his head slowly, his eyes glittering. "No, my darling girl. Even I am not capable of that."

"Of course you are!" I rolled my eyes in exasperation. "It takes courage to live a good life, Harry, but it also takes courage to live like a blackguard. Both require difficult choices. Both require hardship and endurance and patience. There is, in the end, little difference between the good and the bad. Only one of these lives requires you to look over your shoulder all the while and the other one makes it a little easier to sleep at night."

He gave a short laugh. "God, I cannot imagine what it would be like to live without that constant worry. I embarked upon this life for security, you know."

"No, I didn't," I reminded him. "You never told me much about your family, and I am not even certain if what you did tell me was the truth."

"I have no idea which story I spun you," he admitted.

"Then perhaps the truth this time?" I suggested.

He shrugged. "Why not?" He sighed. "If you want a story of great tragedy and pathos, I do not have one. I was born to a gentry family in Norfolk. On the coast. I grew up with the smell of the sea in my nose and I never lost the love for it. My mother died when I was a lad and my father was busy, a common enough story. My brothers were at school so I was left in the care of my grandmother. A formidable old dame," he added with a fond smile.

"Like Lady Hathaway, you said," I ventured.

"Very much. Call me a sentimentalist, but staying at Hathaway Hall, even for a short while, made me feel like a boy again. Someone to fuss over you and worry if you've eaten your vegetables or wrapped up warmly enough for your walk on the moor. It was nice."

"What happened to your grandmother?" I asked.

"Dead," was the succinct reply. "I was fourteen. I'd been sickly as a child, so my grandmother indulged me, kept me at home with her. I'd never been to school before. When she died and Father sent me away, it was like being transported to a penal colony."

I choked a laugh.

"I am serious," he protested. "Have you ever met boys of that age? Absolute savages, every one of them. It was vile. I made up my mind I wasn't going to stay, so I left. I walked home—quite thirty miles. I thought Father would be glad to see me, or at least give me a little credit for my initiative and pluck. Instead, he packed me off to a wretched boys' school in Ireland. And the only thing worse than adolescent boys are nuns," he added with a shudder. "They were determined to beat the devil out of me, and they damn near succeeded. But I bided my time until Father sent me to London to read law, the dullest of all the occupations. He handed me my allowance for the quarter as well as money for my lodgings and expenses, and it was the most money I had ever seen in my life. It was enough for three months' training to be a lawyer, or one great, magnificent gamble. I wanted to see the world, so that is what I did. I might have signed on as a deckhand, working the ships that haul freight, but it seemed like devilishly hard work. And terrible for the complexion," he added with a grin. "So I used Father's money and booked first-class passage on a ship bound for New York. And it was on that voyage that I discovered my true talent."

"Cheating at cards?" I guessed.

He flapped a hand. "Anyone can do that. It is a skill, not a gift. No, my gift is an intuitive one. It is the ability to see what people want to believe and giving it to them."

I stared at him across the narrow compartment and his gaze was unwavering. "That is indeed your talent," I agreed.

"I ought never have used it against you, but believe me, Veronica, I was fooling myself far more than I was deceiving you."

"How?"

"I believed, I hoped, I could be satisfied with normality. I wanted to be . . . content. It seemed a reasonable thing to want, but it has always eluded me."

"Because your contentment so often comes at the expense of others," I pointed out.

His mocking smile returned. "You see? I am right to think poorly of myself. But sometimes, occasionally, I think about that hope of normality, and I dream of it when all other dreams are lost to me."

"What does it look like, this dream of normality?" I asked gently.

"A house, not a large one. Just a house, solid and plain. But facing the sea."

"Which sea?"

"It does not matter. The sea is the sea wherever you go. I want only to sit and watch the wind on the waves and feel small for a while. I want to feel my own insignificance."

"Then why do you not do that?" I pressed. "Surely you have possessed sufficient resources?"

"It has never been the right time," he said. There was no evasion in his glance, but it would have meant nothing even if there had been. Harry was skilled enough in deception that he could squarely meet one's gaze with a lie on his lips. "I have some money put aside. I have spent the last two years trying to retrieve my nest egg, such as it is. But one thing after another has interfered, and so I am still here, adrift as you see me." He grinned suddenly. "Do not look so sad, sweet Veronica. Someday very soon, I will have my little nest egg once more in my grasp. And when I do, I shall be master of my own fate at last."

"I hope so," I told him.

"Do you mean that?" He cocked his head, his eyes bright.

"Almost."

"Progress then," he said in a more cheerful tone. "And now, look lively, love. We have arrived."

We alighted at the station to find the place entirely deserted. The dozing clerk had closed his window for the night and drawn the shade. No one else got off the train and we were not followed as we struck out once more across the fields. I had brought a packet of vestas, but there was no need. The full moon still hung low in the sky, a trifle less brilliant than in Devon but illumination enough to guide our way. The windows of the villa were dark, and as we drew near, I gripped Harry's hand.

"If they have gone—" I began, scarcely daring to give voice to the possibility that they might have taken Stoker away.

"They won't have gone," Harry promised. "Isabel wants that diamond far too much, I am certain of it. There is black cloth tacked over the windows to prevent light from showing through. See there? That is the room Isabel has fitted as a sort of boudoir for herself. You can just make out the glow of light around the edges of the cloth. Now, be quiet," he urged, guiding me towards the coal cellar doors. They had been left open when we made our escape, but they were closed now, the rope knotted clumsily through the handles.

"Ha!" He turned to me with an air of triumph. "I tossed the lock into the shrubbery and that oaf Göran has not found it. He could do no better than the rope, and we shall make quick work of it," he promised. He bent to the knots and mastered them in short order, securing one end whilst I eased one of the doors back a fraction. A warm bar of lamplight fell upon my face. A single lamp hung in the cellar, just enough light to see the dark form at the base of the column.

The rush of emotion I felt at seeing Stoker once more was indescribable. I had to restrain myself from hurtling through the doors like a force of nature. Instead, I opened them carefully, taking the rope from Harry and playing it out silently through the opening so that it fell without a whisper of sound. As the rope wavered in front of him, Stoker lifted his head. A gash on his forehead had bled furiously, and one of his eyes was swollen shut.

But through the blood and bruises, he smiled, and I found myself grinning broadly as I swung out onto the rope. A lash of pain seared my ribs and I almost fell until Harry grabbed hold of me, wrapping his body around mine and grasping the rope.

"Move with me," he ordered. "Right foot down to the next knot. Just like that, I have you. I won't let you fall. Now the left." Harry was slighter of build than Stoker, and his arms trembled with the effort, but he held me firm and helped me to the bottom. I dropped the last two feet, landing with a painful jar. I dropped to my knees at Stoker's side.

"Thank heaven," he said lightly, "the cavalry has come."

I surveyed his face. "It could be worse," I murmured.

"Believe me, it is," he said, lifting his shirt. A network of shallow cuts crisscrossed his torso. Some of the blood had dried; some flowed freely.

"I will take her apart," I said to no one in particular. "Slowly."

"I would not advise that," Harry said.

Something in his voice warned me before I turned. He stood next to the door, smiling grimly. And in one hand he held a revolver pointed at my head.

"Sit down, Veronica. This will not take long." He knocked sharply upon the door, and it opened instantly. Isabel MacGregor entered, dressed once more in her traveling costume. The dour Göran waited behind her, blocking the door.

"You unmitigated *bastard*," I said to Harry.

"There is no call to be rude," he said in an injured tone.

I launched into a tirade that included quite a few choice words I had most definitely not learnt at the vicar's knee.

"She has quite a colorful vocabulary," Mrs. MacGregor said to Harry.

"And a tongue sharp enough to cut glass," he agreed. "It diminishes her attractiveness, I've always thought. But I suppose we might excuse her this once. She does, after all, have considerable provocation. I did just betray her. Again."

"And planned your act of heroics with Mrs. MacGregor's cooperation?" Stoker guessed. "I imagine you broke the key on purpose in order to deliberately leave me here, guessing that Veronica would want to bargain for my life with the diamond."

"Well, she certainly wouldn't have bargained for *mine*," Harry pointed out. "And I would very much like my neck out of the noose. Besides, I knew if Isabel and I had a chance to talk, she would realize that I was playing fair with her. I always intended she should have the diamond, and it was not my fault someone else took the bloody thing. But now I have got it for her, and we can be friends again," he finished with a fond look at his conspirator.

"So, I guess bygones will be bygones?" I inquired.

"Something like that," Isabel MacGregor said.

"If this was all a plot between you, then why torture Stoker whilst we were gone?" I demanded.

Isabel MacGregor's smile was mirthless. "I bore easily and you took such a long time." She turned to Harry. "Do you have it?"

"She does," Harry said with a jerk of the chin towards me.

Isabel smiled. "Excellent." She came near and put out her hand. "My diamond, please."

I reached into my pocket, but what I pulled out was no diamond. It was a knife, thin and beautifully sharp. I had only one chance to strike, but Isabel MacGregor, perhaps with a caution born of long experience, dodged as my hand came up. She feinted to the side and my blade grazed her cheekbone but bit no further. Instantly she turned, backhanding me with a resounding crack. With a roar, I lowered my shoulder and rushed into her, driving the air from her lungs as I forced her to the ground. I had just wrapped my hands in her hair and lifted her head, preparing to dash it against the stone floor, when I was yanked into the air, my feet flailing. The unlovely Göran had come to her defense, plucking me off her as easily as a bit of thistledown. He shook me, like a dog will shake a rat, and dropped me hard, the impact setting my ears to ringing. He put out a hand to help Isabel to her feet. A thin line of scarlet raked one cheek, and she touched it, smiling.

"Wanted a bit of your own back, did you?" she asked. She bent near and slapped me hard, twice, making certain her ring bit. I snapped my teeth at her the second time and she stepped back sharply as I tasted blood.

"Harry, deal with her." She took the revolver from him and he smiled at her.

"Very well, my dear. But first I think we ought to draw her claws," he said, moving for one of the loathsome iron cuffs.

He signaled to Göran to hold my arms tautly behind my back whilst he locked it about my ankle. Then he reached into my pocket, slowly, teasingly.

"I know it is somewhere in here," he said, a tiny smile playing over his lips. His hand closed over the parcel in my pocket and he drew it out. He handed it over to Isabel, standing in front of me whilst she opened it. She unknotted the string and folded back the oilcloth just enough to make certain of the contents.

"Marvelous," she said, putting it into her own pocket.

She turned to Göran. "Are the horses ready?" He grunted something in Swedish and she smiled. "It is time for us to take our leave of you," she said, looking from me to Stoker. Her eyes lingered on his face and the smile deepened. "It will be an absolute wrench to leave you behind, I must say. I do hope you manage to work your way free in a few days. I should hate to think of you starving to death in here. It would be the most dreadful waste." She looked back at me. "You, I shall not miss at all." She waited at the door whilst Harry came to where Göran still held my arms behind my back.

"Why did you bring me back here?" I asked. "You might have overpowered me at the Belvedere and taken the diamond for yourself."

He shrugged. "You are a loose end, I am afraid. And we cannot have that."

He clucked his tongue. "I doubt we shall meet again, so you must have something to remember me by."

Without further ado, he placed his hands on my shoulders and bent in to kiss me. The kiss was . . . comprehensive, involving a significant length of time and effort on his part. When his lips touched mine, I reared back, resisting, but he moved one hand to cup my head, holding it firmly in place as his mouth covered mine once more, urgent. Dimly, I heard Stoker behind me, emitting a low growl, but I ignored him as my lips parted and I gave way to Harry's deft manipulations.

My knees were trembling when he released me, and I stumbled back into Göran, who set me on my feet again with a coarse laugh.

"Good-bye, Veronica," Harry said, grinning broadly. He inclined his head to Stoker in a formal salute and left without a backwards glance.

I kept my lips pressed tightly together while Isabel took a final look at our sad tableau. Stoker was on the floor, chained and scowling like one of Lucifer's lesser devils. I was unsteady on my feet, covering my mouth where Harry had left my lips bruised.

"Adieu," she said. Then she signaled to Göran, who slammed the door closed and locked it, immuring us once more in our prison. After a few minutes, I made out the faint sounds of the wheels turning on gravel and then silence, no sound at all except for Stoker's heavy breathing and the quick-fire beating of my own heart.

"I think," he said in a bland voice, "that my first priority upon escaping this place will be to hunt down Harry Spenlove and administer the beating he so richly deserves."

"If I find him first, there will be nothing left for you to beat," I assured him darkly.

He settled himself onto one of the mattresses and arranged his chains.

"What are you doing?"

"Making myself as comfortable as possible," he said. "I suggest you do the same. We shall most likely be here for quite some time."

"But where is your spirit of adventure?" I demanded. "What has become of your thirst for . . . oh, *blast and damnation*." I threw myself down onto the mattress next to him, wincing. "I surrender. I am hungry. I am tired. I have ribs that may well be broken. And I have, once more, been duped by a man who does not deserve to wipe my boots. And we must not neglect the fact that my actions have also caused the one man I truly love to be imperiled, once again."

"Once again," he agreed. "It has become something of a habit. But it was my idea for you and Harry to retrieve the diamond. And as much as I complain about the rota of beatings and stabbings, I rather think I should miss it all if it went away."

"Went away?" My voice rose on a sob. "Stoker, we are chained in a stone room with a locked door. We have no weapons. No tools. No food. No water. I cannot think when our situation has been more dire."

"Can't you? I can think of half a dozen worse times we have endured."

"Your equanimity astonishes me," I told him.

"Perhaps I have simply decided that if such misadventures are the price I must pay to have you in my life, I am content to pay them."

I turned my head. He opened his arms and I settled against his chest, gingerly, for I could see from the bloodstains on his shirt the hatchwork pattern of cuts Mrs. MacGregor had made upon his torso. "Stoker," I began, hardly knowing how to form the words. "There is something I have not told you about Harry Spenlove."

"Go on," he said softly. He began to stroke my hair, just as Harry had done. Stoker was less gentle, perhaps, but I knew whose hands I would rather have.

"You know that Harry and I had a relationship of an intimate nature." I paused.

"Yes."

"That was not the extent of our connection," I said. "In fact, we were married. We are married."

His hand stilled, but he said nothing. Then he began to stroke my hair again and I went on.

"I did not mean to deceive you," I told him. "I believed myself to be a widow. Harry left me as Krakatoa was erupting, and I thought him killed in the blast."

Still, he said nothing, his hand moving slowly on my hair, never faltering in its rhythm.

"Regardless of what I believed, I ought to have told you at some point in these past months. At the very least, I ought to have spoken of it when Sir Hugo involved me in this business. But I did not. I failed to take any one of the many opportunities I might have seized upon to tell you the truth. Instead, I carried on, lying by omission. And I hope that you can forgive me."

He turned me to face him then, and I saw that he was angry, not the fiery rages which I so enjoyed provoking, but a cold fury the likes of which I had never before seen in him.

"Veronica, what sort of fool do you imagine me to be? *I knew.*"

"How? How could you possibly have known?" I breathed.

"Because I searched his things at Hathaway Hall," he said. "Your husband quite touchingly carries a copy of your wedding lines."

"Our wedding lines? Are you certain?"

"It was an official-looking document with his name and yours and the date under a very pretty scroll reading 'In Holy Matrimony.' I did not bother to read the rest," he said, his mouth tight.

"And you did not tell me? You never even hinted."

"How could I? Do you have any notion of how devastated you looked the day in the park when Sir Hugo said that Jonathan Hathaway might be alive? It was as if the ghosts of your past had risen up all at once. I thought he might have been an old lover, and you said nothing to contradict that suspicion. Instead, you withdrew into yourself when you might have come to me."

"I know it was wrong of me," I said slowly. "But I wanted to put it all behind me as quickly as possible. I had shut the door upon that time, the most terrible time of my life. I never imagined I would see Jonathan or Harry again."

"Then why did you accept Sir Hugo's request?" he challenged.

"Because I wondered . . . Jonathan was Harry's closest friend. I thought, perhaps, if this man who appeared at Hathaway Hall *were* Jonathan, he might know . . ."

"Might know what?" Stoker demanded.

"Whether it had always been a game to Harry or whether he had really loved me," I burst out. "Harry had stood before God and man and promised to love and care for me to the end of his days, and within six weeks, he was gone. He left me, alone and defenseless, in the face of disaster. Why?"

Stoker looked nonplussed. "What do you mean 'why?' Because he is an unmitigated *ass*."

"Is he? Or did he find some flaw in me? Something fundamentally unworthy of love?"

"How can you think that?" Stoker shook his head.

"Because not one person has ever stayed," I told him, my voice breaking. "Not my mother. Not my father. Not my husband. Everyone who ought to have been with me left—not because they were forced. Because they *chose*. What does that say of me?"

"It says that you have been unlucky, not unworthy," he said sternly. "Do you think I haven't had precisely the same thoughts about Caroline? My own wife committed adultery with my dearest friend and left me to die in a jungle. She turned the whole world against me simply because she could not accept that she was the authoress of her own crimes."

"You have your brothers," I pointed out.

"Do I?" His smile was mirthless. "We cannot speak without argument. I can go years without seeing one of them. I may be legally a Templeton-Vane, but I am the cuckoo in the nest, the reminder of my mother's one indiscretion. Do you think I was ever permitted to forget that?" He leaned near, his jaw tight. "Do you think there is a single person in the whole of this world who could understand you better than I?"

"No. But if I had told you—"

I broke off and he leaned nearer still, his emotion palpable. "Go on."

I shook my head. "I don't even know. I simply wanted it all to go away. And you have been so strange with me, so obviously at odds, and I did not know why. Now we are come to this, where you are so angry with me, you can hardly bear to look at me."

He blinked. "Angry with you? Veronica, I am angry with myself. No, you did not confide in me about Harry, but I did not confide in you about Caroline. You discovered the truth because she intruded into our lives.* When the tables were turned and I realized you had a secret that you held rather than entrust to me, my first reaction was rage— not because you did not tell me but because I wanted you to."

"I do not understand you."

"How could I, in all justice, demand from you a trust I had never willingly given? I never told you the worst of what Caroline made me feel. You saw the scars but never the wounds. It was little wonder you felt you could not confide in me."

"I wanted to," I told him.

"I know. And every day that you did not felt like another knife twist to the gut," he replied. "Another proof that I am not a man upon whom you depend."

"The fault is not yours," I insisted. "It is mine. I have been my whole life in the habit of solitude, of trusting no one but myself. The one time I allowed myself to rely fully upon another, he betrayed that trust so completely, I vowed never again to put my happiness in the hands of another."

"Yet another reason to break Harry Spenlove in half if I ever see him again," he said through gritted teeth.

Before I could reply, the door was flung back on its hinges and Harry stood in the doorway. His clothes were mussed, the knees of his trousers heavy with mud, twigs adorning his hair. But he was smiling broadly, the smile of a buccaneer.

"All right, then, who wants a rescue?"

---

* *A Treacherous Curse*

CHAPTER

29

I lunged for Harry, muttering the sorts of words never found upon
ladies' lips, but Stoker caught me just before my ankle irons would
have yanked me backwards.

Harry looked hurt. "I say, that is no proper way to greet a fellow
who has taken great pains to set you free. *Again.* I fell in a mud puddle," he said, surveying his trousers with distaste. "At least I hope it
was mud."

Stoker sniffed deeply. "I think it safe to say it was not."

Harry sighed. "For a civilized country, England is absolute death
to a nice wardrobe." He produced a key from his pocket and bent to
unlock Stoker's wrist irons. "There you are, old man. The other key is
still broke off in your ankle iron, so you must make the best of it with
a hacksaw," he advised, producing the tool in question. He freed me
then, and I resisted the urge to box his ears.

"Would you mind," I said icily, "explaining exactly what you are
doing here?"

He rolled his eyes heavenwards. "I have already told you. I am res-
cuing you. I am being *heroic*, Veronica. It has been my ambition ever
since I read of the ancient Greeks. Theseus, Perseus—all capital lads

with all sorts of daring. Although, I must say, I always imagined the ladies being rescued demonstrated a good deal more gratitude. You are not exactly being appreciative, Veronica."

Stoker flicked him a glance. "She is always bad-tempered when she is hungry. She needs feeding."

"Ah!" Harry patted his pockets and produced a pair of gently squashed sausage rolls wrapped in a handkerchief. "One for each of you. And I've a pork pie in another pocket, but I think I might have sat upon it."

I devoured the sausage roll and Stoker waved at me to take the second as well. I would have resisted, but then I recalled the succulent seductions of his duck dinner and took it without remorse.

"Better?" Harry asked when I had finished.

"Much," I admitted. "I apologize for my churlishness. The rescue is appreciated," I told him humbly.

He grinned and turned to where Stoker was still working away at his ankle irons. "We ought to be speedy about this. If Isabel returns, well, I shouldn't like to be caught is all I will say upon the matter."

"When did you leave her?" I asked.

"On the road to London—and I mean that quite literally," he said with a grimace. "I waited until Göran was whipping the horse up a hill and then I flung myself out of the carriage. I rolled down the hill and flagged a hansom going the opposite direction. They had not even got the carriage turned round by the time I was well and truly gone."

"And you think she will come here to look for you?"

He shrugged. "Isabel is a mercurial creature, as are all women," he added with a meaningful look in my direction. "She will most likely deduce that my precipitate flight means I intended to return here and free the pair of you. In which case, she must decide either to take her diamond and flee or come back here herself and finish us all off—in which case I would vastly prefer not to be at hand when she arrives."

He stroked his chin thoughtfully. "Of course, if my departure has struck her as suspicious, she may well examine the diamond, in which case, she will most definitely come here and we are all well and truly sunk."

"Why?" I demanded.

"Because," Stoker said coolly. "She does not have the Eye of the Dawn." He rose, dropping his ankle irons to the floor with a clanging flourish. "I do."

I stared from Stoker to Harry and back again before pressing my fingers to my temples. "I beg your pardon?"

Stoker nodded to Harry. "Clever of you to have figured it out."

Harry gave him a modest nod. "Well, it was clever of you to have hid a false diamond. It very nearly fooled me."

I held up a hand. "If the pair of you might possibly leave off admiring one another for just a moment and explain?"

"Not now," Stoker said in a tone of unmistakable command. "Harry is quite correct. We need to leave, and quickly. Did you keep the hansom?" he asked.

Harry nodded. "It will be a bit of a squeeze with three of us, and we shall have to pay him over odds to keep quiet about this."

Stoker looked at his clothes ruefully. His shirt was still missing and his trousers were liberally stained with blood. Harry had found his coat and Stoker managed, wincing, to drape it over himself to conceal the worst of his wounds. "Not much I can do to remedy this."

Harry shrugged. "We shall tell him we were engaging in some country fisticuffs and I beat you."

"A likely story," Stoker muttered, but he did not stop to argue. He pushed me out of the cellar ahead of him, and Harry brought up the rear. We hurried through the house—pausing only to snatch up a cold duck leg that Mrs. MacGregor had left behind—and hurled ourselves into the hansom. The driver looked startled and grumbled at the extra distance and the demands upon his horse with a third passenger until Stoker flung the contents of his notecase at him and ordered him to drive.

The fellow complied, much happier with his pockets stuffed with banknotes. I huddled between Harry and Stoker, a thousand questions tangling in my mind. But the driver was too near, and the events of the day too fresh; the hour too late, and the moment too impossible. We hurtled along under that April moon, the heavy scents of the country flowers bearing down upon us in bursts of exquisite sweetness as the rushing hansom brushed the dew from the leaves. We were jolted and jostled, and yet there was something magical about that moment, that liminal time between our liberation and our arrival back in London. We could do nothing but be carried along like so many leaves upon the surface of a churning river. The leaf so moved does not think, and neither did I, content to feel the whip of the wind against my cheeks as we dashed through the night.

Stoker had ordered the driver to leave us some distance from Bishop's Folly lest a pursuer be watching. But we saw no one as we made our way on foot the last half a mile through the dark streets of London. We wended around Marylebone High Street, keeping to the narrow alleys until we came at last to the back gate.

Once more I led the way through the estate until we reached the Belvedere. The dogs, exhausted by our nocturnal adventures, did not even stir as we entered. Stoker locked the door behind us while I lit the lanterns. I instructed Harry where to find food and he retrieved more slabs of fruitcake and a bowl of apples gone only a little soft. I looked around for Stoker but he had vanished. I found him with his thylacine, bent over the creature with a solicitous air.

"I assure you I did not damage it," I said, bristling. "I cut only the stitches you placed and did not so much as nick the hide." Its teeth seemed even more menacing, its lips curled back in a snarl that might well have been a fair imitation of my own. Stoker was at the far end, beneath its belly, lying on his back as he maneuvered his tools. To my intense irritation, he said nothing but continued to work, doing something—I could not imagine what—to the scrotal pouch.

After an interminable interlude, he rose, dusting himself off. "There," he said in a tone of quiet triumph. He held out his hand, and there, burning its cold fire upon his palm, was the diamond.

I gaped at him. "It's true then." I sat down heavily as Harry came to stand behind me, crunching loudly into an apple. After a few deep breaths, I looked at Stoker. "This is no trick? This is the real Eye of the Dawn?"

He displayed the jewel again and Harry and I stared. "Explain."

Stoker shrugged and held the diamond up, watching the play of light as it shimmered through the facets, into the heart of the stone, and back again. "It occurred to me that Harry might prove tenacious about retrieving it," he began.

Harry shrugged. "A reasonable precaution under the circumstances," he said through a mouthful of apple.

Stoker went on. "So I put the real diamond aside for safekeeping last night, just as I said I would. But I also concealed a second jewel as a sort of decoy, something to throw him off the scent should he decide to play the villain."

"Where exactly did you find a diamond of appropriate dimensions?" I asked. He seemed mesmerized by the stone in his hand, answering my questions almost as an afterthought.

"In the costumes Lord Rosemorran acquired from the French opera company. You will remember he said they performed *Le roi de Lahore* by Massenet. One of the characters is a king from India. Luckily, there was a paste jewel approximately the same size, so I pried it from its setting and hid it."

"But a paste jewel could never be mistaken for the real thing," I protested.

"And it wasn't," Harry said. "At least not by me. I caught only a glimpse of it in your hand and I knew at once what he had done. And that is when I realized I had a choice to make—expose you to Isabel or go along with the charade and try to save all our necks. And the diamond."

"Your motives being, I conclude, not entirely altruistic," I put in.

Stoker spoke quietly. "He needn't have come back for us, Veronica."

"Of course he did—he did not know where the real diamond was!"

Harry shook his head ruefully. "She will not credit me with any nobler purpose, and I cannot blame her. I have been, as you know, the great tragedy of her life."

"Tragedy!" I cried. "You were a youthful mistake."

"Mistake? You wound me," he said, putting a hand to his breast. "I have oft thought of us as Pyramus and Thisbe, Orpheus and Eurydice, Apollo and Daphne . . ." He trailed off with a dreamy look.

"Stabbed, cursed to the underworld for all eternity, turned into a tree," I said, ticking off the endings on my fingers. "I do not much care for the fates of your heroines," I told him.

Stoker clapped his hands abruptly. "Do you think we might return to the matter at hand?" He turned to Harry. "Does Mrs. MacGregor know where we live?"

Harry shook his head. "I never spoke of any connection with Lord Rosemorran. She knows Veronica and I were meant to go into London to fetch the stone, but I was deliberately vague as to exactly where we were going."

"How did she know where to find us in the first place?" I challenged. "Is it an accident that she was lying in wait for us outside the Sudbury?"

Harry colored. "Well, as it happens—"

"I knew it! You reprehensible, custard-spined, maladroit—"

Stoker held up his hand. "Harry, I presume that you sent a message of some sort to Mrs. MacGregor at the villa indicating when we would be in the vicinity of the Sudbury? And provided her with a handy description?"

Harry's color deepened. "I had a lapse, a moment of weakness, all right? I lay awake a good long time last night, thinking of everything Isabel might do to me if she didn't get her hands on that diamond, and I panicked. It is not worthy of the man I wish to be, but it is the truth. I thought she might spirit you off to the villa and persuade you to give up the location of the diamond. And then it would be finished—I could start my life anew without the threat of her hanging over my head like a veritable sword of Damocles."

"What changed your mind?" I asked with narrowed eyes. "You were willing to betray us and play the coward ten hours ago—why have you now decided to dance to a different tune?"

"That is my business," he said, folding his hands over his chest. It was an imitation—albeit not on purpose, I suspected—of Stoker's posture. It was the pose of a man who was stalwart, determined. And I saw a resolve in Harry's expression I had never seen before, a firmness to his chin. Could it be possible that the feckless creature I had married had finally decided to grow up at last?

"When did you realize the diamond we were taking to Mrs. MacGregor was false?" I asked.

"At once," he said. "I handled the real one, remember. I made note of the weight of it, and I have considerable experience with precious gems. You found an excellent substitute," he told Stoker, "but anyone who had seen the real thing would have known the difference."

"I didn't!" I was indignant.

Harry canted his head with a thoughtful look. "You saw it briefly at Hathaway Hall and did not hold it. I felt the heft of it when it rested in my palm. Real gems are usually far heavier than paste imitations. And I suspect when we collected it earlier, your mind was on other things." He flicked a glance towards Stoker.

"I suppose I was rather preoccupied with what punishments your inamorata might be inflicting upon him," I admitted. "How is it that she did not discover the substitution at once?"

"I was careful to unwrap the thing in poor lighting and she was in a hurry. Like most people I have deceived, Veronica, she saw what she wanted," he finished with an inscrutable expression that I might have interpreted as sadness. "If she examines it closely, she might well notice its relative lightness and wonder, but she will not know for certain until she decides to sell it."

"What reputable jeweler would touch such a stone?" Stoker asked.

Harry shrugged. "Most, I should think. Isabel could present herself as a grieving widow or bereaved daughter fallen upon hard times, trying to sell a bit of her inheritance for a fraction of its value simply to have money in hand. Or she will go to a receiver of stolen goods, the sort of fellow who has little interest in provenance because he already knows the jewel has been pilfered. It will be discovered for a fraud immediately, but she will have no means of finding us."

"She has tracked you before," I pointed out.

"I underestimated both her skills and her commitment," he said dryly. "I have taken precautions now that I did not when I was in America. London is an excellent place to lose oneself, although I do not mean to remain here for long."

"What are your intentions?" I asked.

He looked at the diamond still glittering on Stoker's palm, and a light flickered in his eyes, something unholy and avaricious. I knew then that he was tempted, and badly so, to reach out and snatch it.

Stoker must have intuited the same, for he gave me a long look. If

Harry made any intemperate move to seize the jewel, we were both prepared to defend it.

Instead, Harry closed his eyes and, after a moment, opened them. He smiled, a small melancholy smile. "Do you know, that is the single most valuable item I have ever had in my possession, and what I want most is to see it restored to its rightful owner."

"The rightful owner is not Lady Hathaway," Stoker pointed out.

"I did not mean Lady Hathaway," Harry said with new resolve. "I mean the maharani. Let us right an old wrong."

CHAPTER

30

And so our peculiar little band of adventurers made our way to the Sudbury Hotel. We had taken a few moments to wash and make ourselves presentable, but there was only so much one could do about the bruises and visible wounds. Stoker's chest was so thickly wrapped, he seemed to be wearing a breastplate of bandages, and one eye was blooming into a spectacular bruise of violet and mauve. He had donned his eye patch, a sure sign that his sight was fatigued, and I saw fresh lines at the corners of his mouth.

As for me, the cut on my cheek was still vivid scarlet and inclined to drip onto my clothes. I dressed in a two-piece ensemble of heavy black silk. It fastened smartly up the front with a row of tiny buttons that led to a narrow, fitted collar, neatly concealing the wound Mrs. MacGregor had inflicted upon my throat. The ensemble was appropriately sober for the occasion, and I had instructed the dressmaker to include wide, hidden pockets inside the seams of the skirt. Into these I slipped a few of my favorite weapons and one or two new finds, including the cheese wire. Stoker stared as I patted it into place.

"Do you really plan on garroting someone in the Sudbury?" he asked pleasantly.

"One can never anticipate when one will be forced to garrote," I informed him as I pinned my hat into place. I favored wide brims when I butterflied, but in town I preferred smaller confections, wisps of feathers or flowers to suggest a head covering. But on a whim, I had asked the dressmaker to fashion a sort of soft cap of the silk left from sewing the dress. The result was a type of tam-o'-shanter, the headwear much favored by the Celt. To the narrow band I had pinned a small feather and the effect was jaunty. I looked like the sort of woman who could keep her composure in difficult circumstances, I decided. There was nothing frivolous or unserious about my costume; even the feather was narrow and stiff, no voluptuous plumes or lacy ruffles for me.

Harry dressed in a suit borrowed from Stoker, artfully pinned to hide the extra length. He had padded out the extra breadth with a bit of stuffing, arranging it to appear as though he had a comfortable and prosperous belly rather than Stoker's admirably developed musculature. He stood with rounded shoulders, and the effect was to make him appear older and shorter. But the greatest change was in his face. I poked the ginger hair glued to his face with a tentative finger.

"Where on earth did you find that set of moustaches?" I inquired.

"I took a leaf from Stoker's book and searched the costume boxes," he informed me happily. "I have decided it is far safer to go about in disguise until I am able to take my leave of London."

"It looks as if you skinned a gnome," I told him. "And those moustaches do not even match your hair."

He smoothed his moustaches and pulled his cap low. "Do not touch what you cannot appreciate," he said loftily. "I intend to present myself as an Irishman visiting London on matters of business," he added in a nearly impenetrable brogue.

"Heaven help us all," I muttered.

. . .

In spite of the lavish red moustaches, we looked, from a distance, like a perfectly respectable trio. Up close, we were disreputable as pirates, and I could only hope we would not frighten the maharani.

We rode in silence to the Sudbury, none of us inclined to conversation. It had, after all, been an exceedingly long and tiring day, but none of us would rest easily until the diamond was safely in the maharani's possession. I could not know what thoughts occupied Stoker's mind, but I was considering Harry's contradictory actions. He had conspired with Mrs. MacGregor, but he had returned to help us escape. For every stroke of red I lettered in his ledger, I must, in fairness, add one in black. It was a distinctly unsettling experience to think anything but the worst of him, and I was not pleased at the ambiguity. I had long ago put him firmly in the category of villain, and it was unreasonable of him to try to weasel out of it.

Such were my thoughts as we drew up in front of the hotel. In spite of the lateness of the hour, the beau monde was just beginning its pleasures. The hotel was ablaze with artificial lights and the lobby was thronged with people, most dressed far more grandly than we—the women bedecked in satin with perfumed and powdered décolletages draped with jewels, whilst the men fussed with their satin-lined capes and pearl tiepins. We garnered one or two curious looks from the more fashionable, but I ignored them, striding through the crowd and directly to the front desk. The night manager, a fellow I did not know, was standing with an expectant expression, his moustaches neatly waxed, his shirt front starched to perfection.

"How may I be of service, madam?" he inquired in a low voice.

"I wish to see the Maharani of Viratanagar," I replied.

He blinked. "I am sorry, madam. But there is no guest by that name in this hotel."

I opened my mouth to contradict him, but Stoker clasped my hand. I remembered then what Julien had told us about the maharani's insistence upon privacy. After her photograph had been published in the *Daily Harbinger*, she had instructed hotel staff to preserve her incognita.

"Blast," I muttered, turning to Stoker. "What was her *nom d'hôtel*?"

He shrugged and I sighed as I turned back to the manager. "We know she is here, my good man. Now kindly send up a note that I will write and—"

The manager held up a hand. "Madam, I cannot send up a note to a guest who is not registered in this hotel."

His voice was reasonable, the sort of overly patient tone one uses with difficult children or people of dubious intelligence. Stoker plucked a coin from his pocket and slid it across the desk.

"Perhaps you can carry the note up now," he suggested with the cool hauteur of a viscount's son.

The manager swept the shiny guinea from the desk and into his pocket with a practiced gesture. "Thank you, sir. And I repeat, I cannot send up a note to a guest who is not registered in this hotel."

"Then you owe us a guinea," I muttered.

His expression was grave. "I am sorry I cannot accommodate your request, madam, but I am afraid I have other matters to which I must presently attend." He inclined his head as a gesture of dismissal, after which he simply stood, looking vacant.

My fingers reached for my garrote wire, but Stoker grabbed my hand and pulled me away from the desk and behind a potted palm, Harry following meekly behind. "Veronica, for the love of all that is holy and good, tell me you were not actually intending to take out your cheese wire."

"*Cheese wire?*" Harry's voice rose in disbelief.

"She carries it in case she is called upon to garrote someone," Stoker explained.

"I did not intend to harm him," I said sulkily. "But I thought the sight of it might prove persuasive."

"If we manage to get through this night without finding ourselves in the cells at Scotland Yard it will be God's own miracle," Stoker said through gritted teeth.

Suddenly, he seemed seized by an idea. He jerked his head towards the door leading to the hotel's inner offices. "Julien will be long gone by this hour," I told him.

"Exactly," he said, leading the way. Concealed by the bustle of the crowd, we slipped through the door and hurried downstairs. Hotel staff, accustomed to odd comings and goings, did not give us a second look. The pastry kitchen was dark, scrubbed clean and ready for the following day. On a hook behind the door hung one of Julien's white coats, which Stoker buttoned over his own. A tray of prettily arranged petit fours, no doubt at hand should any guest ring in the night for a bit of sustenance, lay on a table, and he took it up.

"There is my disguise," he said in some satisfaction as he turned to me. "Where is yours?"

I cast my eye around the room and found only a stack of clean towels. I tied one at my waist to approximate an apron and grabbed an enormous whisk, some two feet long. We were rummaging for another coat for Harry when we heard footsteps approaching.

"In here!" Harry urged, holding open a door. We dove inside, and Harry closed the door after us. We were in a room lined with shelves, each one stacked high with pristine white sheets and towels, the air heavily scented with the odors of starch and clean linen.

Stoker laid a finger over his lips and we held our breath, waiting for the footsteps to pass.

But they did not pass. Instead, they stopped just outside and the door was yanked open.

"What the devil—" The woman outside had no chance to finish. Stoker reached out and jerked her inside while Harry once more closed the door.

"J. J.," I said, sagging in relief.

"You know this chambermaid?" Harry asked, surveying her from starched white mobcap to stiff bombazine skirts.

She gave a sniff. "I am not a chambermaid. I am a *journalist*," she corrected loftily. "And who are you?"

"Henry Trismegistus Spenlove," he said, sweeping her a bow.

"Your second name is not Trismegistus," I hissed.

"No, but I don't much care for Walter. I thought I might try something new," he replied.

Stoker sighed. "J. J., we are in need of assistance," he began.

"So I deduced," she said, a thoroughly mercenary light in her eyes.

"We need an audience with the Maharani of Viratanagar," he explained.

"And your manager is *most* unhelpful," I put in.

"I can get you in," she told us. "But it will cost."

"J. J., really," I remonstrated. "I thought we were friends."

She held up a hand. "Friends keep other friends' secrets," she said with a meaningful look. "Which I have done. And now friends can help friends get a story."

"That is a convoluted statement," Stoker told her.

She bared her teeth in something that was not quite a smile. "And yet you understood me."

"We did," I told her. I sighed. She was entirely correct. J. J. had learnt the truth of my parentage some months back, and although the story would have been the making of her career—she would, in short, have gone down as nothing less than a journalistic legend had she published it—she had said nothing, in print or otherwise, to betray me. Furthermore, when she discovered I was masquerading as Her Royal Highness, the Hereditary Princess of the Alpenwald, she had asked for comparatively little to keep her silence.

"Very well," Stoker said. "We will give you a story. You can print nothing of the maharani and our business here tonight, but I swear we will give you something worth your while. Do I have your word that you will keep quiet with what you are about to hear?"

"My word," she said, putting out her hand to shake. Stoker took hers soberly as she jerked her head towards Harry. "Who is he really?"

"A thief and a confidence trickster," I said. Harry reared indignantly.

"That is mighty rude, considering," he protested.

"What business has a confidence trickster with the Maharani of Viratanagar?" she asked.

"None that you may print," I told her firmly. "But we have something far more interesting for your readers," I assured her.

She gave me a narrow look, then fetched an armful of towels for Harry to carry. "Hide your face with these and follow," she ordered. She took a look at my disguise and snorted. "Speak to no one and keep your eyes down," she instructed me. She poked her head out of the linen room to make certain the corridor was clear before beckoning to us. "Walk fast and stay close."

Unlike the older hotels, where the most august suites were located at the bottom, the Sudbury had been built with lifts, allowing them to give the higher floors over to luxurious rooms far from the bustle of the street and lobby. Everything was hushed here, courtesy of the thick carpets that stretched from wall to wall. Staff spoke only in whispers on these floors, and the air smelt of privilege.

"Which suite?" Stoker asked as he moved down the corridor.

"The Empress Suite," J. J. informed us. "Here." We stopped in front of the door, a tiny brass plaque proclaiming the name of the suite in elegant script. An empty chair sat outside and J. J. grinned. "The maharani's bodyguard has a tendresse for one of the other maids. She finishes work at eleven and he always slips off to see her."

"Rather slipshod if he is supposed to be protecting her," Harry put in.

J. J. rolled her eyes. "There are half a dozen plainclothes detectives in the lobby at any given hour. This fellow is ceremonial."

J. J. rapped sharply and the rest of us gathered behind her. The door opened almost at once, and I peered under Stoker's arm to see that it was our intruder from the previous night.

He looked at Stoker's chef's coat and the tray of pastries as well as Harry's stack of towels. "We ordered nothing," he said, shutting the door. Stoker put out his foot, catching the door before it closed, just as I stepped out from behind him. The young man's eyes widened in shock. I smiled to put him at his ease, but he let loose a string of words in a language I did not speak and turned, fleeing into the suite as if all the devils from hell were hard upon his heels.

We entered and closed the door. The foyer of the suite was furnished with a heavy walnut table carved with assorted fruits and animals. Stoker left his tray of pastries there—not without a longing look at a cream horn—and dropped his chef's coat beside it. We saw ourselves into the sitting room, where our intruder stood in front of a seated woman, his legs spread in a warrior's stance, a sword held aloft in his hand. He was clearly prepared to die in defense of the lady, and I smiled, recognizing her at once.

"I am sorry, I do not know the correct way to address a maharani," I told her.

She raised her hand to stem the flow of chatter from her grandson and gave me an amused look. "You should not address me at all until you are spoken to, but I do not expect you to know such things."

The maharani was dressed in the same style of ensemble she had worn in her photograph, beautifully draped silks, heavy with embroidery. Her hair, thick and black with only a few threads of silver, was coiled at her neck, and she wore a parure of gold jewelry set with enormous gems. Her grandson was also dressed in traditional clothing, with a long silk coat over narrow trousers of the same material. He maintained his martial posture and the meaning was clear—we might intrude, but we would never get near enough to harm his grandmother. The gesture was touching, although one look at the set of the maharani's jaw told me she was a woman accustomed to looking after herself.

"This is my grandson, Bhairav, and you may address me as Excellency or madam," she said. "Let us be casual together." She made a brief signal and her grandson lowered his sword but kept a watchful eye upon us.

"We are sorry to intrude so abruptly," I told her. "But I am afraid the manager at the front desk proved uncooperative to our request to announce us."

Her smile was thin. "It is of little consequence. I know who you are." She waved a hand towards the sofa opposite her and Stoker and I sat, perching on the edge of the settee. Harry stood behind us, and I suspected J. J. was still in the foyer, listening to every word.

"Mr. Templeton-Vane and . . . Miss Speedwell, is it not?"

"And our associate, Mr. Spenlove," I told her. "I must congratulate you on your sources," I said.

The smile deepened. "I have friends in your government. Discreet friends who sympathize with my politics."

"With independence for India, you mean?" Stoker inquired.

"Self-rule," her grandson corrected sharply. "We are dependent upon no one."

"I meant no offense," Stoker replied, careful to keep his voice neutral.

There was a cut high upon the young man's cheek, marring the smooth perfection of his skin. "I am sorry for that," I said, nodding towards the injury. "If I had known who you were, I would have been perfectly happy to hand over what you came for."

He snorted, and his grandmother patted his hand, murmuring a few words in Hindi. "I do not ask you to excuse my grandson," she told us. "His skepticism of Europeans is an honest result of the invasion and occupation of our country. I hope in time he will come to trust that we have some friends here, although not as many as I would like."

"You may count us among them," Stoker said boldly.

She laughed, a strong, mirthful sound from low in her belly. "I am not surprised, Mr. Templeton-Vane. Several of my meetings this week have been with a Sir Rupert Templeton-Vane. A close connection of yours, I am told."

"My elder brother," Stoker said in obvious surprise. "But you astonish me. I knew he worked in some capacity for the Foreign Office. I was not aware he had a stake in the affairs of India."

She shrugged. "At the beginning of the week, he was merely open to the possibility. Now he supports us, albeit quietly. I have asked him not to make his feelings known publicly. He can do far more for our cause by working from within."

She tipped her head to one side. "But I do not think you have come to discuss politics?" She did nothing so vulgar as hold out her hand, but the intent was clear. Stoker reached into his pocket and withdrew one of his red bandanna handkerchiefs. He had knotted it securely around the jewel and he presented this to the maharani.

"An interesting choice," she said. "Your bandanna comes from India, did you know that? We call the technique of dyeing it *bandhani*. It came to this part of the world when there was a fashion for snuff. The habit left white handkerchiefs badly soiled with the stains of tobacco, so these patterned handkerchiefs from our country were the perfect solution. Of course, we make them in all colors, not just this Turkey red, but it is possible the Englishman has a limited imagination."

With deft fingers, she unknotted the cloth and folded it back to reveal the diamond's shimmering fire. Even in its humble wrapping, it was mesmerizing. The maharani said nothing for a long moment, then touched it with a fingertip, her expression reverent.

"It is just as I remember it," she said softly.

"Did you wear it?" I asked.

She nodded. "On my wedding day. The parure was a gift from my husband. It was stolen from us during the rebellion."

"We suspected as much," Stoker told her. "When Lady Hathaway spoke of how she acquired it, she was less than informative."

The maharani gave a short laugh. "No doubt. The Hathaways were staying with us when the rebellion broke out. My husband, the maharajah, and Sir Geoffrey worked closely together. They were friends, and the Hathaways often spent summers with us at our palace in the hills. My relationship with Lady Hathaway was not as close as that of our husbands," she said dryly. "I found her badly educated and unsympathetic. But we were cordial. Our positions and our husbands demanded it. As the troubles began, the Hathaways decided to withdraw to the English fort for their own security. There was much confusion at the time, you understand, and so when the jewels went missing, there was no way to prove who had taken them. But I knew," she said.

"How?" Stoker inquired.

"A woman knows when another woman wants something of hers," I replied.

The maharani inclined her head. "Exactly so. The envy of a woman is not always easy to conceal. I had seen her eyes linger too often upon my jewels, and I confess, I wore them constantly when she was in our home. I knew she had nothing to rival them and it rankled her to see them around the neck of a woman she considered inferior."

"She stole them," her grandson burst out. "Like a common thief."

"But we could not prove it," the maharani went on. "I went to my husband with my suspicions and he refused to broach the matter with the English government. He said matters were at a delicate pass and we could not afford to bring trivialities into the mix."

"Trivialities!" I exclaimed, looking at the diamond.

"It was a point of pride with him that he could afford to replace them," she said. I eyed the elaborate collar of emeralds and rubies at her throat.

"He certainly did," I remarked.

"This? Paste," she said. "Like all of my jewels. Everything he gave me has been sold to raise money for the cause in which we believe so passionately."

"All of them?" I gaped at her, looking from the heavy girandole earrings to the stacks of bracelets encircling her arms from wrist to elbow.

"All," she said firmly. "I would sacrifice everything to see my country free of English rule. Even to the greatest of my jewels." She patted her grandson's hand. "Although I would prefer this one to take rather fewer risks."

"You fuss too much," Lord Bhairav said, ducking his head. "I was not harmed, and even if I were, it was a small price to pay to return the Eye of the Dawn to its rightful home." He looked to us, and for the first time, I saw humor in his dark gaze. "Have you worked it out yet? Our plan to restore the Eye of the Dawn?"

"Almost," I said slowly. "Let us return to the theft of the jewels. They were taken during the mutiny by Lady Hathaway, who later brought them to England. The maharajah refused to raise the matter with the English authorities in India, so she got away with them, but you never forgot they were your property," I said, nodding to the maharani, "and you raised your grandchildren with the story."

"Grandchildren?" Stoker asked.

"Anjali," I told him. "She is your granddaughter, is she not?" I asked the maharani. "Sister or cousin to Lord Bhairav?"

"She is my sister," he said.

"How the devil— Pardon me, Your Excellency," Stoker said to the maharani. "How the deuces did you figure that?"

I gave him a narrow look. "I had a little time to think whilst you were occupied with Mrs. MacGregor."

He blushed deeply and I went on. "And so the three of you concocted a plan. Anjali was to insinuate herself into the Hathaway household. That must have taken some effort."

"Anjali was at school with Euphemia Hathaway," Lord Bhairav said.

"But Anjali is miles older," Harry put in.

"Not if you look carefully," I corrected. "She wears smoked spectacles so you cannot see her eyes. The grey in her hair must be powder. I did not realize it at first, but when I considered it later, I realized what had been bothering me about her. I had detected an incongruity, and I could not, at Hathaway Hall, discover what it was. It was only when I had time to think that I hit upon the fact that, in spite of being told she was a person of some maturity, I recalled that she moved with the lightness and grace of a much younger woman."

"Very clever," said a low voice from the doorway.

"Anjali!" I cried.

It was she, although I am forced to admit that had I encountered her in her present state, I might not have immediately made the connection to the quiet dowd of Hathaway Hall. Her hair, freed of its dulling powder, shone rich and black as her brother's, and her eyes were bright and shining with youth without the mask of the smoked spectacles. She was dressed, not as a wren in dull grey, but as a peacock, in shifting blues and greens, the silks rippling as she moved into the room and took a chair next to her grandmother with a graceful gesture. She looked at the diamond in the maharani's palm and gave a nod of satisfaction.

"I must thank you for returning it to us," she said with an air of authority she had not sported in Devon. "And I must apologize for the stratagems we employed. They were not meant to make you feel foolish or to alarm you."

"They had nothing to do with us at all, I suspect," I replied.

She smiled. "You are correct, Miss Speedwell." She looked with interest at Harry. "Your disguise is as imperfect as mine was. You are the man who claimed to be Jonathan Hathaway and yet you are called Spenlove? Then you were engaging in an imposture of your own?"

He had the grace to duck his head. "I am not Jonathan Hathaway," he acknowledged. "But I knew Hathaway, and I can confirm he is, as his family feared, buried in Sumatra."

She pursed her lips. "To give them hope was a cruel thing to do," she said with all the dignity and authority of her grandmother.

Harry bowed his head further still and Anjali turned to Stoker and to me. "Ask what you like. You have earned it, I think."

"I presume Euphemia Hathaway knew of your masquerade," Stoker put in.

Anjali nodded. "She did. The fact that we were at school together was a coincidence, you understand. But there are not many schools which provide the rigor of scientific education we both wanted. Effie's school fees were paid by her grandfather, who encouraged her studies, and her future seemed promising. She dreamt, we both did, of attending university. But a series of tragedies befell her family."

"Jonathan Hathaway's death," I murmured.

Anjali went on. "With the deaths of his son and grandson, Sir

Geoffrey lost much of his vigor. He seemed to age overnight. He no longer studied the stars or guided Effie in her observations. It seemed as if his very will to live had been taken from him."

"Effie must have known she would have a very different life with Charles as head of the family," Stoker suggested.

"She did. She lived in dread of the time he would inherit. Charles is not a monster," Anjali clarified, "but what he is doing to her *is* monstrous. He has taken all from her that matters, her studies, her passions. He allows his wife to reduce her to a shadow, less than a person. She is permitted nothing of her own, not a dream, not an ambition. He gives all control over to Mary Hathaway, and because she fears what people will say more than anything, she strives to break Effie's spirit as one would break an unruly horse. It is an untenable situation."

"Mary Hathaway is the worst sort of provincial," I put in.

We smiled at one another, bonded—as women frequently are—by our mutual dislike of another.

"How did you come to conspire together to steal the jewels?" Stoker asked.

She folded her hands primly in her lap. "We discussed it often. I knew Lady Hathaway still had the diamond, but Effie said it was always locked away in a bank vault, and for all our cleverness, we could not imagine how we would break into a bank vault and steal it," she added with a smile that revealed two deep dimples. "But I pointed out to her it would be a very easy thing to take it if it were in Hathaway Hall. First, Effie suggested to Mary that Lady Hathaway needed a companion and she mentioned that she knew of a gently born woman of Indian parentage who needed employment."

A wry smile twisted her lips and she went on. "Mary Hathaway liked the idea of having Effie further under her thumb, and Effie would have more time for her little chores if the old woman was tended to by someone else. Effie pointed out that even the queen has an Indian servant, and since Mary was often tired of Lady Hathaway's endless stories of life in India, she thought someone from there would provide her a more willing ear. She was easy to persuade. And Effie put me forward as a candidate."

"How did she explain knowing you?" I ventured.

Anjali smiled. "She gave me a different surname and said I had been a poor scholarship student at school so that no one at the Hall would connect my name with my grandmother's. I came to stay at Hathaway Hall—lightly disguised so I would not be recognized leaving London."

She shifted her head and her hair gleamed in the lamplight. "After that, Effie began to work on Mary Hathaway, very subtly, you understand. Asking her grandmother to tell the story of the jewels so that Mary would hear of them. And because she is acquisitive and grasping, Mary knew that she wanted them. They would complete the picture she is painting for herself of a society hostess of great grandeur. Effie played into this, telling Mary that she ought to be painted in them and suggesting to Charles that he commission such a painting for Mary. That would have worked, I believe, were it not for the return of Jonathan Hathaway."

Her lips compressed into a thin line as she paused, and the maharani spoke. "It grows late and there is still much to tell. Let us ring for refreshments," she suggested. We did as we were told, and in a very few minutes, the maharani's maid emerged from another room with platters of seed cakes and pots of tea flavored with spices and rich with milk and sugar.

The maharani sat back, holding her glass of tea, and gestured towards her granddaughter. "You may continue."

Anjali bowed her head towards her grandmother. "We realized if the diamond went missing but no one in the house left, then the house would be searched. So we hatched a clever plot to get the diamond out whilst we remained inside."

"Clever?" The maharani gave her granddaughter an exasperated look. "It was the scheme of melodramatic children."

"The ghost," I said. I slanted a look at Lord Bhairav. "I presume that is the role you played?"

He grinned, baring teeth as beautiful as his sister's. "I made a very good ghost," he said, raising his arms into a menacing stance. "Were you not frightened by my spectral ball of light?"

"No," I told him calmly. "But you terrorized the villagers to no end."

He shrugged. "I gave them a good story to raise their hairs. They will talk of it for generations. Can you guess how I did it?"

"A glass ball with galvanic effects?" Stoker guessed. "Carried against a black robe so it would appear to be floating in midair?"

"Exactly right," Lord Bhairav said. "But the construction of the orb was Anjali's doing," he added with apparent pride in his sister.

"Of course!" I exclaimed, turning to Anjali. "We spoke at length about Galvani and Volta when I visited the observatory. But your interest is not merely theoretical, is it?"

"My scientific studies," she said modestly. "My speciality is electrical fields. Bhairav and I had to meet occasionally to discuss matters, and I could not always get away at convenient times. And, of course," she added with a wry smile, "we did not want the villagers to note a man of Indian appearance upon the moors. So we met at night, a treacherous proposition for him since the moorland is full of dangers. I developed the orb as a sort of lantern to guide his way across the moors, but also to frighten the local folk should they see him. We could not risk anyone seeing him close and asking questions."

Another piece of the puzzle slotted neatly into place. "You stayed with Nanny Burnham in her cottage on the moor, did you not?" I asked Lord Bhairav. "I heard someone moving about when I called upon her. She told me it was the cat, but the cat was sleeping on the hearth."

"Nanny Burnham was forcibly retired by Mary Hathaway," Anjali volunteered. "Not refined enough to teach her children, she said. So it was not hard for Effie to persuade Nanny Burnham to help us. All she need do was give Bhairav a place to stay hid during the day. His only problem was Nanny Burnham's cooking," Anjali added with a glance at her brother's slender midsection. "He ate too much of her nursery fare and was growing fat."

He grinned and patted his belly. "Nanny Burnham made a very delicious rice pudding and something called a jam roly-poly."

"Damson jam?" Stoker asked hopefully.

"Raspberry," Lord Bhairav told him.

"Even better." Stoker's expression was wistful. His fondness for natural science was rivaled only by his fondness for nursery foods.

"At long last," Anjali said, picking up the thread of the conversation, "the Eye of the Dawn was retrieved from the bank vault and the time was at hand. Effie broke into the casket and took it, leaving behind a handkerchief marked with Jonathan Hathaway's initials."

"In order to implicate me," Harry volunteered.

Anjali shrugged. "Anything to bring confusion to the matter would serve our purposes. Within the family there was dissension as to whether you really were Jonathan Hathaway. If Jonathan's handkerchief were found, apparently dropped during the theft, then it was a certainty that Charles would insist upon a search of the house. But the diamond would not be there. It would have vanished, into thin air," she said, fluttering her fingers.

"But everyone in the house would have lived under suspicion, most of all you," I pointed out.

"I was never going to stay," she replied. "A few days to let them search my things and find nothing. Then I would quietly disappear, remove my disguise, and become myself again."

"And if anyone decided to circulate your description, they would be looking for someone considerably older," I finished. "It would appear you thought of everything."

"Except that without a clear resolution to the crime, without a proper solution, the atmosphere would have become poisonous," Stoker objected. "Everyone would have been under suspicion, always wondering who might have taken it."

Anjali shrugged again. "That is what I told Effie, but she did not care. She is very, very angry—with all of them, even Lady Hathaway. No one in that house understands or cares about her feelings, so why should she care about theirs?"

"I deplore her actions, but I also comprehend them," I told her. "It is diabolical to set out to create an atmosphere of disharmony, of actual malice, within a household. But that is more Mary Hathaway's doing than Effie's. Charles has permitted it, and Lady Hathaway is too old and infirm to make an objection, even if she wished."

"I am not surprised you understand," Anjali said. She met my gaze with her own, level and without judgment.

"Effie Hathaway has a far twistier mind than I suspected," Harry said in a tone of grudging admiration.

"Effie knew suspicion would fall, but she must have known it would always fall hardest upon Anjali, Jonathan—that is, you, Harry—and herself. Lady Hathaway would have no cause to steal her own jewel, and Charles and Mary would never suspect one another. And by causing a search to take place, it would clear the rest of the staff, ensuring they were not touched by her revenge upon her family."

"And I might have swung for it with no consideration from her," Harry said, turning slightly green.

"Hanging, I am informed, is no longer the penalty in this country for theft," the maharani said by way of consolation. "Have another seed cake," she urged. He shoved it into his mouth, still looking darkly at Anjali. I was rather impressed by the ruthlessness of the plot, but not surprised. There are few people on earth more capable of hatred than the female sex when caged.

"So, she plotted a course for restitution," Stoker summed up.

I looked from the maharani to her grandchildren and shook my head. "It was indeed restitution for the theft committed so long ago, but this was about much more than that. I know you have the diamond and to you a wrong has been righted, but Effie was not driven by a desire to expiate the crimes of her family against yours. She has struck out against them as a tigress will turn on its tamer." I addressed the maharani. "She does not seek to benefit you, Your Excellency. She seeks to wound *them*."

The maharani nodded. "Of course, this is true. But I also do not care."

"You were content to take advantage of a young woman's misery?" I asked sharply.

"Yes," she said without apology. "I have what I wanted, what justice required. No blood was shed, so I consider that a victory, Miss Speedwell." She turned to Anjali. "Finish the story, child."

Anjali went on. "Effie took the diamond and wrapped it into a piece of oilcloth. She passed that to me and I went out to the summerhouse, where I was supposed to meet Bhairav to hand the jewel to him. It was essential this happen as quickly as possible because we did not know when Lady Hathaway would realize it had been stolen and the diamond must be out of the house before the cry was raised."

"But before you could hand it over, I appeared," I put in.

She smiled thinly. "I was not pleased to see you, Miss Speedwell."

"Nor was I," Lord Bhairav said in a fervent voice. "I tripped twice over those abominable robes trying to get away from you."

Anjali picked up the thread of her narrative. "There was no time to think, so I shoved the jewel into the watering pot in the summerhouse and pretended to faint."

"Why the watering pot?" Harry asked.

"Because if the Hall were searched and it were found there, it would implicate no one in particular," Stoker guessed.

Anjali nodded. "It was an imperfect solution, but it was the best I could do under the circumstances. I had to stop Miss Speedwell from discovering Bhairav. Feigning unconsciousness would delay her pursuit of him and allow him time to get away, but there was no place to conceal the diamond on my person. If she found it, all would be lost."

"The best of a bad situation," Stoker agreed.

"How did the orb vanish?" I asked.

He grinned. "I shoved it into my robes to conceal the light until I was on the far side of a boulder. Then I hurried away, back to the safety of Nanny Burnham's cottage. I dressed in my own clothes and was waiting for some message from Anjali. Nanny Burnham's cat came in with a shrew, a messy thing," he added with a moue of distaste. "I took it outside to throw it in the midden when I saw a figure in the moonlight, crossing the moor. It was the man calling himself Jonathan Hathaway," he said with a gesture towards Harry. "I thought it curious he would be out so late, and I followed him. He went to the station and caught the first train to London. I did also, although I cannot say I was driven by anything other than instinct. He acted furtive, suspicious. And I wondered if he had something to do with the reason Anjali had not been able to hand over the jewel. I was prepared to follow him and see where he went, but no sooner had he alighted in London than he was taken, abducted really, by a tall man with very blond hair and a woman in a veil."

"We are familiar," Stoker said dryly.

"You saw them snatch me and did nothing to help?" Harry demanded. "I was kidnapped, you know. A rescue would not have gone amiss, my good fellow."

Lord Bhairav gave him a lofty look. "It is not my purpose to involve myself in the domestic matters of Englishmen. Besides, they were suspicious and very watchful. I had to keep well back so they did not see me, and in my efforts to remain discreet, I lost them. I returned here and sent a telegram to Nanny Burnham for Anjali to collect. We used a sort of code, and through that Anjali was able to respond."

His sister picked up the story. "It was Effie who hit upon the idea of how to get the diamond out of the house by secreting it in the orrery. I found your address on the letter in Charles Hathaway's desk and cabled it here to Bhairav with instructions to retrieve it as soon as you had returned to London. Which he almost did," she added, a touch of asperity spicing her words.

Her brother flared. "I would have managed it if it were not for the dogs," he protested. "So many dogs."

"There are rather a lot," I consoled him.

"When he failed to retrieve it," Anjali went on, "I decided to come myself. I thought I could pay a call upon you and perhaps manage to take it. I would have thought of something."

I turned to the maharani again. "Did you know about the scheme to retrieve the diamond?"

She pressed her lips together in an expression of disapproval, but I had a sense she was not entirely displeased. "Not at first. Anjali was supposed to be staying at the Hall as the guest of her schoolfriend, and Bhairav was meant to join her for a visit. It was not until I announced my intention to come to London that Bhairav broke down and told me the truth." She looked complacently from one grandchild to the next. "I am exasperated with their flair for melodrama, but a sense of theatricality is not the worst thing if one means to spend one's life in politics."

"What now?" I asked Anjali. "Will you give up your studies into galvanism?"

"One of the best ways for India to demonstrate her worth is to develop new technologies and means of production," she said coolly.

"There is nothing more political than the ability to take care of one's own people."

The maharani rose smoothly and the rest of us followed suit. She shook hands with Harry. "I believe your motives were not good, and I think your character is entirely defective, but that is not our affair. On behalf of my family, I apologize for any inconvenience you may have suffered."

He gaped but recovered his composure swiftly. "Thank you, Your Excellency," he murmured.

She extended her hand to Stoker. "Mr. Templeton-Vane."

Stoker kissed her hand and she moved to me. "Miss Speedwell." Her mouth twitched a little. "I recognize in you a similar spirit to my granddaughter. I think you might well have become friends under a different set of circumstances."

"I hope, if it is not too presumptuous, she might consider me one now," I said.

Anjali smiled and shook my hand. "Good-bye, Miss Speedwell."

Anjali even shook hands with Harry, who had the grace to look abashed. "I am sorry if I distressed Effie. She is a nice girl, all things considered, and I hope she did not take it too hard."

Anjali laughed. "Effie? She never believed you for a second. She is the only one who knew the moment you arrived that you could not be Jonathan."

He stared at her in astonishment. "But how?"

"Ask her yourself," she said, lifting her chin. "I am finished answering the questions of Englishmen."

We left, collecting a wide-eyed J. J. from the foyer as we went. We hurtled down the stairs and she whisked us into the linen closet again. She scribbled notes on her cuff until Stoker gently plucked the pencil from her grasp.

"You cannot write any of it," he reminded her.

"Blast and damnation," she began.

"But we have something better for you," I promised her. "Come tomorrow for tea and we will tell you everything you want to know about a fiendish villainess who swindled thousands out of the cream of Brazilian nobility."

Her eyes widened and she looked at each of us in turn. Harry gave her a miserable sigh. "Very well. Yes. Come to tea and I will tell you whatever you want to know. Print it all."

J. J. tweaked his moustaches and sent us on our way.

As we settled into a hackney for the drive back to Bishop's Folly, I felt oddly deflated. "I do not like it," I said, my brow furrowing.

"What? The mystery of the ghostly light on the moor is solved, the diamond has been returned to its rightful owner—"

"And Harry Spenlove will soon be taking his leave of you," Harry put in lightly.

"But Effie Hathaway is still at the mercy of a family who respect neither her abilities nor her ambitions," I protested.

"She has got the last laugh," Stoker reminded me. "She carried out a criminal enterprise under their noses."

"Rather too well," Harry protested. "I might have done hard labor because of that little harridan."

"She is unhappy," I said simply. "And she is likely to be for the rest of her life."

Stoker and Harry and I were still gently bickering about Effie Hathaway when we returned to the Belvedere. There was a strange sense of unfinished business about the whole matter, I decided, and it seemed odd to realize how much had happened in only a few short days.

"Shall we sleep here again tonight?" Harry suggested. There was something boyishly hopeful in his tone, and when I looked at him, he blushed a little. "It's just that, I mean to leave by tomorrow night. The longer I stay, the likelier that Isabel will find me, and I'd just as soon not have that happen. And spending the night here felt . . . matey," he finished. "I haven't had that in a while, you know."

I looked at Stoker, who shrugged. "I will fetch the aguardiente," I said. We took a bottle of the heady stuff to the snuggery, where we settled in with the dogs. It was both reward for the successful conclusion of an investigation and anaesthetic for our various injuries. Bruises and swelling had begun to set in, and we were soon nodding over our cups.

Sometime after the clocks chimed two, I felt someone tuck a blanket over me, and I drifted for a long while until I heard Stoker's voice, a low, soft rumble in the darkness. "Do you really think of her as the Eurydice to your Orpheus?"

"Sometimes," Harry said on a sigh. "She is a difficult woman to forget."

"The mistake you made was in thinking she was a bit player in your story," Stoker told him. "She is mistress of her own fate and she bends to no man."

"Not even you?"

A laugh in the darkness that was not entirely mirthful. "Sometimes I think especially not me."

They fell to silence then, and in a few minutes I heard Harry's quiet snores and Stoker's deep, even breaths. They slept, but long into the night I lay wakeful, thinking of what they said.

CHAPTER

31

I woke late the next morning, considerably subdued in health and energy—a regrettable aftereffect of aguardiente when consumed in large quantities. None of my companions was in evidence, not even Vespertine. I assumed they had all risen earlier and were enjoying a hearty breakfast without me. Stiff and moaning gently from my various aches, I washed and descended to the main floor of the Belvedere, where Stoker was staring balefully at a plate of cold eggs and taking tentative sips from a scalding cup of tea. Wisps of steam wreathed his head, giving him the look of one of the lesser satyrs.

"Where is Harry?" I asked.

"Gone," he told me, clipping off the word sharply.

"Gone where? Did you let him take a turn in the Roman baths?" I asked with a forced smile. Stoker has a notoriously proprietary attitude towards the baths. Lord Rosemorran built them to soothe his occasional bouts of rheumatics, but Stoker is the one likeliest to be found in them at any hour of the day or night. Since Stoker and I had discussed the fact of my marriage, something unfinished had lingered between us—something I was not entirely ready to conclude. I had no notion of his feelings on the matter. The fact that I was afraid to discover them did not reflect particularly well upon my character or my courage. So, I concealed my uneasiness behind a quip and was not surprised that he did the same. When he spoke, his tone was pleasant, studiedly so.

"I have not seen Harry this morning," he told me. Stoker handed over the scarlet leather box, stamped with the papal tiara, but I already knew what I would find when I opened it.

"Oh no," I moaned.

I flicked open the clasp and lifted the lid. The collection of papal cameos was gone, and in its place a single scribbled word in a hand I knew only too well.

Sorry.

I flopped into my chair with another moan, folding my arms upon the desk and dropping my head onto them. "He was so nearly good."

When I raised my head, Stoker was watching me closely. I sighed. "I shall have to make good with his lordship."

He sighed heavily. "Would you like me to—"

"No," I said quickly. "Harry is my responsibility."

"Yes," he said, his expression inscrutable. "He is after all your husband."

There was an unmistakable note of bitterness in his voice, something dark and angry. He had behaved with considerable bonhomie towards Harry, but I understood he had done so whilst it was expedient—when we were in the midst of abduction and the potential threat of violence. And he had been courteous enough upon our return to the Belvedere, but it was only at that moment that I understood precisely what that civility had cost him.

He turned on his heel and left me then, and I added Stoker to the list of problems yet unsolved.

During a painful interview with Lord Rosemorran, I accepted responsibility for the missing cameos—I simply said they ought to have been locked up and my neglect had resulted in them being lost.

He waved away the subject, uncomfortable as he always was when discussing matters of finance. But I insisted and we at length came to an understanding that I would recompense him for them at their current market value by having a certain sum deducted from my pay packet each quarter. The result was that I would be beholden to Lord Rosemorran for the next forty or so years, I reflected darkly. I had no plans to leave his lordship's employ in the near future, but the very fact that such an option would be impossible was yet another crime to lay at Harry's door. I cursed him soundly as I left Bishop's Folly and made my way to the Hippolyta Club, known affectionately to its members as the Curiosity Club. The steps had been freshly washed, and the brass plaque proclaiming the club's motto—*Alis volat propriis*—was gleaming with fresh polish. A pair of tall, arrow-shaped topiary flanked the doors like living sentinels, and I sniffed appreciatively as I entered the club. Inside, the odors of beeswax and rose and woodsmoke mingled with the enticing aromas of the luncheon being served in the dining room. But I was bent upon other business. I signed in and briskly took myself up to one of the smaller private meeting rooms on the first floor. I had reserved it for my own use for only half an hour, and I hoped my guest would be punctual.

In fact, she anticipated me, for she had already been shown to the room before I arrived and was sitting in one of the chairs before the fire, clutching a reticule in her gloved hands and playing with the clasp. The Italian greyhound, Al-'Ijliyyah, shivered at her feet, dressed in a little coat made from an old jumper. She looked distinctly miserable, but not more than her mistress, who regarded me with dull eyes as I entered. She rose politely but seemed on the verge of collapse. I rang at once for refreshment, guessing she suffered from inanition. We spoke of meaningless things until the food arrived, and I insisted she drink two strong cups of heavily sugared tea and consume a plate of sandwiches and another of cake before changing the subject.

"I am certain you wish to know why I asked you here," I began.

"Asked?" Her expression was faintly mocking. "You insisted. To the point that you included a train ticket. It led to the most furious row with Charles. You do understand that I have run away, Miss Speedwell. It was the only way to escape my family in order to do as you asked. I have come as instructed, and I am penniless and alone in the world now, so I hope you will provide me with enlightenment and possibly employment before I starve on the streets," she said, and I heard a note of hysteria creeping into her voice. She was so very young, I reminded myself. Almost the same age as when I had married Harry Spenlove. Scarcely more than a child, but determined to survive—nay, to *thrive*.

"You will understand shortly," I promised her. Without further delay, I launched into an explanation in the simplest and most straightforward of terms. But the swift reversal in her fortunes confused her and she could not accept the facts until I explained them, and even then she queried me at length.

"I am to study with the Misses Marvell in Scotland," she said in a small voice.

"Yes. In exchange for doing light domestic and secretarial labor in their observatory—writing up notes, dusting instruments—you will be given lodging and board and tutelage."

"And a stipend," she breathed.

"A very tiny one," I said. It would be even tinier than I had intended now that my own salary had been reduced. But her expenses would be few, and I had every expectation that Effie would prove up to the challenge. "You will live a hand-to-mouth existence, but you will not starve and you will be doing what you love. Moreover, you will be given opportunities—if you prove a dutiful and diligent student—to do your own research and to write. The Misses Marvell maintain a voluminous correspondence with fellow astronomers throughout the world and are happy to provide the necessary introductions when you have proven worthy of them. All you need do is work hard and think about the stars, Effie."

She had held herself taut throughout the conversation, but it was at this point her resolve seemed to falter. Her hands shook and she forced out the next words through a throat that must have been tight with emotion.

"But Al-'Ijliyyah, I cannot leave her," she lamented. "And she would never abide the cold in Scotland."

She held tightly to the little animal, her feelings clearly at war. Her own desires were in conflict with her responsibility to her pet, and the fact that she hesitated to leave the dog behind, even at the expense of her work, made me like her even better.

I sighed, knowing I would regret the next words I spoke.

"I will take her," I told her. "There are already four dogs. Why not a fifth? Besides, Stoker is handy with a needle. I suspect he will enjoy making little coats for her." Effie wept then, liberally dropping her tears into Al-'Ijliyyah's fur as the dog stared at me with what looked like an entirely human expression of resentment.

"I do not know how to thank you," Effie said, mastering her emotion at last.

I handed her a small portfolio. "You haven't time, my dear. Your train leaves in an hour. There is your ticket and some money for food. I have included the latest journal of the Society for Astronomical Studies. I thought you might enjoy some reading for the train."

She fell into weeping again, and it proved much more difficult to dislodge her the second time. But at last, I managed to persuade her, still sniffling and petting the dog, out of the room, down the stairs, and into a cab, whilst I held an indifferent Al-'Ijliyyah in my arms.

"Wait," I called, and Effie put down the window. "I am certain that

Anjali has told you by now that the man calling himself Jonathan Hathaway was not your brother."

She nodded, sniffling hard. "I knew from the beginning."

"How? When everyone else in the family was uncertain?"

Effie's smile was cool. "Because one of the tasks Mary liked to set for me was collecting the boots to be polished. I took his and compared them to the brogues that I wore. The brogues were Jonathan's, you know. The newcomer's boots were fully an inch shorter."

"And a man's feet may grow, but they will not shrink," I said, shaking my head. "So stupidly obvious. And yet everyone overlooked it but you."

She put her hand out the window to shake mine. "What is overlooked is often the most significant, Miss Speedwell."

She said a final farewell to Al-'Ijliyyah. "You will write and tell me how she fares?" she asked, an anxious line etched between her brows. But her eyes were bright with anticipation, and I knew in her heart she had already begun her grand adventure.

"I promise," I vowed. Effie waved again and was still waving long after the driver sprang the horses and moved smartly into traffic.

I looked down at the dog and she gave me a long, baleful look. "We are going to be friends," I warned her. "Whether you like it or not."

CHAPTER

32

The matter of Effie Hathaway had been settled to my satisfaction; the matter of the cameos slightly less so. But it was the best I could do under the circumstances. I returned to the Belvedere and threw myself into my work, hoping that the methodical cataloging and restoring of lepidoptery would, as it had so often done in the past, soothe my troubled spirits. Yet too often in the following days, I would find my attention wandering and my thoughts elsewhere.

Stoker and I spoke little during the days that followed our adventure with the impossible impostor, as I had come to think of Harry Spenlove. I had, true to my word, entertained J. J. to tea after my sending Effie on her way. Without alluding to the Hathaways or my own personal entanglement with Harry, I told her everything I knew about Isabel de Armas MacGregor, relating the details of the Brazilian railway affair. J. J. took copious notes and then went to ground. When she surfaced, two days later, it was with an exposé published on the front page of the *Daily Harbinger*. LADY ADVENTURESS SWINDLES BRAZILIAN ROYALTY screamed the headline, and there were several illustrations of her, enabled by my description. Göran, I was interested to see, warranted little more than a footnote. It was the notion of a lady criminal that intrigued the public.

"You realize you will have only enraged her further," Stoker pointed out.

I shrugged. "She hates me in any event. And she cannot be certain that I was the one who told J. J. about her endeavors."

"It would take precious little to find out," he said.

"If she is as clever as Harry says, she will have brushed the dust of London off of her shoes and taken herself far away. In making her crimes public, I have made England a dangerous place for her."

"And won yourself an implacable enemy," he said, his eyes never leaving my face.

"I am not afraid of her," I told him, squaring my shoulders. "If she wants a fight, she is welcome to bring one. We have unfinished business in any event," I added, touching the length of velvet ribbon at my throat. The cut had healed cleanly, leaving a slender pink line. I had taken to tying a ribbon to conceal it, but I was reminded of her every time I had occasion to use the looking glass.

I would have continued the conversation, but Stoker had already turned away, as he had so often done in the preceding days. We had spoken little and never anything of real importance. We discussed the collections and evaluated one another's articles for publication; we exercised the dogs, and Stoker, as I anticipated, spent a good deal of his free time sewing small coats for the eternally shivering Al-'Ijliyyah. But further than that, we did not tread. We walked carefully around one another, as if picking our way across the dangers of Dartmoor, fearing to step into a bog and drown if we moved too quickly or in the wrong direction.

And finally, one brilliant morning, I could bear it no longer. I had been working in the vivarium, attending to a particularly beautiful and demanding brood of *Agrias claudina*—the adults feed on rotting fish and the smell, as has been pointed out to me on several occasions and by numerous people, is less than wholesome. Suddenly, as I watched the brilliant scarlet slash of wings, I was filled with a melancholy I could not bear. Division from Stoker, in any form, was like an amputation of the soul, and I would do anything to bridge the abyss between us.

I made my way to the Belvedere, where I found Stoker precisely where I anticipated—with his thylacine. He had made great progress with the beast, conjuring a lifelike appearance so convincing, I could fairly hear the snarl from its open jaws. But Stoker, like all genius, is never content with the obvious. Besides the creature's ferocity, he had paid homage to its intelligence, fashioning eyes of such cunning coupled with understanding, I should not have been surprised if the beast spoke to me.

"It is extraordinary," I told him truthfully. Stoker turned in obvious surprise. So intent had he been upon his work, he had not heard me enter. As he often did when in the throes of his efforts, he was stripped to the waist, covered in sweat and sawdust and streaks of glue. His hair, always overlong, was a tumble of black waves, his jaw heavily shadowed by unshaven beard. He was filthy and looked every inch the disreputable pirate. And he was the loveliest thing I had ever seen.

He looked at his trophy. "Yes, he has come along well, hasn't he," Stoker said, but it was no question. He knew the value of his work. There was no one in England, indeed in all of Europe, to touch him for skill and for artistry.

"You should be very proud," I ventured. "His lordship will want him in pride of place when the museum opens."

"In another forty or so years," Stoker agreed with a small smile.

"Stoker, you must know how sorry I am—" I began.

His jaw tightened. "The fault is as much mine. I understand why you did not tell me about Harry. I understand why you married him, and I understand why you wanted to leave. I even understand why you did not wish to speak of him after you believed him dead. There is no power or pain as devastating as a first love."

He stepped towards me and raised his hand as if to touch me but dropped it back to his side. "I understand all of that, and I can even forgive it. I have done as much. As we have always known, Veronica, we are the same, you and I."

"Quicksilver, we said. And the rest of the world is mud," I reminded him.

"Just so. And yet, for all that I understand and all that I forgive, I cannot forget. I cannot forget that when you might have relied upon me, you felt that you could not. And I have to wonder, where does that leave us?"

I stepped towards him and reached for his hands. Filthy and scarred, strong and sensitive. I pressed a kiss to the back of one. "For too long I have resisted allowing anyone else to be responsible for me. I have loved you but held you at bay, determined to withhold part of myself. I am willing now to put my happiness into these hands."

My head was still bent when I felt the pressure of his lips upon my hair. Gently, slowly, he withdrew his hands and stepped back.

"Oh," I said quietly.

"Veronica, you are his legal wife," he replied, his eyes bleak with heartbreak.

"If you think for a moment that I care for him—"

"Of course not. I admit that I have wrestled with jealousy as any mortal man might, but I am content that whatever feelings you once had for him are long dead."

"Then why?" I asked.

"Your feelings must have changed, but I am not certain that his have," he told me.

"What does that matter to me?" I demanded. "To us?"

"If he did not care for you, he would have secured a legal separation, a divorce even."

"If he *did* care for me, he would not have abandoned me to die in a volcanic eruption," I reminded him icily.

"You are his legal wife," he repeated. "And I know what it means to have someone break that bond. I want to believe that you are entirely mine, but in the eyes of the world, you belong to him."

"I belong to no one," I reminded him. "Except myself. And I wish to be with you. Harry Spenlove made himself irrelevant to me when he left me six years ago. Do not let him come between us now."

For an instant, I thought I had swayed him, but he said nothing for a long moment, and when he spoke, it was in a voice thick with emotion. "I need time, Veronica."

I forced a smile. "We have all the time in the world," I assured him. "I will be here."

The next day, I arrived at the Belvedere to find Stoker absent. The thylacine had been finished, eyeballs brightly polished, the coat brushed and gleaming. Two envelopes and a parcel lay upon my desk. The first envelope was stamped, the address written in a hasty scrawl. I withdrew several pieces of paper. On top was a legal document followed by a brief note.

My dearest Veronica—Please accept this as a token of my gratitude. I do not expect that you will think of me, but I hope that this ensures that if the name of Harry Spenlove ever crosses your mind, a smile will follow. H.

I turned to the legal document. It was the marriage lines Stoker had spoken of—a record of my wedding to Harry Spenlove. And my eyes fell upon the space where the attending clergyman ought to have signed. It was blank. So too were the spaces for witnesses. Without those, there was no marriage, I realized with a dizzying rush of emotion. I had married him in good faith, but Harry, ever the opportunist, had—through some sleight of hand—ensured the proper legalities were not fulfilled. I had, it seemed, lived in sin with him in Sumatra. Delicious, liberating, unfettered, and unbinding sin. Whatever his intentions in keeping the document, in giving it to me, he had ensured that I knew I was free. It was thoroughly typical of him to keep the information from me and then present it as though bestowing a royal favor. I was conscious of relief, deep and profound—with an equal certainty that if ever I saw Harry Spenlove again, a smile was not what he could expect.

My gaze fell then to the postscript. "*I must thank you for the loan of the cameos. I needed traveling money in order to retrieve my nest egg, but have now done so and am happy to enclose the pawn ticket and sufficient funds for their retrieval.*"

Wrapped neatly in a sheet of paper was the ticket from the pawnbroker and a thick stack of fifty-pound notes. As soon as I restored the cameos, I could consider my obligation to Lord Rosemorran at an end, I realized with another rush of happiness, followed almost instantly by irritation that Harry had not simply *asked* for the loan of some traveling money. If he could only be bothered to deal forthrightly, I reflected, he would be a good deal less irritating.

The last items in the envelope from Harry were a handful of banknotes in exactly the amount that I had made him a loan of for a suit of new clothes and a shave. A small slip of paper read, "*Debt discharged.*"

The parcel was wrapped in brown paper and bore the label of

Wycherly & Sons in Bloomsbury, the purveyors of the highest quality impedimenta for natural historians. I opened it to find a butterfly net. Fashioned of ash, it was elegant and lightweight, each ring painted with a narrow, smart stripe of hyacinth pink. The handle fit my grip perfectly, and the net was dark green silk, supple as a flower petal. I gave it an experimental swish and it cut through the air with a whisper. At the end of the handle, my initials had been embossed in gold.

It was not a mere love token, I realized, but a gift from someone who truly understood what mattered to me. Any man might present orchids or jewels, but Stoker had given me back my joy.

In the wrappings was an envelope marked only with the letter "V" in a bold, familiar hand, the paper smelling of honey drops and smeared in one corner with dried glue, and I smiled as I anticipated some line of Keats.

Instead, it began without preamble, and it was no poetry.

I have accepted an invitation to survey a collection of mounted wolves in Bavaria on Lord Rosemorran's behalf. I expect to be gone for some weeks. I have had word from Charles Hathaway that the butterflies he promised are en route, and I am certain you will enjoy the study of them.

I stared at the page, then turned it over, certain I would find more writ upon the back. There was nothing.

My hands trembling only slightly, I laid the net carefully aside and picked up the third envelope. The letter inside was headed with the Templeton-Vane crest. It was from Tiberius, Viscount Templeton-Vane and Stoker's eldest brother. He, too, began without preamble—a family trait, I thought in some irritation.

I am in Rome and have discovered the most exciting collection of birdwings—Southern Tailed, Ornithoptera meridionalis—*which my hostess is willing to donate to Lord Rosemorran's burgeoning museum provided they are treated with the utmost care by an accomplished lepidopterist. You have only to come and claim them.*

I picked up Stoker's note and sat for a moment, holding the letters—Stoker's in my right, Tiberius' in my left. Then I pulled out the atlas, turning the pages from Bavaria to Rome and back again.

After a long while, I rose, whistling for George, the hallboy. He trotted in, his expression expectant.

"Yes, miss."

"You will need to watch the dogs, George," I told him as I unearthed my carpetbag and began to pack. "I am going on a journey. Excelsior!"

ACKNOWLEDGMENTS

Much love and many thanks to everyone who helps keep my particular ship afloat and on course: my family, my friends, my writer pals, my professional team, and all of the readers, booksellers, librarians, and reviewers who share their book love.

To the Berkley/Penguin team, I send bouquets of thanks with particular gratitude to: Craig Burke, Loren Jaggers, Claire Zion, Jeanne-Marie Hudson, Jin Yu, Jessica Mangicaro, Jenn Snyder, Ivan Held, Tara O'Connor, Alaina Christensen, and Candice Coote. The art, marketing, publicity, production, sales, and editorial departments have been Veronica's stalwart champions from the beginning, and she would not be here without them. Special thanks to Ellen Edwards for bringing Veronica to her Penguin home, and to Eileen Chetti for deft and elegant copy edits.

This book is dedicated to Danielle Perez and Pam Hopkins. To have an editor or an agent with such talent, integrity, and warmth would be a gift. To have both is an embarrassment of riches.